JAY S. SCOTT

ASCENSION

—•WARDENS OF THE RIFT, BOOK ONE•—

For information regarding subsidiary rights, permissions, or bulk purchases, please contact the publisher at:

Email: jaysscottauthor@yahoo.com

Website: https://authorjaysscott.org/

Edited by Jonathan Jones

Cover design by Miblart

Interior design by Atticus

Contents

Foreword

Before you step into the world of *Ascension*, I just want to say—thank you.

Thank you to my wife. For dealing with my periods of late-night writing stints and listening to endless story arc ideas (she only likes non-fiction)—I know it was exhausting to you. To Pam for encouraging me to finish this project. To Wendy for telling me my story was amazing and worth publishing.

Thank you to my readers for picking up this book. Whether you stumbled across it by chance, followed a recommendation, or have been patiently waiting for something new to sink your teeth into, I'm glad you're here. Writing this story has been a long, often chaotic journey—and seeing it in your hands (or on your screen) is more meaningful than I can put into words.

This book is about survival, transformation, and finding your place when the world no longer makes sense. It's a story that mattered to me long before it made it to the page, and I hope, in some small way, it resonates with you too.

If you enjoy the ride, I'd be incredibly grateful if you'd consider leaving a review. Your thoughts—whether a few words or a full breakdown—help other readers find the book and keep stories like this one alive.

Thanks again for being here.

Prologue

The street was silent as Jax stood on the front porch. The patter of rain on the roof, and the creak of the porch swing were the only sounds that intruded on his quiet brooding.

He inhaled the sweet-scented smoke from a cigarette he couldn't seem to quit, savoring the weight of it between his fingers. Of all the vices he could have chosen, he'd picked one of the worst—though, for someone like him, lung cancer wasn't a concern. The rapid healing of his kind rendered diseases irrelevant.

Death, however, was still on the table. He knew it was coming for him even now.

He flicked the cigarette's glowing stub off the porch and watched it spiral down to the wet grass before fizzling out.

With a resigned sigh, he made his way down the porch, following the cobblestone path that cut through the pristine lawn.

He paused at the curb and looked back one last time at the quiet house behind him. Leaving the sleeping woman behind, filled him with a deep sense of emptiness.

Ellen Tomlinson—she had been worth it. Every risk, every law broken. In all his centuries, he'd never met a woman like her.

There was a magnetic pull to her he'd felt the moment they'd met. He didn't know why, but she made him feel something he hadn't felt before—peace.

He had known the punishment for sleeping with her was death, but she'd been worth it.

A part of him hoped he'd get more time. That the universe might turn a blind eye just this once.

But the universe had other plans.

He felt it before he saw it—a ripple in the Rift, that ancient barrier protecting Earth from the violent races of the Seven Realms.

It came as an electric pulse, dancing over his skin like a static charge. He turned, already knowing who it had to be.

Akron.

Across the street, a jagged tear in reality widened and the First Warden stepped through. Rain hissed off his long coat as it met the still-dissipating energy arcing around him.

Warden battle armor covered him from foot to neck. His favored twin swords, etched in blue-white runes, rose from behind his back.

Jax swore under his breath.

There were only two reasons Akron ever dressed like this: Rift patrol... or executions. And Jax knew which one had brought him here today.

So much for more time.

Akron's eyes, hollow and heavy with a millennia's worth of burdens, locked on him.

"Jax, my brother," he said, voice low and thunderous, "what have you done?"

Jax offered a crooked smile, lifting his chin toward the overcast sky. "I think it's fairly obvious. You're here dressed like that, aren't you?"

Akron stepped forward, boots splashing through shallow puddles. "You've endangered everything. We lose too many Wardens as it is. Now, your actions force me to take the life of one more."

A familiar bitterness rose in Jax's throat like bile.

"You ever feel it, Akron? That hollowness? That aching quiet after centuries of existence?"

He paused, eyes searching.

"I found something worth dying for. She gave me peace."

"And your Oath? Did this peace make you forget the words you swore?" Akron asked, jaw clenched.

A gust of wind whipped between them, stirring leaves and tension alike.

"No," Jax said quietly. "I remember every word."

Akron's hands twitched at his sides. The Oath bound him—he couldn't defy it even if he wanted to. Onos's laws, anchored in his very essence, always forced his hand.

"Do you think you are the only one who feels that way?" Akron's voice sharpened, cutting like a knife. "That I, who have lived for millennia, haven't known loneliness? What you feel pales compared to the weight I carry. And yet I stand here, not breaking sacred oaths. Instead, I'm forced to uphold them—to take the life of a brother."

Jax drew a deep breath, eyes fixed on the man who had been more of a brother to him than a commander.

"Do what you must, Akron." His voice was steady.

"I only ask that you do one thing for me. Leave the woman out of this. She is ignorant of what we are. I made sure of it."

"I'll spare the woman," Akron said. "She did nothing wrong by loving you."

"Thank you," Jax whispered.

Akron didn't speak again. The moment had passed.

He drew his blade from the sheaths on his back with a metallic hiss. The air shimmered between them as he drew on the Rift energy, casting a glamour that wrapped the street in a veil of concealment.

Across the street, Jax mirrored him. The blade in his hand trembled slightly. Like a rookie, facing his first Rift breach.

"I know you don't have a choice," Jax said, a sad smile tugging at his lips. "But don't think I'm going to make it easy on you."

Akron let out a bitter chuckle. "You never did."

He saw the strike form in his former pupil's mind before it reached his limbs—telegraphed in a shift of weight and a tensing of his shoulders.

Akron was already moving before Jax had taken his first step.

The two Wardens met in a clash of blades in the middle of the street, their battle adding its own thunderous music to the angry skies overhead.

Five heartbeats later, it was over.

Jax collapsed, eyes wide with surprise, his blade slipping from limp fingers as he fell.

Akron stood over him for a moment, grief etched in the deep lines of his face. He sank to one knee beside his fallen brother, gently cradling the hand that had once held unshakable resolve.

"What happens now?" Jax asked, voice barely a whisper.

"When you die, your Essence returns to Onos. You will finally be at rest," Akron said, eyes damp.

Jax gave a faint smile, and then he was gone.

Akron sat still for a long moment. Then he unclasped the pendant from around his neck, opened the small vial from within, and held it above Jax's chest.

The reddish mist of Essence lifted from the body, drawn upward like smoke from a flame, funneling into the vial.

When it was done, Jax's body dissolved. Centuries of life and dedicated service reduced to ash, carried off by the breeze into the waiting darkness.

Akron rose, soul-weary, his heart heavier than it had ever felt.

He looked at the house across the street.

Drawn to it like a moth to flame, Akron crossed in silence, stopping at a window. He needed to see what would cause a Warden, loyal for centuries, to risk everything by falling to temptation.

Inside, Ellen slept peacefully, her face serene in the glow of a bedside night-light. She was beautiful, yes, but there was something more. Something deeper that pulled at him beyond the physical—a quiet warmth, a calm yet insistent gravity.

He lingered longer than he should have, struggling to admit the truth taking shape in his heart.

That maybe... just maybe... this woman had managed to give Jax the peace he'd searched for.

But duty called.

Akron turned away and stepped back into the Rift, unaware that behind him—deep within Ellen's womb—a tiny flicker of red-gold light pulsed once... then twice...

A new life had begun.

One that would change the world forever.

Chapter 1

Twenty-Eight Years Later

A wet sound of flesh tearing under claw echoed faintly off the alley walls—sickening and intimate, like meat being pulled from bone. The Drakyn purred low in its throat, reveling in the hot gush of blood that sprayed across its scaled muzzle. The still-beating heart in its hand throbbed once before its serrated teeth sank in.

Another meal. Another kill.

It stood nearly seven feet tall, its body covered in dark, metallic scales that gleamed like oil-slick armor beneath the city's dim light. Four thick limbs ended in clawed fingers, each tipped with razor-sharp bone talons capable of tearing through steel, let alone human flesh.

Its elongated snout curled back to reveal jagged, interlocking fangs—designed not only to rip but to consume. Sparse, wire-like hair trailed down its spine, and a ribbed tail jutted from its back, swaying with lethal grace, tipped with bone ridges sharp enough to slice concrete.

It had been five days since the Drakyn crossed the Rift into this realm, and already five lives had ended beneath its claws. Humans were weak, uncoordinated prey—soft and slow.

The Drakyn had stopped trying to hunt discreetly. No one could stop it, so why bother?

The Seven Realms liked to breed killers, creatures that could slip through weaknesses in the Rift, leaving death and destruction in their wake.

Breaching the Rift demanded sacrifice. Countless creatures died in the effort, their lives consumed to force it open. But the rulers of those realms hated humanity enough to pay the price.

The Drakyn was such a killer, bred from the Realm of Shadow and Thought, where the ruling power dreamed only of humanity's extinction or subjugation.

In its overconfidence, it missed the dark figure that stepped from the shadows like smoke gathering shape—a tall man in a long coat, face shrouded, with twin swords strapped to his back.

The Drakyn only had time to sense the presence, to begin turning, when the first blow landed.

The alley exploded in sound. Steel flashed. Bone split. The creature couldn't even scream before it collapsed in a heap of twitching limbs and fractured scales.

Akron exhaled slowly, sheathed his swords, and surveyed the carnage with disgust.

He'd tracked this Drakyn for five days. Brutal. Animalistic. Relentless.

He'd been too late to save its first few victims. Too late to save this one too, damn it. Ending the creature though—that brought him a measure of satisfaction, however small it may be.

Akron knew the local authorities were investigating the crime scenes—centered on the brutal murders of the Drakyn's four previous victims. He was trying to get ahead of it but wasn't having much luck.

Due to some unknown magic or law of the Rift, generally any race that died in the Earth Realm reverted to human form upon their death. Thank Onos for small blessings—he would take them when he could.

As he knelt, in an effort to stage the scene—setting several blades next to the body—he hoped the authorities would make the connection between the killer of the four previous victims, and this "man" that was lying next to the fifth victim.

He knew the blades wouldn't match the cuts on the victim. There really was no way to explain how the man this Drakyn turned into, was strong enough to rip through a chest cavity.

But where evidence fell short, humans were great at filling in the gaps to help them explain the inexplicable.

He wouldn't hold his breath though. The two detectives assigned to this case were almost supernaturally perceptive.

He needed more time. He needed to find the other Drakyn and quickly, before it struck again. The beasts always hunted in pairs, usually mated pairs.

An inhuman roar pierced the quiet a few blocks east.

Akron straightened slowly, the tension coiling tight beneath his skin. The second Drakyn had felt its mate's death. Good!

He smiled...This Drakyn had been too easy to kill, and it did nothing to ease the anger burning within him at the destruction of five human lives.

He reached into his coat and withdrew a pair of customized titanium-alloy 'brass' knuckles. Warden-forged by his armorer, Teliz—designed to shatter scale and bone alike.

They glinted dully in the alley light as he slid them over his hands.

Akron tilted his head, catching the faint pulse of energy ahead where the Drakyn had vanished into the Rift, and leapt effortlessly to the rooftop. He was looking forward to hunting it down and working out his anger the old-fashioned way.

This wouldn't be a swift or painless death when he caught up to it.

That thought gave him a sense of satisfaction as he raced along the rooftops after his prey.

He didn't notice the security camera mounted above the bank across the street, or that a repair tech had accidentally left it facing the alley. He didn't feel the faint, rhythmic blink of its recording light, quietly capturing every brutal second.

He didn't know that this footage—grainy, obscured, and damning—would find its way into human hands.

And that it would change everything.

Chapter 2

M arek Tomlinson's day was already off to a shitty start, and it wasn't even 3 a.m.

Captain Greggs, with a gravelly, unapologetic voice, had called and informed him that sleep was canceled, and he needed to be at the station in an hour. Another body had been discovered.

So much for recovery mode.

He and Tucker had closed a rough case the night before and, like always, that meant a drink or six at Dudley's.

They'd earned it.

Dudley's had soul. Low lighting, worn booths, and a bar counter polished by decades of elbows and Dudley's bar towel. A dive, sure, but it had a kind of working-class sanctuary feel—like it understood that sometimes you just needed to sit with your pain for a while—or drown your memories, if that was your preference.

The case had been a nightmare. Kid dead. Mother too. Stepdad with a drinking problem and fists that didn't know when to stop. The piece of shit cleaned up afterward—tried to play innocent.

It almost worked—would have too, if Tucker hadn't made a breakthrough; coming through again with that insight of his that made him so valuable.

Now the man was looking at back-to-back life sentences, but Marek couldn't get the image out of his head.

The kid's small body, and the mother's broken face. Even when they cuffed him, Marek didn't feel like they'd won. Not really.

That's what Dudley's was for. To forget, if only for a few hours.

Dudley himself was a neighborhood legend. Six-foot-five, three hundred pounds of retired heavyweight boxer turned barkeep and bouncer. He'd bought the bar with his prize money in the late '90s and had been running it like a benevolent dictator ever since.

He greeted every customer personally, kept a Louisville Slugger behind the counter, and had a strict code: respect each other and keep the peace, or get tossed out.

Marek respected the hell out of him.

A few years back, Marek and Tucker helped Dudley deal quietly with a situation involving his daughter and a boyfriend who thought "love" meant bruises. Since then, they'd never paid full price for a drink.

That loyalty extended beyond drinks too—because Marek didn't even remember getting home. He found the receipt folded in his wallet next to a napkin that just read:

"Took a twenty for the trouble. The guys drove your truck home. Rest up—D."

He smiled despite the headache. Dudley always had his back.

But any good mood evaporated as soon as Marek's thoughts turned back to their current case.

The body captain Greggs had called about—fresh, mutilated, and dumped in an alley uptown, matched the others. This brought the total victim count to five.

The killer left no pattern or connection between the victims, only that each had been torn open and their hearts removed. Literally.

Gaping chest cavity. No heart. In at least two scenes, someone found the mangled, chewed remains of the organ nearby. Marek had floated the cannibalism theory once, half-joking, trying to push the squad into a new angle. One rookie made a crack about a Hannibal copycat. Next thing he knew, the nickname was born.

The Cannibal.

He hated how catchy it was.

Now the Feds wanted in. SCU—Special Crimes Unit. Not exactly the most known entity in the Bureau. From the little he could gather, they dealt in "weird" crimes. Cold cases. Superstition and shadows. Which meant someone, somewhere, thought this case wasn't just brutal—it was unnatural.

Marek wasn't sure what he believed. But the bodies didn't lie.

He texted Tucker while dragging himself toward the shower:

—*Morning sunshine. You get the captain's call yet?*

The response came two minutes later:

—*Fuck your damn sunshine.*

Marek chuckled, wincing as it rattled his skull, and texted back:

—*See you at the station in 40.*

If he were a betting man, he'd have made money on Tucker's reaction.

Tucker Daniels was a man of habits, hangovers, and a dark history he didn't speak of. He didn't bounce back from these nights like Marek did, and he sure as hell didn't suffer in silence. But he was loyal, brilliant, and one of the best detectives Marek had ever known.

They'd been partners since the academy—became detectives together. Seven years of crime scenes, stakeouts, and finding their way through moral gray zones—they were brothers in all but blood.

Tucker looked like hell most days—unshaven, messy hair, beat-up boots and threadbare Polos. He'd gotten stopped once outside a crime scene because someone thought he was a passing homeless guy, not the one assigned to the case. The other detectives still gave him shit for it.

But he saw things no one else did. Could read a crime scene like a diary. And when he went quiet, Marek knew something bad was coming.

Marek looked like trouble on a SWAT team. Six-foot-four, linebacker frame, always dressed in tactical gear instead of the standard detective uniform. Black NYPD shirt, cargo pants, combat boots. It made people underestimate his brains. He liked that.

He didn't know where his bulk came from, since his mother was tiny. Five-four, delicate, all grace and softness. His father? He'd left them before Marek was born. No photos. No records. Just stories. According to Ellen Tomlinson, Marek was "just like him."

He never asked what she meant by that. He figured anyone who'd leave them, wasn't worth asking questions about.

Showered and dressed fifteen minutes later, Marek felt... normal. No hangover. No headache. He should've been curled around a bottle of aspirin, but he wasn't.

Ever since he turned seventeen, things didn't stick like they used to. Cuts healed faster than normal. Bruises faded in a day or two. Headaches disappeared in minutes. It still amazed him, even now—but he wasn't going to look a gift horse in the mouth.

Marek slipped on his jacket and stepped out into the chill of early morning. The streets were mostly empty—just garbage trucks, cabbies and people who didn't want to be seen.

He got in his gunmetal-gray truck, started the engine, and cut through the quiet darkness, headed toward the station.

The Cannibal had claimed another victim, and this time, the Feds were getting involved.

Whatever was happening in his city... Marek had a feeling it was just getting started.

Chapter 3

T ucker Daniels hated mornings, and this one was shaping up to be a contender for the worst. The sun hadn't yet risen, and streetlights still illuminated the precinct parking lot.

He parked his rusted-out Dodge next to Marek's truck with a groan of protesting metal and killed the engine. The resulting silence only made his headache worse.

He rubbed his temple and muttered something unkind under his breath about Marek's iron constitution. Of course Marek would already be here. Probably bright-eyed and cheerful—likely sipping black coffee as if he hadn't consumed six rounds the previous night.

The hangover from last night was lingering like a sour taste. Dudley's whiskey wasn't top-shelf, or at least the kind Marek and he usually ordered, but it got the job done. Unfortunately, it also had a mean after bite.

As Tucker trudged up the precinct steps, he wondered what the FBI wanted. He wondered why it had taken them so long to get wind of the serial murders, and why the Bureau was coming in to consult now, at this god-forsaken hour? Couldn't it wait?

This case was really getting to him. Not because it was a string of serial killings; after all, he and Marek had seen a couple of those. It was because neither of them could get a read on the motive of the killer. There was no pattern to the killings, no specified preference of targets.

The victims ranged from old to young, wealthy to poor, and muscle-bound men to slender females. Nothing in any of the killings gave a hint about what the killer was after and provided no way for them to anticipate when—or whom—the killer would strike next.

Tucker had always had a knack for profiling—it first surfaced during the Police academy, where it disturbed and impressed his instructors in equal measure.

He could get into the mind of a killer, building out a psychological profile, even when the evidence was thin. But with this one? Forget it. So far, the sheer range of victim types cancelled out any profiles he'd tried to establish.

"Sir, may I ask you to step to the side and come through the line?"

The question snapped Tucker out of his dark musings, and he flashed his badge at the rookie officer manning the check-in station. Tucker's irritation evident on his face.

He pushed through the secure access point normally used by officers, ignoring the rookie's stammered apology and surprise when he realized who Tucker was. His worn-out jeans and ratty collared shirt under the faded leather jacket was far from the required attire of a detective.

Jim, the old desk sergeant and veteran of thirty years, was standing to the left of the rookie and chuckled to himself as he nodded his head at Tucker in greeting.

Tucker really liked the old man and was surprised that he hadn't retired yet. There was a betting pool going around the precinct for when he was going to retire, but three-fourths of the department had already lost out on their bets. Rumor was that Jim knew of the bets and had placed his own through a proxy, just to spite everyone.

Tucker smiled at the thought. It was just like the old man to try to screw everyone over before he left.

The elevator ride up to the fifth floor gave him a chance to catch his breath. The homicide division was quiet at this hour. A few night-shift detectives hunched over reports, faces pallid in the blue glow of their monitors. Tucker gave a few of them a nod as he passed, receiving a few in return.

As he got closer to the captain's office, he spotted his partner through the open door. Marek was standing with his arms crossed, broad shoulders relaxed but alert, dressed in his usual black tactical shirt and cargo pants.

Unconventional for a detective, sure, but no one on the force questioned it anymore. Marek got results.

The woman standing across from the captain was unfamiliar. Tall, tanned, with sharp eyes, brown hair, and a stance too coiled to belong to anyone just pushing paper. Tactical gear. Pistol at her hip. Confidence radiated off her in waves. Tucker's instincts pricked up: Fed.

Marek had noticed Tucker the moment he rounded the corner. Of course he had. Bastard seemed to have a sixth sense about him—always had. He gave Tucker a raised brow and the barest hint of a smirk.

Tucker walked through the open door. "Morning, Captain. Marek. Mysterious government lady."

Greggs looked up, exasperated and already massaging the bridge of his nose. "Agent, this is Detective Daniels. Daniels, meet Agent Kaycee Gordon. She's our new liaison from the FBI's Special Crimes Unit."

◆

Fifteen Minutes Earlier

Marek arrived at the precinct about ten minutes prior to Agent Kaycee Gordon's arrival, and well before his partner showed up. He had taken a moment to get up to speed on the case.

Apparently, this case had made it onto the radar of the Feds due to a possible overlap in one of theirs. He was no stranger to working with the FBI, as some cases required partnering because of jurisdiction issues. In this instance, he was drawing a blank on how there could be any overlap.

Even more disconcerting, and why Captain Greggs was spewing obscenities at the moment, was how fast they had found out about the recent murder. Greggs suspected someone was already watching this case and had their 'grubby fingers' deep into the investigation details already.

"How the hell did they find out so fast?" Captain Greggs questioned no one in particular.

The captain's eyes were bloodshot, and his face was lined with worry. He looked like he hadn't slept in days. This case had been eating at them all, little by little, and the FBI getting involved before they found any hard leads was only making things worse.

"I suppose I don't need to tell you to play nice with this Agent Gordon, right?" Greggs asked Marek.

He removed his glasses, pinching the bridge of his nose as he attempted to, by sheer willpower, prevent a building headache.

"FBI Director himself deemed it necessary to send me an email... damn Feds."

Marek gave a reassuring smile as he eased Greggs' fears. "Don't worry Captain, I'll give Agent Gordon my full support; and before you ask, yes, I will make sure Tucker gets on board too."

"Ok... Alright. Where the hell is he, anyway?" The captain questioned as he checked his watch for the tenth time since Marek had arrived. "I called you right after I called him. Gordon is almost here, and I wanted to bring you *both* up to speed."

Marek couldn't help but chuckle as he replied, "We spent a couple hours after shift getting drinks at Dudley's. Tucker and I had a little more than usual, seeing as the last case we closed hit a little too hard. That, along with how this one is going, didn't make for a stellar combination last night... for either of us."

Greggs took in Marek's appearance and raised a skeptical eyebrow. "Well, you're here, looking chipper as ever and none the worse for wear. Did you even drink last night?"

"Sure did, and Dudley had to get a cab for me. I don't even remember getting home last night—Dudley somehow got my truck home too." Marek replied with a shrug of his shoulders.

He didn't have a good explanation for why he always bounced back so quick; it had been that way since his seventeenth birthday. Hangovers weren't the only thing he bounced back from either; injuries healed a little faster, and he hadn't been sick since.

Captain Greggs just grunted, clearly not believing Marek's obvious attempt at trying to excuse his partner's inability to show up on time.

Marek chuckled at the skeptical look the captain threw his way and thought back on that period when his life had seemed to change directions literally overnight. He had some time to take a trip down memory lane before the Fed showed up and the shit hit the fan.

Chapter 4

Eleven Years Earlier...

U ntil his seventeenth birthday, Marek remembered living a laid back and average life.

Good grades, decent friends, a tight bond with his mom—a future as an engineering student at Columbia waiting just a year down the road.

He was an average sized kid. He got sick, injured, and had all the same problems every teenager has when growing up.

Life was orderly. Predictable. Safe. Then one day, without warning, his life changed.

It started small. The morning after his birthday, he woke before his alarm, wide awake at six a.m.—a phenomenon so foreign to him it felt like someone had hijacked his body.

He wasn't tired, wasn't groggy. Instead, he felt energized. Buzzing, almost—as if every cell in his body was humming with the need to do... something.

Maybe it was just a high from how good the party had been last night—he'd read somewhere that adrenaline and serotonin could do weird things to your system.

But then the hunger hit. Not teenage-boy-hollow-legs hunger. This was an aching, insatiable need that had him cooking an entire breakfast—a feat in itself for those who knew him.

He inhaled an entire stack of waffles, a pound of bacon, and every single Pop-Tart in the pantry before his mom, Ellen, had even shuffled down the stairs.

She'd stared at the carnage, blinking blearily. "Jesus, Marek. Did you eat all that? It looks like a tornado hit our kitchen."

He'd laughed it off. No big deal, it's normal. He'd heard of hunger pains before in his friends who'd had massive growth spurts. He tried to convince himself this was nothing more than that.

But that was only the beginning. Over the next year, Marek began to change in more noticeable ways.

He shot up from five-foot-ten to six-foot-four. His muscles filled in like he'd been living in a gym, though he hadn't changed his routine.

It didn't stop there.

He started noticing other things. His hearing was just a little sharper. Conversations from across crowded rooms somehow found their way to his ears—whispered conversations in class became clearer.

His reflexes improved beyond anything he'd had before. His balance felt more stable. He moved with more grace, more control.

His doctor was baffled. His mom—even more so. They ran tests. Checked hormone levels. Everything came back normal.

"You're just growing into yourself," the doctor had said. "Some boys are late bloomers."

But Marek wasn't buying it. Not really.

Still, he kept quiet. He didn't want to worry his mom. He didn't want to believe something was wrong.

His growth spurt stopped by the end of the summer before his senior year, and that's when the really weird shit started happening.

———◆———

He hadn't meant to sign up for mixed martial arts, it just kind of happened. His friend Luke needed to run an errand for his uncle, Pete Nelson, so Marek decided to tag along.

The second he walked into Nelson's Gym and saw the sparring mats, punching bags, and fighters moving through their paces, something inside him locked into place—like a switch flipped. A hunger, different from food, flared in his chest. He didn't know why, but he had a sudden urge to learn everything he could about what he was seeing.

Pete Nelson owned the gym and had been training fighters for twenty years. He'd seen Marek's interest right away, had given him a shot, and Marek took to it like he'd been born for it.

One month in, Pete called him a prodigy. Two months in, Marek knocked a regional fighter out cold in the first round of a friendly sparring match. The fighter had been training for years.

Through it all, Marek tried to ignore the nagging fear in the back of his mind. That maybe this wasn't normal. That maybe this wasn't just a growth spurt, or some buried knack for fighting.

He kept that fear tucked away. Until the alley. Until the girl. Until he saw what no human was meant to see.

———◆———

It was a Saturday night, late.

Marek was walking home from a midnight action flick—the kind where the plot was paper thin and the fight scenes were the only reason to buy a ticket. He'd just stepped off the sidewalk to cross the street when he heard a scream.

Sharp. Frantic, and Female. Tearing through the quiet, it seemed to come from a narrow alley to his right.

Marek didn't hesitate. He sprinted toward it, boots hitting the pavement hard.

"Hey!" he shouted. "What's going on down there?"

Four men stood halfway down the alley, clustered around a girl who couldn't have been much older than him.

The girl's jacket was torn, with one sleeve ripped clean off. She struggled like a cornered animal, kicking and twisting, but they had her boxed in—laughing like it was a game.

Their faces were the kind you didn't forget. Hard lines. Greasy smiles. The kind that said you were now a part of something terrible. The kind that promised retribution for interrupting their fun.

As he got closer and the grisly scene became clearer, that part of Marek's brain controlling fight-or-flight started screaming out warnings. He came to a stop only feet away from the three men who'd turned to greet him.

The largest of the three took a step forward, a dark and wicked smile forming on his lips, arms spreading out wide.

"Well hello friend, what brings you to our humble alley this fine evening? Come to join in the fun?" His buddies snickered behind him.

Beside him, another man—the one holding the girl—didn't laugh. He just watched Marek with unsettling stillness, his expression unreadable, his head titled slightly as if studying prey. Something about him felt... wrong. Not just cruel, but *off*.

Marek tore his gaze away, looking once more at the girl—shivering, trapped, her torn jacket hanging from one shoulder. Her eyes snapped up to meet his—the fear and desperation he saw there caused something inside him to snap.

Never one prone to lose his temper or crave violence, what unfurled in his chest was a white-hot anger unlike anything he'd felt. It started in the center of his chest and spread out through his body, burning away any fear or doubt about what he had to do.

Every part of him vibrated with a need to protect this girl, by any means necessary—the anger feeling like a beast trying to claw its way out of him. He clenched and unclenched his fists, vibrating with the need to protect. To punish.

He smiled as he spoke, keeping his voice cold and unfeeling. "You guys need to clear out right now before you do something we'll all regret."

The men just chuckled at that, and one of them addressed the leader of their group.

"I don't know about you Jim, but I'm not planning on regretting anything tonight, and I'll be damned if I'm going to let some young kid ruin our fun. You just run along now before you end up joining her."

"I'm afraid I can't do that." Marek stated bluntly.

"Well then, I guess we'll just have to take care of this little shit real quick-like and get back to our fun-filled evening." Jim said to the other two as he removed a knife from his coat pocket and advanced on Marek.

As Jim made his way toward him, he glanced back at the man holding the girl, and said, "Harley, make sure the bitch stays quiet for this. I don't want her screams to draw any more attention."

"Sure thing, boss," the quiet one—Harley—finally said. His smile was lazy, but his eyes didn't match it. They were too still. Too sharp. Marek couldn't explain it, but something in his gut twisted, warning him that this one wasn't like the others.

He leaned his head down to whisper softly in her ear as he pressed his blade tighter against her neck, breaking a little skin, "you'll be a good little bitch and stay quiet, or I'll make sure you never speak again."

Marek's eyes narrowed back in on the blade in Jim's hand. He stopped waiting; Pete Nelson always said, "*If you know a fight's coming, throw the first punch.*"

He used the distraction to do just that.

The two men shouted to their leader in warning as Marek surged forward. Jim whipped back around, his knife arcing toward Marek, but the swing was wild and too late—easily blocked.

A second later, Jim was screaming in pain on the ground, taken out by a brutal kick that shattered his knee. Marek hammered a punch to his face, ending any more complaints from him.

Quiet descended on the alley, and the other two goons shared worried looks with each other. Harley still wore a relaxed smile, like he was enjoying the show.

It didn't take the other two long to find their courage. They charged him—sloppy, uncoordinated, hoping numbers would win out.

Marek met them head-on. No hesitation, and no warning.

He waded into them with an intensity that would bother him later—when adrenaline faded and he had time to unpack the details. Time to wonder why part of him had enjoyed it.

The first man went down with a vicious punch to the throat—gagging, clutching at his windpipe. Marek side-stepped, pivoted, and landed three body shots on the second before slamming a right hook into his jaw. It shattered under his fist with a clean, satisfying *crack*.

The man collapsed—but somehow, through pain or a desperation, he forced himself up. Sobbing. Face bloodied and eyes staring hate-filled daggers. He scrambled to help his friends, dragging Jim's limp body as they staggered toward the end of the alley.

They had fled, leaving Marek standing there, chest heaving as post-fight adrenaline pumped through his system.

Disgusting. Pathetic. *Amateurs*. A small voice whispered in the back of his mind. He turned his attention to the last man who was still holding the girl.

"Now it was Harley, wasn't it? You've seen what happened to your buddies, so you can either let the girl go and be on your way, or you can get the same treatment as your friends." Marek said

Harley's eyes darted to the three men hobbling off, then to Marek, and finally to the girl he was still holding.

Harley got a nasty little smile on his face. "Now why did you have to cause all this fuss, and all over a single girl? You should have just moved on, human. Instead, you had to come to the rescue, play the hero."

"Now you get to watch what happens when a hero picks the wrong fight." He said with a sneer as he backed up against the chain-link fence with the girl.

It happened all at once—like a mask sliding free.

Harley shifted. Not in the way a man might brace for a fight or puff his chest in bravado, but in a way that felt... wrong. Unnatural.

As if something inside him had been waiting, coiled and patient, for the exact moment his friends were out of the picture.

His body stilled. No more nervous glances. No swagger. Just stillness—pure and chilling.

His eyes sharpened. Gone was the greasy bravado and slack jaw. What replaced it was something ancient and calculating. A predator taking off its borrowed skin.

The air around him shimmered. Like heat rolling off asphalt in a dead summer—only this wasn't warmth. It pulsed with cold intent. The shadows near him bent inward, subtly, as if drawn to his presence.

Then his eyes flashed. Not the white of adrenaline or rage, but violet. Glowing as if lit from within.

His skin paled, bleaching toward albino white as his body lengthened—his frame stretching taller, more imposing by the second.

Darkness erupted from his body and wound its way around Marek.

Marek couldn't move. His body refused—every limb stiff with a sudden influx of terror as the man before him transformed into a nightmare.

Harley smiled. Long, gleaming fangs slid down from his gums—cruel and elegant.

Then, without a word he sank his teeth into the girl's neck.

The sound was worse than the sight.

A wet, visceral tear of flesh. The spray of blood was sudden and sharp, painting the bricks behind them in a wide arc. Her scream—brief and panicked—cut off in a wet gurgle as her body went slack in his arms.

Marek's stomach lurched.

Harley raised his head slowly, almost reverently.

Blood painted his face, dripping from his chin and staining his shirt collar like a grotesque baptism. His inhuman eyes glowed faintly in the dark, twin violet coals gleaming beneath a twisted expression of satisfaction.

Marek couldn't breathe.

Couldn't think.

Couldn't move. As if something nailed his feet to the pavement. His fists, once burning with intent, now hung useless at his sides. The fire inside him had gone out. All that remained was cold and *fear*.

Then Harley spoke, his voice light and singsong, like a nursery rhyme turned wrong.

"I see I have your attention now," he cooed, baring a wide, red rictus grin.

He inhaled deeply, nostrils flaring like a predator savoring the scent.

"Innocence lost. That fear rolling off you... mm." His grin widened. "Absolutely delicious."

Marek's heart hammered in his ears.

"Time for me to go," Harley said, licking blood from his mouth. "I think I'll leave you alive—let you wonder, every night, if she'd still be breathing if you'd moved faster. Hadn't frozen. Hadn't failed her."

He turned, muscles coiling, and added with a chuckle, "Here. Catch. Maybe you can still save her. Maybe not."

He flung her at Marek dismissively. Like one would a sack of potatoes.

She hit Marek, and he dropped to his knees with the impact. Her body was limp. Her head lolled against his shoulder, blood soaking through both their clothes in seconds.

Too late, he knew. She was already gone.

By the time Marek looked up, Harley had leapt—ten feet in the air, clearing the chain-link fence. Like gravity had no say in the matter.

He turned, gave a mocking salute, and was gone, swallowed by the dark like he'd never been.

Marek stared into the silence. His breath hitched in a half-sob. He looked down at the girl in his arms.

Eyes open, unseeing. Neck mangled. Blood still dripping from the wound. His hands pressed against the wound out of instinct, but he knew it was useless. She was past saving. Gone before she even landed in his arms.

Still—he made himself move. He pulled his phone out with blood-slick fingers, thumb shaking as he dialed.

"911, what's your emergency?"

"I need help," he rasped. "Lower East Side. Alley off Rivington Street, between Christie and Bowery, close to Freeman's. Someone's attacked a girl. She's—she's not breathing."

"Is the attacker still present?"

"No. He ran. Please—just send someone."

He gave what details he could. Description. General height. The knife. Left out the violet eyes, the teeth. Left out the impossible jump and change of appearance.

His voice cracked halfway through, but he forced the words out.

By the time the dispatcher said help was on the way, the girl's body had grown cold and stiff in his arms.

He sat there, silent, covered in her blood. And something in him broke.

It wasn't dramatic. Not a scream or a sob. It was a quiet, devastating fracture. A line drawn deep across whatever innocence he'd carried until this moment.

He'd tried to fight. To save her, but in the end, it hadn't mattered.

He'd failed. He should have been faster, should have done more.

His thoughts continued to spiral in a vortex of guilt and failure.

Red and blue lights painted the alley in alternating flashes of judgment and salvation. Sirens cut through the night as uniforms arrived in pairs, followed by an unmarked cruiser with a grizzled detective behind the wheel.

The EMTs carried away the girl—what remained of her. Marek barely noticed.

A man with sunken eyes and a brown trench coat, crouched beside him.

"Name?"

"Marek Tomlinson."

"You the one who called it in?"

Marek could only nod.

The detective—Randall, his badge said—tilted his head. "You want to tell me what happened?"

Marek exhaled slowly. Gritted his teeth. "There were four guys. Three jumped me. One had the girl."

"And?"

"I fought the three. Took them down. The last one—the one who... who did this—he was different."

"Different how?"

Marek hesitated. "Fast. Strong. Way too strong."

"Did you see his face?"

"Yeah. I'll never forget it."

Randall hummed, noncommittal. "You said he ran?"

"Yeah, after he threw the girl at me.... Like she was nothing. Like trash." The last word barely made it out—half-whispered and weighted with disbelief.

He rubbed a hand across his mouth, eyes unfocused. "I blinked, and then he was gone. Over the fence like it wasn't even there."

He left it at that. He didn't say he'd seen something impossible. Didn't say he'd watched a man break the laws of nature and grin while doing it.

The truth would lock him in a psych ward faster than it'd take the ink to dry on the paperwork.

"Alright," Randall said after a moment. "You're not in any trouble, and chances are, if those guys are still on foot, we'll catch them soon. You're not being held. But don't leave town. I may have more questions."

Marek didn't argue as he gave the detective his address and contact information. He sat on the curb, blood drying on his hands, as police cordoned off the crime scene around him.

He didn't go right home after that.

He just walked.

City blocks blurred past as his mind ran in loops. Her eyes. Her blood. That monster's smile.

He'd always believed the world made a kind of sense. That even bad people had limits, some kind of buried decency.

Tonight shattered that. There were things out there that didn't care about decency. That may not even be human.

Tonight, he'd seen evil. *Real* evil. And it had a name.

Harley.

And from the moment Marek watched the girl die in his arms, something in him knew—he'd never stop chasing the truth. No matter where it led.

Until this point, Marek hadn't had a plan for what he would do after high school, but he sure as hell did now.

He would get his degree in criminal justice, he would join the NYPD, go through the academy and work his way up.

And most importantly, he would find Harley again. He'd figure out what it was he saw.

And when he found him, he'd provide justice. *Vengeance.* Something stirred inside him at that thought... and smiled.

Chapter 5

Present Day—Captain Gregg's Office

Gordon stood and extended her hand. Her grip was firm. No nonsense. Tucker gave her a quick once-over. Strong hands. Steady gaze. She had a look that said she'd seen some shit.

Marek briefly wondered if Tucker was feeling the same thing he felt when he'd first met Agent Gordon and shook her hand—probably not.

She was stunning. Not in the polished, movie-star way, but in a way that hit him straight in his gut. Strong. Sharp. Gorgeous. Brown hair pulled back in a no-nonsense tie. High cheekbones, a firm jaw and full lips set in a quiet line that didn't give anything away.

It was her eyes especially, that caught his attention. Dark, serious and always searching. She looked like she belonged on a battlefield, not behind a desk. Every line of her body radiated control and lethal grace, and he felt the pull of her before they even shook hands.

When they did... damn. Her grip was firm, warm in a way he wasn't prepared for. And his mind, traitorous bastard that it was, noticed the slight calluses on her palms and imagined how they'd feel sliding over his body—he slammed the door shut on that thought as fast as he could.

God, what is wrong with me? He thought. He needed to get his shit together—and fast.

Gordon had noticed Marek as soon as she exited the elevator, drawn to him as if by an invisible thread. *No cop should be that attractive*, she remembered thinking to herself.

And their meeting should've been professional. Just a standard introduction between fellow law enforcement colleagues.

Instead, she'd felt something electric pass between them the moment their fingers touched. Not visible, not obvious—but undeniable. A quiet recognition. A pull in her chest she hadn't expected.

She'd withdrawn her hand smoothly, masking the flicker of heat that flared low in her gut. Her face hadn't given anything away. But her pulse had jumped.

Marek Tomlinson was a wall of muscle wrapped in tactical black, his green eyes sharp, his mouth stubborn. And somehow, he wore that lethal frame without arrogance—quiet, composed, dangerous.

He was exactly the kind of man she had no business being drawn to—relationships in her line of work never ended well. And yet, standing this close, her skin prickled with an awareness she was having trouble ignoring.

Professionalism dictated she move on, and logic demanded she ignore the sudden flush heating the back of her neck.

But as she turned to address the captain, her heart decided logic and professionalism had no say in the matter as a single thought snuck past her defenses, *Onos help me, he's beautiful.*

She locked the reaction away behind years of training. Attraction was a vulnerability, and she had no room for vulnerabilities.

---◆---

"You're late," Marek said to Tucker, not unkindly, as he handed him a coffee.

"You're lucky I'm upright," Tucker muttered, taking the cup and sinking into the nearest chair.

Turning to Gordon, he said, "So what's the deal, Agent? You here to take over our case, or just tell us we're doing it wrong?"

Gordon smiled faintly, though it didn't reach her eyes. "Well, that remains to be seen and depends on how you react to what I'm about to share with you."

She pointed at Marek and Tucker. "The two of you are currently investigating a case that may have ties to an old series of murders investigated by the FBI's Special Crimes Unit. The cases share... similarities that can't be ignored."

Marek raised an eyebrow, his tone calm and direct. "Let me guess. Hearts missing. Bodies ripped open. No obvious pattern?"

She nodded. "And DNA evidence collected at your most recent scene matches a sample taken from a cold case in 1941. Same exact sequence. No mutations. No degradation."

"That's impossible," Greggs muttered.

"Maybe, maybe not. Let's see what she has to say." Tucker said, scratching his jaw with a faraway look in his eyes.

The room went quiet.

Agent Gordon reached into one of the side pockets of her pants and pulled out a palm-sized device. She flipped a switch. The captain's desk phone let out a brief static burst and went dead.

"Signal jammer," she explained. "This doesn't leave the room. Everything I'm about to tell you is classified at the highest levels. You speak a word of it outside this office, and you'll disappear so fast your grandkids won't remember your name."

"Well," Tucker drawled. "Aren't you just a ball of positivity."

Marek chuckled. Agent Gordon didn't.

She laid out several black-and-white photos from the 1941 case. Gruesome. Detailed. Hearts missing, chest cavities hollowed out. Then came the modern shots. Almost identical.

"This DNA," she said, tapping the photo, "doesn't match any known human genome. It doesn't follow the rules of animal DNA either. We ran every database we had access to. The only match was from this cold case—an unsolved series the Bureau quietly buried decades ago."

"And you think it's the same killer?" Greggs asked.

"We believe it's the same species. Possibly even the same individual in that species."

"Species?" Marek asked, ice skating down his spine.

Gordon gave a single, measured nod. "What I'm about to show you three, doesn't exist, and as far as the public is concerned, it never will."

She pulled out a tablet and opened a video. Security footage. Grainy, but stabilized. An alley. A figure moving fast, dragging something heavy.

That it wasn't human, was clear. Even grainy footage couldn't hide that fact.

Tucker and Marek leaned forward. Captain Greggs gripped the edge of the desk.

The creature was tall, scaled, and lizard like. It lifted with one limb what it had been dragging—their latest victim, a very large man, and clawed the chest open. It tore the heart out and started eating.

"This thing was caught on camera," Marek said slowly. "So why wasn't it reported to us? Better yet, why have the news outlets not exploded?"

"Because this," Gordon said, tapping the tablet, "was wiped an hour after it was recorded. We have a specialist at the SCU who has developed advanced algorithms. They seek out any security camera footage that points to signs of extreme violence and abnormalities. We found this camera and erased the footage. What you're seeing is the only copy."

Marek looked over at his partner.

Tucker, who was looking pale and a little green, grunted.

"I've seen a lot of seriously fucked-up shit in my years on the force, but this..." he drew in a sharp breath as he motioned at the screen, "this takes first place."

Captain Greggs broke the silence following Tucker's words. "It was bad enough having to hunt down the monsters when they were human, but now we have actual monsters running around the streets?"

He leaned forward and rubbed his forehead. "Makes me seriously re-think early retirement."

The captain turned haunted eyes filled with equal parts desperation and anger, to Agent Gordon.

Tucker leaned forward, fixing Gordon with a look. "That thing lifted a 300-pound man—coroner's report confirms it—with one hand. Marek's the deadliest guy I know, and even he wouldn't last ten seconds. So tell me... how the hell do we fight something like that?"

Marek shook his head, a flicker of amusement tugging at his mouth. Tucker wasn't wrong, but still, it would've been nice to think his partner had a little more faith in his skills.

Then again, Marek knew the truth. If this thing ever got close, it wouldn't be a fight—he'd be just another smear on the pavement.

Their questions and comments hung in the dead silence of the office. And that silence was starting to get real uncomfortable, real fast.

Agent Gordon had paused the video on the grisly scene when the guys had started their exclamations. Marek knew they had thrown quite a few questions her way. More as an attempt to process what they had seen, than to get any real answers.

It was into this silence that she threw the next bombshell.

"To answer your question, detective Daniels, it appears that there is already something, or someone, who is aware of this creature. Whoever it is, also is most likely not human, or at least not completely."

She gestured for them to turn their attention back to the tablet, ignoring the looks of disbelief on their faces.

As the video continued, Marek was drawn back to the screen. It was like watching a car wreck; you wanted to look away, but it was just so damn interesting that you couldn't.

Marek made out a shadowy form off to the left of the picture, like liquid darkness that peeled off the alley wall—it formed into a large figure in a leather trench coat.

The newcomer seemed to pause for only a moment to draw swords from somewhere on his back. He abruptly vanished, along with the creature, the victim, and any sign that pointed to what had just taken place.

He looked up in surprise at Agent Gordon, and she waved at him to continue watching. When he focused back onto the screen, the image came back, and the stranger stood to the side of the creature as it crumpled to the ground.

In a blur he sheathed the swords, kneeling next to the victim briefly—but the image was too grainy to see what he was doing. He stood up then and faced the building on his right, tilted his head, as if listening to something.

Then he leaped twenty feet to the fire escape above him. One more jump took the stranger over the roof and out of sight.

Marek dropped into the seat in front of the captain's desk, as the reality of what he'd seen, sank in. There was a silent war going on inside his head.

The practical detective wanted to point out all the ways that someone could have tampered with the video, making him see what they wished.

The other part—the teenager who had witnessed the attack in the alley years ago, which had prompted years of therapy—was screaming out in validation that this was proof he wasn't nuts.

He'd begun to give up hope that he'd find anything. He'd begun to start thinking he imagined everything in the alley with the man—no, the monster—Harley.

Marek looked down at his shaking hands, and up into the eyes of Agent Gordon. He saw no deceit in those eyes, only a hard and callused truth. He resigned himself to the inevitable and turned to address his partner and Captain Greggs.

"While you both may be surprised, or struggle with whether what you have seen is real or not, I am not. Scared shitless but not surprised. Since I was seventeen, and witness to a grisly murder, I've thought I was either crazy or traumatized. That night I witnessed a monster. It was very different from this one, more human-looking, but it was still every bit a monster. What Agent Gordon showed us tonight confirms it."

With deep breath, he continued, "Monsters, the super-natural—whatever you want to call it, exist. And for what-ever reason, they are killing us."

Marek nodded once to himself as if coming to a decision, brushed his sweaty hands against his legs, and looked up at the others in the room.

"We need to find a way to protect people. To ensure this doesn't happen again. Whatever it takes."

Marek saw the agreement on the faces of Captain Greggs and his partner. He glanced over to agent Gordon. She had fixed him with an intense look, and something flashed across her eyes—the hard lines of her mouth loosened as the corner of her mouth twitched in a small smile.

She nodded once, seeming to come to some sort of decision. "Right, then."

She pulled out two envelopes and gave them to Marek and Tucker. "Inside those two envelopes are job offers from me, with the signature of both the President of the United States and Director Green, of the FBI. They request that you accept these offers to join our Special Crime Unit's task force as agents of the FBI. These would be permanent positions, which if accepted, would require you to quit the NYPD, I'm afraid."

"If you accept the offer, meet me at this address tomorrow evening and you will be fully read in on the investigation... Gentlemen." She nodded to each in turn, handed them a business card with a handwritten New York City address on the back—with some instructions, and promptly left the office.

Tucker looked at Marek and the Captain and shrugged. "It's not like you get a chance to help defend mankind against monsters every day. I'm in. Sorry Captain, but I gotta be on board with this."

Marek laughed. "Well shit... there goes years of therapy. Guess I'm on board too. Can't just chalk it up to being crazy anymore."

◆

Agent Gordon stepped out of the precinct and into the cool evening air.

The city buzzed around her in its usual chaotic symphony—sirens somewhere distant, horns blaring in frustration, people moving with purpose. She paused on the sidewalk for a moment, letting the shift settle into her bones. Letting the mask drop.

Because inside that precinct, she was Agent Gordon.

Here—just for a breath—she was Warden Kaycee. And she was rattled.

She adjusted the collar of her jacket and started walking, boots striking pavement with rhythmic purpose. The cold kissed her cheeks, but her thoughts were anything but chilled.

She'd done it. She'd shown them the video. The Drakyn. The execution. And worse—the shadowy savior who didn't exist on any record the Bureau had ever admitted to keeping.

Her footsteps slowed as she passed a darkened shopfront. The city lights reflected in the window, ghosting her reflection back at her—composed, cool, unreadable. But beneath the surface, adrenaline still hummed.

She didn't know how Akron would respond. He knew that she differed from him in her beliefs—that humanity needed to be more aware of what was happening.

She'd known from the moment she cued up that video that she was skirting a line—a thin, sacred line etched into Warden history like a commandment.

Akron had given her explicit orders: she was *not* to speak about the Wardens or the Realms. Orders from Akron weren't just commands—they were binding, sealed by swearing upon one's own Essence.

She physically couldn't say the words.

But like all oaths, there were... loopholes. The kind you had to know how to slip through. As long as she didn't *explicitly* mention Wardens or the Realms, she was still within the letter of the order.

Well, she thought, *I didn't say those things, now did I?*

She wasn't sure if Akron would interpret it that way, but she'd done what she had to. Because when the next creature came clawing through, and if Akron appeared to stop it, she needed her team to hesitate just long enough not to shoot the one guy who might save their lives.

It wouldn't kill him, but it would piss him off. And no one wanted Akron pissed off.

She stopped walking and leaned against the corner of a graffiti-stained brick building. Pulled her phone out of her pocket. No messages.

Akron hadn't reached out. She didn't know if he would. Sometimes he was confrontational and direct, and sometimes he would sit back and wait to see what happened.

She stared at the phone a moment longer, then slipped it back into her pocket. Whatever came next, she'd face it head-on with no regrets—like she always did.

Kaycee pushed off the wall and vanished into the night.

Chapter 6

Marek stood beside Tucker outside the federal building... nervous tension etched into both their stances.

It loomed in front of them—just four stories of unmarked concrete—tucked between a pair of warehouses on the edge of the Brooklyn waterfront.

No markings, plain exterior. Forgettable, even. Exactly the kind of place you wouldn't look twice at unless you knew what was inside.

"Never thought I'd willingly join the Feds," Tucker muttered, eyeing the building like it had personally insulted him.

Marek gave a quiet snort of agreement.

They'd accepted the Bureau's offer. Signed the contracts. Handed over their weapons and badges from NYPD Homicide like it was the end of one life and the start of another. In a way, it was.

This wasn't just murder and motive anymore. It was the unknown. Creatures out of some supernatural story, unknown killers on the loose. A case file so far out of left field, it made every precinct story Marek had ever heard sound tame by comparison.

And somehow, through it all, he couldn't shake the feeling that he belonged in this moment. That he was finally on the track to finding answers about what had killed that girl and changed the trajectory of his life all those years ago.

The security checkpoint was quiet when they walked in. One agent—young, serious, sharp-eyed—checked their new IDs against a tablet and buzzed them through a thick steel door that led to a stark hallway lined with fluorescent lights. Not a word spoken.

Agent Gordon was waiting.

◆

She'd heard footsteps before she saw them, but the moment Marek stepped into view, something in her chest tightened—a quick, involuntary catch of breath she masked with a subtle shift of her weight. *Down, girl.* She told herself. *Keep it professional.*

She stood just inside the elevator at the far end, arms crossed, expression unreadable.

Dressed in black boots, cargo pants, and a tight, high-collared tactical jacket—she knew she looked like she was prepared more for a firefight, not a personnel orientation.

"Glad you made it," she said. Her voice was steady, but Marek caught the quick glance she gave him. Like she was assessing something only she could see. He nodded back.

Tucker offered his usual grin, though it was dulled around the edges. "Can't resist a job where there's a promise of death at the hand of monsters."

Gordon didn't laugh, but her lips twitched. "Come on. The team's upstairs. We'll do introductions and then get right into it if you're both ok with that?"

Marek and Tucker nodded and followed her into the elevator.

The elevator ride was silent. Marek watched her in the mirrored wall, catching the way her jaw tightened, how her gaze flicked to him once, then quickly away. She was watching. Calculating. But it didn't feel hostile. It felt... curious. Like he was a puzzle she was trying to figure out.

What Marek didn't know, was that Gordon was feeling a tug she couldn't fully explain. The closer Marek stood, the more aware she became of him—not just physically, because he was stupidly handsome—but on a level that brushed against her instincts like a faint pulse. There and gone again just as fast.

It was easy enough to ignore. Easy to chalk up to gut instinct or professional interest—but somewhere in the back of her mind, it lingered.

They stopped on the third floor, which looked more like an operations bunker than a workspace.

Cables snaked across the floor. Monitors flickered with surveillance footage. A whiteboard on one wall was filled with names, case IDs, and autopsy photos. A small team of Agents were gathered around a central conference table, their conversations hushed but urgent.

This was SCU—the Special Crimes Unit. The real one. The one everyone in the Bureau turned a blind eye to until they showed up to take over when someone higher-up cleared the way.

"Everyone," Gordon said, raising her voice. "Meet Marek Tomlinson and Tucker Daniels. They're officially part of the weird and the strange."

The agents turned. One by one, they looked up from their work, taking in the two newcomers with varying degrees of interest.

Gordon motioned to each in turn. "This is our core team. You'll be working closely with them. They have specialties, but all are trained in weapons, tactics and combat."

She pointed to the corner of the room. "Agent Marcus Velez. Surveillance and data aggregation specialist. If it has a camera or leaves a digital trail, he can find it."

The tall man with closely cropped hair and an unreadable face nodded once. "Welcome to the madness."

"Agent Harper Lanning. Forensics and bio-anomaly analyst. Former CDC pathologist. She's a double major in Pathology and Medicine. Our resident field medic when she's not in the lab. She's the reason we even know how weird the evidence is." Gordon said.

A petite woman with a sharp jawline and tired eyes gave them a wry smile. "Don't bleed on anything until I can study it. I may even patch you up first."

"Agent Malik Grant. Tactical response and extraction. Former Delta Force. If you ever get in over your head, pray he's nearby." The mountain of a man gave them a solemn nod and returned to cleaning his weapon on the table.

"And last but not least, Agent Riley Chen. Linguistics and pattern recognition. Languages, codes, anything with structure—she'll crack it."

Chen, a woman with a pixie cut and a sharp gleam in her eye, gave a half-wave. "Glad to have more boots on the ground."

Tucker gave them a casual salute. "I'll do my best to remember all your names, but I hope there's not a pop quiz at the end of this."

Marek nodded to them all. "Nice to meet everyone. Also, just call us Tucker and Marek—less of a mouthful."

"I like it. Nice and informal. You'll fit right in here," Chen said dryly. "Just don't get eaten."

Marek smiled faintly and took it all in. He couldn't help noticing the way Gordon carried herself—alert, controlled, quietly fierce. There was a calm intensity in her movements, a quiet storm always just below the surface. It intrigued him. She intrigued him.

It wasn't just her skill or presence—there was something deeper he couldn't put his finger on. And maybe it was just the adrenaline or the strangeness of the last few days, but the way she looked at him caused his heart rate to jump.

The low murmur of activity. The tension. The quiet competence. This wasn't a team of paper-pushers. These were professionals standing between the rest of the world and what went bump in the night. And now, he and Tucker were part of it.

Gordon gestured toward the far corner where a long table had been cleared. "We got something an hour ago. You should see it."

She tapped a tablet and brought up video footage. A parking garage camera, low angle, grainy. It showed a man walking to his car. Then the shadows moved.

A shape—too tall, too fast, too wrong—stepped out of nothingness and grabbed the man. No struggle. No sound. Just a flicker of motion, and the man was on the ground, chest torn open.

Tucker swore under his breath.

Gordon zoomed in on the attacker. The form was distorted, flickering in and out of frame like bad reception. But the outline was clear enough. Bipedal. Long limbs. Something like a tail. Not human.

"This is the sixth one this month," Gordon said.

She looked at Marek and said, "We still haven't been able to make sense of the locations, victim types, anything."

"Looks like the same creature as the video you showed us at the precinct. Before we knew what we were facing wasn't human, we were in the same boat as you all." Marek said as he gestured at the screen.

Tucker jumped in with an eager light in his eyes, one that generally precluded a breakthrough idea. "What if we've been thinking about this all wrong?"

Gordon shot a look to him, "We're all ears. What's running through your mind?"

"Well, what do we know for sure? We know that it isn't human and there's no pattern. That's not getting us anywhere, so what if, instead of looking for the next victim, we try to anticipate the next location?"

Marcus perked up at that and set to typing away at his computer, a couple minutes later, he spun around and exclaimed, "Got it! I started looking for similarities in the video recordings of each location, looking for commonalities, repeat occurrences. That's when I noticed that the cameras surrounding each location were picking up a strange frequency surge before each attacker showed up."

"This may be just a theory, and is kind of out there, so save your judgement," Marcus said, mouth pursed in concentration. "What if they are utilizing some way of traveling through the city that is based on some sort of dimensional travel? We already know they just pop into existence somehow, so what if wherever they are coming from, emits some sort of energy when they cross over?"

A short silence followed. Chen exchanged a look with Harper, then raised an eyebrow.

"Okay, that's officially the weirdest pitch I've heard this month," she said.

Harper nodded slowly, fingers drumming the table.

"We've had stranger ideas pan out though. I say we give it a try... what say you, boss?"

Gordon stayed quiet for a second... deep in thought.

Then she grinned and addressed Marcus. "You know, that may not be so far-fetched. Let's test your theory. I want you to build into your search algorithm any unusual frequency surges in cameras throughout New York City."

Marcus was already buried in code, fingers flying across the keyboard. "Alright, I'm adjusting the scanner parameters—tracking electromagnetic fluctuations, thermal spikes, and any shortwave anomalies across the city's surveillance grid. Give me some time to compile the data."

Gordon nodded.

"Good. Flag anything in real time. Whatever these things are, if your theory is correct and their appearance triggers the surges, I want to have as much advanced warning as possible."

Tucker leaned back in his chair; arms crossed behind his head.

"So, we sit on our asses and wait for another monster? If that's the plan, then let's just hope sword-guy shows up, otherwise we'll have another body on our hands."

Chen perked up and chuckled at that, "Sword-guy, I like it. Real original."

Tucker shot Chen a smirk, "I do live to please."

"No," Gordon spoke over them. "We prepare."

Gordon turned, keyed in a code on the wall panel, and stepped aside as a recessed cabinet slid open with a soft hiss. Inside were a series of matte-black cases stacked neatly and marked with SCU seals.

"Since you're both officially part of the team now, it's time you upgraded."

Tucker's eyebrows lifted as he and Marek walked over to the wall and took a look. "Gotta admit, I'm starting to like this job already."

Gordon flipped open the first case, revealing sleek, reinforced sidearms and compact carbines with custom etchings along the barrels. The weapons shimmered faintly beneath the overhead lights—nothing flashy, just the suggestion of something... different.

A second case held field gear: modular armor plates, tactical comms, ammunition, cartridges, and rows of combat knives. All with the same faint shimmer.

Gordon was expecting questions about the faint shimmer on the weapons and the weight that felt just a little too dense for their size. She didn't volunteer anything—and neither man asked. Not yet.

The weapons had been made for her team. Crafted by someone in the Warden ranks who owed her favors. Someone who knew how to make weapons that could kill monsters.

Both Tucker and Marek, however, didn't seem fazed—instead they were acting like kids at a candy store. She smiled.

Marek holstered the sidearm he'd removed, after examining it briefly, and clipped the carbine to the sling across his chest. Next, he strapped on two of the knives—one on his belt and the other in a thigh sheath.

Gordon flipped open the next case and pulled out a reinforced tactical vest, holding it out. Marek reached for it at the same moment. Their fingers brushed—brief, accidental—but it was like touching a live wire. Marek felt the jolt shoot straight down to his gut, fast and hot.

Gordon suppressed the sharp flare of heat that raced up her arm at the contact. It was just a touch. It shouldn't have affected her like this.

Except her traitorous brain was already cataloguing the width of his chest, the way his shirt pulled tight across it and the way his pants hugged that perfect ass—*snap out of it!*

She closed the case with a sharp snap, forcing herself to focus. Mission first. Everything else—everything she wasn't supposed to want—locked down hard.

Gordon masked her reaction well—but not quickly enough for Marek to miss the hitch in her breath, the light flush of her cheeks. *Does she feel it too?* He thought.

Before either of them could speak, Marcus's voice broke the silence.

"Got something."

Everyone turned.

He swiveled the monitor around. The live feed showed a stretch of cracked pavement and chain-link fence outside an old meatpacking plant in East Harlem.

A faint flicker pulsed in the corner of the screen, where one of the nearby street cams shimmered with a static distortion.

"I did what you asked. In each situation where a creature comes through, there was a slow build-up in thermal energy readings. A sudden spike in those readings always precedes a creature showing up on the cameras. With that metric, I reset my algorithm to seek these thermal energy build-ups—it just flagged a low-level surge spike."

"Anything moving in the area on thermal scans?" Gordon asked.

"Nothing yet, but there's a blind spot near the west loading dock. If something moved fast, we wouldn't have caught it."

Gordon was already moving. She grabbed her vest off the back of a chair and snapped the clips shut with practiced ease. "Suit up everyone. Marek, Tucker, no time for training wheels. Let's roll out."

Tucker gave a tight nod, his usual grin gone, replaced by the hard focus of a man switching into field mode. Marek said nothing, but his pulse had started to race. Not from fear—but from something else.

That awareness he got during high-stress combat situations kicking in. He felt eager, focused, and a little excited as he followed Gordon out the door to the armory.

The corridor outside the armory buzzed with quiet urgency. The team moved with purpose—checking gear, loading weapons, syncing comms. No panic, no chaos. Just routine, sharpened by readiness.

Marek adjusted the carbine across his chest and followed Gordon down the hall, Tucker on his heels. The elevator opened to the underground garage, where black SUVs sat in a neat row, engines already idling, headlights slicing through the dim light.

Tucker peeled off toward the lead rig, climbing in with Malik's response team. Marek hesitated just long enough for Gordon to glance back at him, then motion toward the passenger side of the middle vehicle.

"You riding with me?"

Marek smiled faintly. "If that's not a problem?"

The interior of the SUV was cool and quiet, the muted chatter of the SCU comms channel filling the silence between them as Gordon pulled the vehicle into gear—merging with the small convoy exiting the garage.

For a while, neither of them spoke. The city flashed past in a blur of streetlights, pavement, and metal buildings—the rain having just begun again in a thin drizzle that whispered across the windshield.

Marek watched the road, then risked a glance at Gordon. She was calm. Composed. But not stiff. There was a controlled intensity about her, like a coiled spring that never quite relaxed.

"You've been doing this sort of thing a while now, haven't you?" he asked finally.

She chuckled, low in her throat. "You could say that."

Marked continued, "I can tell. You're different from the rest of the agents I've worked with in the Bureau. The way you assessed the situation back there—how you moved. Calm, confident. Like someone more used to combat than a desk job."

She was quiet for a second, then said, "Let's just say my path into the SCU wasn't exactly traditional FBI academy, a desk first and then field work."

He gave her a sideways look. "And I'm guessing the full story's classified?"

She didn't answer right away, but the corners of her mouth lifted just slightly. "Something like that."

Silence settled between them—less awkward this time, more thoughtful. Gordon tapped the steering wheel lightly with her fingers, then said, "What about you?"

"What about me?"

"You've been in the SCU for what... twelve hours? And already you're walking into what could be a fight with a monster and barely a flicker of hesitation. Most recruits take weeks to stop flinching at the thought of facing something unknown. You didn't even blink."

Marek didn't answer right away. His eyes stayed on the road. "That thing I mentioned yesterday in Captain Gregg's office? I've been chasing it since I was seventeen. I just didn't know what it was... or if it was even real."

He let out a breath and shuddered slightly. "It looked human. That's what messed me up the most. It moved like a man, even smiled like one. But underneath... it wasn't. And that's the part that stuck.

"A monster that looks like a monster? You can brace for that—it's less scary because you expect it to look like it does. But one that hides behind a human face? That scares me more—it messes with my head."

She turned toward him slightly, her expression unreadable but open.

"That night," he continued. "A girl was attacked. I tried to stop it. I did everything I could, but... whatever the bastard was, he wasn't human. And the way he changed—shifting before my eyes—I thought I was losing my mind."

His voice had dropped, quieter now, almost introspective. "I've spent years trying to make sense of what I saw. Some therapy—then denial when that didn't work. Now I'm here, and I don't know if that means I've finally found answers... or if the rabbit hole just goes deeper."

Gordon was quiet, her eyes on the road, but something softened in her posture. Understanding, maybe. Or something like it.

"You're not crazy," she said.

He looked at her, surprised by the certainty in her voice.

She glanced over at him. "You're not the only one who's seen things that shouldn't exist."

The air between them shifted—subtle, but there. Marek felt it in the warmth that spread through him, in the awareness of how close they were in the tight confines of the vehicle. Her voice. Her scent—clean, faintly metallic, like ozone before a storm.

He cleared his throat, trying to shake the feelings he shouldn't be having for his superior. "So, what's the deal with the gear? That sidearm you handed me... it's not standard issue either."

So much for them not asking questions. She thought to herself, *I should have known this one wouldn't miss it.*

"No, it's not," she admitted. "The SCU works with a few custom suppliers. Everything's tailored for high-impact, non-standard engagements."

"You mean monsters."

Her lips twitched. "Something like that."

He chuckled to himself, "yeah, something like that, huh?"

They reached a red light, and the SUV rolled to a stop. Gordon drummed her fingers on the steering wheel again, thoughtful.

"I meant what I said earlier," she said quietly. "You don't move like a regular cop. I've worked with enough to know. You've got instincts. Awareness. When Marcus called out that sensor spike, you were already gearing up before I gave any direction."

He looked at her, something stirring behind his eyes. "You always analyze your teammates this much?"

"Only when they make the hair on the back of my neck stand up," she said without missing a beat.

Marek chuckled, the sound low and genuine. "Good to know I'm making an impression."

Marek leaned back into the seat and let his gaze drift over her. Gordon drove with effortless control—one hand resting lightly on the wheel, the other poised near the gearshift. His eyes had a mind of their own, as they were drawn to the rise and fall of her breasts as she breathed evenly and steadily.

Fuck... He was acting like a teenager again. *Eyes upfront!* He scolded himself, snapping his gaze to the road. He shouldn't be thinking that—not now, not ever. But the image was there anyway, unbidden and vivid.

Beside him, Gordon stayed outwardly composed, but she wasn't immune either. She felt the heat of him, the way his arm nearly brushed hers across the console, the casual power in the way he lounged in the seat.

His eyes felt like a physical caress when she caught him looking at her just now. Marek Tomlinson radiated strength—and worst of all, he didn't seem to notice the effect he was having on her. Or maybe he did. She couldn't tell, and it was *frustrating*.

Damn it! She exhaled quietly and fixed her gaze on the road. No distractions. No entanglements. Especially not ones built like sin and packaged as her subordinate.

The light turned green, and the convoy moved forward again.

For a few moments, the city faded around them. And in the silence that stretched between one breath and the next, something unspoken sparked and lingered between them—just beneath the surface.

Something neither of them was quite ready to name.

Chapter 7

Meatpacking Plant—3:14 am

The convoy rolled to a stop in the shadow of an abandoned meatpacking plant, engines humming low
against the early-morning quiet. The building loomed
like a concrete tomb—four stories of soot-stained brick,
its broken windows like dark, watchful eyes.

Marek stepped out of the passenger seat and scanned
the surroundings. The air was dense with the smell of
rust, and something faint beneath it—something sour
and animal. It raised the hairs on the back of his neck.

Gordon joined him a second later, silent as a shadow.
She moved like a jungle cat—calm, confident and lethal.
She glided across the ground, head on a swivel, and
shoulders loose but ready.

"Looks abandoned," Tucker muttered as he climbed
out of the SUV behind them. "Which means something's
probably inside waiting to eat us."

"Harper, Marcus—set up perimeter feeds," Gordon
ordered, eyes rolling at Tucker's comment. "Thermals,
motion sensors, full sweep. I want eyes on every inch of
this place."

"Copy that," Harper said, pulling her helmet on.
"Deploying motion sensors—forty-five-degree coverage
pattern."

"Running infrared calibration," Marcus added. "Thermal feed up in sixty seconds."

Gordon nodded. "Take your time—do it right. I want zero dead zones."

Marek glanced at her. "You expecting company?"

"I always do."

Malik emerged last, already suited up, rifle slung across his chest.

"North and west alleys are blind," Malik said in his deep rumble. "Too many obstructions for line of sight. I'll post at the west entrance, cover movement from the rooftops."

"Do it."

Marek stood at Gordon's side as she surveyed the building. Her face was unreadable, but he could feel the tension humming off her—like she already knew something was off but wasn't ready to say it.

She turned to him without warning. "You feel it?"

He blinked. "Feel what?"

She didn't answer immediately. Her eyes tracked along the broken fence line, then back to the flickering streetlamp at the far corner of the lot. "Static in the air. Like before a lightning strike."

Marek inhaled slowly. The air *was* off. Charged in a way he couldn't explain. It settled against his skin like dust from a fire. His chest tightened slightly, not from fear, but from pressure. He also became aware of a low thrum just behind his eyes, faint but there.

"I feel something," he admitted. "But I can't name it—just a faint buzz in my head."

Her eyes met his for a beat longer than necessary.

Interesting instincts for a human, she thought.

Instead, she said, "Let's check the south entry. You're with me."

Tucker rolled his eyes. "Of course he is."

Gordon shot him a dry look. "Cut the sarcasm, Tucker. Sweep the exterior. Stay on comms, report anything out of place. And take Chen—everybody gets a buddy."

Chen quipped, "What about Malik? Doesn't he get a buddy?"

"No, because he's a badass," Gordon said, a rare grin tugging at her mouth.

Chen muttered, "Unfair workplace favoritism," but fell into step with Tucker, anyway.

Tucker smirked. "Chen, we're not badass enough—we'll just have to try harder."

Then to Gordon: "Boss, if we trip over anything with scales, I'm blaming you personally."

"You can file a complaint later," she said with a chuckle, already moving toward the plant.

Marek followed, boots crunching softly on broken glass and gravel. The side door of the plant stood crooked on its hinges.

Marek stepped closer, inspecting it without touching. The metal wasn't just warped—it had *bowed inward*, as if something huge had busted through, and recently.

"Looks like it was strong enough to not notice a door in its way," he murmured.

"Not surprised," Gordon said. "Whatever it was, probably wasn't concerned about being subtle."

She pulled her carbine, checked the load and chambered a round. She nodded toward the open door. "Stay close."

Inside, the air was even heavier—humid and stale, like the inside of a forgotten basement. Rusted meat hooks dangled from the ceiling. Large metal tables, long unused, were arranged in disarray. Old conveyor belts and walk-in freezers lined the far wall. The faint sound of dripping water echoed somewhere in the dark.

Gordon swept her flashlight across the floor, and spotted blood.

A thin trail, already drying, ran in uneven spatters across the concrete toward the stairwell in the back. No body. No drag marks. Just drops—like something would make if it was injured and still moving.

"Shit," Marek muttered.

Gordon crouched and examined the blood. "Too fresh for this to be old. And no smear pattern. Whoever was bleeding... they were upright. Moving fast."

She rose to her feet. "I'm thinking something was waiting for our creature when it crossed over and maybe injured it."

Marek frowned. "Could this be like some kind of entry point to our world from theirs? Always open if they know where to look?"

Gordon hesitated. She didn't like theorizing out loud—especially when she already knew more than she could explain. But Marek's instincts were good. Maybe better than she'd accounted for.

"It's possible," she said. "We've seen patterns before—surge sites appearing in clusters, locations used more than once. This building's isolated enough to serve as a temporary staging ground."

Marek's gaze swept the darkness beyond her shoulder. "I don't like the sound of that."

They shared a glance, tension sharpening between them—not just from the scene, but from something else. A quiet pull neither could fully name. Gordon was the first to look away.

Her comm crackled in her earpiece. Malik's voice came through, steady but clipped. "Movement on the north roof. One shape. Bipedal. Limping but moving fast."

Gordon tapped her earpiece. "Marcus, can you confirm?"

A pause.

"Negative. It's staying in the blind spots."

She spoke to Malik again, "Human or something else?"

"The giant tail would suggest otherwise." Malik deadpanned.

Tucker chuckled over the comms "My kind of guy,"

"Bunch of smartasses we got here," Gordon said in some exasperation. "Quiet on the comms, if I wanted jokes, I'd hit up a comedy bar."

She rolled her eyes, and glanced Marek's direction, "Teenagers... I work with teenagers."

A thud echoed from above, followed by the screech of metal dragging across concrete.

Marek tensed. "Malik's right, that sounds like it came from the roof and it's moving."

"You ready for a little exercise?" She asked.

He grinned. "Lead the way."

Chapter 8

The metal stairs groaned under their boots as Marek and Gordon climbed, weapons drawn, flashlights now turned off. Gordon didn't want to risk whatever was up there, getting advance notice that they were coming.

Rain tapped against the steel railings in a soft hiss, the city stretching out around them in a wash of shadows and orange streetlight. Every instinct in Marek's body was on high alert.

There was a buzz behind his eyes which was growing stronger the higher they climbed. Some sixth sense, something he couldn't put a name to, told him that whoever—or whatever—was up there, wasn't human.

They reached the rooftop access door, rusted shut and half-hinged. Gordon didn't hesitate. She pressed her back to the wall, nodded once, and Marek kicked the door open, him taking point and Gordon moving out behind him low and fast.

Empty air and concrete met them, but no movement.

Gordon continued on, gliding low across the rooftop's surface like she'd done this a hundred times. Marek followed without thinking, sweeping his carbine left to right, breathing steady despite the adrenaline thrumming in his veins.

They moved like they'd been training together for years, aware of each other in a way that defied explanation.

The rooftop was cluttered with old HVAC units, tangled piping, and moss-slicked vents—plenty of places to hide.

Marek stayed close—too close—and every time their bodies shifted in tandem, Gordon felt the proximity like static brushing her skin. His heat an almost physical presence against her back. Solid and steady. The faint scent of him—leather, soap, and something darker underneath—threaded through the humid night air.

Marek caught a flash of her profile—sharp cheekbones, full mouth tight with focus—and had to wrench his gaze away before his mind wandered somewhere dangerous.

Eyes on the mission. He reminded himself. Not on the curve of her hips beneath the gear. Not on the lithe strength of her frame clearing the debris ahead.

The static in the air was stronger now, prickling across his skin. That strange buzz in his head was getting worse, slowly easing into headache territory.

He glanced at Gordon. She felt it too—he could tell. Her movements were sharper, faster, like she was moving towards something her eyes hadn't caught yet.

"Malik," Gordon whispered into her comm, "do you still have eyes?"

A moment of silence, and then. "Negative."

Gordon cursed under her breath. *Damn it.* She was aware of exactly where the creature was, but if she spoke now, they'd start asking questions she wasn't allowed to answer.

So, she motioned for Marek to stay close. He did, showing trust in her leadership—which did funny things to her insides.

They moved in silence, weaving between vents and low ducts, eyes scanning every angle.

Then the wind shifted—carrying a sharp, metallic tang that hit Gordon's enhanced senses like a slap.

Blood. More of it.

Her gaze snapped toward a dark smear trailing across one of the HVAC units—barely visible in the low light, but crystal clear to her.

She switched on her tac light and panned it toward the smear. Once illuminated by the light, she was able to motion for Marek to check it out.

He moved in silently, crouched beside the smear and touched it with a gloved hand.

Still wet.

"Trail's fresh," he said quietly.

Gordon's eyes tracked to the far corner of the rooftop. Butting up against a neighboring roof, there was just enough room for a person to clear the distance in a well-timed jump. An easy distance for the creature they were hunting.

"It's either injured, or fresh off a kill. I haven't seen a body yet." Gordon said.

"My money is on sword-guy," Marek said with a faint chuckle. "He could have injured it when it got here, and we could be in the middle of his hunt."

"Please don't encourage your partner with the nicknames," Gordon replied, rolling her eyes.

"Let's try catching up to see if we can't find ourselves a creature, or better yet... our sword-guy." Gordon said, glancing at Marek—a smile tugging at the corner of her mouth. Signaling them to move forward, they advanced in sync, weapons raised.

Marek's pulse thudded in his ears. Something wasn't right. He didn't know what he was feeling. It wasn't... fear, but something else. The buzz in his head had turned into a full-on headache now.

He didn't realize he'd slowed until Gordon turned to look at him.

"You feel something?" she asked softly.

He nodded. "Yeah, maybe nothing—but the buzzing's a full-on headache now."

It wasn't just the trail. The rooftop *felt* wrong—like a drumhead drawn too tight. Pressure against the inside of his skull. Every step forward made it worse.

Suddenly, a blur of motion swept past them—fast and low, like a shadow breaking from the vent system. It clipped Marek's elbow and Gordon spun, weapon raised.

"Contact!" she said into her comm.

Marek pivoted, but it was gone before he could track it. A faint scuff of claws on concrete echoed across the rooftop.

Then silence.

"Something's toying with us," he muttered, wincing still against the building headache.

Gordon's jaw clenched. "Yeah, or it's on the run from something worse."

From the corner of his eye, Marek caught it—for a brief moment. A silhouette, crouched on the far corner of the building they were on. Tall, scaly with a tail. Large—probably seven feet tall. Definitely not human.

It tilted its head at them—slowly, deliberately, its eyes a reddish glow against the early morning darkness.

"You see that?" He pointed with his carbine.

Gordon raised hers, and whispered, "don't move."

But the thing was already heading away from them—launching from the rooftop with inhuman grace. It cleared the distance between the two buildings easily and disappeared on the other side.

Marek moved instinctively, sprinting after it. Gordon cursed and followed, both leaping the gap between rooftops. They hit the far side hard, Marek rolling to absorb the impact—Gordon landing with a grunt but never breaking stride.

They gave chase, leaping the next gap, boots slamming onto the crumbling concrete of the building's roof.

The creature had been fast—blindingly fast—but it seemed to be slowing down. Like it was running out of steam.

They cut through an upper catwalk, ducked beneath sagging power lines, climbed over rusted ductwork.

"There!" Gordon called out, pointing to a flash of movement one rooftop down from them. The figure was hunched, its limbs jerking unnaturally, skin slick in the moonlight, head swiveling back and forth. It stopped for a half-second—long enough to turn its head and stare back at them.

Marek felt something in his chest lurch, a deep, primal warning that vibrated through his bones.

His headache increased to a level that almost took him to his knees.

Then the thing moved again, loping like a predator toward a dilapidated rooftop billboard. But it wasn't alone.

There was a flash of blue-white lightning—and immediately, Marek's headache vanished, like something released the building pressure.

That's when Marek saw a figure stepped out of the disturbance, moving quickly.

It hit the creature mid-run in a blur of motion. A shockwave cracked through the night air as both forms collided, skidding across the rooftop in a blur of violence.

Marek and Gordon came to a stop, ducking behind the edge of the rooftop.

The fight played out in brutal silence—almost too fast to follow. Steel clashed with claws. Sparks lit the dark like miniature lightning strikes. The creature shrieked, a raw, guttural sound that echoed down into the alleys below.

Gordon stood frozen for a moment, *Shit, Akron showed up without a veil. He's got to be pissed to not be aware that humans are in the area.*

Marek's breath caught. He looked to Gordon, but didn't find the surprise on her face he was expecting.

Her eyes flicked to him and whatever he saw, disappeared behind that cool mask of steel, as she turned back to look.

The second figure—tall, cloaked, blades flashing—moved like a controlled whirlwind. Every strike was deliberate, surgical, and landed with the force of a freight train. The creature tried to break away, clearly outclassed and desperate as it lunged toward the fire escape.

It didn't make it.

Sword-guy caught it mid-leap with one arm and drove it into the rooftop. The creature writhed on the ground briefly, then there was a flash of steel, blades driving deep.

The creature twitched once, then stilled.

Marek didn't move. Couldn't.

The cloaked figure—taller than Marek, broad-shouldered, face obscured by shadow—stood over the body for several seconds. Then, as if sensing them, he slowly turned his head in their direction.

Even at a distance, Marek felt it—pressure, like a memory that wasn't his pressing against the inside of his skull—recognition without reason.

He didn't know the figure, but some deep part of him did. And it scared him more than the creature had.

What the hell? He thought to himself. He then looked in Gordon's direction.

She crouched lower, rifle slightly lowered. Like she was trying to make herself smaller.

Then, as fast as he'd come, the stranger was gone.

He stepped into nothingness—disappeared. No flash of light. No sound. Just... gone. Swallowed by the shadows.

Marek surged forward instinctively, sliding down fire escapes, making his way over to the building's rooftop. He sprinted across to the site of the battle, Gordon on his heels.

They arrived, weapons up, but it was too late.

The creature's body was already beginning to change—its elongated limbs shriveling, its skin paling to a greyish hue. Changing to human right before their eyes.

"Impossible," Marek whispered.

Gordon grimaced, standing over the body. "That's probably why these creatures have stayed hidden for so long."

Marek took a deep breath, "Probably why sword-guy doesn't bother cleaning up. No one's going to ask questions about a homicide that leaves no evidence—I wouldn't even know where to start if this crossed my desk."

Gordon crouched beside it, inspecting the massive gashes across its torso.

"I'll have to check the video feeds again, but I think this is the same type of creature as the others," she murmured.

Marek knelt beside her, eyes still scanning the shadows. "I think you're right. And someone took it down like it was nothing."

Gordon felt like a puppet master—trying to point them to what they were dealing with, without actually giving information that would violate her orders. She was getting quite good at asking the right questions. At pointing her team in the right direction—and Marek was sharper than most.

Marek was still trying to make sense of what he'd seen. The speed. The precision, the sheer strength required to lift that creature one-handed.

"If it weren't for the video feeds, I'd probably seriously question my sanity, what with the changing corpses, and sword-guy appearing out of lightning." He shook his head.

This wasn't his first glimpse of one of these creatures. But seeing it in real life was different. Seeing someone fight it and win, was something else entirely.

Destroy is more like it, he thought, *the creature didn't stand a chance.*

Malik's voice crackled through the comms. "Team one, sitrep."

Gordon tapped her earpiece, her eyes still locked on the mangled body.

"Target neutralized," she said. "But not by us."

There was a long pause on the line.

Then Malik's reply: "Say again?"

"You heard me," Gordon muttered. She stood, gaze drifting toward the place the cloaked figure had vanished. "Seems like we're not alone in this fight."

"Was it sword-guy?" Tucker's voice broke in excitedly, "Please tell me it was sword-guy!"

"Tucker!" Gordon shouted

"Yes boss?"

"Shut up."

"Yes boss."

Marek chuckled to himself, glad someone else had to deal with Tucker's antics for a change.

His mirth vanished as he remembered the draw of the figure—sword-guy. The shiver of recognition he felt within himself when he'd turned in their direction

Whatever that man was, and wherever he was, Marek had the suspicion that they'd see him again.

Chapter 9

Akron stood at the rooftop's edge, one boot perched on the rusted railing of a forgotten water tower, his long coat fluttering in the wind. Below, the city murmured in restless sleep—traffic lights blinking in isolation, a distant siren wailing in the silence. Blood still clung to his gloves.

The Drakyn was dead. This was the second one—the one that had escaped him the night he'd killed its mate. He'd arrived too late, then. Too late to save the fifth victim.

Tonight, he thought with satisfaction, had balanced the scales, but it wasn't victory. Not really.

Akron's eyes swept the rooftop below where the Special Crimes Unit gathered around the cooling corpse. Their postures spoke volumes—tight grips, sharp glances, the unsettled edge of professionals shaken by what they'd seen. And in the center of it all was Warden Kaycee.

Of course she was here.

She was supposed to be watching. Advising, maybe. Not fighting. Not getting involved. He should have pulled her out months ago. But she would've fought him—and he hadn't had the energy for that.

She always had been stubborn—this was her section of the rift to patrol after all. She also had her own agenda. She thought the humans should be made aware of what was going on. She'd always felt that way.

She believed they need to know so they could try to learn how to fight back. And now, it seemed, she was right in the middle of things—trying to do just that.

Akron had been explicit. The command wasn't casual—it had been sworn upon her Essence, a binding order. She was forbidden to speak of what she was, the Wardens, or the Realms. So far she was complying... barely.

He understood that she meant well—and maybe she was right—maybe humans deserved to know about the Realms...

But he didn't see how they'd stand a chance against Realm creatures—human weapons had no effect on them. So why even try when they'd just panic? It was the Warden's job to keep the humans safe and protected. Had been since their creation.

Kaycee thought she'd found a way to change the human's weapons—giving them a fighting advantage. Well, that remained to be seen.

She thought Akron didn't know about Teliz helping her craft rift-forged weapons—but he did. Sometimes he felt like a father with unruly kids. They all thought they were being so sneaky.

His gaze flicked to the man beside her.

Tall. Strong. His stance was disciplined, but something in it was... familiar. A confidence not often found in one his age. And there was a rhythm to the way he moved—like he was reacting on instinct more than training.

Akron frowned. He didn't recognize the man, other than that he was one of the detectives who'd been following the case several days ago.

He wasn't a Warden. No tether to the Realms. And yet—a vibration in his pocket derailed his thoughts.

Akron drew out the obsidian disk—ancient, Rift-forged by his own hands millennia ago, meant to monitor the Rift's structural integrity.

It was warm. Pulsing. Pulsing was always bad. It meant weakness.

The Rift had closed. But it was still weak in this section of New York City.

That was the real problem. Not the Drakyn, or the killings—those were symptoms of a larger problem.

It was that a Rift had thinned enough to let a Realm creature pass through.

That wasn't supposed to happen. Onos's power wasn't supposed to wane. He had been a Titan, after all.

The Rift was Earth's last defense, a barrier holding back the chaos and power of the Realms. And now, it was thinning, wearing down.

Not in a single catastrophic collapse... but quietly. Gradually. Like sand slipping through a crack in the foundation.

Beasts that once needed a gatekeeper now seemed to slip through on their own. And those that did still need a hand? Their handlers wouldn't stay put for long. Not if they smelled blood. Not if they saw an opportunity.

Earth already housed a scattering of Realm citizens—those who had fled their home realms. Exiles. Refugees. Some harmless. Some dangerous. But they kept quiet. They kept hidden.

This though? This would break the balance, if it hadn't already. Akron wasn't sure how the Wardens would keep up with their already reduced numbers. He'd been unable to make any new Wardens in the past three centuries—not since Warden Kaycee. No human so far had been found worthy of the Essence.

He clenched the disk in his hand—still pulsing red—and pocketed it again.

The Realms hadn't figured it out yet—not fully. But when they did, when word spread that Earth's barrier was thinning... faltering... the flood would come.

Akron turned away from the city, fading into the shadows that gathered behind the water tower. He looked back one last time—toward Kaycee. At Marek beside her, and the mortal agents cleaning up the corpse of something that should never have made it through to begin with.

Something had changed in the last century. Something that was escalating the breakdown in Onos's protection. He didn't know what it was, but he needed to find out, and fast. Earth was running out of time.

As he opened up a Rift portal and stepped through, his thoughts were heavy with the weight of responsibility and a need to find answers.

◆

The Rift pulsed shut behind Akron as he stepped out into his personal study within the Warden stronghold—Arckus.

He crossed to the map on his desk and updated locations in New York City where the Rift was showing signs of weakening.

One spot in Central Park, was particularly worrisome, so he made a special notation by that area.

Rift weakening—paper thin—flag for special follow-up. Concern about complete failure.

At that moment, his phone chose to buzz. He checked it and sighed heavily. The Council. Again.

—FROM: *Warden Council*

—TOPIC: *Warden losses & Rift Stability Concerns—The Council is having a special session of the Five. Your presence Is respectfully requested.*

Respectfully. He snorted. *That would be the day.*

For centuries, he had allowed the formation of this so-called "Council"—a concession to give the Wardens a voice. A way to surface concerns: gaps in training, threats from the Realms, failures he might not catch himself.

He never intended for them to grow teeth.

And now they were biting. Gaining traction. Becoming more than a formality—becoming a problem. And frankly, a major headache.

He pocketed the phone without replying, and headed to the Council Chamber.

The corridors were quiet at this hour, but Arckus itself thrummed with power—Rift energy pulsing through the walls lining his passage, like a distant heartbeat.

◆

The Council chamber was located slightly above Arckus, in floating cliffs connected by a winding stone staircase that—like everything in Arckus—defied the laws of physics by its existence.

He opened the double doors and walked into the chamber, exuding power and quiet authority. The chamber itself was built into those cliffs above Arckus—dark stone hewn by Rift energy manipulation.

Riftlight filtered through slits in the rock, the walls pulsing faintly with Rift energy.

A vaulted dome arched above the central table—massive, round, scarred by centuries of arguments. Five Wardens stood within. The five who were the most vocal, and who had the strongest voice.

Althis, upright and rigid, arms folded behind his back.

Vara, statuesque and composed, every movement precise.

Halros, hunched slightly with his usual air of concern.

Elyos, robes perfectly arranged, face calm with the ever-present smile of a seasoned diplomat.

And Malen—by the far edge, half-shadowed, brooding and unreadable.

Akron stepped forward, scanning each of their faces before speaking. "I've read your message. Say what you wish—I do not have much time."

Halros was first. "We've lost twenty Wardens in the last thirty years—one of them by your own hand."

Akron's gaze did not flinch.

"And you've found no new Warden recruits to replace them in that time," Althis added sharply. "We used to number five thousand strong—and over the past five centuries we've been whittled down to twenty-five hundred."

Elyos interjected, tone measured, words chosen with surgical care. "We're over-extended, Akron. Rift breaches are increasing, and more and more creatures are slipping through. I'm covering four territories now—and I'm not even the worst case."

Vara's voice was low and precise. "The pattern is unsustainable. We're burning through our strength, and Earth's current trajectory offers no return."

Akron tilted his head. "Return?"

Vara held his gaze. "Earth gives nothing back now. No new Wardens. No awareness of the Realms. We are ghosts to them, and we die as such, while they go on oblivious."

Akron's voice was calm, but absolute.

"We were never promised rewards. Onos gave us Earth to protect—your duty... your whole reason for existing is to protect them. That is the charge. That is part of the Oath. One each of you took when you became a Warden. I know because I was the one who saved you from death and gave you the opportunity to serve."

"That is the problem, Akron. You have not made any new Wardens in the last two centuries," Elyos said, arms spread in weary exasperation.

"None have been found worthy," Akron replied, jaw clenching.

Malen stepped away from the wall, his voice darker than the others.

"Maybe because humanity is no longer worthy. You've seen them over the past two hundred years, Akron. Becoming more morally bankrupt. Killing themselves. Warring with themselves—it causes our Warden brethren to question why we die to protect a species that seems intent on self-destruction."

"Maybe it's time we question whether that Oath makes sense?" He added, his voice sharp, the final word like a blade on stone.

The chamber went silent. Akron's gaze turned on him.

"You speak like one who has forgotten that the Oath is not something you get to back out of because it's hard."

"Hard?" Malen snapped. "It's suicide. And you refuse to adapt. The Realms are not unified anymore. We have potential allies out there—"

Akron cut him off. "You FORGET! Your singular reason for existing is to serve humanity. Without them, there is no reason for you—for us. And the realms are NOT our allies. They simply bide their time. Their hate is ancient. We protect the humans from Realms that wouldn't hesitate to enslave and destroy if presented the opportunity."

Elyos raised a hand, placating, shooting daggers at Malen. "We're not suggesting we abandon Earth. Just that we open channels—formal overtures of diplomacy to the Realms. Define our terms, protect our strength. This isn't betrayal, Akron. We're weak, and our numbers are getting smaller. When strength in numbers becomes a problem, strategy should be the solution."

"You think a treaty will protect you if the Rift collapses? It will not. When that happens, make no mistake: every Realm will unite to subjugate or destroy humanity," Akron said. He reached into his coat and pulled out the obsidian disk, glyphs glowing a dull red.

"This burned in my hand the moment the second Drakyn crossed into New York City. It shouldn't have been possible, yet It slipped through anyway. Further evidence that the Rift is continuing to weaken."

Vara frowned, voice unshaken. "Then we should be using our energy to reinforce the Rift, not to just keep bleeding for a species that wouldn't blink if we were erased."

Malen spoke again. "Maybe Earth is no longer worth the sacrifice."

Akron turned slowly, meeting his gaze. "You would abandon the world that Onos sacrificed his divinity to protect? That the last of his power forged the Rift to shield?"

He stepped closer, voice low and dangerous.

"To speak of withdrawing from Earth—to consider alliances with Realms who once sought to rule or destroy humanity—is bordering on treason. Do not speak of it again. This Council was created to advise me. To elevate the voices of Wardens who felt unheard—not to question your sacred Oaths, or your duty as Wardens."

Akron turned and walked back toward the exit of the chamber. He paused to look back at them.

"Let me be clear. If any of you reach out to the Realms without my explicit order, you will be stripped of your mantle and killed for treason. That is not a threat. That is a promise—one I am oath bound, and enthusiastically willing to enforce."

He left the chamber without another word.

Malen remained motionless as the doors shut behind Akron.

Vara exhaled. "Well, that is that I guess. He won't change."

Elyos folded his hands. "He's right to fear the Realms. But fear can be as blinding as faith."

Althis sighed, removing his robe and draping it across his chair revealing black Warden armor beneath.

"Well, best be back to our patrols... not much more we can do. We've shared our thoughts, and Akron took it about as well as we all thought he would. Better—actually, since we're all still breathing."

Malen said nothing. Just watched the Riftlight flickering... seething inside at Akron's unwillingness to hear reason... Again!

He would need to find a way to get in touch with his contact from the Realm of Shadow and Thought, and soon. He'd have to be quiet. Careful. Akron had confirmed his contact's suspicions—the Rift was weakening.

Malen hadn't confirmed the exact location... not yet. But he would. Akron had to know more than he was sharing... had to.

And when he did confirm it, then Dharken Mohr would be ready... And when he was, there'd be no more protecting these worthless humans.

No more dying in order to save a race that was no longer worth saving.

Everyone would bow to the Elvahr General or be killed—and Malen would be there—ruling alongside him.

Chapter 10

Rooftop—Meatpacking Plant—4:05 a.m.

The rooftop was quiet now. Too quiet. The air still carried the echo of violence—cracked asphalt, and the metallic smell of blood.

The creature was dead, and the man who had killed it—if he *was* a man—was gone.

Marek stood near the mangled corpse, trying to process what he'd just seen.

Whoever the cloaked figure was, he had taken down the creature with brutal efficiency. There was no hesitation or wasted movement. He fought like he'd done it a thousand times.

No—scratch that. 'Fought' wasn't the right word. That wasn't a fight. A fight was two sided, when both sides at least had equal chance of victory.

This had been a one-sided, quick execution. Like watching a predator dispatch prey. It was swift, practiced and inevitable.

And that sword-guy, as Tucker dubbed him? He hadn't broken a sweat.

Marek's breath steamed in the cool air as he turned his head to look at Gordon. She stood a few feet away, her back to him, eyes scanning the skyline where the figure had disappeared.

Her jaw was set, her weapon still half-raised—like she expected something else to come lunging from the dark.

She hadn't said a word since the man vanished.

Neither had he.

But Marek was watching her now. She'd handled the entire chase like a veteran, like someone who'd seen monsters before. And that... that kind of strength was impressive.

It drew him in like a magnet. He'd always had a thing for strong women, and she was stronger than most.

Marek tried to shake the feeling, but it settled deeper still. The adrenaline was fading, but the sharpness in his chest wasn't. It was turning into something else now—something warmer—something he shouldn't feel for his superior.

"You okay?" he asked quietly.

Gordon nodded, still facing the skyline. "Yeah. Just... thinking."

"About that guy? Who he could be?"

"About *what* he could be."

She turned then, meeting his gaze. Her eyes were storm-dark, calm on the surface but hiding too much beneath. It hit Marek harder than he expected—how composed she was. She was beautiful, in a way that had nothing to do with symmetry or softness.

It was strength. Poise. And something else. Something wild under the surface she hadn't let out yet—though he'd only caught brief glimpses of it.

"You've seen a lot," he said, his voice lower than usual. "More than you're saying."

She didn't flinch. "So have you."

"You handled yourself like you've done this before," he said after a moment. "Like hunting monsters is just another Tuesday."

"Not just monsters." Her voice was quiet, and there was something brittle underneath—like she wasn't talking about the creatures anymore.

That answer didn't help the burning curiosity building in his chest.

She moved toward the edge of the rooftop, glancing once more at the place the cloaked figure had disappeared. Marek followed her a few steps, close enough to notice the subtle shifts in her breathing, the controlled tension in her jaw. She was still on edge. Still wired.

She shifted just slightly, like she wasn't used to people standing that close. Or maybe she was afraid of what he might see if he got too close.

"I've worked with a lot of agents," he said quietly. "Most of them... they get loud when they're scared. They overcompensate. You don't."

She glanced at him sideways with a little smirk. "You always analyze your teammates this much?"

He laughed—deep, smooth, confident—and she hated the way her thighs clenched at the sound. "Touché."

Her lips quirked, just barely. "And what's the verdict?"

He hesitated. "You don't move like any agent I've met."

She arched a brow. "No?"

"No. You move like a soldier."

Their eyes locked again—longer this time.

Gordon didn't respond. She didn't have to.

The moment stretched thin between them, pulled taut by adrenaline, proximity, and everything they weren't saying.

Gordon sighed and said, "It's been a long night and an even longer morning. Go home, Marek. Take some time today to rest and try to get some sleep tonight. We'll debrief tomorrow morning."

He nodded. His thoughts were tangled. Not just about the creature. Or the cloaked figure.

But *her*.

His rational mind screamed at him to back off, to keep things professional. But something deeper—instinctive, primal—leaned toward her. Wanted more. She pulled to something in him like a magnet.

He was trying to keep it professional. Keep his distance. But the way she moved, the way she thought, everything about her—it was becoming a temptation he wasn't sure he could resist.

Chapter 11

Marek's Apartment—The Next Day.

The shower hissed behind him, steam curling through the small apartment bathroom as Marek leaned on the edge of the sink, shirtless, palms pressed flat to the cool porcelain.

His reflection stared back at him from the mirror, jaw tight, dark hair damp with the moisture in the enclosed space.

After running some errands and re-stocking his fridge—he still had to eat, after all—he called his mom, and had a good, long talk.

She was always a light in the darkness, had been ever since he joined the NYPD. She didn't ask too many questions, and was always just there to talk when he needed it.

She grounded him. Always had.

Sleep that night, if you could even call it that, had been restless.

Every time he closed his eyes, he saw it again—the creature's silhouette crouched in the moonlight and the blur of motion. The way sword-guy took it apart.

And then Gordon standing steady beside him, eyes sharp, voice calm, and not a tremor in her hands.

He'd seen hardened cops who'd get weak in the knees at less.

She handled everything that was thrown at her with that same calm, unflappable demeanor. And God help him; he couldn't get her out of his head.

He scrubbed a hand down his face and tried to chase the thought away. It was stupid. Complicated. She was his superior and a federal agent. He wasn't about to be the rookie who couldn't keep it in his pants.

And yet...

The way she moved. The way she looked at him. That moment on the rooftop—when their eyes had met, and something passed between them—had tied an invisible thread around his chest.

It hadn't been there before. But it was there now—like gravity—connecting to her.

And it scared the hell out of him.

She was off limits. His mind knew that, but his heart didn't seem to care.

He'd always been one to follow rules. Always professional.

She made him want to break every damn rule. And that—more than anything—was what scared him. He was someone else around her, and he didn't know how to handle that.

He turned the faucet on cold and splashed water on his face, forcing a breath through his nose. It didn't help.

He wanted to know more about her. More than what the files said. More than what she was willing to give.

She was holding something back—he could see it in the small silences, the way she deflected questions, the way she had responded when sword-guy showed up—unsurprised and expectant.

And maybe that was part of the pull, too. The mystery. The locked door.

But the other part? She'd faced a monster and didn't flinch. She commanded like she'd been born to lead. And when the shit hit the fan, she never once looked to someone else to take point.

She was exactly the kind of person he wanted at his back in a fight.

Exactly the kind of person he wasn't supposed to want in *any* other way—given their positions.

He leaned on the sink a little longer, breathing in the steam—searching for calm but unable to find it.

Then he finally looked up, stared into the mirror, and said aloud—half to himself and half to the echo of her presence still lingering in his mind.

"Yeah, this is gonna be a problem."

Chapter 12

SCU HQ—Gordon's Office—7:12 a.m.

Agent Kaycee Gordon sat alone in her office, the blinds drawn. She'd stripped down to a plain black T-shirt and cargo pants, the stiffness of her field jacket discarded in the corner.

Her sidearm lay on the desk beside her. Field reports were stacked neatly in front of her—untouched for over twenty minutes.

Instead, her eyes were fixed on the security footage frozen on the screen before her—grainy rooftop camera footage. No audio. Just the silent blur of the cloaked figure—Akron—taking down the Drakyn with inhuman precision.

And in the corner of the frame was Marek.

Leaning over the ledge. Watching. Jaw clenched. That steady posture that didn't waver, even after what he'd just seen.

She should have shut it off. Logged it in as evidence and moved on to her reports.

But she hadn't, and she didn't know why.

He was a problem.

Not because he was impulsive—he wasn't. Not because he lacked control—he had that in spades. It was because she couldn't read him. Not fully. There was something beneath the surface of Marek that didn't add up.

Something that tugged at her instincts—making her hesitate. And she did *not* hesitate. Not as an SCU agent, and not as a Warden.

She'd hunted creatures from realms that humans would never even dream of. Been alive for centuries.

And yet... something about *him* got under her skin. The way he looked at her. The way he *felt*—his subtle yet insistent pull when he was near.

It wasn't just attraction—though yes, that was there in plenty. She'd be stupid trying to deny it.

He was infuriatingly handsome, sharp, and carried a quiet kind of kindness that had no business surviving the career he'd chosen.

No—this was something else.

A hum in her blood when he was near. Like pressure building in a sealed room. Like standing at the edge of a storm.

She hated that she noticed it. Hated more that she was starting to look forward to it. To seeing him.

Her hand curled into a fist on the desk. She flexed it open again slowly, breathing once, grounding herself.

He can't know what you are.

Not yet at least. Maybe not ever—her orders forbid it.

The Wardens didn't get involved with humans—not like this. It was punishable by death if it crossed a line. Not to mention he was her subordinate too.

She was already pushing the boundaries of Akron's binding orders by joining the SCU. He'd rip her a new one if he knew how deeply she was embedded.

Maybe he'd already found out, but for whatever reason, he wasn't saying anything.

If Akron knew what she was starting to feel for Marek—if it continued to grow and she acted on it—she'd follow in Jax's footsteps.

She cared too much for her fellow Wardens to be selfish enough to take that route.

She clenched her fists again. Damn Jax for leaving her to handle this corner of the world alone. If he was here now, she'd kill him again—just on principle.

She sucked in a deep breath, held it, and released it slowly. Regardless of her attraction to Marek, she'd soldier on, just as she always did.

She sat back down at her desk to go back over those field reports. She had a debrief with the team in a couple hours and the reports wouldn't read themselves.

Chapter 13

SCU HQ—Conference Room—9:14 a.m.

The entire SCU team had gathered in the conference room. Tucker lounged in his usual chair, halfway through a donut. Marcus was hunched over a tablet. Harper flipped through forensics readouts, and Chen tapped one foot under the table like she was trying to keep herself from getting up and pacing.

Malik stood against the back wall, arms crossed, silent and stoic until needed.

Marek sat near the far end of the table, half-watching, half-listening—still wired from the night before.

At the head of the room stood Gordon, arms crossed, focused on the big screen. At the grainy rooftop footage looping over and over. The creature fleeing. The cloaked figure intercepting. The kill, brutal and precise.

"This doesn't strike me as random," Marek said. "He wasn't just passing through. He must have been tracking it somehow... Waiting for it."

"I think Marek's right," Tucker said, nodding his head at the TV. "He seems to show up at the same time as these monsters. Pretty damn effective, too. He came out of nowhere and beat that thing like it owed him money."

Marcus leaned in. "I've been over every camera in a ten-block radius. He didn't show up on any approach. No entry point. No thermal trail before the attack. The only thing I can find is a spike of energy similar to the ones our creatures make. Only this one doesn't slowly build. It just appears, and boom, there he is. I think they're traveling the same way, but it's different somehow—I can't put my finger on it."

"Anyone think he's human?" Harper added. "Because I'm pretty sure no human can move like that."

"He's *something*," Marcus replied, not looking up. "But human? I wouldn't bet on it."

Chen twirled her pen once before pointing at the freeze-frame. "And no tattoos. No insignias. He's not broadcasting an identity. That feels deliberate."

Marek's gaze stayed on the still image—the cloaked figure standing over the creature, swords wet, shoulders squared like it was just another day on the job.

"You said there've been three surges in the last thirty-six hours?" he asked.

Gordon tapped the console, shifting the projection to a heat map. Red pulses glowed at three locations across the boroughs—tight clusters, each marked by elevated electromagnetic readings and sensor interference.

"Localized, and short-lived," she said. "But they're increasing. And not only in number—in intensity too. Whatever's causing them is picking up momentum. The next one might not be as clean."

"Clean?" Harper scoffed. "That body down there barely had a spine left after sword-guy got done with it."

"I meant *contained*." Gordon gave her a look. "This one didn't result in any human deaths. It didn't draw attention. We got lucky, but that won't last."

Malik finally spoke from the back wall. "If these surges keep climbing, we won't be the only ones who notice."

"And if our mystery guy's tracking them," Marek added, "we either get there first... or clean up whatever he leaves behind."

"Assuming he's on our side," Tucker said.

There was a short silence at that statement.

Marek noticed Gordon's jaw clenching, like she wanted to disagree—that was interesting. She was just as in the dark as they were... wasn't she?

His instincts perked up—her reactions so far, both on the roof and in this meeting, didn't seem to line up with the surprise everyone else on the team felt.

"Do we even *want* to find him?" Chen asked. "Not sure he'd stick around for questions even if we did. I doubt we could force him to for that matter. Something tells me we couldn't even if we tried."

"We don't chase him," Gordon said. "We follow the trail. Focus on the next surge, not him. If we find him, and he talks, great. If not, that's fine too. Our primary mission is to contain and neutralize."

Everyone looked at her, but no one pushed back.

Marek stayed quiet. He was watching her now—not just listening but observing the way she took control of the room. She was calm—didn't flinch under pressure. Didn't hedge her orders. And when she talked, people *listened.*

It got under his skin—*she* got under his skin. The way she moved, the way she owned every space she stepped into. It was attraction—visceral and unsettling.

She stirred something inside him, a sharp-edged and raw kind of desire. The longer he was around her, the stronger it got. And no matter how hard he tried, he couldn't shut it off.

He turned away from her slightly, clearing his throat. "Where's the next spike most likely to hit?"

Marcus tapped a few keys on his tablet. "We've got a pattern starting to emerge. Industrial zones. Places with low foot traffic, old infrastructure, weak surveillance coverage.

My algorithm's narrowed it to five hotspots. One of them is already flaring."

He brought it up on the table—a warehouse complex near the Brooklyn waterfront. Isolated. Dense. A hell of a place to fight something if it went sideways.

"How long do we have?" Gordon asked.

Marcus didn't look up. "If it continues to build at this rate—based on the previous data we have of the last breach—we've got about two hours until another breach manifests."

"Just enough time to make it there before something tears through," she muttered, more to herself than the room.

Gordon stared at the projected hotspot for two seconds longer, then nodded once.

"We roll out in forty-five minutes," she said, voice clear. "Load for heavy contact. Marek and I will take point. Tucker, you're with Chen. Harper stays in the mobile ops van with Marcus."

"Harper never gets to play," Tucker said.

"Harper's the reason you'll still be breathing if you get hurt out there," Gordon shot back without missing a beat.

That shut him up.

She turned off the projection and straightened. "We don't know what we're walking into. We don't know who else might be watching. Eyes sharp. Guns holstered unless it's a creature—we don't want to accidentally hit... sword-guy."

"And Tucker—for god's sake—try to control yourself if he shows up," she said, pointing at him.

"I can't make any promises, boss." He said, laughter in his eyes.

He looked over at Chen in the next breath and said, "See Chen? Even the boss is calling him sword-guy..."

Chen rolled her eyes and muttered under her breath… but her lips twitched like she was fighting a smile.

Everyone chuckled at that as they nodded or murmured agreement to Gordon's directive. Chairs scraped back as the team stood and scattered to gear up.

Marek lingered as the others filed out. Gordon didn't move.

"You sure about just the two of us taking point?" he asked.

"I trust you," she said without looking at him.

That landed heavier than she'd probably intended.

Marek nodded once and turned to follow—her words staying with him, taut and humming like a wire pulled tight between them.

Chapter 14

Brooklyn Waterfront—11:05 a.m.

The convoy rolled up quietly along the crumbling edge of the old pier district—two black SUVs and a large Transit van that looked out of place among the sleek SUVs. The air reeked of low tide, rust, and old concrete soaked in decades of oil and rain.

Marek stepped out of the passenger seat and took in the scene. The warehouse ahead looked like it hadn't been touched in years—two stories of dilapidated walls, rusted roll-up doors, and shattered windows veiled by grime. The kind of place people knew better than to ask questions about.

It was perfect. A perfect place for creatures to congregate. A perfect place to die if they weren't careful.

Gordon exited the driver's side and came around the front of the SUV, eyes scanning every corner. She didn't speak right away. Just took in the structure like she was committing it to memory.

Marek found himself watching her again.

The way she moved. The sharp turn of her head. She didn't just survey the scene—she read it, like every shadow might contain a threat. Tactical and fluid. Dangerous and beautiful.

"Motion sensors show no recent activity," Marcus said through comms from the van.

"But the energy surge is climbing. It's coming from inside the northeast portion of the warehouse—right near what looks to be the loading dock."

"Could be something trying to break through," Chen offered as she and Tucker approached.

"That makes me feel better. Let's walk into an ambush, why don't we?" Tucker muttered.

He adjusted his jacket and looked at Marek. "I hate abandoned warehouses. Something bad always happens in warehouses."

"You hate mornings," Marek said. "And vegetables. And paperwork. Pretty sure warehouses are just another item on the long list."

Tucker snorted a laugh, but didn't argue.

Gordon gestured the team into a loose semicircle. "Alright, listen up. Marcus has us on a fifteen-minute countdown before this thing hits peak flare. That gives us a window to get in, map the interior, and prepare to engage. If it escalates while we're inside, we try to fall back and re-group together. If it comes through, I don't know if we can handle a creature like the one at the meatpacking plant alone."

Everyone nodded.

"Marek and I will take point and move to the northeast of the building. Tucker, Chen—you sweep the western side. Watch out for structural instability; creatures aren't the only thing that can kill you in these old buildings. Malik, take perimeter coverage and overwatch. Harper, stay on comms with Marcus. I want you both to monitor vitals and be ready to provide back-up if needed."

"Got it," Harper said, already sliding into the back of the van beside Marcus.

Gordon turned to Marek. "You ready?"

He gave her a warm smile. "Always."

She tossed him a side glance, the smallest lift of one brow. "You know you don't have to flirt every time we suit up."

"That wasn't flirting," he said, following her toward the warehouse entrance. "If I flirted, you'd know."

The corner of her mouth twitched. But she said nothing—the flush creeping up her neck speaking volumes.

The interior of the warehouse was worse than it looked. Cold, dark, and filled with the scent of damp wood and mold. Sunlight filtered through the shattered windows in pale shafts that barely reached the floor. Crates sat abandoned under layers of dust, and every step echoed like they were walking through a tomb.

The silence wasn't natural.

Marek felt it instantly—like the air had weight, a pressure behind the eyes that didn't belong.

His hand slid to the grip of his pistol as Gordon raised her rifle, sweeping left while he moved right.

"You feel that? Feels like the meatpacking plant," he whispered.

"Yeah." Gordon said.

"Stay close to me. We watch each other's backs, and we'll be just fine."

◆

The deeper Marek and Gordon moved into the warehouse, the worse he felt.

It wasn't just in his head anymore. The air crackled around him, thick with static, brushing his skin like ghostly fingers. His jaw clenched as they crossed through the northeast part of the warehouse, light thinning the farther they went as the windows became fewer—until only their tac lights cut the encroaching darkness.

"Marcus, how close are we to that energy spike?" Gordon asked into her comm.

"Twenty meters, give or take. Directly ahead, just past the steel support wall. Readings are volatile and starting to spike erratically."

Marek glanced sideways at her. "Volatile's never good."

"No. It's not," she murmured, voice tight.

They passed the remains of a collapsed loading platform and rounded a corner into a narrow corridor half-buried in debris and broken pallet racks. The flicker of the energy was building in intensity, causing another headache. He slowed.

Then the wall *breathed*.

Or at least, it looked like it did. A ripple passed through the far end of the corridor—then, with a soundless shudder, a jagged tear split open in the wall like a gash in reality. A churning mass of blue-white energy surged in its place.

Marek felt it crackling against his skin like electricity—the buzzing behind his eyes vanishing. It left him strangely energized. Like he'd been hit with a shot of adrenaline.

And from it... something stepped through.

It looked like the same type of creature they'd faced at the meatpacking plant—only this one was bigger.

Nearly eight feet tall, its body coated in dark, metallic scales that gleamed, catching the dim corridor light. It moved with a kind of coiled power—four thick limbs ending in clawed fingers tipped in bone talons that clicked against the concrete with every step. A ribbed tail dragged behind it, twitching—tipped with spikes.

Its head was reptilian—an elongated snout filled with jagged fangs and lips that flexed and curled but never quite closed. Sparse, wire-like hairs ran in a line down its spine like a frayed mane. Its eyes glowed red in the darkness, unblinking, locked on them with predatory focus.

Marek barely had time to shout before it lunged.

"Contact!" he snapped out, as the thing came at them.

They scattered. Gordon rolled left and came up firing—three shots center mass. They hit, tearing through the scales like paper—the modified rounds from her Warden contact doing their job.

It roared in anger, blood dripping from its wounds.

Marek fired twice, aiming high. One shot struck home, blood trickling from its throat. The second missed as the creature reared back, bellowing in pain.

Then, creature turned on *him*—faster than he thought possible.

"Oh Shit," he swore.

Its tail hit him like a truck. Marek slammed into a steel support beam five feet away with a dull, bone-jarring clang. His carbine skidding across the floor, out of reach. He stayed conscious... barely.

Energy still coursing through him, he was able to twist out of the way just in time, as it tried to rush him—to finish him off.

He kicked up at the creature with a strength born of desperation, and something else.

It was like kicking a tank, the impact numbing his legs, but the creature staggered half a step back.

Gordon moved fast, firing again as she circled wide. *Onos, he's actually fighting it. How's he even moving after that hit he took?*

Even as the thought crossed her mind, Marek was picking himself up off the ground and moving back in.

His body moved on instinct, faster than it should. That strange energy buzzing in his veins.

He ducked a swipe that was meant to take his head off, planted a boot against the creature's thigh, and *vaulted* up—slamming a pipe he'd grabbed from the ground across the back of its skull.

The metal bent under the force of his blow, connecting with a dull thud.

The creature roared—an awful, guttural sound that rattled the walls—then backhanded him across the floor before he could plant his feet.

Marek hit the ground and skidded before a shipping crate stopped his progress—wood splintering around him.

The impact should've knocked him out—or at least broken some ribs. Hell, the last hit should have done him in, but Marek gritted his teeth and got up. Bleeding. Bruised. But standing... Again.

Gordon had stopped, staring in stunned silence. It wasn't very often she was surprised by a human, but he'd managed to do it twice in as many minutes.

What the hell is going on? Who is Marek... really?

The creature roared and charged again, just as Gordon raised her rifle for a final shot.

She didn't get the chance.

The same jagged tear from before split the air between them, spilling out arcing swirls of blue-white energy.

A cloaked figure stepped through, coat catching the air like wings. Blades in hand. No hesitation.

Akron, she thought—not surprised he'd shown up.

He didn't move like a man. He moved like a force of nature.

The creature had a second to turn before Akron's first strike hit—a slash across its neck that left sparks and dark fluid in its wake. He shattered its leg next with a brutal kick. The third strike buried both blades deep into its chest.

The creature dropped in a heap, twitching, then stilled. A heavy, charged silence followed.

Akron stood over the corpse, chest rising and falling, in an easy rhythm.

Then he turned.

His gaze stayed fixed on Marek—studying him, searching for something, anything that would explain this feeling of familiarity he got whenever he saw him.

"You shouldn't be here," he said, voice low and thunderous.

"We had it handled," Marek said as he swayed on his feet

"No," Akron said with a meaningful look. "You didn't."

"This isn't your war," he continued quietly. "Stay out of it—while you still can."

And then he was gone—slipping back through the rent in the air—that same blue-white energy crackling against Marek's skin.

Silence returned.

Marek exhaled, slow and ragged. However energized he felt, he was still bruised and bleeding—tasting blood in his mouth.

Gordon lowered her weapon. But her eyes were still locked on him.

"You okay?" she asked, her voice quieter now. Not clipped, or commanding.

"Not dead," he said. "That counts."

She didn't reply.

But the look she gave him?

It was one of uncertainty—skepticism. Like she wasn't quite sure what to make of him now.

Chapter 15

SCU Command Van—11:31 a.m.

The inside of the van was quiet except for Harper's mutterings as she gathered her supplies to treat him. Something about idiots trying to be heroes.

Marek had an idea of who she thought the idiot was.

Tucker paced outside, shooting concerned looks Marek's way every so often.

All Marek could focus on was the static feeling of energy still coursing through him. Like electricity.

Pain lanced through his ribs, dull and thudding—but not debilitating. He was still amped up by the strange energy moving under his skin.

He sat on a bench near the back of the van, shirt off, dark bruises blooming across his torso like storm clouds under his skin.

Gordon hadn't said much since she'd helped him walk out of the warehouse.

She stood across from him, arms folded tight—expression unreadable. Her posture was taut with unasked questions as Harper came over and prodded his torso, feeling around Marek's ribs and spine for injuries.

"No breaks from what I can feel," Harper said.

"You're banged up, but nothing's broken. Which is...a miracle, honestly."

Marek grunted. "Felt like something broke."

Harper gave him a look. "You hit a steel beam. I've seen less serious impacts leave someone on a ventilator."

Marek didn't answer right away. He stared at the bruises darkening his ribs, the echo of the impacts he'd sustained still humming in his bones.

She's right. I should be in pieces, he thought. Instead, he was breathing. Alert. Alive.

It didn't make sense—unless something was changing... again.

He remembered what that felt like when he was younger. The hunger. The growth spurts. The way reality had started to tilt sideways just before his life had gone off the rails at seventeen.

He'd buried that chapter of his life. He really didn't need or want a sequel.

He let out a breath and forced a grin. "Guess I'm lucky."

Harper didn't answer—only pressed a cold patch against his side. Her brow furrowed, just slightly.

Gordon watched it all in silence. Her eyes never left him—not while Harper patched him up, not while Marcus relayed an incoming report about secondary energy anomalies, not even when Tucker and Chen traded snarky banter in an attempt to lighten the mood.

She was thinking—hard.

Remembering the fight and his bursts of strength and speed.

Once Harper moved on to pack up her supplies, Gordon stepped closer.

"You sure you're okay?" Gordon asked.

"Little sore," Marek said, adjusting his posture with a wince. "But yeah, I'll live."

Tucker paused his pacing and shot him a sidelong glance. "You don't get points for acting tough, dumbass."

But there was a flicker of something deeper in his voice—worry, buried under sarcasm like always.

Gordon didn't smile. Her arms stayed crossed. "*Living* is the part I'm surprised about."

Marek looked up, surprised at the edge in her voice. "What does that mean?"

"You got tossed across a room like a rag doll—twice. You got up swinging both times. Your body should've been in shock from the first hit. Instead, you went back at it like you were trying to kill the damn thing."

"Isn't that what we are here for? To stop them? Plus, I've taken worse." Marek said, defensively.

"I doubt it," she muttered.

The air in the van grew thin between them—tighter, tenser.

Gordon's gaze held his. It wasn't hostile. But it was probing. Like she was trying to strip away the layers—searching for a truth that was just out of reach.

"You're healing fast," she said.

Marek flexed his fingers. No more tremor. No pain.

Part of him—some buried, vicious part—was pissed he hadn't finished the fight himself. That sword-guy had stolen his kill.

He swallowed hard, forcing the thought away. *My kill? Where the hell did that come from?*

What the hell is happening to me? He thought.

He cleared his throat. "Adrenaline," he offered instead.

"Mhm." She didn't buy it. But she didn't push. Not yet.

Marcus cleared his throat from the front of the van. "Surge readings are dropping. Whatever was fueling that spike—it's gone. Or dead."

"Probably both," Tucker muttered, "thanks to sword-guy again."

Gordon didn't respond. She was still watching Marek.

"Get some rest," she said finally. "I want you on light duty for the next twelve hours. Full eval if you so much as wince."

"Yes, ma'am," Marek said, trying not to wince.

She turned to leave but paused just before the door.

"Did you see him come in?" She said quietly.

Marek's brow furrowed. "Who?"

"Cloak. Blades. You know, sword-guy."

"Yeah. Kind of hard to miss someone stepping out of blue lighting." He hesitated before adding, "he looked at me like he recognized me. Sounded like he was... disappointed maybe?"

Gordon nodded once. "He told you to stay out of it?"

"Word for word."

She glanced over her shoulder at him, and for the first time, Marek saw something in her expression he couldn't quite place—concern. Not just for his injuries, but like something else was weighing her down.

She didn't say anything else.

The door shut behind her with a soft hiss, leaving Marek in the hum of the van and the low static in his own thoughts.

◆

The door hissed shut behind her, as Gordon exited the van—sealing her outside—away from *him*.

Out here, the night felt colder. Sharper. Sirens echoed a few blocks away—distant, but not far enough to ignore.

Her boots slowed to a stop beside the rear bumper of the van. She exhaled a breath—slow and shaky—only then realizing she'd been holding it.

Marek should be dead.

She'd seen enough bodies—enough humans injured by forces less powerful than the Drakyn was—to know how that kind of impact usually ended. Internal bleeding. Shattered ribs. The vacant look of a teammate gone too fast.

But Marek had gotten up. Had kept getting up. And how he had moved against that thing—*Onos*, it wasn't normal.

Not just fast. Fluid. Like his body already knew the rhythm of that creature's movement. Like something inside him had recognized the threat before he had.

She crossed her arms, fingertips digging into her sides.

And then there was the way Akron had looked at him. That pause. That flicker of something she couldn't name. Recognition?

She shook her head. It didn't make sense. Marek was just a cop. A stubborn, reckless, frustratingly loyal pain in the ass.

Good instincts, sure. Tough, definitely. But not trained for this. Not built for it.

Except—what if he was? Her eyes drifted back toward the van. She could still feel his presence like heat on her skin—bruised, bloodied, sitting on that bench like he hadn't just taken damage that would have folded a normal man in half.

He looked at me like he recognized me. That's what he'd said about Akron.

She swallowed hard, running a hand through her hair. There were too many questions stacking up in her mind regarding Marek. She felt like she could only see a small piece of the picture.

Marek was supposed to be a wildcard. A fluke. A perceptive cop that could help the team... help her answer questions. He wasn't supposed to create more of them.

But this? This felt like something else. Something more. Like he was something more than human.

Gordon exhaled through her nose and rubbed the bridge of it between thumb and forefinger, grounding herself. She couldn't afford to spiral. Not now. Not when the team was watching her. Not when the next surge was only a heartbeat away.

Still...

She glanced back toward the door once more.

What are you, Marek?

Chapter 16

The soft glow of her laptop lit the dim room, washing Gordon's face in pale light. She sat in her chair. One hand under her chin—files scrolling across the screen. Nothing about Marek Tomlinson was adding up the way it should.

Not after what she'd seen.

Not after the way he moved. Fought. Held his own against the Drakyn.

She'd worked with seasoned agents, and combat veterans alike.

Marek's pain tolerance, his reflexes, his *recovery*—they weren't just impressive. They bordered on the impossible.

So, she'd started digging.

She told herself it was a precaution. That it was her job.

But it wasn't just about the mission anymore. It was about *him*. The strangeness that kept piling up around him.

She pulled up his background again—public records, archived school reports, medical logs. On the surface, it was normal. Clean.

Too clean.

His father: listed as "deceased before birth." No death certificate attached. No name on record. No next of kin, no birth announcement, not even a family obituary. It was like the man never existed.

She narrowed her search. Looked into old NYPD recruitment files—psych evaluations, academy reports. He'd passed everything. But there were small anomalies buried in the comments.

"Exceptional physical strength relative to size and muscle mass."

"Unusually fast reaction time under duress."

"Medical clearance confirmed—however, healing rate on minor injuries was noted as accelerated."

Then there were his school records.

Middle school: average grades. Some disciplinary notes for fighting—defending other students.

High school: upward shift. Sudden spike in athleticism. Coach's note:

"Growth spurt unlike anything I've ever seen—nearly five inches in one summer. It's like he woke up someone else."

Doctor visits from that same year after his growth spurts dropped to zero. Just... stopped.

Like his body had stopped needing outside help.

Gordon leaned back, staring at the screen. She was circling a shape in the fog—it just didn't have a name... yet.

Her instincts screamed that he wasn't entirely human—but she had no facts to go on, not yet. Just centuries of combat experience dealing with the supernatural and humans.

A knock on her door pulled her out of her thoughts.

Tucker stepped in without waiting for an invitation, holding a data pad.

"Marcus says you need to see this," he said. "We've got another one."

Gordon stood instantly, already grabbing her jacket. "Where?"

"Midtown," Tucker said grimly. "Underground transit line. Old track section they shut down ten years ago."

Gordon's head snapped up.

"Not just a flare this time," he added. "Three maintenance workers are unaccounted for. And Marcus says the energy readings are spiking off the charts—erratic, unstable."

Gordon's jaw clenched.

Midtown. Civilians. Missing workers meant the breach was already past containment, and they were behind the eight-ball. *Shit.*

Worse, a confined space like a tunnel meant no fallback. No clear sightlines. No clean perimeter.

"Get the team," she said, already reaching for her gear.

"Full tactical load-out. I want to be on the road in ten."

Then, lower—more to herself than anyone else:

"This could get loud... messy."

Tucker nodded and turned to go but paused.

"You alright?"

She didn't answer right away.

Then, "Not sure."

She didn't explain. She just stared once more at Marek's file, then shut the screen off.

SCU Headquarters—Locker Room—1:42 p.m.

Marek stood under the punishing stream of the locker room shower, palms pressed against the tile, head bowed.

Steam filled the space, coiling around the tension knotted in his back. His bruises throbbed, but less than they should've. The pain was already fading into something distant, manageable.

That wasn't normal. Then again, nothing about him had been normal since joining the SCU—and the more strange shit he ran into, the stranger he felt.

He exhaled sharply, water rushing down his face.

He wasn't stupid. He'd felt how fast his body was bouncing back. He remembered the creature's hits—how it launched him into a metal beam.

How it'd then knocked him across the floor. He *should've* blacked out. Should've needed a hospital. Instead, he'd been able to walk away from it all—nothing worse to show for it than some bruises.

And Gordon had *seen* it. He'd only seen curiosity in her eyes, not shock or incredulity. That threw red flags for him.

She hadn't said much since. But it was in her eyes—that narrowed stare, the quiet calculation that followed the curiosity.

She was looking at him like he was a puzzle. Like she was waiting for the pieces to reveal something she'd already started to suspect.

He wished she'd tell him what that was, because he didn't have a goddamn clue.

Marek shut off the water and stepped into the open space, toweling down. He moved to his locker, opened it slowly, and pulled out his phone.

He hesitated.

If she was watching him like that—if she thought she knew something he didn't—it was only fair he started watching her too, right?

He paused before unlocking his phone, staring at his own reflection in the locker mirror.

Bruises already fading. Breathing steady. Muscles loose and eager—like his body *wanted* more.

He didn't recognize the man staring back. Not really.

You used to know who you were.

That thought lingered as he opened his phone and started typing.

He searched what little he could without setting off flags: FBI placement records, law enforcement academy rosters, public-facing casework. Kaycee Gordon was clean. Too clean.

No early assignments. No law enforcement history that he could see. No birth records he could verify. Just a clean five-year file that started with her placement in the Special Crimes Unit.

It's like she appeared out of nowhere.

His jaw clenched. It could've been federal clearance or deep cover. But it *felt* like something else.

And now she was digging at him like he was the only one with secrets.

His phone buzzed with an incoming text:

—*Team Rollout in 10. Suit up. Load for heavy contact.*

Marek stared at the message from Gordon a moment longer, then tossed it on the bench and began pulling on his gear.

He'd play along for now, but he was watching her too.

Chapter 17

SCU Convoy—En route to Midtown Underground—2:02 p.m.

The convoy rumbled through New York City—two black SUVs in formation with the mobile command van trailing behind. Sirens weren't their protocol.

After all, the stuff they hunted needed to stay classified. Lights and sirens attracted unwanted attention.

Inside the lead vehicle, Marek sat in the passenger seat, fully geared up, trying to stretch the stiffness out of his shoulder without looking obvious.

He was definitely trying not to wince, and it was getting easier. The aches and pains were fading with every passing minute.

Gordon drove with her usual laser focus, one hand on the wheel, the other flicking through data on a mounted console synced with Marcus's feed.

The silence between them wasn't uncomfortable. But it wasn't casual either.

Marek broke it first. "So why tunnels? Why abandoned infrastructure instead of, I don't know, Central Park at noon?"

Gordon didn't look away from the road. "You afraid of confined spaces?"

"Not afraid. Just... prefer places with a little more room to move. Less echo."

She gave a faint nod. "You'll have enough space. But probably not the kind you want."

Marek smirked, then glanced at her. "You always this warm and sunny on a mission?"

"Only when someone flirts with death and walks away like it's just another day."

He raised an eyebrow. "Is that what this is about?"

"You tell me."

Marek didn't answer. Instead, he looked out the window as the city passed by. His reflection stared back at him—worn, thoughtful, and still rattled from what happened in the warehouse.

Not just the creature. Not just the cloaked stranger, but the way Gordon had looked at him afterward.

The questions she asked that he couldn't answer. She thought he was hiding something. And he wasn't sure she'd believe him if he said he didn't know what it was.

The second SUV held Tucker and Chen. Their voices filtered through the shared comms channel—Tucker ranting about tunnels and rats the size of raccoons.

Chen patiently ignoring him as she reviewed schematics of the subway tunnels.

In the command van, Marcus and Harper monitored the surge and the team's vitals—providing updates.

"Energy levels have plateaued for the moment," Marcus reported over comms. "But there's a persistent flicker in the signal. Something's moving down there."

Gordon keyed her mic. "Any thermal signatures?"

"Maybe, hard to tell. Too much interference. The lines are old, shielded weirdly, and there's minor flooding in some sectors. You'll be half blind down there."

"Perfect," Tucker said. "Because nothing says safe like blind spelunking with potential monsters."

"I told you to stop calling it spelunking," Chen muttered, "it's not a cave."

Tucker grumbled something too low to pick up on the mike.

"What was that you just said?" Chen asked.

"I didn't say anything," Tucker griped back.

"Mhm, that's what I thought." Chen smirked.

Marek chuckled under his breath and looked over at Gordon again. "You trust them down there?"

Marek let their voices fade into background noise as he watched Gordon, her jaw set, eyes forward.

"I trust everyone on my team to do what they're trained for," she said. Then, more pointedly: "Even when they're holding things back."

That caught him off guard with how hard it hit.

Marek held her gaze for a moment. She didn't flinch.

There was something in her eyes now—a knowing glint that hadn't been before.

"You looked me up," he said quietly.

Gordon didn't blink, only raised an eyebrow. "Should I not have?"

He didn't answer, and she didn't deny it.

It was her prerogative as his superior, but it still rubbed him the wrong way.

They drove the rest of the way in silence.

As the city skyline gave way to Midtown's industrial corridor, the convoy slowed near a gated construction zone just beyond the old MTA maintenance line. Marcus's voice crackled in their ears.

"You're at the access point. Third stairwell leads to an abandoned Line—decommissioned fifteen years ago. No traffic. No tourists. But those maintenance workers haven't reported back since this morning. That's the last known location before the surge started."

Gordon killed the engine.

"Alright," she said, glancing at Marek. "Let's see what we're walking into."

Marek followed without a word, the weight of everything unspoken settling like a blanket over his mood.

◆

Midtown Underground—Stairwell—2:41 p.m.

Tucker's boots echoed with every step, the narrow stairwell spiraling downward into flickering darkness. The air was damp, stale, and full of that metallic tang old tunnels never seemed to lose.

Beside him, Chen walked with a kind of quiet purpose that made him feel like the amateur.

He muttered, "You'd think the city could at least upgrade some damn light bulbs."

"Budget cuts," Chen said, deadpan.

"Always budget cuts," he grumbled.

"Even when we're hunting interdimensional monsters, it's still duct tape and water damage."

"I'll make sure to file a formal complaint with the City Manager. You know, make sure it gets seen," she replied.

Tucker snorted a laugh and kept walking, his flashlight beam bouncing off rust-streaked walls.

He glanced back. "You notice anything off about those two?"

Chen didn't ask who. The whole team felt something off.

"Yeah," she said after a moment. "Mom and dad have been circling something since the warehouse."

Tucker chuckled, "Mom and dad... I like that. You know what it's about?"

Chen gave him a sideways look.

"Don't take this the wrong way, because I know you two are close, but something doesn't add up about Marek and I think it may be driving Gordon crazy."

He raised a brow. "You mean what happened at the warehouse? My boy has always been a tough sonofabitch."

Chen didn't answer right away. "Yeah, but you heard how hard he got hit, right? Then to just walk away with only bruises? I've seen bigger guys laid low by a lot less."

Tucker was quiet for a moment before he spoke.

"You may have a point," he said, more quietly now.

"Something may be different. I've known Marek for years—I *have* seen him injured by less than what hit him in the warehouse. He's changing somehow. It's slow, but I've noticed."

Chen didn't reply.

"Maybe all this weird shit we're being exposed to is changing him." Tucker continued, almost to himself.

Chen reached the door and pulled the latch, keeping her voice level. "We've all got things we don't talk about. But whatever he is hiding—or isn't—does it matter if he's with us?"

Tucker stared at her a second longer. Then nodded.

"You're damn right it doesn't," he said, flicking off the safety on his weapon. "Now, let's go find out what the hell's waiting for us down there."

The door groaned open into blackness, and the tunnels swallowed them whole.

———◆———

Midtown Underground—Northeast Entry—2:41 p.m.
The tunnel swallowed the light as Marek and Gordon descended the final steps and stepped into the aban-

doned spur. Flashlight beams barely cut through the gloom ahead, catching glints of wet track, broken tile, and graffiti-scrawled support columns.

Gordon moved ahead, her footfalls silent on the concrete. Marek followed close behind, eyes adjusting to the darkness.

Every sound around them felt too loud—his own breathing, the metallic creak of pipework overhead, the soft splash of water as his boot caught a shallow puddle.

He hated the quiet. It gave too much room for thoughts to creep in.

Like how Gordon had looked at him in the SUV. Cold. Analytical. With a little distrust sprinkled in for good measure.

Like something about *him* wasn't adding up—and that pissed him off, because he couldn't give answers to things he didn't even understand.

He didn't blame her for being curious. Not really. He had always bounced back quick from things, but even he could concede when things were getting too weird.

And weird shit was going on with him ever since he took this gig.

But it didn't give her the right to dig into his personal life, right? That was a violation of trust he wasn't prepared for. He didn't know how to reconcile what he still felt for her—with what she'd done... and what he'd done in return.

Her voice broke through the noise of his thoughts.

"Marcus says there's a drop-off ahead on the schematics, and the tunnel splits."

He nodded and angled his light toward the edge of a collapsed service platform. Even before the beam landed, he could already make out the shape of the drop—the jagged break in the concrete, the twisted rebar jutting from the edge.

A part of his brain took note—that the tunnel was too dark for him to be able to see this clearly. That the light wasn't coming from his flashlight at all—that he was able to see in the dark.

He frowned, the thought dissipating like smoke, and stepped forward, falling into place behind Gordon.

Beyond it, the tunnel narrowed and dipped sharply into a passage that looked like it hadn't been maintained since the Nixon administration.

"Perfect place to die," he muttered.

Gordon looked back at him. "You planning to?"

"Not today." He grinned.

She gave the faintest twitch of a smile, then crouched low to inspect a splatter on the wall.

Marek stepped closer and knelt beside her. "It looks like what we found in the meatpacking plant. Blood maybe?"

She touched the splatter, then seemed to breathe deep, almost like she was... scenting it?

Well, that's different Marek thought.

Her eyes widened just slightly in recognition before she quickly schooled her features again.

She wasn't fast enough for Marek though. He caught the look—she recognized something about the blood, but she didn't say anything.

She got to her feet. "Let's keep going and see what we find."

It irritated him, all these secrets and unanswered questions, but he grudgingly let it go for now.

As they moved on, deeper into the tunnel, the silence grew thicker the farther they went. As if the air itself was watching them. Marek's instincts prickled, causing his hair to stand up.

Gordon stopped abruptly and raised her hand, signaling him to freeze.

They listened.

No sounds of movement up ahead, but something was wrong.

The static in Marek's head buzzed. Not loud. But there. Just like in the warehouse before something tore out of the wall.

And then the wall seemed to move—no, it wasn't the wall, but something massive peeling off from the shadows.

Marek lifted his weapon on autopilot.

Gordon swept her light down the corridor—and the beam caught it.

A massive figure halfway turned. Just a glimpse.

Marek caught the glint of scales, and a spiked tail, clear to him despite the oppressive darkness of the tunnel.

It darted out of sight before either of them could fire—moving faster than should have been possible for something that large.

Gordon was already moving, weapon up, voice low. "We've got company."

"You think?" He snapped, irritation creeping into his voice—he still wasn't quite over her digging into his personal life.

She mumbled something he couldn't make out as they pressed forward carefully, steps quiet now, back-to-back as they rounded the next bend.

Five minutes later, they came to another junction—where the SCU team had agreed to regroup.

Emergency lights clung to life on one side of the chamber—dim, yet casting reddish shadows across the stone walls. Old maintenance rails and rusted scaffolding crossed the area; a relic of whatever construction had once been abandoned here.

Marek spotted Tucker first, he was standing at the split with Chen at his back. Both were silent, weapons up, eyes sweeping every inch of dark.

"You took your sweet time," Tucker muttered.

"We were playing hide and seek with something," Marek replied. "Didn't want to come running if it meant bringing it to you."

"Gee. Thoughtful," Tucker said, but there was a flicker of tension in his eyes. "You see it?"

"Just a glimpse," Gordon answered.

"It looked similar to the creatures we've been dealing with—scales, a barbed tale, large but fast."

Chen spoke quietly. "We saw movement ahead of us too. To damn dark in here to see past our flashlights, and it was moving to fast to make out—it stayed just out of line of sight."

"Then it's herding us," Gordon said.

Marek turned toward her. "You think it's that intelligent?"

"It's a possibility we'd be stupid to ignore."

From his spot near the edge of the platform, Tucker swept his flashlight across the mouth of the tunnel, trying to peer into the darkness. "Man, I hate it when the monsters are smart."

Chen handed Gordon a small field scanner. "Energy surges have shifted again. Readings are tighter now—more concentrated."

Gordon studied the display. "Which means it's not moving around as much. Either it's stopped... or it's waiting for us."

"Just fucking great," Tucker muttered, as the team fanned out, moving carefully.

Each member checking blind corners, walkways, and ventilation shafts with quiet, practiced precision. Anywhere something could hide, was scrutinized.

Marcus's voice crackled through their earpieces. "Still tracking faint signals from your position. But it's unstable. Interference is getting worse—signal static's spiking across multiple sensors including your bodycams. You've probably only got... minutes... efore... lose... entirely."

"You're already breaking up," Gordon said. "We'll move fast."

Tucker swept his rifle, and its mounted tac light at a corridor to their right, illuminating a thin trail of blood that led deeper into the dark.

"So, is this the part where we all split up and die horribly, or the part where we stick together and *still* die horribly?"

"Stick together," Gordon replied. "And try not to be so optimistic."

"You know I only complain when there's a legitimate concern." Tucker replied.

"I don't think that's true," Chen added under her breath.

Marek chuckled at their banter.

Gordon moved to the front of the group, flashlight aimed ahead, jaw tight. Marek took her flank, rifle up, eyes sharp. Tucker and Chen fell into step behind, watching their six, as they tried to pick up the pace.

The air down here was heavy. Dense. There was a malevolence hanging in the air that made everyone's hairs stand on end.

The sound of their footsteps echoed farther than they should have, bouncing into places the light couldn't reach.

Marek adjusted his grip on his weapon and swept the corridor, continuing in Gordon's wake.

Ahead, the tunnel curved left—narrow, pinched by fallen concrete and twisted rebar. The dark pressed in tighter.

As they continued through the tunnel systems, Marek was on edge. He could feel the tension in the rest of the team.

Something wasn't right. It was too still. Too quiet.

Marek's skin prickled. Every breath felt thick, the buzzing in his head was building to a crescendo. He swept his gaze through the corridor again, slower this time.

"Gordon, I think we're getting clos—"

That's when it hit them.

A blur of motion dropped from the ceiling, shattering grates and slamming into the space between them, cracking concrete. There was a deafening roar that briefly stunned Marek.

Rookie mistake, he managed to think, as Gordon shoved him sideways—hard—with a strength that didn't match her frame.

She shouldn't have been able to reach him that fast. Shouldn't have been able to throw him that far.

A taloned arm tore through the space where his head had been, followed by a snarl—the creature having targeted Marek first.

Sparks lit the tunnel where its claws impacted.

Marek hit the ground several feet away, rolled, and brought his weapon up.

Then he saw it. The same type of creature they'd fought in the warehouse, although this one was smaller... relatively speaking.

Dark, oily scales shimmered like armor. Four thick limbs, an elongated snout, and rows of jagged teeth—familiar, but somehow worse in the tight, narrow corridor. A ribbed tail curled behind it, bony ridges scraping the tunnel floor.

It locked eyes with him—and then with Gordon.

There was an animalistic intelligence in its red, glowing eyes. Cold. Predatory. *Hungry.*

Gordon fired first—three controlled shots to the torso. The rounds imbedded, digging deep furrows into the beast's hide, leaking blood.

It let out an ear-splitting roar of rage and pain, looking down at its wounds like it was confused as to why it hurt.

It turned its glowing red eyes her way and lunged.

Marek's instincts chose that moment to kick in. He didn't think, he just charged.

The beast twisted, one massive arm already arcing through the air to meet him—

And then time fractured. Slowed.

He dodged low, drew his knife blade from the sheath on his thigh, and hammered the blade into the beast's chest. He felt it connect.

The beast snarled in rage, its taloned hand clawing the knife free—tossing it aside like it was no more than an irritation.

Then it went on the offensive.

One massive limb caught him across the ribs, and his world turned sideways.

Pain lanced through his abdomen from its claws—hot and immediate. The next thing he knew, the wall slammed into him like a sledgehammer.

Pain exploded through his back, his shoulder, his chest. He hit the ground hard and didn't get up.

Something was cracked. Maybe more than one something. He was also bleeding.

Through the haze, he heard Gordon shout his name—but she wasn't yelling in panic.

She was calling a command, but he couldn't make out what it was.

The beast took a step toward him, as if to finish him off.

Then the tunnel shifted—a sudden pulse of pressure hit the space like a soundless thunderclap.

Blue-white light split the gloom—blinding, radiant, alive.

For a heartbeat, the tunnel became something else. The air shimmered, folding outward from a ragged tear in reality, pulsing with a kind of radiant energy that was both alien and familiar.

And then he felt it again—the same surge from the warehouse. Like adrenaline, but different in its intensity.

It rolled over his skin like static and shot through his chest, snapping every nerve awake.

And from that tear, a figure stepped through.

The coat. The blades. The impossibly calm stride.

Marek's breath hitched—not from pain this time, but from recognition.

Him. The man from the warehouse. The one from the meatpacking plant.

He didn't speak. He didn't hesitate. He just moved—straight at the creature.

What followed wasn't a fight. It was a brutal, merciless one-sided beating. Like the man had an axe to grind and decided using the dull edge was going to be more satisfying.

The creature roared, whirled, struck—and missed. Every attack was deflected. Every defense shattered.

Sword-guy destroyed the creature, systematically. It never stood a chance.

Marek could barely follow him and his movements—they were a blur.

He wasn't using swords this time. Just brass knuckles—heavy, brutal things designed for blunt force trauma.

Every punch he made, connected. Each strike was a shockwave that Marek felt in his bones,

The power behind those strikes had to be immense—the kinetic force was rattling his eardrums. The beast could do nothing against the onslaught.

Sword-guy didn't slow. He drove the beast backward, blow after blow—until finally, the monster slammed into the far tunnel wall with enough force to crack concrete.

It slid to the ground, silent and bleeding. Dead.

Silence fell.

Marek blinked up through pain and disbelief.

The man turned to him. Studied him for a brief moment and said, "Stay out of the dark, Marek. Stop hunting where you don't belong."

Then, without another word, he vanished, the blue-white energy swallowing him whole and snapping closed—Marek blinked, and he was just... gone.

Gordon dropped beside him seconds later. Her face was calm, controlled—but her hands trembled as they hovered near his ribs.

"Stay still," she said.

Marek stared up at the cracked ceiling. His voice was hoarse. "It would've killed me back there if you hadn't moved me out of the way."

He turned his head toward her, eyes narrowing. "How did you get to me so fast? Did you hear it coming? Everyone else was dazed—but not you."

She didn't answer.

Not right away.

And when she did, her voice was distant. "I was closer than you remember."

Marek narrowed his eyes. "I could've sworn—"

But then he stopped, the words falling away as his mind went back through the last few encounters. The blood in the tunnel—how she'd smelled it like she knew what it was.

The way she hadn't flinched when the creature dropped from the ceiling. The way she always moved first—like she had been aware of it on a level no one else on the team had.

As he reflected on other encounters with these creatures, he realized there was the same pattern.

She responded the same way each time they came up against one.

Immediate action. No hesitation—like she was just waiting for them to arrive.

◆

Marek leaned against the tunnel's cold wall, one knee drawn up while the other was stretched out, throbbing with pain. Every ragged breath sent sharp spikes through his ribs, a relentless agony accompanying the warm streak of blood along his side.

His head pounded, a dull echo compared to the barrage of unanswered questions swirling in his mind.

Beside him, Gordon crouched, a field med kit sprawled open on her thigh. She said nothing—her jaw set, her focus clinical—but her hands moved with a lingering hesitation, fingertips brushing against bare skin as she peeled away the torn fabric of his shirt.

Her touch was steady, yet her breathing betrayed a tremor, a flicker of vulnerability in the woman who never flinched. Marek picked up on it immediately.

With gauze, she methodically wiped away blood from his ribs, her fingers trailing against his skin and lingering just a moment too long.

"You didn't hesitate back there," he whispered, low and rough. "You never hesitate. Like you know they're there before we do."

Without meeting his gaze, she replied, "I was as surprised as you."

"Bullshit," Marek muttered. "Stop lying to me. You always seem to know."

Her silence spoke louder than words, giving him the confession he'd expected. Finally, Gordon's eyes lifted. Behind her guarded expression burned an intensity—conflict and heat that wouldn't fade, eyes locked on him without flinching or turning away.

Marek's breath caught, not from pain this time but from the charged space between them. "So, what is it, Agent Gordon?" he asked in a husky tone. "What is it you're not telling me?"

She said nothing, her eyes drifting downward to his chest—the wounds that had already stopped bleeding—then to the stains on her gloves.

"You heal too fast," she murmured.

Her fingers now traced his ribs like a gentle caress, no longer searching for hidden damage but simply touching.

Her palm came to rest over his heart, its warmth palpable even through the pain. "You should be unconscious by now," she said softly, almost to herself.

Her thumb skimmed the line of a bruise along his collarbone, drawing a flush from Marek that he neither resisted nor welcomed.

"You've got secrets too," she observed.

"I never said otherwise," he rasped. "I just don't know the answers to mine."

Their eyes met, a silent struggle suspended between them—tension, adrenaline, pain, and something unspoken.

Then, in a quieter tone, she admitted, "This thing between us... it's a problem."

"Gonna file a report on it?" he joked, voice rougher than he meant it to be.

She didn't smile. She leaned in—barely—close enough that her breath warmed his skin.

"I should," she whispered, lips just a breath from his.

Get it together, she told herself. But she didn't move. Didn't pull back.

Why don't I pull away?

It was him—something about him. Like he carried his own damn gravity, and she was always drifting too close.

Dangerous. Reckless. Inevitable.

Marek swallowed. His hand trembled slightly as he reached up, fingers brushing the back of her neck, drawing their foreheads together.

She didn't resist. He didn't let go.

Whatever spark lived between them, it was real—undeniable.

Yet Gordon, ever the professional, pulled back just before the flames could fully catch.

Her hands resumed changing his wound, pressing firm bandages against his aching ribs, though her breaths remained shallow—her fingers still shook.

When she finished, she straightened on her heels and scrutinized him once more.

"Can you walk?" she asked, voice husky.

"Yeah," he exhaled.

She extended her hand, and he grasped it. This time, she held on just a moment longer, making slow circles on his hand with her thumb.

"We'd best get this cleaned up and head back." She said, dropping his hand and turning to walk toward the rest of the team.

As Marek followed her, he knew that whatever this was between them, it wasn't going away. Not here. Not now. Not ever.

Chapter 18

T he team filed into the briefing room, each face taut with tension and frayed nerves. Not a word was exchanged.

Chen and Tucker even fell silent, the usual bickering and quips nowhere in evidence.

They'd gone home for a few hours of sleep before reporting back, but the mood was heavy. Not just from post-nap grogginess, but from the weight of what they'd faced in the tunnel—from the ever-increasing number of surges.

Marcus worked methodically at the console, pulling up a detailed schematic of the tunnel network alongside time stamped bodycam footage and sensor data. Nearby, Harper lingered by the wall with arms crossed, eyes fixed on the grainy footage cycling in eerie silence.

Gordon took her place at the head of the conference table, while Marek sank into the seat at the far end—still limping from the fight. His ribs, though no longer screaming in agony, were grumbling their own protest.

Tucker, seated next to Marek, leaned over to Chen and let out a low whistle.

"This is getting way too crazy. I haven't been able to even put together a decent explanation for what I've seen since joining this team."

"I'm right there with you," Chen agreed in a low murmur.

Marcus didn't tear his eyes away from his screens. "Whatever that thing was, it scrambled every sensor we had and turned nearly all the body-cam footage into useless static."

He continued, "Harper and I didn't get any thermal readings; the place was essentially in darkness, aside from our comm chatter."

Harper added, "And even then, we never got a clear image—everything blurred whenever it moved."

Tucker shook his head. "I couldn't make out a thing—it was too dark and everything just smeared together. I even missed sword-guy. All I saw was a flash of light, and then nothing... damn it! If I had to guess, it was the same thing that hit us in the warehouse—I only snagged a passing glance at it in the tunnels before it ambushed us."

Marek stayed quiet. He didn't want to call attention to the fact that he had seen everything—that it had all been crystal clear to him in the tunnel—it would invite questions he couldn't answer.

Marek thought back—back to before the attack, to when they first entered the tunnels. There'd been no ambient light, no working fixtures. But he'd walked confidently. Seen the walls. The debris. The blood on the walls—beyond what his tac light brought into focus.

He remembered seeing the twisted rebar and jagged concrete near the dilapidated service platform, before his light shined on it.

During the ambush, the team had been exactly where he was, but Tucker mentioned it was chaos, and too dark to make out any details.

Seems it was another change he'd undergone since starting with the SCU. Another shift that set him further apart from the rest.

He knew Gordon felt the same way, having witnessed enough to see that her perception rivaled his own. And the way she'd moved him out of the way like he weighed nothing?

When he looked at her, he found more questions than answers. She was different, maybe not in the same way as him... but she *was* different—she had to be, in order to react the way she had.

Leaning forward with palms flat on the table, Gordon said, "We can all agree we faced another monster down there. From what we saw before it attacked us, it seemed to be the same type we encountered at the warehouse and the meatpacking plant."

Tucker nodded, glancing at Chen. "This one felt more calculating, though. It let us see it, led us, practically herding us into an ambush."

The team nodded in agreement at his words.

Gordon cut in, her gaze locked on Marek. "I think you're right, Tucker. It picked its target deliberately. It knew exactly where to strike—and it went straight for Marek here."

Tucker frowned. "How could you tell? I couldn't see a damn thing down there."

Chen cut in, brow furrowed. "If that's true... then why Marek?"

Marek raised an eyebrow, giving Gordon a look that dared her to actually answer—for once.

She didn't.

True to form, she sidestepped the question.

"Maybe," she said, her eyes never leaving him, "because he just keeps surviving."

Meeting her eyes, Marek's expression seemed to ask, *really? You're still not letting that go?*

Gordon smirked, seeming to reply, *can you really blame me?*

She tapped the display screen and addressed Marcus, "How about this area you sent me? How long until the next energy surge hits the threshold?"

Marcus's fingers flew over the keyboard as a graph appeared—a series of red lines spiking unevenly with overlaid coordinates.

"At this rate, we're looking at maybe ninety minutes before we hit the next peak at those coordinates," Marcus explained.

Gordon nodded slowly. "Then we head back out in forty-five minutes."

Marek's eyes widened. "Really? That soon?"

Gordon met his gaze. "Whatever's happening—it's accelerating. We can't afford to wait until another attack catches us off guard. You good to go, or do you need to sit this one out and recover?"

"I'm good," Marek said, realizing it was true. His ribs hurt less than they had when he sat down, and the stiffness and pain in his leg was wearing off.

Gordon nodded, "Good."

"Harper and Marcus, pack up the mobile command van—you'll stay in reserve. Harper, be ready to provide medical assistance."

The two of them nodded.

Tucker groaned. "Aww boss, I just got comfortable—I haven't even had time to restock my trauma snacks."

"Can't you do that on the way?" Chen muttered under her breath.

Marcus grinned, "I already packed the med kit with protein bars. You're welcome."

"You the man, Marcus." Tucker said, as he and Marcus fist bumped on the way to the armory.

Chapter 19

SCU Headquarters—Sublevel Armory—6:40 p.m.

T he sublevel prep bay was quiet, punctuated now and then by the click of locking mags or the measured thump of boots on concrete.

At the far end, Marek methodically fastened a fresh tactical vest, each movement loose and easy. His ribs barely throbbed, his cuts didn't burn, and his leg felt fine.

He'd never healed this fast before—it both thrilled and terrified him. *What's happening to me?*

It was a thought he'd asked himself regularly the last couple days.

Across the room, Tucker leaned casually against an open locker door, a protein bar held between his fingers as though it were a personal affront.

He took a bite, cringing at the flavor, then swallowed with a wry grimace. "These things taste like drywall."

Marek stayed focused, not lifting his eyes. "You always complain when you're nervous."

Tucker shot him a look. "I always complain. Nervous or not."

He crossed over, discarding the wrapper into a nearby bin before sliding a couple mags into his belt-mounted pouch. "You good?" he asked in a quieter tone.

Marek tightened the last strap on his vest, meeting Tucker's gaze. "Still breathing."

"That's not what I asked."

A beat of silence passed.

"I'm fine," Marek offered.

Tucker raised an eyebrow. "Uh-huh. Sure. Because guys getting slammed into walls by hell-beasts usually bounce back in under an hour."

Marek's look remained flat.

"Don't do that," Tucker urged. "Don't be stoic and try to handle all this shit on your own. We've been through too much for that."

Marek exhaled, jaw locked tight. "I don't know what to tell you, Tuck. Something's happening, and I can't explain it."

"You don't have to explain it." Tucker said.

They sat in silence for several minutes. Marek's gaze drifted to the open rifle rack on the wall.

"I don't know... weird stuff has been happening to me ever since we started with the SCU," he admitted. "And I think Gordon knows more than she lets on—I know she thinks I'm hiding something."

Tucker nodded without argument. "Yeah. I've seen the way she watches you—like she's trying to figure you out."

"I mean, I had bruises hours ago, Tuck..." He lifted his shirt and pointed to his ribs.

"Now they're gone. That's crazy, right? I mean, I was always a fast healer, but this..." he trailed off.

Tucker leaned forward for a closer look, then drew back and whistled. "Besides being really fucking awesome, you're right, that is some weird shit."

Turning serious again, he grabbed Marek's shoulder. "Whatever this is, man—whatever's happening to you—we'll figure it out."

Marek met his eyes steadily. "I hope so."

"We will." Tucker turned back to the lockers.

"And when the real shit hits the fan, it's gonna be me and you like it's always been. Weird abilities or not. The rest of the team can tag along too, of course. Except Chen, she's annoying."

Marek laughed, "I think she likes you, bro."

Tucker's face looked like he'd eaten a lemon, and Marek laughed harder.

"Glad you're sooo amused with yourself." Tucker griped, but a small smile tugged at the corner of his lips.

At that moment, Gordon entered the prep bay, dressed and ready for war. Her presence shifted the air—everything controlled, calm—but her gaze locked on Marek, lingering a split-second too long before moving on.

"Ten minutes," she called. "Final check. We move out on Marcus's coordinates in ten minutes."

The team nodded as tension sharpened every corner of the room.

Marek did a last check of his weapons and adjusted the collar of his jacket. Gordon said nothing more, yet as she passed him en route to her own gear locker, her hand reached out and grabbed his—squeezing gently.

It wasn't an accident, and it wasn't professional.

Marek didn't flinch, didn't even look at her. But he squeezed back, her touch grounding him.

———◆———

Mobile Operation's Van—7:00 p.m.

The light from the array of screens lit the interior of the van like a bank of watchful eyes. Marcus sat hunched at his station, stylus twirling between his fingers as a sequence of biometric readouts scrolled across the main display—heart rates, core temps, environmental readings—Harper's area of expertise.

He kept his eye on them, trusting that they'd squawk or something—his attention was split between the data on his own screens and the creeping unease at the base of his spine.

Up front, Harper was driving, following closely behind the other SUVs.

Marcus leaned in slightly, tapping a finger on one of the screens. "The energy surge signature is still rising. Slower than last time, but steadier."

Harper didn't look away from the road. "That's almost worse."

"Because it's not a spike," he said softly. "It's a climb."

They both knew what that meant.

Surges that built like this weren't random. Something was getting ready to come through.

"Any anomalies on the other cameras?" She asked.

"Couple minor distortions in lower Manhattan. One building's grid is giving me gaps—sensors still reporting, but there is some interference." Marcus confirmed.

"That's consistent with the last breach, right?"

"Yeah. Same pulse pattern." Marcus tapped his keyboard again, then leaned back in his chair. "It's got to be the energy. Whatever's leaking through those surge points—it's shorting out the data as it crosses. Not on purpose. Just... proximity."

"Like a solar flare hitting a comm array," Harper murmured.

"Exactly." Marcus nodded.

She shifted slightly in the driver's seat, jaw tight. "So, you don't think it's deliberate sabotage by these things?"

"No. I think it's just a by-product of them crossing through wherever they come from. I don't think the monsters know we're blind when they cross over." He paused, then added quietly, "Not that they'd care if they did."

"They're not hiding then, they're hunting."

Marcus looked her way, his eyes hard. "Seems like that's their modus operandi."

Harper's attention shifted sideways to the laptop mounted to the dashboard on her right—at the monitor showing Marek's vitals.

Elevated heart rate, steady blood pressure. Normal under most circumstances.

But she had seen the erratic spikes earlier, after the ambush. And she'd pored over the records herself: the wound he had sustained hours ago, inconsequential on the surface, was now almost completely healed.

No red flag adorned his file. His background was clean.

And yet...

"There's something off about him," she murmured, as she slowed down for a pedestrian in the road.

"Marek?" Marcus inquired.

"Yeah, he and the boss both."

Marcus didn't press further, simply returning his focus to his terminal.

"Well, whatever it is," he said dryly, "I hope it works in our favor."

Harper remained silent, one eye on the road and one eye tracking the slow pulses of red lights on the display and prayed none would turn into a flatline in the next couple hours.

Chapter 20

Downtown Manhattan—Service Alley—7:50 p.m.

T he convoy had pulled up a block away, turning off their lights in an attempt at blending into the cityscape—less attention was always better for their operations.

They exited their vehicles, and started toward the alley where Marcus said the energy surge was cresting.

From an outsider's view, they resembled a few government agents on a casual stroll—tactical vests discreetly hidden beneath black jackets, arms at the ready yet weapons under wraps, channels muted unless absolutely necessary.

In the distance, downtown Manhattan hummed with life.

Gordon led the team down a cramped service alley—brick buildings rising above them on either side. The air was heavy with the reek of old refuse and that same sour animal smell from the meatpacking plant.

Above, the streetlights flickered inconsistently while neon signs from a nearby deli splattered garish hues across the cracked pavement.

At the far end, a chain-link fence buckled inward, sporting a jagged tear—as if something had violently passed through.

"Marcus, can you confirm this is the spot?" Gordon murmured, her tactical flashlight sweeping the tight corridor.

Her earpiece sputtered to life. "Confirmed. Surge origin point is within ten meters. Energy signature is still on the rise."

Marek trailed close behind, his gaze wandering toward the rooftops. The air itself seemed marred by an inexplicable sensation—beyond grime, stench, or even the eerie quiet.

It was an internal pressure. A faint pulse starting behind his eyes, a subtle buzzing coursing just beneath his skin like a captured electric current. He paused; jaw set in a firm line.

"You okay?" Gordon asked, glancing back.

Marek gave a tight nod. "Just a headache, the same one before the tunnel and the warehouse incident."

Gordon's jaw tightened visibly, and she spoke over their comms. "Heads up, team—Marek's got a bad feeling about this."

"I hate it when Marek gets a bad feeling—it generally ends in growls and screams," Tucker muttered.

"Aww, poor Tucker. Did you leave your big boy pants at home?" Chen asked.

"Children please, the grown-ups are talking." Malik cut in before Tucker could respond, "No civilians nearby. Foot traffic's been dead for half an hour. Perimeter's secure."

Tucker crept along the side of the alley, weapon poised. "This place feels staged... like something's just waiting for us to walk right in."

Chen indicated some crumbling brickwork overhead. "Brickwork's smashed and chipped. Something slammed into it—something big."

Marek closed his eyes for a moment as the pulse intensified—not audible, but a bodily sensation. His skin prickled, his breathing quickened.

Something was coming.

He opened his eyes and looked upward. High above, something caught his attention—a pulsing shimmer.

"Gordon," he whispered. "I think something's coming through."

Without hesitation, she raised her hand in a silent halt signal, directing the team to tighten formation. Her sidearm materialized from her belt in an instant.

The overhead lights flickered again before cutting out—one after another.

Pop.

Pop.

Pop.

Darkness engulfed the alley.

Marcus's voice cut through the comms, sharp and focused. "Surge just spiked—crossing the threshold. Distortion readings are localized to your area only."

Chen responded grimly, "Here we go, it's coming."

Tucker hefted his rifle. "No shit."

And then Marek felt it. The low-level buzzing, spiking into a full-on headache—accompanied by a feeling of static electricity washing over him. The same feeling he'd had in every previous creature encounter.

His body reacted before his mind could catch up, muscles contracting, jaw locking shut. He spun back to Gordon—just as she lifted her head.

A blue-white pulse of light and energy ripped into existence on the rooftop above and ahead of them.

Something massive shot out of the tear in reality, and the flash of light cut off abruptly.

It landed on the rooftop, and in the next breath, leapt off and dropped, a blur of darkness in freefall.

With a bone-rattling CRACK, the creature landed in a crouch—its muscled limbs absorbing the impact, shattering concrete in a concussive blast.

The shockwave knocked debris from ledges—windows exploding outward.

Reacting instinctively, Marek lunged and swept Gordon aside just before the shockwave hit, shielding her as the force rippled through the narrow corridor. Concrete fractured, windows shattered, and the comms buzzed with static.

Then the thing rose.

Seven feet tall, its skin was a layer of dark scales that shimmered with shifting hues in the low light.

Its eyes—red, like burning coals—locked instantly on Marek and Gordon.

And it *smiled.* Or that's what it seemed like to Marek.

Shit, another Drakyn, thought Gordon. *Why is it always a Drakyn?*

The muscles of its snout curled to reveal more teeth than should fit in a mouth that size. It exhaled with a low, grinding *snarl.*

Then it charged, and the alley erupted into chaos.

Chapter 21

The creature lunged at Marek first. It came in low and fast, too fast. Marek barely had time to drop into a crouch, weapon raised, before the thing was on him.

Gordon fired—a short, tight burst to the head. The rounds struck, jerking its head back, it stumbled, giving Marek time to reset.

Blood splattered the brick wall behind it, dark and shimmering, but it shook off the hit like a punch-drunk boxer and kept going.

Tucker opened fire from the far end of the alley, distracting it further.

Chen swung wide to cover their right side. Malik moved to flank left, drawing its attention with quick bursts, trying to force it into the open.

The creature crouched, then launched sideways and up—concrete cracking beneath it from the sheer force of the jump. It slammed into the wall of a nearby building, four clawed limbs digging in deep.

With a flex of its arms, it pushed off, twisting mid-air as its tail curled for balance.

It landed in the center of the team with a bellowing roar—primal and wrong, the kind of sound that grated against the inside of your skull.

The tail came first, a spiked blur that clipped Malik and sent him skidding into a metal dumpster. The impact dented the steel, and Malik dropped like dead weight, eyes rolling back as he hit the pavement.

"Malik!!!" Chen shouted into the melee, trying to move to check his vitals.

As the creature turned to find its next target, something snapped in Marek—white-hot rage flooding his limbs at the sight of his teammate crumpled on the ground.

There was no hesitation on his part—only the pull of instinct as he surged forward.

The world dragged in slow motion around him, as if he was the only one moving at full speed.

Ducking beneath a sweeping claw, he drove his fist into the creature's gut. Amped up by that same surge of energy, the impact landed like a sledgehammer, slamming the beast back a step.

It snarled, jaws splitting wide to reveal rows of thick, pointed fangs.

The creature lunged again, and Marek pivoted, arm snapping up, driving his knife home dead-center of the chest. He'd drawn it from his thigh sheath at some point during the chaos.

It stumbled back, hissing in anger.

Then, without hesitation, it yanked the blade free and flung it aside—continuing its advance.

Time snapped back into place. The world caught up to him just as the creature spun and slashed, claws raking across Marek's chest in a brutal, jagged sweep.

Pain. White-hot, seared across his chest. But Marek didn't fall. He stayed on his feet despite the pain.

Gordon was there a second later, blade flashing. She sliced deep across its back, cutting through tendons. The thing shrieked, whipping around.

"Move!" she shouted.

Marek spun clear, as Gordon took his place, driving the creature back a step. Its movements were faster now, erratic. Blood streamed from the wound on its back where her blade had caught bone.

Chen threw a flash bang into the center of the alley—their surrounds exploding with white light. The creature shrieked again, disoriented.

"Jesus, Chen! A little warning next time." Tucker yelled, momentarily blinded by the burst.

Marek didn't stop. He felt the trickle of blood slowly soaking through his vest, but his stride never faltered. He gripped Gordon's arm and jerked her back, just as the creature slammed its tail down in the spot where she'd been. Concrete shattered beneath the blow.

She turned to him—eyes wide. First with shock. Then fear. Then something else entirely. *Rage.*

Not panic. Not weakness. But something fiercely protective.

"You're hit," she said, voice tight.

He managed a grin. "It's noth—"

The creature coiled again, muscles bunching, readying itself to attack.

The rest of the team was still off-balance, blinking through the aftershock of the attack and Chen's misplaced intervention, but not Gordon—her reaction was immediate.

She twisted, impossibly fast, coming around it. She grabbed it by its shoulder and threw it into a wall. It fell to the ground, thrashing, and twisted back to its feet.

It went back at Gordon, claws slashing, but she sidestepped in a blur, faster that should have been possible. Grabbing the creature's arm, she bent it backwards with a *snap*, breaking it at the joint.

She pulled a blade from her hip sheath—while it was distracted by pain—and proceeded to tear into it with a viciousness that stunned Marek, slicing through tendons, muscle, and flesh.

Each strike was surgical, brutal, and efficient. It tried to fight back, but it was outmatched. Then, with a final thrust, Gordon drove the blade into the side of its skull.

The creature buckled—its legs giving out all at once. As it fell, she grabbed its head in both of her hands and snapped its neck with a grunt. The audible *crack*, echoed in the stillness of the alley, sharp and final.

It hit the asphalt with a wet slap, spasming once, then going still.

Silence fell.

He looked at Gordon and blinked, not believing what he just saw.

"Where the *fuck* did that come from? That was..." He trailed off, still stunned.

Gordon didn't respond. Rage had overtaken her the moment she saw Marek get hurt—instinctive and absolute.

She hadn't really thought. She'd just reacted. Because in that moment, the only thing that flashed through her mind was: *How dare it touch what's mine.*

The realization hit her an instant later—*mine?*

The word rattled in her skull, unwelcome and unprofessional. He was her subordinate. A teammate. Not someone she was supposed to feel this way about—not someone she could claim.

And yet, in the heat of battle, that primal instinct had surged forward like a tidal wave, drowning out everything else.

She stood next to the body, breath coming in slow, controlled pulls. Her chest felt tight, her heart hammering; not from exertion, but how it always did whenever he was near.

She desperately wanted to look at him—to see how badly he was hurt. She kept her eyes on the ground instead. On the body. On anything but him.

Afraid of what she'd see in his eyes after she'd let her leash slip. After giving into the rage that came when the Drakyn had hurt him.

"You're not even going to deny it this time, are you?" Marek said. "How you moved...it's impossible."

Gordon said nothing, lips pressed into a tight line. "What are you?" He whispered.

She finally met his gaze. Her eyes were dark, storm-dark, but not hiding now. "Not what you think."

Marek took a step toward her, then winced as pain flared across his chest again.

"You are one to talk," she said softly. "I saw how you moved too—like we were all standing still. You going to shed light on that?"

He shook his head, a humorless laugh escaping, "If I knew, believe me I'd let you know."

His eyes didn't leave hers. He still felt the heat of her in the tunnel yesterday, when she'd leaned in close enough for him to feel her breath against his lips.

Close enough for him to know they were both hanging on to their professionalism by tattered threads.

Chens's voice cut through the silence between them "Uh, guys? Little help here?"

Marek turned to see her dragging Malik to the side of the alley, where Harper was coming up with a med kit—having just pulled up in the van outside the alley.

"Is he breathing?" Marek called out, urgency overriding everything else. Putting a stopper, however temporary, in his exchange with Gordon.

Out of the corner of his eye, he saw Tucker go over to the creature's body—now turned human—and start kicking it, cursing.

Harper didn't look up, but her voice carried a hint of relief. "Yeah. Pulse seems strong. He may have a concussion when he wakes up, but he's stable for now. No thanks to Chen dragging him like a sack of potatoes."

Harper looked at Chen like she was judging her intelligence. "You do know what a stretcher is, don't you?"

Chen shuffled in place, looking at her feet "Sorry," she mumbled.

Harper shook her head and sighed. looking at Gordon, she said, "I want to get him back to HQ to get an MRI."

She looked at the dent in the garbage can meaningfully. "He hit hard, so I want to make sure there's no internal bleeding."

"Harper, you and Chen get Malik loaded up and back to HQ," Gordon called out.

Gordon looked back to the alley with an exasperated eye roll. "Tucker, stop kicking the dead body and call in a clean-up crew for this scene, will you? We need to get out of here before the locals come to investigate."

Tucker grumbled, "Yes boss," and gave one final kick, "Fucker," he muttered.

As the team sprang into action, Gordon returned to Marek. On her way to him, she knelt to retrieve his knife.

When he reached for it, she gently pushed his hand aside and slid the knife back into his thigh sheath.

She fastened the clasp, her hand lingering a moment too long on his thigh as she looked back up at him—heat and hunger in her gaze.

For *him.*

Marek took a slow breath, trying to calm his racing heartbeat. He reached for her hand—carefully, deliberately—and held it.

Her touch burned him, the echo of it seared into his skin where it had scorched his thigh. Even now, as their fingers intertwined, the heat lingered.

The pulse of attraction between them was unmistakable—like a live wire.

"We're going to have to figure this out eventually, you know," Marek said, his voice low and husky—rough around the edges in a way that made Gordon's toes curl.

Heat bloomed low in her core—sharp, sudden, and impossible to ignore.

"Yeah," she murmured, looking up at him. "But not tonight."

Her other hand came to rest on his chest, "You need to get this bleeder checked," she added softly—her signature move: changing the subject—slipping back into professionalism with practiced ease.

Then she stepped back, breaking the contact, and headed toward their SUVs.

Marek watched her go for a moment before following—still feeling the warmth of her touch... and the desire threatening to fry his brain.

Chapter 22

T he silence that night in the SCU operations room was charged—an undercurrent of excitement permeating the space.

Marek stood with one hand braced on the edge of the conference table, the other gripping a cooling cup of coffee he'd forgotten to drink. Around him, the rest of the team filtered in—Malik, conscious now and fully cleared by Harper.

Then came Chen, Marcus, and Harper—each moving with a strange mix of tension and wonder, the aftermath of something monumental that no one quite knew how to process.

They'd killed it. Not contained it. Not fled. Not watched sword-guy dispatch it in some blur of power and fury. They'd killed the damn thing. Them... together.

Well, mostly Gordon—but the rest of the team wasn't quite aware of how one-sided that contest was.

Marek remembered.

Gordon stood at the far end of the room, her arms crossed, her weight shifted subtly to one leg in that casual-coiled way of hers.

She scanned each face in the room, cataloging reactions the way only she could. But when her gaze found Marek's, it lingered—just long enough to say *I see you.*

He offered her a warm smile and was rewarded with a flush that crept up her neck to her cheeks.

She looked away a beat too late, slamming the mask of professionalism back into place—but not before mutual desire passed between them, hot and undeniable.

A continuation of what had taken place just minutes before in her office.

Gordon scolded herself silently. *Stop thinking about his lips and how they felt. You're a damn professional—start acting like it. And that smug smile of his—damn him! Don't let him get to you.*

It had been chaos in the alley. Blood, claws, and smashed pavement. But somewhere in aftermath, there'd been a realization.

They *could* fight these things. And maybe... just maybe... they could win.

"Alright," Gordon said, coming back to herself. "Let's not break our arms patting ourselves on the back. That thing is dead, but we're not done."

Marcus wheeled around from his station. "Before we dive into debrief, I need you all to see this."

He tapped a few keys and brought up a wide-angle city map. Three red marks bloomed across it—tiny pulse points across New York's boroughs. The room leaned in.

"Surges," Marcus said. "Low-level energy readings so far. These are just the ones we picked up in the last twenty-four hours. There's been a slow uptick."

"Slow?" Harper asked, stepping closer.

"Slow, but steadily climbing," Marcus replied. "We're seeing two, maybe three every day. Not big enough to trip our threshold and let one of our creatures through from... wherever it is they come from. My concern is that we only used to see one small surge point a day, if that."

Gordon nodded. "Start building a grid. Let's keep a close eye on those three and if any of them get close to our threshold, I want the system to trigger an alert. I want at least a couple hours of response time so we can try to head off anything coming through."

"Yes, ma'am."

She turned back to the team, tone sharpening just enough to cut through the buzz.

"We did take one down today, but we didn't get out unscathed. I don't want anyone thinking we're invincible. The thing we killed tonight bled, but others won't go down as easy. Stay ready. Stay smart. And don't get cocky."

The room slowly began to disperse, agents peeling off to their workstations or to snag sleep in one of the bunk rooms. Tucker gave Marek a light elbow nudge.

"Briefing room in ten? If you have a moment, I'd like to talk," he said.

"Make it fifteen," Marek said.

He needed air. The heat and tension in the operations room—between him and Gordon, layered with what had happened earlier—was making his head spin.

* * *

Gordon's Office—Ten Minutes Earlier

The blinds were drawn, the lights low. Outside, the faint hum of operations continued—radio static, typing... quiet voices. But inside her office, the world felt suspended.

Marek knocked on the open door to her office, and leaned on the doorframe, unsure whether to come in and sit, or stand.

Gordon had called him in to her office to "discuss things," before the team's scheduled debrief.

He didn't know what to make of it. They had shared an intimate moment in the alley earlier after the fight, but that didn't mean she wouldn't shut him out again.

She was good at that—putting up walls between what she felt and what she showed.

Still, when she looked up at him—just a glance in response to his knock—

God, she was stunning, he thought.

All sharp lines and quiet authority. Those eyes read him like a book—thorough, and unflinching.

Her arms crossed beneath her chest, and that's when he noticed.

The way her shirt stretched with each breath—the subtle rise and fall of her breasts, pressed just tight enough to draw his eyes before he could stop himself.

And her mouth. *Don't even think about her mouth* he scolded himself.

But he did anyway. He couldn't shake the memory—her breath, warm and measured, lips just shy of his in that tunnel.

She'd only been checking for injuries. Still, it had felt like something more.

Then he remembered the alley and how the air still smelled of blood and gunpowder. How she'd strapped his knife back into its sheath, her hand lingering a second too long on his thigh—like she didn't want to let go.

He remembered the way her lips parted, like she was about to say something—or do something—and didn't.

And he remembered wanting to close the space between them and take her right there.

———◆———

Gordon leaned against her desk, her arms uncrossing—gaze locked on him.

It was stupid how handsome he was. She thought.

No man had a right to look like that. Leaning against the door frame, looking like some damn romance novel character come to life.

She inhaled deeply and then let it out, looking for control. It didn't show up.

It wasn't fair what he did to her. And those eyes, smoky and smoldering, looked at her like he wanted to strip her bare and have his way with her.

Her thighs pressed together at the thought, that low, familiar heat already blooming—just like it always did when he was near, and her thoughts turned south.

Snap out of it, she told herself. *He's your subordinate, and he's a human. You know what the Warden's Oath says about that.*

If only her body would comply, life would be so much simpler.

Marek shifted slightly, one shoulder still propped against the doorframe. His lips curled into that half-smile he wore when he was trying not to smirk—and failing.

"You wanted to see me?"

Gordon nodded once, keeping her expression neutral. "Close the door."

He did, and the soft click of the latch seemed louder than it should've.

She gestured toward the chair across from her desk, but Marek didn't move.

"You gonna sit?" she asked.

"Depends," he said, voice low. "Am I here for a reprimand... or something else?"

Her jaw tightened, just a little. Not in anger—restraint.

"You were reckless and impulsive in the field today," she said. "You engaged that thing on your own. What were you thinking?"

"I was thinking about trying to save Malik's life," he said calmly.

"I know. But it was reckless, and I need you alive—not dead because of some damn heroics," she said, clearly exasperated.

"I could say the same thing about what you did. You stepped in to save me. Impulsive—reckless, even. Wouldn't you say?" he asked, throwing her question back at her.

Her face flushed, *the nerve of this man!*

He cut in before she could think of a response. "You called me in to say that?"

"No," she said, and suddenly she wasn't leaning on the desk anymore—she was moving, slowly, deliberately, around to the side.

She needed to create some space between them—she was having a hard time breathing when he was this close.

Maybe inviting him into the office—into a tight intimate setting—hadn't been the best idea in hindsight.

She reined her thoughts back in, saying, "I called you in because what happened in that alley... what happened *after*—we need to be clear on it."

Marek's gaze didn't waver, filled with heat. "I thought we were."

Her throat worked around a response. She wasn't used to being thrown off balance—not by anyone. But Marek Tomlinson had a way of making the walls she'd built around herself—the ones propping up her orderly life—crumble.

His heart pounded, but he stayed outwardly calm—just watching her move around the office, like a warrior: graceful, yet strong. It made him want to do reckless things.

She had that effect on him—always had. From the second she'd stormed into his precinct with that badge, dressed in formfitting tactical gear that seemed to hug her every curve, he'd been lost.

She'd lit something in him. Something primal. Something he couldn't name, but it burned for her.

"I can't afford to be distracted," she said finally. "Not with what we're facing."

"And I'm a distraction?" he asked, moving slowly around the side of the desk in her direction, eating up the space she'd created.

"You're starting to be," she said softly.

She didn't look up, but she could feel the heat of his body stop just inches away. His presence like a tangible thing that sent shivers through her.

She didn't move away.

He hovered there, the tension in his frame barely leashed.

"Funny, because when I thought I was done for—before you saved me—the only thing I could think about was you."

Her breath caught. *Damn him. Damn him to the darkest hells. If he'd just kept his mouth shut.*

She didn't answer. Couldn't. The silence stretched taut between them.

Then, slowly, Marek reached up with one hand and tilted her chin, forcing her eyes to meet his.

"Beautiful," he said, his voice husky and his eyes burning with desire.

Her breathe caught in her chest at that look—like he was a man dying of thirst and she was water.

"This is probably a mistake," he murmured as he moved both hands to the side of her face—gently, like she might bolt if he moved to fast.

"Probably," she whispered back.

And then he kissed her.

Oh. My. God.

Her world didn't just stop—it *fractured*, coming apart at the seams with a breathless, aching kind of violence.

Thought vanished, wiped clean by the press of his mouth against hers. There was only heat. And want. And the raw, searing gravity of him.

And *Onos*, could he kiss.

He started slowly, mouth moving against hers, mapping every curve and edge like she was the only thing that existed.

His tongue teased her bottom lip, coaxing her open with maddening patience—a question and a claim all in one.

She answered, opening to him with a soft whimper, her hands fisting in his shirt, dragging him closer until there was no space between them—no distance, no air, just *him*.

Hard muscle pressed flush against her body, and her bones went liquid beneath it. When he deepened the kiss, it turned *carnal*—his tongue sliding against hers, rough and perfect and devastating.

She met him stroke for stroke, her breath catching when he growled low in his throat. In that moment of surrender, her body betrayed every oath she'd sworn, every wall she'd built. She was on fire—nerve endings lit like a bonfire—and still it wasn't enough. Would never be enough.

She pulled back after a few heartbeats, breathing hard, still drunk on the feel of him. Her lips tingled. Her heart raced. Her body ached to close the distance again—but her mind clawed for control.

She tried to get her bearings. Tried to come back to earth.

"We can't—" she began, voice rough.

"I know," he said, still close enough that she could feel the warmth of him. His voice was husky, low, threaded with restraint. "I know."

Her gaze dropped to the floor. She couldn't look at him. Not right now.

"You should go," Gordon said softly.

Marek stepped back, just enough. "I'll see you in the briefing."

And then he was gone. His footsteps faded down the hall, and the door clicked shut behind him.

Gordon stood frozen, every part of her aching and alive. She dragged her hands over her face, trying to scrub away the heat still clinging to her skin—the burn of his mouth on hers.

Shit.

Her fingers trembled.

I'm in so much trouble.

◆

Operations Room—9:30 p.m.

The lights hummed faintly, casting long shadows across the table strewn with printed reports and left-over coffee cups.

The rest of the team had already cleared out, when Marek and Tucker came back in fifteen minutes later, leaving them alone with the silence and their thoughts.

Tucker leaned back in one of the conference chairs, feet kicked up on another, his sleeves rolled up and shirt half-untucked—like he was daring someone to call him unprofessional.

Marek sat by the wall-length whiteboard, arms folded across his chest, eyes fixed on nothing, nursing a cup of cold coffee.

He'd taken to drinking it cold after many late nights at the office and on stakeouts—it just wasn't worth the hassle of heating it up every five minutes. Tucker gave him shit, saying it meant he was a psychopath.

"So..." Tucker said, dragging out the word like he was unwrapping a present. "You gonna tell me what the hell that was before the meeting?"

Marek blinked. "What?"

"You know what. I walked past you going into the boss's office, and then ten minutes later, you walked into the room looking like you'd seen God—or a very attractive angel... who either kicked your ass, or kissed you, judging by the tension in the ops room after."

Marek didn't respond right away.

Tucker sat up, dropping his feet to the floor. "You kissed her, didn't you?"

Marek sighed and sank into the chair beside him. "Yeah. I did."

Tucker grinned. "Well, shit. Did she punch you? Slap you? Stab you? Please tell me she stabbed you."

"No," Marek said. "She kissed me back."

Tucker let out a low whistle. "Okay, now *that's* a twist."

"It was—is... complicated," Marek admitted.

He scrubbed a hand over his face, the memory of her mouth still burning on his.

"She told me I was a distraction. That she can't afford that right now. But I couldn't—hell, I didn't even think. It just... happened."

Tucker's shit-eating grin faded, replaced by something softer. "You care about her."

Marek didn't answer, but he didn't need to.

"Look, man," Tucker said after a pause, "I give you crap, yeah, but you know I've got your back. Always have. And I've never seen you like this."

"Like what?"

"Like someone who's finally found something that makes the nightmares a little quieter."

Marek looked down at his hands. "She's not like anyone I've ever met, Tuck. She's... sharp and dangerous and focused, but underneath all that, there's this storm she keeps barely under control. I see it. I *feel* it. I'm drawn to it, and I can't even help it."

Tucker watched him for a beat, then leaned forward on his elbows. "And the other thing?"

"What other thing?"

Tucker raised an eyebrow. "The part where you held your own against a creature that tossed Malik like a rag doll. Don't think I missed that. You moved faster than I've ever seen you move. And you healed fast—again."

Marek's shoulders tensed. "It's getting worse. Or better—I don't even know anymore. Every time we get close to a surge point, something in me starts to hum. My skin itches. My head throbs like I've got a headache. I get this surge of energy—like adrenaline. My instincts go haywire. It's like I can feel them before I even *see* them."

"And Gordon?"

"She knows I'm different," Marek said quietly. "I just don't think she knows what I am... Hell, I don't either."

Tucker let out a long breath. "You think she's the same?"

Marek met his eyes. "I think she's more than human. I don't know how much more. But yeah—I think she's hiding something. And I think whatever it is... it's something she either won't tell me or can't. It's frustrating."

Tucker nodded slowly, then clapped a hand on Marek's shoulder. "Well, if it makes you feel any better, I've always known you were a freak. But you're my freak."

Marek huffed a quiet laugh.

Tucker leaned back in his chair again, suddenly thoughtful. "So what now? You gonna keep kissing your boss in dark corners and pretending everything's normal?"

"God, I hope not," Marek muttered. "But I'm not sure I could stop, even if I wanted to."

"Then I suggest you figure it out, and fast," Tucker said, half-serious now. "Because one of these days, something's gonna hit us harder than we can hit back. And when that day comes, you need to know who you are—and who she is to you."

Marek nodded, the weight of the words settling deep in his chest.

"Yeah," he said. "You're right."

At that moment, they got a text from Gordon:

—*Lower East Side surge. Abandoned tower. Marcus confirmed the threshold. Suit up. Parking garage in twenty.*

"Damn, it's like she knew we were talking about her," Tucker said, glancing around the room like she might pop out of the walls.

Marek chuckled as he stood, reached for the cold coffee, and tossed it back without flinching.

"I'm sure that's it. Alright, nothing for it then. Time to get back to work."

Tucker winced. "Jesus, Marek. Still a psychopath... I don't know how you drink coffee like that and not vomit."

Marek grinned. "Wouldn't be me if I couldn't."

They both laughed as they headed out the door, and to the armory.

Chapter 23

Abandoned Tower—Lower East Side—10:30 p.m.

T he wind howled between steel beams, threading through shattered windows like whispers.

Marek stepped carefully across the cracked floor of the abandoned high-rise, his boots crunching over loose gravel and glass.

The building loomed over the Lower East Side like a monument to unfinished ambition—forty stories of exposed girders, rusted scaffolding, and half-installed paneling.

It had been condemned mid-construction a decade ago. Now it was just another forgotten scar on the city's skyline.

And tonight, it was pulsing with energy.

Marcus had flagged it three hours earlier—a surge point that was building toward the threshold. An hour ago, he'd moved it to the priority board, and that meant they had to check it out.

They'd taken a still-operational freight elevator up to the 39th floor, and were clearing it methodically, searching for signs of a creature, distortions in the air, or anything out of the ordinary.

"I hate heights," Tucker muttered, his voice low in Marek's earpiece. "Why can't the weird shit ever show up in a nice ground-level spot?"

Marek smirked. "We've done ground-level recently—remember the warehouse? It wasn't that nice."

Gordon moved ahead of them, her steps silent despite the unstable flooring. She didn't respond to the banter—just kept scanning the shadows, her sidearm drawn and held low, her posture tight. Always in control. Always watching.

Marek watched her, that familiar heat stirring again. The way she moved—precise, deliberate, lethal.

Even now, during an op, he still couldn't stop remembering the way her lips had felt against his an hour ago. The way she'd tasted. The way she had softened against him—so different from her controlled professionalism, that no nonsense exterior she always wore.

Focus, he told himself. *This isn't the time.*

They moved in staggered formation—Tucker covering the rear, Gordon and Marek in the lead, Malik and Chen flanking wide. The wind whistled through the skeletal frame of the building, and every sound echoed too long, too loud.

"Picking up energy outputs gaining strength at the far end just above us," Chen said, consulting her scanner. "They are just at the levels we saw with our last encounter, and holding steady. Something will be coming out to play soon."

"Awesome, can't wait for a repeat," Marek said dryly.

They had climbed a set of stairs and had just reached the 40th floor, where the ceiling gave way to exposed sky. Torn tarps snapped in the wind. Rebar curled like ribs from broken concrete. Plastic sheeting fluttered across makeshift barriers.

"Eyes ahead," Gordon said quietly. "Stay tight."

Marek's skin started to itch. That now-familiar hum buzzed behind his eyes—and it was getting stronger, which wasn't a good sign.

To his left, Chen moved to check the far edge of the floor. Malik followed behind her with his carbine up, sweeping left and right, up and down in a methodical pattern. The rest of the team held their positions, forming a perimeter around the exposed central platform.

"Something's here," he murmured.

Then, the air crackled with blue lighting, that familiar energy crashing against his skin. Except this time, some of it seemed to lick at him—questing, almost like it *wanted in.*

Before he knew what he was doing, he reached out to it. And, as if it had been waiting permission, it slipped under his skin.

He gasped, as fire and power seared through his veins. Like someone tried to jumpstart his heart with pure adrenaline while he was still conscious.

His body brimmed with energy. It felt like he'd been blind his whole life and now he could see. Like he'd been weighed down with bricks and had finally shrugged them off.

His breathing was even, and time slowed as he felt something enter the world.

It stepped out from behind a slatted column of concrete and steel.

It was massive. Ten feet at least—a hulking, predatory creature. Bigger than any other dragon creature they'd encountered up till now.

"Shit!" Tucker yelled, as he brought his carbine up.

"Contact! Engage!" Marek barked, as he brought his rifle to bear.

The creature turned its head from side to side, surveying the humans who had surrounded it.

Then, it locked eyes with a target and with a bellow of animalistic rage, surged forward—its tail whipping outward in a deadly arc.

Chen barely had time to scream before the tail struck her, mid-torso hurling her into a support beam. She hit with a sickening *crack*, and crumpled to the ground in a boneless sprawl of twisted limbs.

"Chen's down!" Tucker shouted, voice cracking.

"Engage—now!" Gordon ordered.

She opened fire, controlled bursts—two center mass, one to the head. The creature flinched, staggered. But it didn't fall.

It came straight for her instead.

Marek saw it—every movement slowed, like the world had been dipped in molasses; everyone else moved in slow motion, except him.

He intercepted the creature before it had crossed half the distance, slamming into it with a full-body tackle—his shoulder crushing into its ribs hard enough to send them both skidding across the floor.

It twisted mid-fall, claws slashing out, scoring his forearm through the sleeve of his jacket.

Pain flared—and then vanished. The world narrowed. The creature lunged again.

Marek *met it*.

Brimming with a power he didn't yet understand, he caught its arm mid-swing and twisted—feeling the bones snap under his grip. He didn't stop. Something inside him—some dam—had broken, and he gave in to his rage.

He drove a knee into its chest, then twisted—still holding its ruined arm—and hurled it into a pillar. Metal groaned and bent on impact. It rolled, tried to rise—but he was already there.

Fist. Elbow. Fist again. Fueled by anger, fear for his team—and something else—each blow landed with brutal force, wet crunches accompanying the spray of blood.

The thing roared—ancient, alien, and laced with something like fear.

Marek roared back. He seized the creature by its throat, leapt into the air with it, and slammed it back down—hard enough to crack the concrete floor.

The creature sprawled in a dazed heap, but Marek grabbed its head and drove it down again.

And again.

And again.

Blood splattered across the floor, he felt it spray his face—warm and metallic.

His vision tunneled. His muscles burned with a power not his own. His pulse boomed in his ears like a bass drum.

He was going to kill it. He *wanted* to kill it. Needed to punish it for what it had come here to do. To him. To his team.

For what it had already done to Chen.

It thrashed once more—and in that moment, he felt something pass between them.

A flicker of understanding. Of recognition. Its gaze locked with his, wide and burning.

Like it had seen its death in the eyes of this human who was something else entirely...

Then, in a burst of shimmering energy, it was ripped from his grasp—sucked backward through the same type of tear in reality it had come through.

Marek felt the energy pouring from it—pulsing in time to what was coursing through him.

Then with a pop of sound, the tear vanished, taking the creature with it.

The surge of power cut off abruptly, like a switch had been flipped. Marek dropped to one knee, chest heaving, limbs trembling as if he'd gone fifteen rounds in a heavyweight title match.

The spiderweb of shattered concrete and blood, was the only sign of what had just happened. That—and his team, scattered around him, trying to regroup.

The silence was deafening.

Behind him, Tucker was kneeling beside Chen. Blood-slicked hair clung to her scalp. Her arm was bent at an unnatural angle. She was alive—but barely.

Gordon hadn't moved since firing her last round—hadn't needed to.

Marek looked at her.

A silent exchange passed between them, too deep for words. She'd seen everything. But there was no judgement in her eyes.

Then her eyes flicked to the others—Tucker, Marcus, Malik—just for a second. A silent signal. *Not now. Not yet.*

Instead, she walked over to him and said, "You almost killed it."

Marek didn't answer. His mouth was dry. His hands still trembled with the aftershocks of power that hadn't felt like his own.

He glanced down—blood caked his knuckles. Knuckles that weren't damaged at all.

A gash ran along his forearm, but it was already scabbed over. He was healing faster than ever. Too fast. *Again.*

"I wanted to. I *needed to*," he said.

"I know." She said softly, "You don't know how much I know the feeling."

Chapter 24

The rooftop was quiet now. The chaos had been cleared. The medevac had lifted Chen out only ten minutes ago, its red lights dwindling against the midnight sky.

Somewhere in the city, Chen was fighting to hold on, tucked inside SCU's underground trauma facility. But here, above the city that never slept, the world felt muted. Distant.

Marek stood near the edge, arms resting on a rusted crossbeam, eyes fixed on nothing.

The city stretched out before him—lights blinking, cars crawling—it felt worlds away. People were down there somewhere, living normal lives, safe in their homes and cars.

Safe from monsters. Unaware that something inhuman had walked in their midst just an hour ago.

His breathing was mostly steady now. Mostly. But every muscle in his body felt like it had been wrung out and hung to dry. The wound on his forearm—scabbed over now—had started to itch.

He could've sworn it was getting smaller by the minute.

He flexed his fingers, trying not to think too hard about it.

Behind him, he heard footsteps. He didn't turn.

"You gonna brood up here all night?"

Gordon's voice. Soft. But there was an edge to it—a rawness he hadn't heard before.

He didn't answer. Just closed his eyes and let the wind cut across his skin. The scent of concrete dust, sweat, and ozone still lingered.

She stepped up beside him, hands tucked into the pockets of her jacket, eyes scanning the skyline like it might offer answers. For a few minutes, neither of them spoke.

"She's gonna make it," Gordon said. Not a statement as much as it was a prayer.

"Maybe," Marek replied. "But she shouldn't have to. These... *creatures* shouldn't even be here."

The words sat heavy between them.

He turned his head, finally looking at her. "I lost control out there—I don't know what happened to me, how I did what I did. It's like it happened to someone else."

Gordon didn't respond for a long moment. "You saved me."

Marek ran a hand across his face. "I nearly killed that thing. I wanted to kill it. I wanted it to bleed. To suffer. That... that was rage. Lack of control. That's not who I am."

Her gaze flicked toward him then, sharp and unreadable. "It wasn't just rage."

Marek held her stare. "Then what the hell was it? Because it didn't feel human... I don't feel human anymore."

Gordon looked away again, back at the city. Her fingers twitched in her jacket pockets.

"You're not going to let this one go, are you?"

"I need answers, Gordon. I feel like I'm going crazy—and you're acting like its normal, which is crazy..."

She frowned for a moment, visibly wrestling with something—then seemed to come to a decision.

"You felt the energy coming from the Rift. You connected to it."

He blinked. "Rift?"

She pursed her lips, the same look on her face she got when she didn't—or wouldn't—answer a question.

He straightened, eyes narrowing. "Gordon..."

She sighed and shook her head, leaning forward against the rail like the confession cost her something.

"I've already said too much as it is. There are things I haven't told you. Things I can't."

"Why?"

"Binding orders mostly. But even if I could, the whole team would be in danger. Because not everything out there can be explained. Because some truths get people killed. And some truths I physically am unable to share—aren't mine to share."

He turned away, jaw tight, frustration evident on his face. "Chen almost died anyway."

Gordon swallowed hard. When she spoke, her voice cracked—for the first time, "And that's on me. I froze. I hesitated. Because I didn't want to expose myself. I wanted to protect the mission, the team, *you*. But she paid the price."

Silence.

Then, softer:

"And I watched you become something tonight, Marek."

He turned back to her. The anger had drained from his face, replaced by... acceptance. "It scared me. But it also felt right. Like... like I'd been holding back my whole life and didn't even know it."

She nodded. "You were."

"You know what I am, don't you?"

She met his eyes. "Not exactly. I don't know what that means moving forward, but we'll find out together."

The wind shifted. Somewhere below, sirens echoed off the buildings.

And up on the rooftop, two people stood together in silence—not as superior and subordinate, but as something else.

◆

SCU Headquarters—Locker Room—11:45 p.m.

Marek sat on the bench between rows of half-lockers, his uniform jacket discarded and balled at his feet. The warm water from a shower hadn't done much to rinse away the night—his bones still ached with it.

He was struggling to understand it all.

Footsteps echoed in from the hall.

Tucker appeared in the doorway, face pale, eyes red-rimmed but dry. His usual sharp sarcasm was nowhere to be found.

"Hey," he said.

Marek didn't look up. "Hey."

Tucker came in slow, dropped onto the bench across from him. Elbows on knees. Hands clasped tight. For a while, they sat in silence.

"They said Chen's in surgery," Tucker said finally.

"Broken ribs, collapsed lung, fractured arm—possibly more. They don't know if she'll breathe right again when she wakes up... *if* she'll even—"

He stopped abruptly, unable to give voice to the possibility.

Tucker exhaled. It shook on the way out. "I should've had her six. I was too slow."

Marek leaned forward, grabbed his shoulder.

"It wasn't your fault," was all he could think to say.

"Maybe not," Tucker said. "But it still feels like I failed her. Like we all did."

Marek looked up and met his eyes. "You didn't fail her. That thing... It wasn't like the others, it was massive. You didn't stand a chance."

Tucker studied him. "But you did, though. You weren't like yourself either."

Marek didn't reply.

"I saw what you did," Tucker said, softer now. "Hell, I *felt* it. You beat the shit out of it—moving like we were all standing still. Leapt into the air with it—like it weighed nothing."

He continued, voice lowered. "That was more than instincts, more than your normal level of weird. You were... you were something else, man."

"I don't know what that was. What I am. How I did what I did," Marek said softly, opening and closing his hands, staring at them like they weren't his own.

"Gordon has suspicions but she won't... or can't share."

Tucker offered a bitter smile. "Maybe you don't need to know. Would you change anything about yourself if you did? Maybe just keep being the guy who steps in front of the monsters—cause that's who you are."

They sat together, quiet in their grief, in their shared failure, in the bond that hadn't broken—even when life tried its hardest.

"We still have a debrief in twenty," Tucker said.

"Yeah," Marek muttered. "Can't wait."

Tucker stood, offered a hand.

Marek took it. Whatever came next, they'd face it together.

———————◆———————

Briefing Room—12:05 a.m.

It was quiet in the room. Too quiet.

No idle conversation. No sarcastic quips. No rustle of case files or hum of laptops. Just silence—heavy and suffocating.

Marek sat at the long table, fingers laced, head bowed ... and completely healed—he was going to keep that fact to himself.

Malik leaned against the far wall, arms crossed, the faintest tremor in his jaw betraying the emotion he was holding back. Harper and Marcus hovered by their screens, but the monitors remained unchanged. No new data.

Chen was in surgery. Internal bleeding from a punctured lung. Broken shoulder, ribs, and arm. A fight for her life with no guarantees.

Tucker entered quietly, setting two coffees on the table without a word. One for Marek and the other for himself.

Then the door opened again, and Gordon walked through. She looked like hell.

Still in her gear. Still radiating that command presence. But tonight, it was fractured—a tear in the fabric. Her eyes rimmed with exhaustion. Her gait half a second slower.

She didn't speak right away. She didn't have to.

Everyone straightened. Her gaze swept the room—steady but weighted.

Then, finally, she spoke. "We were overconfident."

No one challenged her.

"We killed one of them in the alley. We thought that meant we understood what we were dealing with. We thought we were ready."

A pause. No one filled it.

"We weren't." Her voice cracked—just barely—but the team heard it.

"What happened tonight is on me. I led us in. I didn't coordinate backup. I thought we could handle it. And Chen almost paid for that with her life."

Marek raised his head. "We all signed on for this. You didn't force anyone. We walked in as a team. We take the hit as one."

Tucker added: "And we sure as hell continue as one... for Chen."

That broke something behind Gordon's eyes. Not visible to the rest of the team—there and gone again just as fast—but Marek saw it.

Her voice softened. "Then we need to adapt. We need to stop treating these things like one-offs. We train harder. We prepare better. We get ahead of it. Because it seems like these breaches are escalating and we can't afford to fall behind."

Marcus nodded from the monitors.

"I'll go through every second of the data. We'll find patterns. If it blinked in and out, I'll find out how. Why."

Malik finally spoke. "And we hit back harder next time."

Gordon jerked her head in a quick nod. "Yes. But smarter, too. No more half-measures. We learn from this, or someone might die next time."

The team nodded slowly.

She turned and gave one long look at Marek. He saw it in her eyes—something was shifting behind the steel. The leader was still there. But the woman underneath was starting to peek through. A testament to how rattled she was. She just wouldn't show it to the team.

Only to him. And maybe not even on purpose

◆

Gordon's Office—12:10 a.m.

The hallway outside her office was dark, quiet. Most of SCU had gone home or scattered to corners of the facility to decompress, rest, or drink in silence. But the light was still on under Gordon's door.

Marek knocked once and entered. She was sitting behind her desk, jacket off, and a half-drained bottle of water next to her laptop.

"You didn't have to check on me," she said, voice low.

"I saw your light on. Still working when everyone else is home," he said. "I didn't want to go home without checking on you. See how you were dealing with... everything."

She didn't respond to that. Didn't want him to see just how much that meant to her. She just motioned for him to sit.

They were quiet for a while. A silence that shouldn't have been so comfortable.

She eventually broke the silence. "We weren't ready. I wasn't ready—I froze."

Marek shook his head. "Even the best agents and officers freeze. But you know you couldn't have saved Chen, right? You were too far away. What you did was what any good team leader does—you pulled the team together. You rallied us."

Her eyes lifted to meet his. "I still hesitated. I don't do that."

He didn't know what to say to that. So, he stayed quiet.

She leaned back in her chair, rubbing at her face with one hand. "Chen... I keep replaying it. I saw it coming. I *felt* it. And I still didn't stop it."

"You're not a god, Gordon."

"No," she said. "But I'm something else. And maybe it's time I stop pretending I'm not."

Her eyes drifted to him again, and this time the look was different. Less guarded. More vulnerable.

"You scared the hell out of me tonight," she said. "But you also saved us. You saved *me*."

He nodded. "It felt... right. Like I stepped into something I didn't know was mine."

"You should get some rest," she said finally.

He stood slowly. But he didn't move toward the door.

"Are you really okay?" he asked.

She gave a faint smile. "No. But I will be."

He nodded and turned to leave, stopping at the door. "Kaycee?"

She jerked up at the sound of her first name on his lips—not Gordon, not Agent... Kaycee. A testament to how their relationship was changing. Since the alley... since the kiss in her office.

It did strange things to her insides—and she didn't fight it. Didn't correct him—a silent acknowledgement that they'd crossed a line at some point.

"Yeah?" she questioned, softly.

"If you ever need to talk, ever need to just *be*... You know where to find me."

She almost broke at those words. "Thanks, Marek. Night."

After he closed the door, she sat in silence for a long time... replaying his words over and over again. *You know where to find me...*

And that was the problem, if she was honest with herself.

She didn't just know where to find him.

Tonight, she *wanted to.*

Chapter 25

The water was still running down the drain when Marek stepped out of the bathroom. A towel hung low on his hips, hair damp, jaw freshly shaved. Steam curled across the mirror, hiding the reflection of a man who felt like a stranger.

He was heavier now—not in muscle or weight, but in something deeper. Like something had shifted beneath his skin and settled there, permanent and unfamiliar.

He'd just pulled on a pair of loose pants and a soft T-shirt when a knock came at his door. Gentle. Hesitant. But unmistakable.

Something tugged in his gut—low, insistent. He already knew who it was.

Barefoot, he crossed the apartment and opened the door.

Kaycee stood there, hair soaked from the rain falling in gentle sheets outside.

She was still in her boots and black tactical pants, a different jacket thrown over her usual undershirt.

Rain clung to her lashes and threaded down her jacket, soaking through the shirt underneath. Her eyes moved over him briefly—just enough to catch the lines of his chest beneath the shirt—before flicking back up to his face. Her cheeks flushed.

"Can I come in?" she asked, voice quiet.

He stepped aside without a word. The door clicked shut behind her. The apartment falling quiet, broken only by the sound of the rain outside, and the low hum of the heater.

"I couldn't sleep," she said, almost to herself. "I kept seeing Chen...kept seeing you."

"I know," Marek said. And he did.

They stood there for a long beat—both still, both holding the weight of their burdens. It was Kaycee who finally spoke again, her voice unsteady.

"We almost lost her today. I almost lost *you*."

"You didn't," he said. It came out rougher than he'd intended—raw around the edges.

"But if I had..." She took a breath. "I never would've said what I needed to say."

Her eyes met his—vulnerable in a way he'd never seen her.

"I need you to know how much you mean to me."

He stepped closer, barely breathing. All the nights he'd thought about what it would mean for her to look at him like this—raw and unguarded. He'd buried those thoughts. Buried everything, because it was easier to follow orders than admit how much of his heart she already held.

"I'm here," Marek said softly. "Always have been. Tell me what you need, Kaycee."

That undid her.

The rawness of that statement. The sound of her name on his lips—like a promise, like an anchor. The truth in his eyes staring back at her without uncertainty or hesitation.

Screw protocol. Screw restraint. Screw the Warden Oath.

Tonight, she chose him and damn the consequences.

Her eyes darkened—and then she closed the space between them, reaching up and pulling him into a kiss.

She kissed him like she'd been holding back for years—and maybe she had—maybe they both had. Her fingers threaded through his hair, anchoring him, like she was afraid he'd disappear if she let go.

He kissed her back like he'd been starved for her—for this—for the permission to feel what he'd locked away.

His arms circled her, pulling her flush to him. She didn't flinch when his hands found her waist, didn't shrink when he backed her into the wall. Her breath caught—and it wasn't fear. It was heat. It was *need*.

She broke the kiss, and yanked his shirt off in one smooth motion, her palms skating over his chest, tracing every scar, enjoying every twitch of his muscles under her hands. She touched him like she wanted to memorize every part of him.

He let her, as their mouths met again. No defenses. No masks.

"You're soaked," he murmured against her lips.

She smiled, breathless. "You're overdressed."

They stumbled together toward the bedroom, breath hitching, hands wandering, mouths never parting for long. His heart thundered with every step—not just from what was coming, but from what it meant.

What had started as lust and raw desire, had turned into something deeper by the time she landed on the mattress—something neither of them could name, but both felt.

He knelt, not out of obligation, but because he couldn't do anything else. She was soaked and shaking and perfect, and he felt like if he moved too fast, he might miss it—miss *her*.

He eased her boots off one at a time and slowly, started unzipping soaked clothing—removing layer after layer with worshipful reverence. Fingers brushed skin, each contact tender and electric—like touching her was the only thing that mattered.

He kissed the inside of her knee, then the soft skin of her thigh, moving slow—every inch was a revelation. Her breath stuttered—her hands tangled in the sheets.

"Marek," she pleaded, voice thick, breaking. Her strong and guarded eyes were wide—vulnerable now. Open.

And for a moment, the whole world narrowed to the rise and fall of her chest. To the vulnerability in her eyes. To the way she said his name with breathless need.

He looked up, eyes locked on hers.

"Are you sure?"

"Yes."

There was no hesitation. No second thoughts.

He kissed her again, slower now. Like he was memorizing her from the inside out.

When they finally came together, it wasn't frenzied. It was quiet. Fierce. Sacred.

For once, there were no rules. No Oath. No line between duty and want. She wasn't a Warden, and he wasn't her subordinate.

Only two people—raw and aching—finding something close to peace in the storm of each other.

Later, tangled in bedsheets and the hush of post-storm quiet, Kaycee rested her head on his chest—one leg draped over his. Skin to skin, heartbeat to heartbeat.

Her fingers traced faint circles over his chest, grounding herself in the rhythm of his breathing.

"You okay?" she asked.

He didn't speak.

He just turned, kissed the top of her head, and pulled her closer—like he never intended to let her go.

And if tomorrow went sideways—as it very well could—this moment would be the only thing worth remembering.

◆

Akron—Twenty minutes later—Outside Marek's apartment.

He had been following the human male closely the last couple days. There was something about him that tugged at Akron's awareness—a resonance he couldn't place. He was a puzzle that didn't have an answer, and Akron didn't like puzzles.

He had been standing across the street from Marek's apartment, veiled from sight by Rift energy, when Warden Kaycee had arrived.

The look on her face, the way she moved—tight, coiled, grief bleeding at the edges of every motion—told him all he needed to know. He saw the storm in her. Desperation. Remorse. Anger and sadness at the near-death of one of her team. But more than that—something deeper.

She was falling.

And she had chosen Marek, the human, to catch her.

How could she do this?

After all the disdain she'd held for Jax—for the choice Jax made, for the *life* it cost—how could she follow that same path? She knew what it had done to Akron. How it still ate at him, even now.

Still, she chose Marek.

Akron's hands clenched at his sides, fingers twitching with barely leashed energy. Desperation warred with fury in his chest. Logic gave way to memory, and in that moment, he hated how much she reminded him of Jax.

He waited as long as he could, giving the human male time to sleep—to stay ignorant of what was to come.

Then he let a pulse of energy ripple outward—subtle but unmistakable. Any Warden would know that another was in the vicinity.

She stepped out five minutes later. The front door clicked softly shut behind her, as she walked out into the light drizzle of rain. Her boots crunching on loose gravel and asphalt as she crossed the parking lot of the apartment building. She stopped on the sidewalk across from him, the quiet street a vast gulf between them.

Hands in her jacket pockets. Head high. Stubborn to the end.

She didn't wait for him to speak.

"You don't have to do this," she said, voice low, raw with quiet defiance.

"You of all people know that's not true," he replied, each word measured steel. "The Warden's Oath is not a suggestion, Kaycee. It is binding. *Sacred.*"

"Yes, it binds *you* to enforce it, and I am sorry for that—but I still have free will to choose, and I chose him," she said.

"The Oath says we cannot lay with a human." She looked him straight in the eye then, her voice trembling on the edge between hope and fear, "but I don't think he *is.*"

Akron's jaw tightened. "He is not a Warden. He has not taken the Oath. He has not been judged by the Essence—he cannot be anything else."

"No," she agreed, "but he survived things no human could. He heals faster. He ascenses the Rift when others don't. He *used* the Rift energy tonight—like a Warden would."

"You feel it too, don't you?" She asked, "That's why you've been watching him."

Akron didn't respond. His silence was answer enough.

She stepped forward, "I didn't plan this. I didn't want this. But he's... different. I don't know what he is yet, but I know what he *isn't*. He isn't just human. Not like the ones we're sworn to protect."

"That didn't stop Jax either," Akron said bitterly. "He said the same thing. '*She's different. She's worthy.*' He told me that right before I killed him."

She pushed back. "That's different. He knew she was a human—there was no doubt. Here, there *is* doubt."

She continued in a whisper, "That broke something in you, having to end his life. And I hated him for what he did to you. I still do. But I won't hate myself for this, and I won't run from it."

"Then you damn yourself," Akron said.

He blurred. One moment he was across the street, and the next, he was inches from her, the air cracking with displaced force. Rain splitting away from his form as he moved.

He didn't hesitate. The blade arced toward her neck, swift and sure—an execution delivered by the First Warden, unerring and absolute.

Kaycee didn't flinch. Didn't raise a hand against him. Didn't step back.

She simply looked at him—eyes wide and unguarded, lips parted in silent surrender. Not from fear, but faith.

And then—He *stopped*...

The blade hovered at her throat. Barely a breath between steel and skin. Akron's arm trembled.

His heart thundered in his chest, but something was off. *Missing.*

There was no pull. No command from the Essence. No divine compulsion forcing his hand forward to carry out judgement.

There was *nothing.*

His breath caught. His hand jerked the sword back from her neck. Rain pattered on the blade, rolling down its edge like tears.

Kaycee blinked, her voice barely a whisper. "You stopped..."

He jerked back further, as if burned.

She should be dead. She *should* be dead. The Oath was clear—sacred, and absolute. A Warden who broke it had to be executed. The will of Onos bound him to obedience.

So why—

He stared at the blade in his hand. He slowly sheathed it next to the other on his back.

"I don't understand," he breathed.

"No compulsion," she said, stepping forward, her own hands shaking now. "I saw it in your eyes—you were ready. You meant to fulfill what was required, but the compulsion was missing, wasn't it?"

Akron's mind reeled. In all his centuries, the Oath had *never* stopped. Never faltered. The Essence did not bargain. It did not hesitate.

It was impartial. It judged. It commanded.

"Why..." he whispered. "Why not now?"

Kaycee exhaled shakily, voice trembling at the edge of disbelief. "Because he's not human. Not completely. Which means..."

She swallowed. "The Oath doesn't apply to him."

Akron's frowned, confusion written deep across the lines of his face.

She took a breath, stepped even closer. "He's something else, Akron. Something *not* human, I'm sure of it. I don't know what that is, but maybe you should start asking yourself *why* this time is different. See where that takes you."

He turned away from her again, this time not out of anger—but confusion. Conflict.

The storm inside him no longer raged. It churned. Slower. Deeper.

"I need... time," he said hoarsely. "To understand what this means."

She didn't speak. She simply nodded, her eyes rimmed with unshed tears and unspoken relief.

And then, Akron vanished into the blue-white flare of the Rift.

Kaycee stood in silence for a long moment, heart pounding.

Then she turned, climbed the stairs and walked back into the warmth of Marek's bed.

Chapter 26

Light crept across the floor in slow, golden stripes. Marek stirred first—groggy, warm, tangled in sheets and limbs he didn't want to move from.

Kaycee lay tucked against his chest, her breathing slow, one hand resting over his heart like she was staking her claim on him even in her sleep.

He didn't want to wake her, so he lay there quietly, committing her to memory—how she looked in this moment, peaceful and free from the weight of the world.

The night played out in his mind over and over, each detail would be forever seared into his memory. Everything they'd given to each other.

His chest felt lighter this morning. He felt grounded in a way he hadn't felt since he joined the SCU.

In the silence of the morning, he was acutely aware of the strange hum that still pulsed in his veins—the last remnants of the strange power that had entered him on the rooftop last night.

She stirred against him.

Her eyes opened slowly, still half-lidded with sleep. She blinked once, twice, then exhaled a quiet breath and laid her head back down.

"Morning," he whispered.

She smiled faintly, fingers absently brushing his chest. "Is it already?"

"Sadly, yes."

They lay like that for a while. No urgency. No mission. Just warmth and breath and silence.

He kissed the top of her head.

"You okay?" he asked.

She hesitated. "I want to say yes."

"But?"

"I don't know what this changes," she murmured. "Between us. With the team. With everything coming."

He shifted to face her. "It doesn't have to change anything."

Her eyes searched his—guarded again, but not cold. Just wary.

"You don't know what I am," she said.

He smiled gently. "Maybe not. But I know who you are. And that's enough."

The words hit her deeper than he realized. Her throat tightened.

She wanted to tell him.

About the Wardens. About the Oath. About who she really was. About how close she'd come last night to losing him—not to his own death—but to hers. To Akron's judgement.

But Akron had forbidden her from giving those secrets, and unlike the Oath—which didn't apply to Marek—his binding orders still held her in silence.

Sure, the orders themselves were bound to her Essence, but she also followed out of respect and duty—a soldier following orders of a commanding officer.

And besides... those truths weren't hers to give.

"We should get cleaned up," she said instead, slipping from the bed, beautiful curves and naked skin bared as she walked into the bathroom.

He watched her go, and however much he wanted to, he didn't push her for an answer to the burning questions she left him with.

He just laid back, arms behind his head, and breathed.

After her shower and finding her clothes again—*Onos*, they had made a mess of his room—Kaycee sat at the edge of the bed, dressing in silence. Marek had already moved to the kitchen, throwing on a t-shirt and jeans after his shower. He was leaning over the counter, sipping black coffee and watching her with quiet eyes.

She was about to say something—maybe soften the tension still lingering from everything unsaid—when her phone notified her of a text. She dug it out of her back pocket and brought up the incoming message from Marcus:

—Need you at HQ now. This Surge reading's off the charts. Bigger than anything I've tracked. I'm locking co-ordinates.

Kaycee stood immediately.

Marek caught her look and straightened. "Trouble?"

"Big surge. Marcus says it's the largest he's ever seen."

Marek nodded once and tossed the rest of his coffee back. "Let's go."

She didn't stop him. Didn't tell him to stay behind—to protect him like she wanted to.

They moved together, comfortably—him getting dressed in his typical tactical pants and black shirt. They armed up, falling into an unspoken rhythm that now felt like second nature.

When they hit the stairs leading down to the ground floor, Kaycee sent a brief acknowledgment to Marcus:

—On our way.

Shit, she thought as they walked to their cars. She'd said *our*...

Hopefully Marcus wouldn't read too deeply into that. He was sharp—too sharp sometimes—and he didn't miss things like casual phrasing.

Chapter 27

The room was already humming when Kaycee and Marek arrived. There were curious looks as they stepped in together, but no one said anything. Everyone seemed too busy with their assignments.

Marcus stood at the central terminal, the glow of harsh red screens casting deep shadows across his face. A digital map of the city projected on the wall behind him, showing a singular massive surge indicator pulsing near the East River. Harper was at her station, fingers flying. Malik leaned against the far wall with crossed arms and dark circles under his eyes. Tucker, coffee in hand, looked like he hadn't slept—but his eyes were alert, tracking every move.

As soon as she entered, Marcus looked up—and gave her a quick glance. Not long. Not obvious. But enough. A flick of his eyes from her to Marek, then back again. One brow ticked upward—just a fraction.

He'd seen the text. He'd caught the *our*.

Then, like nothing had passed between them at all, he turned and gestured toward the map.

"This came through about forty minutes ago."

On screen, a single large surge had flared near the industrial edge of the Bowery, between Delancey and Canal. It was ground—level in a cluster of aging warehouses and service roads that spanned nearly five city blocks.

"Jesus, that's massive," Marek said.

Marcus nodded grimly. "Told you. It blinked in fast—stabilized for about three seconds, then vanished. Power grids in the area blew, and traffic lights stopped working. No heat residuals, but the energy spike was... unprecedented."

Harper spoke up. "Whatever this was, it wasn't subtle. It didn't care about being seen."

Marek stepped closer. "Any idea what came through?"

He glanced at Kaycee—and caught something flash in her eyes. Recognition. Then, a moment of fear. It vanished just as quickly, shuttered behind the calm, unreadable mask she always wore.

Marcus hesitated. "That's the thing. I don't know if anything did come through. We don't know enough about the creatures we're dealing with. We've assumed there's only one type, since that's all we've seen so far."

He paused, scanning the room.

"What if there's more? Different species? Some that are stronger... that need a higher surge to come through? We don't know where they're coming from... or what could trigger something this big."

A quiet settled over the team. Kaycee turned to Marcus. "Send me all the data you have on this one. I want to study it myself."

Then, with a short nod toward Harper: "Prepare for everything, bring the mobile hospital and have our on-base doctor ready to accept patients. I want to be prepared for anything this time."

Then, to Marek: "I want you with me in the lead vehicle."

She continued in that no nonsense tone Marek was coming to realize was her default, "I want teams ready in twenty. Prepare for heavy contact. I want every angle covered and no one engaging solo."

She had a quiet word with Marcus as she was leaving, then disappeared into the hallway.

Marek didn't ask why she'd asked for him specifically. Just prepared to follow her into whatever hell they were about to jump into.

———◆———

SCU Headquarters—Observation Room

Kaycee stood alone at the edge of the secondary ops room, staring at the surge point on the map. The digital display flickered slightly as if trying to warn her about what they were walking into.

She knew too well, the types of things that could cause a surge this size—and that the surge would need to be much bigger before it broke through. They had some time.

She'd tried contacting Akron but had no luck. She needed permission to act to her full abilities, possibly expose what she was if this went sideways.

Marcus entered; door hissing shut behind him. He held a tablet in one hand, but didn't look at it.

"You wanted to talk?" he asked, voice low.

She nodded, then turned to face him. "This surge... I have a bad feeling about it. We need to prepare for the absolute worst."

He stepped up beside her, gaze on the screen. "We're preparing for full containment. Anything you're not telling me?"

She hesitated.

Then: "You saw what Marek did at the last breach."

Marcus exhaled. "Yeah. I saw it. It's all over the body-cam feed. Doesn't feel human. But it doesn't feel dangerous either. Not to us. He protected the team."

She exhaled slowly. "Good, because I need him at my side today."

She looked up at him, letting the next part land with some weight. "And I need you to ensure that anything... unusual... stays off the radar."

"Can you do that for me? Do I have your support?" She asked him, eyes searching.

Marcus gave a short nod. "Always."

They stood in silence until Malik's voice cracked through her comms.

"Team's ready. Just waiting on you."

Kaycee nodded to Marcus and turned. Her expression hardened. Time to move.

———◆———

The Bowery – Breach Site, 10:02 a.m.

The convoy rolled to a stop just off Broome Street, a half block from the pulse epicenter. Aging warehouses loomed around them—graffiti-stained brick and shuttered bays, some tagged decades ago, others still bleeding fresh paint.

Emergency crews had cordoned off the area due to downed lines and ruptured gas mains, but the SCU's black SUVs swept through the barricade like it didn't exist. Their credentials bought silence.

Kaycee stepped out first. The air was thick, heavy with that same low hum that scraped against the base of the skull.

She looked over at Marek and saw him wincing. He felt it too—another piece clicking into place of the puzzle that he was.

Traffic lights at the nearby intersection blinked uselessly, one stuck on red. Storefronts had shattered glass spilling into the street like crystallized ash.

Marek joined her, eyes sweeping the area. "This place feels... wrong."

Kaycee came to his side. "Like the other sites?"

"No," he said quietly. "This is stronger. It's like my whole head is gripped in a pulsing vice."

"Try visualizing the pulsing in your head as a wave, then visualize building a wall—building it brick by brick—to guard against the wave. It may help," she said.

Marek gave her a skeptical look as he closed his eyes, following her instructions. His jaw clenched as he concentrated, visualizing the pulse as a cresting wave of pressure. He pictured the wall being built in front of the wave, brick by brick.

When it was finished, the pressure faded significantly—it didn't vanish, but he was able to focus again.

He abruptly opened his eyes in surprised relief, turning to her.

"You're welcome," she said with a smirk.

Behind them, the rest of the SCU team disembarked. Malik scanned the rooftops. Harper swept the adjacent storefronts with her drone rig. Tucker crouched near the SUV, rifle in hand, waiting for the all-clear.

Marcus's voice came through their comms. "We're getting some strange interference again. Your heart rates are spiking. You feeling anything unusual?"

"Define unusual," Marek muttered.

The team advanced down the narrow corridor between buildings. The old loading bay doors were ajar—shadows spilling out like ink across the cracked pavement. The scent of ozone and ash lingered, thick in the air.

And then—everything stopped.

A ripple spread through the space, invisible but undeniable.

Marek froze mid-step. "Did you feel—"

Before he could finish, the air broke apart in a jagged tear in reality, hissing and spitting arcs of blue-white energy.

One breath, there was nothing. The next, something stepped out of the tear.

The figure was tall. Slender. Pale as bone. Two of the dragon creatures came out on either side of it—sitting motionless on their haunches like pets.

Black leathers wrapped the figure's body, etched in silver script that shimmered with dark energy. His long hair spilled past his shoulders, obsidian-dark and braided through with crimson beads. And his eyes—vivid violet, glowing, rimmed with shadow—locked on Marek and Kaycee with amusement.

"Well, well, well. What do we have here?" he said with a slow grin.

Marek froze.

He narrowed in on Marek with a flash of recognition... eyes widening slightly. "Well, if it isn't our little hero, all grown up. Do you like my pet Drakyns? You've all been doing such a good job exterminating them recently, that I thought I'd bring more along for extra practice."

That voice.

The alley. The girl. The blood.

It was him.

"Harley," Marek breathed.

The figure grinned, razor-sharp fangs glinting in the morning sun. "Ah. You remember. That warms my heart. What little is left of it."

He spread his arms theatrically. "You know, they call me Dharken Mohr. I rule the Realm of Shadow and Thought. But here, titles and realms are meaningless to you humans, so I always preferred Harley. It felt basic, easier for you primitive animals to grasp."

Kaycee stepped forward. "SCU. You are not authorized to be in this realm. Stand down and return through the Rift, or we will treat this as an act of aggression."

Marek shot a glance at her. *Realm? What is she talking about?*

Harley smiled wider. "Oh, you're cute when you act official. Tsk. You brought children to fight your battles, Warden Kaycee? Come now, how do you think this will end?"

Marek shot a look of surprise at her. *Warden?*

"Oh ho! He doesn't know." Harley laughed, voice bright with delight. "Gods, this is delicious."

"Back away from my team," Kaycee growled.

Harley tilted his head, amused. "Oh, you're still pretending. That mask must be exhausting, darling. Come on, let's play."

Then he moved. No warning, just a blur of motion. And the Drakyn followed in his wake—charging directly for Kaycee.

"Kaycee, look out!" Marek yelled, but she was already moving—engaged with the Drakyn, sword in one hand, gun in the other.

Tucker shouted out a warning, raising his rifle to track Harley.

Wait, what? Where did she get a damn sword?

Marek didn't have time to process it. Harley blurred past him—dark, fast, silent.

A flash of motion. A twist. A sickening crack.

Tucker dropped—his shout abruptly silenced.

Marek froze, breath catching as the world narrowed—stuttered to a stop and started again. His best friend, gone in an instant. Snapped like a twig. No warning. No chance to fight back.

"TUCKER!" he screamed, knees hitting asphalt—numb from shock—from the suddenness of the loss.

"Gordon—Gordon! Tucker's vitals just flatlined! Marcus and Malik are spiking—what the hell is happening out there?! You need to pull them out now!" Harper's voice shrieked from the van, high with panic. "Hhold on, I'm coming!"

She ducked beneath a Drakyn claw and snarled, "Stay in the van, Agent Harper. That's an order! What we're being attacked by... you'd have no chance against it. Do not leave that vehicle!"

"But Gordon—"

"I said stay put!" She snapped, voice sharp with fury. "I need you alive to provide medical support when this ends... Do you understand me?"

A long beat of silence—then a whispered, "Copy that."

Harley turned to Marek, grin wide and mocking. "Oops. Was that your bestest friend?"

Malik roared and opened fire, bullets slamming into Harley's back.

"Move!" Marek shouted, surging to his feet—pushing through his shock and grief. He and Marcus flanked left and right, rifles up, trying to encircle.

Harley didn't even flinch. "Oh my," he cooed, turning. "That tickles."

Malik didn't stop when bullets failed to do the job. Instead, he dropped his rifle and charged, blade flashing. A feint left, a jab center.

Harley caught his arm mid-strike—*snap*—and Malik's scream pierced the air.

Marek fired. Marcus fired. Rounds impacted on Harley's body. Blood sprayed. But Harley twisted, using Malik's writhing body as a shield—effectively stopping their fire so they wouldn't hit Malik.

"Gutsy," Harley said, almost admiringly.

Then his blade flashed—a brutal, upward rip that tore through Malik's torso. Armor and bone split apart like paper.

Malik gasped, eyes wide. Blood poured out in thick rivers.

Marek yelled and advanced, but Harley spun Malik's body like a barrier, forcing Marek back.

"Uh-oh. Speaking of guts, that looks serious." He let Malik's body crumple, entrails trailing behind like spilled rope.

Marcus broke formation and lunged, shouting, rifle blazing.

Harley moved. One blink—he was behind Marcus. Arms hooked in.

There was a pop, followed by a crunch.

Marcus screamed as both shoulders dislocated. Then Harley struck—fangs plunging deep into his neck, drinking greedily as Marcus thrashed.

Marek, unable to get a clear shot, charged in to try and get Marcus away—only to have a foot hammer into his chest, sending him flying as the breath was knocked from him.

Harley ripped free with a growl, tearing Marcus's throat open. As Marcus slid down, Harley drove his blade into the exposed neck and sliced.

Marcus's body collapsed; his head rolled a few feet farther, eyes wide and glassy.

Harley stretched and sighed like he'd just finished a warm meal. "Ahh. Humans. Vintage 2025. Smooth finish."

Kaycee screamed in rage and anguish, still engaged with the Drakyn—unable to get to her hopelessly outmatched team.

"This one screamed," Harley breathed, licking Marcus's blood from his lips. "Oh yes, I liked that. Tell me, little hero... will you scream?"

Marek got up from the ground and charged, rage boiling through his veins.

He swung wild, grief and fury guiding his blade. Harley caught his wrist mid-strike and drove a knee into Marek's gut. Air fled his lungs and he dropped to the ground.

Before Marek could recover, Harley grabbed him by the back of the neck, lifted him and *slammed* him face-first into the pavement.

Then again.

And again.

Concrete cracked. His vision swam. Pain rang through his skull like a bell, but Harley wasn't finished. He hauled Marek up and delivered two brutal punches into his body.

Marek felt things break inside him. Vital things. The pain was almost too much to bear.

"This all you've got?" Harley roared in his face. "You're the one who killed my Drakyn, and *this* is your follow-up act?"

"*Pathetic*," Harley snarled.

He hurled Marek across the street like trash. Marek slammed into the side of their SUV, ribs cracking, blood filling his mouth.

He tried to rise, but Harley was already there.

"Let's see that anger again," Harley hissed, grabbing Marek by the collar and punching him...knuckles thudding against bone. Over and over. "Come on, little hero. Where *is it?!*"

Marek couldn't breathe. Couldn't see. Blood filled his mouth, his nose. But he could hear—Harley's voice drilling into him.

"Worthless humans, the lot of you. Nothing more than an inconvenience. Except for Marcus... Oh, he was *delicious*... you heard the sound of his screams—like music to the ears. You can't seem to save anyone, can you, little hero?"

Something inside Marek shattered—then surged. He grunted with the last of his strength, swinging his blade in a desperate arc. It caught Harley's cheek.

Blood bloomed. A shallow cut. But it was something.

Harley staggered, hand reaching up to touch his cheek. Then smiled. "Atta boy."

The next blow felt like being hit with a truck. Harley kicked Marek in the chest, the force of it lifting him off the ground. He flipped back over the hood of the SUV and tumbled to a stop on the pavement behind—like a bloody rag doll.

"Marek!" Kaycee's voice tore through the chaos as she sprinted toward him—finally free of the Drakyns.

The first beast lay in a twitching heap behind her, its torso split from navel to neck, dark blood steaming against the asphalt. The second had taken a point-blank shot to the face—just enough distraction for her to close the distance and take its head clean in a single, savage arc of her sword.

She was bloodied, but she was alive—and she was pissed.

Harley turned. "Ah, the Warden herself. Took you long enough, Kaycee. Let's see how long you last against me."

Their clash cracked the air like lightning. Her Rift-forged blade sang—a blur of blue-white steel—but Harley met it with a sword of his own—black as night.

They moved too fast for human eyes. Strike, parry, pivot, kick. Sparks flew. Followed by grunts and snarls.

Each blow from Kaycee landed—and each one took its toll on Harley. But he was faster, ancient in his experience, and more precise. He landed more.

She bled from the temple. Cuts on her torso, arms, and legs burned like fire where his blade touched. Her breathing shortened and her stance wavered—just for a second.

That's all Harley needed.

He feinted, then stepped inside, and drove his blade into her shoulder. Twisting it free in the next breath, he backhanded Kaycee into the wall of the building behind her with incredible force.

Marek blinked up from the ground, his vision double and fading. Blood pulsed from a dozen wounds. He couldn't move his legs. His arms twitched.

His heart shattered.

"Get... away... from her," he croaked.

Harley looked over at him with a smile. "Aww, how sweet," he said, voice dripping with mockery.

Then he turned back to Kaycee, crossing the distance in a blur—batting aside her attempt at defense and hammering a fist to her face.

Kaycee, momentarily dazed by the hit, gave him the opening he was looking for.

He drew the blade back—then drove it forward with both hands, slamming the weapon into her chest with brutal finality.

She gasped. Eyes wide. Her blade dropped with a clang.

Marek's world stopped.

"No..." he whispered, vision tunneling. "No—"

Harley let her slump to her knees, still impaled, before casually stepping over to Marek. "You're lucky, you know," he murmured, kneeling beside him. "I won't let you watch her die. I'm not a monster, after all."

He laughed hysterically for a moment, and then slammed his fist into Marek's face—the world went black.

The last thing he saw—through the haze of blood and darkness—was Kaycee on her knees, a blade still in her chest as Harley walked slowly back to her, drawing a second one, curved and wicked—raising it above her throat.

Then the wind shifted.

The air became dense with pressure, with *presence.*

A deep, ancient hum rolled through the street, and sparking, spitting blue-white energy arced into existence as another Rift opened up.

Harley growled in frustration. "Daddy Akron to the rescue. Pity. We were just getting to the good part."

He looked down at Kaycee, bloodied but still alive.

"We're not done here. Your precious Rift is failing. The Realms can sense it. It won't be long until we can break through in overwhelming numbers. And when that happens—I'll be back, and there won't be enough of your kind left to stop me."

The blue-white energy of the Rift opened before him, and he vanished—back the way he came. Bodies and blood—the only sign that he'd ever been.

Chapter 28

Kaycee—Breach Site—Seconds Later

She gasped, sucking in air around the sword embedded in her chest. It had missed the heart—but it hurt. *Onos*, how it hurt.

Her eyes locked on Marek.

He lay still, face pale, blood pooling.

No.

Her limbs screamed as she crawled to him, leaving a trail of crimson.

"Marek—Marek, stay with me," she said as she drew herself to a sitting position next to him.

He didn't answer.

His eyes fluttered once, then closed. She touched his face, hand trembling. "Don't die," she whispered.

"Don't—"

Then she felt it.

A shift in the world. A pulse of Rift energy.

Akron had arrived, but he was too late—Harley was gone, and Marek was dying.

The moment Akron stepped through the Rift, the world greeted him with blood.

The scent of it was everywhere—sharp, fresh, metallic. It coated the pavement in wet spatters, soaked into broken concrete, and pooled beneath twisted bodies.

And he had been too late. Again.

Akron didn't move at first. He simply stood there, eyes closed, inhaling the carnage like a man memorizing the scent of his failure.

When he opened them again, they burned. Tucker. Malik. Marcus. Humans he was supposed to protect... that Wardens were to protect—gone.

He turned and saw Kaycee, dragging herself across the ground, blood trailing behind her, a blade still lodged in her chest.

She drew up to sit near Marek—head hanging low. Her breathing was shallow, but steady.

And Marek—

Akron's gaze locked on him.

Marek lay sprawled in a pool of his own blood, chest barely rising. His face was broken. His chest was crushed—misshapen. There was so much blood—too much.

Akron moved in a blur, crossing to his Warden first. She lifted her head at his presence, wincing as her body screamed in protest.

"He's dying," she rasped.

He crouched beside her, taking her chin gently between his fingers, tilting her face up. "So are you."

She gave a faint, bitter smile. "I'll live—it missed the heart."

His eyes narrowed at the sword buried in her chest. Darkness-wrought steel. Dharken Mohr's design.

He could feel it pulsing. Feeding on her.

Designed not just to wound, but to suppress Warden abilities... like healing and Rift energy manipulation.

"Where is Dharken Mohr?" Akron snarled, as he removed the the sword in one quick tug.

Kaycee gasped in relief. "Thank you…"

Then she shook her head, fury bleeding through her exhaustion. "He felt you. He vanished. He knew he couldn't take you after forcing his way through the Rift."

Akron's jaw clenched. "He took enough."

He turned to Marek. Dropping to one knee, his hand hovered over Marek's chest. Energy flickered there—low, fading, buried deep beneath the surface of his human shell.

But it was there. Essence, where there should be none.

"How can this be?" Akron muttered to himself.

"What?" she said, hoarse. "What is it?"

Akron frowned. "He has Essence within him. It is faint, but it is there."

She stared at him for a minute, then at Marek, and understanding flared in her eyes.

"That must be why the Oath didn't bind you the night I slept with him. That would explain his ability to fight the creatures."

Akron looked back to Marek with confusion. "I do not know how it is possible… How can you exist?"

He looked up at the overcast sky as he whispered, "Is this all part of your plan? Please, Onos, give me a sign… anything to tell me the right thing to do. No one other than humanity has been given the Essence."

As he pleaded for direction, he felt Marek's pulse flutter in and out, his body beginning to shut down.

In the same moment, the Essence in the vial around his neck vibrated, pulsing red, and then flared brightly for a split second. Confirmation, in a sense.

"It has been decided, then." He reached into the folds of his coat and took the small vial out—obsidian glass bound in runes. The Essence of the Titan, Onos.

He stared at it. Then at Marek.

His fingers curled tight around the vial. "Once I give this... there's no going back... We don't know what he is or what he will become—if it will even work."

"*Please, Akron,*" Gordon pleaded.

"He may not be him if he awakens. Are you prepared for that?"

"I'll sacrifice anything for him to live... even if he's different, he'll still be alive."

"So be it," Akron said as he uncorked the vial and placed his hand on Marek's head. "I will need to wake him to take the Warden's Oath—he will be in unimaginable pain."

Akron pulled a syringe from his coat pocket and slid it straight into Marek's chest. Depressing the plunger, he didn't have long to wait.

Marek's eyes snapped open—a pain-filled scream followed soon after.

Agony. Blinding. White-hot. It tore through his chest like wildfire, burning in his lungs, in his ribs... everywhere.

He coughed blood—dark and wet—and clawed at the pavement instinctively, like a man buried alive trying to dig his way out.

Akron's hand pressed against his sternum. "Easy. Breathe. You're not dead. Not yet."

Marek's head turned, vision swimming, locking briefly on Kaycee's blood-smeared form next to him. "Kaycee..." he rasped.

"I'm here," she whispered hoarsely, pain lacing every word.

Then his eyes rolled back, his body buckling again under the weight of pain.

Akron caught him, stabilizing his head with one hand, voice cutting through the fog.

"You're fading, Marek. I can save you—make you like us... a Warden—but only if you take the Oath. There is no other way."

Marek's jaw clenched against the pain. "What... oath?"

Akron's voice was steel. "The Oath of the Wardens. You'll be changed—bound to the Essence. You'll police the Rift that stands between Earth and the Realms. You'll fight to protect humanity—and you'll have the power to avenge your friends."

Marek's lips trembled as he considered. He blinked slowly, memories rushing in. Tucker's scream. Malik's silence. Marcus's body falling. All of it.

Then Marek bared bloody teeth. "Then do it."

Akron nodded solemnly. "Repeat after me."

He placed his hand over Marek's chest, and his voice came out low and reverent:

"I stand before the Rift, between this world and the Realms.

Bound by the Essence and the will of Onos.

I vow to guard humanity, to shield the mortal world from the horrors beyond.

I pledge my life to the legacy of Onos and to the Warden brotherhood.

I will not waver. I will not break.

I will defend the innocent and uphold the ways of the just.

I shall carry the burdens of the ancient war, and walk the line others fear to tread.

I vow never to love a mortal, lest my life be forfeit.

From this moment on, my life is not my own. My death is not my own.

I am Warden now, for eternity, until death. Or until the Realms are no more."

Marek repeated the words, lips cracked, voice thin and raw—but each phrase carried weight.

When the final word left his mouth, the wind shifted.

Akron lifted the vial.

He opened it, and red-gold mist flowed out—like smoke, like breath—and hovered briefly over Marek's chest.

It flared once, then was sucked down, disappearing from sight.

Marek convulsed once—arched, eyes wide—then collapsed, succumbing to the pain and his injuries.

Blood still seeped from his wounds, but already something else had begun to rise beneath his skin—like heat, shimmering just above the surface.

Kaycee crawled closer, weak but watching. "Is it done?"

Akron's eyes didn't leave Marek, but he stood and stepped back. "Now we wait."

He looked up at the rain filled clouds in the sky above. "If the Essence finds him worthy, it will remake him."

"And if not?"

"It will burn through his body until there's nothing left but ash. You know this."

Kaycee said nothing, looking on in prayerful silence.

Then—

A sound. A low hum. Subterranean, and ancient.

Marek's body lifted an inch off the ground as the Essence started pouring out of him, swirling and twisting, entering and leaving his body in a whirling vortex.

His veins lit up red-gold beneath his skin.

Akron's eyes widened, just a fraction. "It has begun."

Then Marek screamed.

Chapter 29

Dharken Mohr

The Rift burned as he entered back through it, sucking at his power and trying to unmake him—as if it found his very existence offensive. It was designed to keep his kind out, after all.

He was ready for it, though, as he always was.

After millennia of growing in power, he had found a way to pass through the breaches on his own.

The smallest breaches were always the worst, the most painful—the Rift energies too concentrated—and this one had been very small.

"Fuck," he swore, as he emerged in a breathless stumble.

It had hurt like a bitch, but desperate times called for desperate measures. He hadn't had much of a choice, really.

He hadn't been ready to tangle with Akron after his run-in with that uppity little bitch of a Warden. And definitely not so soon after having traveled the Rift. If he'd stayed, Akron—still fresh and bloated with Rift energy—would have killed him.

Full stop.

He straightened and stretched, his back shifting and popping in relief.

The Realm of Shadow and Thought greeted him with silence and darkness—comforting in its own way.

He was the undisputed ruler, left as regent when his goddess, Nyxia, went off to fight Onos millennia ago.

He exhaled through his nose, slow and seething. Rage still burned through every inch of him, but he didn't let it bleed outward. There'd be a time for that.

The Warden bitch still lived. The kill had escaped his grasp, and like anything he left undone, it felt like an itch under his skin he couldn't scratch.

He clenched his fists. He'd soon rectify that.

And Akron... damn that infuriating prick. Akron had arrived just in time to ruin everything. Again!

How does he always know it's me and where I'll be? he thought to himself.

I had my best shield up this time, and even though he was delayed, he STILL. FOUND. ME.

The First Warden had made it his life's mission to try to kill him—ever since Dharken started ambushing and killing Wardens centuries ago.

He was one of the few beings who could stand against a Warden and win. Akron wanted him dead at all costs.

Well, the feeling was mutual.

As he turned and started walking, he saw the fortress palace of Nyxia herself—Dreadfall—looming in front of him.

A twisted combination of the Vatican mixed with the Château de Chambord—it stretched out before him.

Obsidian black, with ivory white spirals throughout, its construction had been overseen by Nyxia herself upon her banishment from the Earth Realm. It was an awe-inspiring testament to the glory of his goddess.

Located within the heart of the Realm, it sat atop an obsidian mountain and towered over a churning sea of shadow.

Above it, a sky of darkness mixed with blue-white Riftlight extended endlessly in all directions.

Two Elvahr sentries knelt as he strode forward through the outer wall's perimeter gates—their obsidian armor swirling in spirals of shadow.

The air trembled with his passage, thick with the residue of power. Power he'd been stockpiling for centuries.

Let the other Realms posture and bicker. Let them call him mad, staying insulated in their own realms.

He had tried to galvanize them in support centuries ago—to get them to join forces with him in his endless battle to try to shatter the Rift. To finally subjugate humanity, as his goddess originally intended.

But, like prisoners in their millennia of isolation, they had forgotten the desires of their own gods and goddesses. They had become content to rule their prisons.

They had forgotten that *they* were the rightful rulers of humanity. It was disgusting—unforgivable.

But he hadn't forgotten the mandate of his goddess. Her will lived on in his heart, and he had been making plans for centuries.

Plans that were close to realization.

Soon the other Realms would see he wasn't mad. They would join him in his conquest of Earth.

As he made his way through the inner gates—up the steps into the grand hall leading to the throne room, a silent runner waited. It was an Elvahr youth, thin and silver-eyed, clad in ceremonial black.

Dharken didn't break stride. "Summon my lieutenants," he snapped. "Tell them to assemble in the War Hall for our Council of War. Now."

The runner bowed low and vanished without a word, boots barely whispering against the onyx tile.

He walked on, alone now, down the length of the throne hall. The stained-glass windows shimmered with old memories—Nyxia at her height of power, her hands casting shadow into form, giving birth to the Elvahr.

There she was again—standing defiant against Onos, her siblings standing at her side. And finally... her death. Speared by divine swords.

As he approached the towering doors to the Throne Room, he paused—just for a breath—letting his eyes linger on the mural carved across the arch.

His personal request. A tribute and a reminder. It depicted the Titan at his end—Onos, being laid low by one of his own divine blades.

It was a moment Dharken replayed more than any other. Sometimes, it was the only thing that gave him any kind of happiness.

He remembered hearing the scream of Nyxia's anguish as Onos struck her down with those cursed swords of his—of him, rushing to where she had fallen on the battlefield—far too late to save her.

He had dragged her body back into the Rift, back to her chambers beneath the Throne Room, weeping the entire way.

When she faded into stasis—when her divine soul seemed to slip from her body, entombing her in obsidian darkness—he remembered his oath to her on that blood-soaked battlefield.

Before she had turned and walked into the final confrontation with Onos.

He had inked it into his skin in spiraling tattoos, a reminder to him forever that he would one day rule humanity—or end them all.

That every one of their fragile little lives would one day tremble beneath his boot, or end in a screaming symphony of death and destruction.

Whether they fell to their knees or to his blades mattered little to him.

Since the day he laid his goddess to rest, he had fueled himself with hatred. Hatred of the Wardens, of humanity, of anyone who would stand in his way.

He passed beneath the high archway into the throne room.

Dark spires reached overhead like interlocking blades. The throne itself—black obsidian mixed through with ivory-colored stone—rose above a staircase of silent steps.

But the true heart of the room was the statue. Seven feet tall. Carved from that same ivory stone, with an obsidian crown atop a face so beautiful, it hurt to look at.

It captured her likeness perfectly. Nyxia—eternally beautiful.

He had placed it there with his own hands, bleeding for every cut of the chisel, every rune inscribed into her armored mantle.

He paused before it now, his hand brushing the base of the statue's leg.

"Soon," he whispered.

But he did not linger. He marched briskly to the War Hall.

Walking into the circular chamber, a massive obsidian table sitting at the center of the room, he took a stand at the head. The sound of boots echoed as his lieutenants arrived shortly after him.

There were twelve, each draped in their battle armor, darkness swirling and twisting as if it were a living thing.

Each of them leaders of a division, commanders of elite Elvahr battalions. Their armor whispered as they knelt in unison—a ripple of discipline honed across centuries.

"Rise," he said, voice a blade in the dark.

They stood.

"The time for patience. For biding our time" he said slowly, "is over."

None spoke—but their eyes burned. They had waited as long as he had. Trained. Bled. Built fortresses and drilled new warriors while the other Realms whispered politics, acceptance, or cowardice.

"The Rift is close to crumbling in New York," Dharken continued. "A flaw. A fracture waiting to be shattered. That city is a wound. And we will break it open."

He began to pace, the motion predatory. "Two thousand Drakyn. One thousand Elvahr. The strongest battalions ever assembled. Gather your forces and hold them at the ready. When the time is right, we'll wreak destruction and death upon the humans."

One of the lieutenants stepped forward—Torvahr, commander of the Obsidian Fang division. He was lean, pale, with tattoos of blood-oath script carved into his throat.

"My lord," Torvahr said, voice like silk dragged over razors, "what of the Wardens? Of Akron?"

Dharken paused.

His lip curled.

"Akron has grown tired. He clings to the old ways. And the new Warden Council has already begun to challenge him. I have a mole on the inside—someone I've been grooming for years. He is close to discovering the key to all our plans—the spot where the Rift is the weakest. The Wardens are fractured—ideology bleeding into policy. They'll bicker while we slaughter."

"And the other six Realms?"

"They will not interfere, nor will they help." Dharken said, voice cold. "They've grown fat in their silence. But they forget—they would not exist without Nyxia. She was the first to raise arms against Onos, the first to demand humanity be ruled by those more powerful. And now they dishonor her with their complacency."

He stepped toward them.

"I do not care if they follow," he growled. "We begin the conquest alone. Gather your forces, ensure they're ready to march at my command—the time is almost here."

A moment of silence passed. Then every lieutenant dropped to one knee and drew a blade—holding the hilts across their chests.

"For Nyxia," they said in unison. "For vengeance!"

Dharken smiled.

He spent the next hour finalizing deployment orders, mapping the movements of troops from the lower battalions in the Thought Warrens, ensuring each lieutenant knew their orders and how many of their troops they were responsible for assembling.

When the final orders were given, he dismissed them with a sharp flick of his fingers.

They bowed again and vanished, one by one, into the darkness.

Only when they were gone did he return to the statue.

He stared up at her—the way her eyes had been carved to see forever, the faint tilt of her mouth, the sigils circling her collar.

Dharken reached up, touched the edge of her stone jaw.

"I haven't forgotten you," he whispered. "And I never will."

Kneeling down, he bent low in supplication, forehead resting against her feet.

"The humans will scream your name," he said, voice shaking with something deeper than rage. "Akron will die by my hand—as will every last Warden. That, I promise you."

Chapter 30

Marek—Bowery Breach Site

M arek's scream ripped through the empty street, raw and jagged, cutting across the silence like a blade. It echoed through broken windows and crumbling alleys, bouncing off concrete and dust until it became something feral.

His body arched, slammed back to the ground, then twisted again—caught between what he was and whatever the Essence was trying to make him.

It felt like dying. And not for the first time.

Light surged beneath his skin, pulsing bright and fast—too fast. He tried to breathe, but the fire inside him didn't just want air. It wanted *everything*.

He clawed at the ground, nails catching in cracks and grit as power tore through him. It wasn't just merging—it was colliding with something that was already inside.

The Essence didn't settle into him. It burned through him in a cleansing fire. Muscles spasmed. Bones groaned. Tendons screamed. Every vein searing with agony.

It wasn't stopping—it was building in a relentless tide.

He thrashed, vision swimming in white-hot bursts. He could feel every cell in his body shifting, melding, rebuilding—he didn't know if he could survive this.

Then something deep inside him cracked open. An ancient force—different from what was already burning him from the inside out.

Something dormant and vast seized upon the Essence running through his veins and ignited—adding gasoline to the fire already raging inside.

Then, gold light flared in his chest.

It hit like a roaring freight train, a blinding internal eruption. There was no warmth to it—just raw, untethered power.

For one second, he felt the scope of it. The age. The vastness—like a galaxy of power, unfathomable.

And then it was gone, burrowing down inside him, dormant but aware. Waiting.

The light retreated like a tide. The pressure vanished. He collapsed onto the pavement, chest heaving.

His skin still shimmered faintly, veins lit from within, but it seemed, for now, that the power had stopped trying to kill him.

◆

Tucker—Somewhere unknown

There was nothing.

No light. No pain. No thought. Just stillness.

He was floating in nothingness, gradually being pulled toward something—a door in the distance that felt like an ending and beginning all in one.

Then it hit.

A jolt. Gold-white. Blinding.

It didn't come from the dark. It came through it.

He didn't know where it came from, but it felt familiar—a name pulled at him—Marek.

That gold-white light pulled at him—dragging him further away from that door in the distance. He wasn't ready to go—to move on yet... and neither was that familiar feel of power.

That light and warmth wrapped around him—sunk into him. A thread of impossible light stitching him back to the world he thought he'd already left.

And then... silence again.

But different—not nothingness this time. He wasn't awake, but he wasn't gone either.

◆

Marek didn't know how long he lay there. Just breathing. Just existing.

His hands trembled as he pushed himself upright. The world wobbled. A high-pitched ring pierced his hearing, fading only when he blinked hard enough to bring the street back into focus.

His skin was cool now. The glow fading. His pain gone—injuries healed. No outward signs of scorch marks from the fire that he'd felt burning through him moments ago.

Just him. Whole. But not him as he used to be.

He looked at his hands. Flexed them. They felt different. His whole body felt different... powerful. Unbreakable.

Sounds were too loud, scents too distinct. His vision—he could see the writing on a newspaper blowing down the street a hundred feet away.

The Essence had settled, and with it, something else seemed to have woken in him. His emotions were going haywire. Before this, emotions were distant things that took time to build and had always been easy to manage.

Now? Now each one crashed into him in a rush of feeling as soon as he focused on it—each one so strong, it took his breath away, made it hard to think.

His breath stuttered. *What the hell was he now?*

The question barely formed before another realization hit—sharp and painful: *Tucker's gone.*

Sorrow hit him like a spear to the center of his chest—he almost doubled over with its intensity. The feeling burned his lungs. Crushed his heart like a vise.

Tucker. His best friend and partner. Gone.

And here Marek was. Rewired. Healed. Alive.

The universe wasn't fair.

He forced himself to stand, legs shaking. The sky hung low overhead—clouded, heavy with rain that hadn't yet come. Wind stirred debris across the street.

Every sound was too loud. The air buzzed. The world vibrated.

In the far corner of his vision, he saw Kaycee. Motionless. Watching.

He didn't look at her. He couldn't. Not yet. He was feeling too much. Far too much.

Behind her stood a taller shape. Akron.

Marek's pulse jumped, then steadied—like it recognized him now. Like part of him belonged to whatever world Akron was a part of—what *he* was now a part of.

That wasn't comforting.

Marek dragged in a breath and tried to lock it all down. Grief, anger, guilt. The questions. The power inside him, coiled and waiting.

The world didn't feel real.

He blinked slowly, his vision too sharp... it overloaded his senses.

Shadows pulsed with unnatural weight. Even the wind sounded wrong—louder than it should be, humming with a pitch he didn't recognize.

The Essence hadn't just settled. It had woven itself with him, into his very soul. He could feel the buzz of power—of familiarity—coming from Akron and Kaycee now.

He swayed slightly—a moment of vertigo—legs adjusting under him, and reached out to brace himself—but nothing around him felt stable enough to hold his weight.

The air itself had changed. He could feel it vibrating through the soles of his boots, like the city was still reacting to whatever he had just become.

And Kaycee—she was standing there, just ten feet away, eyes wide, frozen in place like she was staring at a ghost.

"What are you?" she whispered, barely more than a breath.

That wasn't a good sign if she didn't know—she was a Warden, after all.

His jaw clenched. *She was a Warden.* All this time, she had to have known everything. About what they were facing, about what they were walking into.

Feelings of betrayal hit him like a tsunami, followed by a white-hot rage.

Tucker was dead—Malik and Marcus too.

And Kaycee had to have known enough to give them some sort of warning.

Why didn't she? Why didn't she say anything? It could have helped, couldn't it? It couldn't have made anything worse.

Was all the trust he thought they'd built—everything they shared last night—all a lie?

He was too tangled inside by his thoughts to make any sense of it—to know what to feel.

He turned slightly away, hands flexing at his sides, trying to ground himself.

———◆———

Kaycee had seen Warden awakenings before.

She had gone through one herself.

What she'd just witnessed wasn't that. It was something altogether different.

She remembered the flash of golden energy that erupted from him before disappearing again, just as fast. The shockwave of power he released that almost knocked her flat.

Her eyes locked on him, taking in every detail. The way the golden energy had clung to his skin in faint pulses, then abruptly faded.

The way he moved—carefully, like every step was a negotiation with forces just below the surface.

He wasn't breathing like someone in physical pain.

He was breathing like someone trying not to explode.

She swallowed, throat dry. A tremor rolled down her spine, cold and jagged.

*What he must be feeling now—the power, the uncontrollable emotions. It must be overwhelming—*it had been for her.

She didn't want to believe what she'd seen—but the flashes of gold energy, the resonance that echoed through her bones—it all pointed in one direction.

Onos—their creator. Humanity's creator. She'd only ever read about him from brief texts in the Warden archives.

And somehow, that power—if that is what she saw—had ripped through Marek. What did it mean?

She took a step forward, stopped herself. What was she even going to say?

What do you say to someone who has just lost every-thing?

He looked her way, just briefly.

And in that look, she saw it. The moment he came to the realization that *she* was to blame for the deaths of Tucker, of their team.

—◆—

Marek was saying the words before he could think to hold them back.

"You should've told me." He said.

His voice wasn't loud, but his accusation landed in the silence of the street like a bomb.

Kaycee blinked and drew back slightly, as if the words had struck her physically.

Marek took a step forward, the movement slow, deliberate.

"You knew," he said. "What we were walking into. You knew... and you let it happen without saying anything."

The anger inside him had shape now. Edges. Weight. It burned hot, and it was focused on Kaycee.

A needle in his spine, holding him upright when everything else wanted to collapse.

"We could've saved them."

His jaw tightened. The words tasted bitter, soaked in guilt and blame that wasn't all hers. But most was.

Kaycee opened her mouth, hesitated, then said quietly, "It wasn't my secret to share."

Marek stared at her. "No?" he questioned. "But it was my life. Marcus's. Malik's—Tucker's. You kept us blind."

His voice broke at the last name. He hadn't meant to say their names. Hadn't meant to feel their deaths all at once.

But his feelings didn't seem to care.

He looked away, blinked hard, and when he looked back, something had changed in his face. Not anger now.

Something rawer. Betrayal and distrust.

"I was following orders from Akron. Orders that are bound to my Essence. I wanted to tell you everything, but I couldn't!" Kaycee pleaded.

"You stood beside us. You made us believe this was a fight we could win. That we were part of something bigger. That we had a chance!" Marek shouted.

He took another step toward her, power pulsing faintly beneath his skin—responding to his emotions.

"And the whole time, you knew. You knew what—" He looked around and waved his hand at the scene, "—all of this was. What we could be walking into."

Kaycee flinched—just slightly. Sorrow crossed her face.

"No. You don't get to do that," he said, voice low. "You don't get to act like you cared."

She looked like she wanted to speak again, eyes shining with unshed tears—but he kept going.

"Everything's gone. Tucker's gone. The team is gone. And I'm standing here, I'm alive. I'm *this*, because you followed orders."

The accusation hung in the air like smoke. Thick. Clinging.

He shook his head, then looked over at Tucker. "I didn't even get to say goodbye... it all happened so fast..." he said in a broken sob.

———◆———

Kaycee wanted to reach for him, but she didn't move.

Marek looked like he was barely holding himself together—and the truth was, she wasn't doing much better. Her arms felt heavy. Her heart was breaking.

The weight of everything she had kept from him was now sitting between them like a wall too thick to breach.

"I didn't want this," she said quietly.

He didn't respond.

"I didn't want any of this," she tried again. "But I didn't know what would happen. I didn't know it would end this way."

He turned his head slightly, watching her through a sideways glance.

"You knew enough," he said. "Enough to stop it. Enough to say something. You didn't have to let us walk into that fight blind."

Kaycee shook her head. "It's not that simple."

"It *was* that simple," he shouted back.

His voice, raised now, cut into her with its bitterness.

"You chose silence. You chose loyalty to them—your people, your Wardens—over the people bleeding beside you. Over me."

She looked down, jaw tightening, then looked up and met his eyes.

"I was trying to protect you," she yelled, getting angry now. "You don't understand the pressure, the history, the rules, how orders bind us—"

He interrupted her. "I don't care about your rules."

The words hit like a slap.

"You should... They're your rules now too," she shot back, regretting it as soon as the words left her mouth.

"And whose fault is that? You say you were protecting me," he shouted. "But I don't feel protected. I feel *used.*"

She saw it in his eyes then—saw the wound she'd left. Not just from the lies, but from the trust she'd let die.

"Marek—"

He held up a hand.

"No. I need time," he said, voice cracking again. "I need space. To figure out who the hell I am now, and whether anything between us was ever real."

She froze. Her hands twitched at her sides, like she might try to reach him, but she didn't.

"Was there *ever* an us?" he asked.

The question landed like a death knell.

Her mouth opened. Closed. "Yes. What we shared—," she whispered, "it meant everything to me."

He snorted. "Obviously it didn't, or you wouldn't have kept secrets."

She said nothing, because she was breaking apart inside.

He looked at her like she was a stranger, and then he turned and walked away.

◆

Akron watched it unfold with the quiet patience of someone who had seen centuries of things fall apart.

The confrontation had gone how he expected. Painful. Honest. Brutal in its necessity.

Kaycee's shoulders had slumped. She looked smaller now, stripped of her certainty.

Marek didn't look back at her as he walked past Akron.

Akron reached out—placed a hand on Marek's shoulder.

"We leave now, to Arckus for training," he said, his voice calm but final.

Marek just nodded, shrugging his hand off, and continued on—stopping several feet away.

"Training?" Kaycee asked, disbelief in her voice. "Now?"

Akron walked up to her. "He's not ready to be here," Akron said quietly, "and you're not ready to face what he's become."

She didn't argue.

"You remember what it was like," he added. "The early days. How sharp everything feels. How loud. How raw. Every emotion clawing at you?"

Gordon nodded, silent.

Akron's voice dropped lower. "This isn't just a transformation," he said. "This is something else—the flare of power we both saw. I don't know what it means. The answers have to be in his past. I will find them."

She didn't ask for clarification as he walked back toward Marek.

Akron stopped and glanced back once, just briefly. "He needs time to become what he's meant to be. And when he does... he'll need to decide where you fit in that space. You won't be able to force this."

She didn't speak.

She just watched them walk away, Marek's silhouette already fading, taking her heart with him

◆

The Rift loomed ahead of Marek—shifting, churning, pulsing with colors that didn't have names. Clear in a way it hadn't been before... whatever it was that had happened to him.

Marek could see it now, could feel it. It wasn't a doorway. It wasn't a gate. It was a wound in reality. Open. Raw. Alive.

Marek slowed his pace as they approached. The closer he got, the more his senses warped. Air turned dense, electric. His skin prickled with static. His ears popped twice in a row, like pressure was building around him, then releasing, only to build again.

It smelled like ozone and electricity.

The wind died completely. Even the city behind them seemed to fade. No distant sirens. No hum of traffic. Just the low, resonant thrum of the Rift calling them forward.

Marek's breath hitched.

The air ahead shimmered like heat off pavement, except this heat bled light, and the light didn't stay still. It twisted, spiraled, fractured—blue-white colors folding over themselves and bleeding into one another.

Time flickered in his chest.

He took another step. His boots crunched against shattered glass and debris, but the sound echoed oddly. Drawn out. Fragmented.

Akron walked ahead of him, unbothered. The First Warden's coat didn't flutter, though the air around them churned like a cyclone. He moved with the same quiet confidence he always had.

They reached the beginning of the edge of the Rift. There was no real line. Just a moment where the world went from real to... something else.

Akron stepped through without hesitation. He turned halfway through and held out a hand.

"You will need direct contact your first time traveling. I will guide you."

Marek hesitated, only for a second, then took his hand and followed.

It was like being swallowed.

There was no tunnel. No straight path. Just movement.

Up was down. Down was up. He felt weightless, like he didn't possess a physical body.

The Rift didn't transport—it rearranged.

Light blurred past him in streaks and ripples, slipping through the seams of his vision.

Every sense was overloaded. His skin buzzed. His bones ached. He felt like he was stretching and collapsing at the same time.

He tried to speak—couldn't. The air here didn't carry sound the same way.

He kept moving, following the tether to Akron—what was a hand moments ago, now an invisible tether connecting them. Something felt rather than seen.

The swirl of motion narrowed. Colors stopped bleeding together. Light began to organize.

He sensed Akron slowing, and then there was an abrupt shift—a hard tug as Akron's tether pulled him the rest of the way through.

◆

Kaycee watched the Rift vanish.

One heartbeat it was there, pulsing and alive—colors twisting through impossible angles, vibrating with soundless power. The next, it was gone.

And Marek was gone with it. Swallowed whole.

Kaycee stood frozen in place, arms at her sides, unable to move. The space where he had stood, where he had turned away from her without looking back—this was where it all caught up to her.

Her breath felt shallow and thin. Like she couldn't get enough air.

He was gone, and it was her fault. Everything was her fault.

She stood there as the wind picked up again, swirling dirt and ash around her boots. The street felt too big. The city too far away.

Her senses, usually sharp, honed, trained to track and analyze—were muted now. Like something inside her wanted to shut down... everything.

She had watched Marek become something she had no name for.

And then, the argument. The look of anger and betrayal in his eyes as he traded hard words—true words—and then walked away.

She didn't even know when she had started crying.

Tears burned down her face, unnoticed. Her vision blurred, but she didn't lift a hand to wipe them away.

The truth had weight. And now it was sitting on her chest, heavier than it had ever been.

She had followed orders. Kept secrets. Told herself it was to protect the mission, the team, him.

But Malik... Marcus... Tucker—they were all dead. Marek had walked out of this world—out of her life, following Akron without a backward glance.

And she was standing in the wreckage with nothing left but silence and regret.

"*We trusted you...*"

"*I trusted you...*"

His voice echoed in her memories, raw, quiet, and final.

She sank to her knees. It wasn't graceful. It wasn't composed. Her legs just gave out, and she let them. The concrete dug into her pants, the grit sharp beneath her palms as her hands hit the pavement.

Her chest heaved once. Then again. And then she broke.

She didn't scream. Didn't sob. It was quieter than that. Worse than that.

It was the sound of someone realizing they had become the villain in someone else's story.

Her fingers curled into the asphalt, powerful nails digging furrows until they caught on something sharp. She barely noticed. She couldn't feel anything except the pressure building inside her—pressure she had tried to balance for weeks.

She had thought she could control this. That if she walked the tightrope just right—she could have it all—her secrets, and him. But she had lost both and had nothing to show for it except the dead bodies of her team.

"Gordon!"

The voice slammed into her like a brick through glass.

She flinched hard, hands lifting like she'd been struck. Her head snapped toward the sound.

Harper.

The analyst's boots hit the pavement hard as she ran toward her, tablet in hand, eyes wide and wild—tears streaked down her own face as she closed the distance.

"You need to see this," Harper said breathlessly, skidding to a stop beside her.

Kaycee blinked, dragging herself back to the surface. "What?" she rasped, her voice shredded.

"I'm picking up something. It's... it's Tucker."

Her whole body went still. "What did you say?"

Harper crouched beside her—trying not to focus on the bodies of her team lying like broken dolls around them—trying to keep it together.

Pulling up a screen, she showed her. "I got a hit from his monitor just now... his vitals—they were redlined for several minutes... but seconds ago, his heartbeat registered. It's faint, but it's there."

Kaycee leaned over, eyes locked on the signal displayed on the tablet. She saw the pulse.

"And?" she asked, voice steadier now.

"They are weak, but they are growing stronger by the second," Harper said.

Kaycee stared at the data for another second. Then straightened.

The weight in her chest was still there—but it had shifted. Reorganized itself. A new shape.

Hope. Not the warm, glowing kind. Not yet.

This was just a small ember in the dark, but it was enough.

She got to her feet. Her knees shook a little, but she didn't fall as she walked over to Tucker's prone form.

"Get the stretcher—we need to get him into the van and to Headquarters as fast as possible," she said.

Harper sprinted off and returned quickly.

The wind had changed direction.

As the SCU clean-up team arrived on site. As they loaded Tucker into the van, and his vitals remained steady, Kaycee made a promise that she'd do whatever it took to keep him alive.

She hoped it would be enough—needed it to be enough. Without Tucker, she didn't know if Marek would make it through the darkness.

Chapter 31

Marek

The Rift closed behind them with a final pulse—a current of power snapping shut like turning off a TV. Marek stumbled, boots scuffing across a surface that wasn't stone but felt older than Earth itself.

He fell, still off-center from the transition to his physical body. He caught himself, one hand bracing instinctively against the ground—feeling the pulse beneath his feet.

The ground thrummed. Not metaphorically. Literally. Like energy... a heartbeat.

Like he was standing on the chest of something alive.

He looked up—and forgot how to breathe.

Akron had said they were going to Arckus before they stepped into the Rift. This had to be it.

The word echoed in his head the same way the city echoed across the wind-blown sky that stretched in all directions. There were no stars here—no sun, no moon. Just swirling auroras of Rift light, painting the heavens in moving hues of silver and blue.

The stronghold was perched on the edge of a floating landmass, suspended between Realms. Below, rivers of glowing energy cut through the dark like molten veins. Other floating islands drifted in the distance—some with crumbling ruins, others shrouded in permanent storm clouds.

Arckus itself looked like it was carved from the bones of the world. A fortress that had once been a cathedral. Or maybe a cathedral that had always been a fortress.

Massive spires pierced the sky like obsidian spears, each inscribed with curling, ancient script that shifted subtly when you weren't looking directly at it.

Between the spires, arched walkways stretched like stone bridges over nothing, held up by energy—as if the laws of physics were as foreign to this place as magic was to Earth.

Towers spiraled into themselves, winding with impossible architecture that suggested the builders hadn't been bound by gravity—or human imagination.

The entire structure shimmered faintly with power. Not magic, exactly. Something older. Heavier. Something Marek felt in his bones—familiar in a way he didn't yet have the knowledge to grasp.

"This is Arckus," Akron said beside him, voice quiet, reverent. "The last bastion of the Wardens. Forged by Onos for Wardens before the end of the final war and my creation millennia ago. A time when the Realms were young.

"I think some part of him knew it would end the way it did—that we would be the earth's protectors, and that even we would need a place of solace."

Marek didn't answer. He couldn't. His thoughts were scattered across the impossible skyline and the steady thrum of power that resonated deep within him. The city was silent and loud at the same time—full of echoes, like everything here contained a memory.

The stone under his boots was dark gray, almost black, veined with glowing threads of gold and red. It felt warm—not from sunlight, but from whatever energy kept this place tethered between worlds.

Ahead, wide gates led into the heart of the stronghold—an enormous open courtyard flanked by towering statues of armored figures.

Wardens, Marek guessed. Carved in their prime. Each bore a different weapon—swords, glaives, spears, twin axes... the list went on.

Their armor looked nothing like what he thought armor should look like—his only reference being what he had seen in museums. Heavy, thick, and clunky.

It was as far from it as a kite was from an airplane. Sleek. Shimmering. Like liquid metal covering the body. Every surface was etched with runes that pulsed faintly as Marek passed.

"They're watching you," Akron said.

Marek blinked. "What?"

"Their Essence still lingers. Every Warden who bled for this place left a mark. You'll leave one too, if you survive."

That *if* sat heavy in the air.

They stepped through the gates and into the main training square—and suddenly, the quiet grandeur of the outer city gave way to life.

The clash of blades rang out to the left, where two Wardens trained in a walled pit, swords clanging with bursts of light. Farther back, a row of what had to be newer Wardens—maybe five in total—moved through a kata drill under the sharp eye of another. Across the square, energy flared as another pair practiced manipulating Rift energy into shields and weapons.

Marek felt all of it.

Not just the sounds, but the pressure—like every motion, every breath in Arckus was part of a living system, and it was testing him. Weighing him.

"Where is everyone?" he asked. "This place could house tens of thousands."

Akron nodded. "And it once did. Now there are fewer than twenty-five hundred active Wardens. And only one new trainee this cycle—you."

"And the others?" Marek asked. "They're all—?"

"Dead or broken beyond recovery." Akron turned toward the eastern corridor. "Which is why you get one-on-one training. Your training process is personal. It has to be."

Marek followed him down a narrow hallway lined with glowing crystals embedded in the stone. The walls shifted slightly as they walked—runes reacting to their presence, flickering with a strange light.

A figure stepped out from the next chamber, tall and massive. His armor was the same liquid metal that the Warden statues at the entrance wore—that everyone seemed to wear.

His didn't have any runes or etchings and was not polished for show. It hugged his body, covering every surface, leaving only his hands, neck and face uncovered. It flexed and moved with him as he stalked toward them. His eyes were sharp, gray-blue like steel left out in rain. His expression was unreadable.

He looked Marek up and down like someone inspecting a blade just pulled from the fire—and unhappy with the results.

"So, this is him?" the man said. "The newb?"

"Cael," Akron said with a small smile. "Meet your new trainee."

Cael turned back to Marek. "You look like you want to kill something, boy."

Marek met his stare, fists clenched—burning rage rolling through him. "I do... badly."

Cael looked at him and then at Akron. "Akron's always bringing me the angry ones. Are you going to be a problem?"

"I'll do anything you ask—anything that will help me find and kill the fucker who killed my team. My friends."

A slow smirk curled Cael's mouth. "Ah, anger... Rage. Good. You will need both, and then some to get you through what I'm about to do to you—when all you want to do is quit. Just don't let it consume you."

"Too late," Marek said.

"We'll see..." Cael murmured.

He turned to Akron, lifting an eyebrow in question. "Who's this 'fucker' he's referring to?"

Akron clenched his teeth. "Dharken Mohr."

Cael's eyes narrowed and he spit on the ground in disgust.

Turning to Marek, he explained, "Dharken Mohr is an Elvahr... a vampire, to put it into a context you'd understand. They get stronger as they age, and he has been around for longer than Akron here. You've got a long way to go before you'll be able to handle an Elvahr—much less *that* Elvahr—and you can't do it filled with anger."

He stepped forward, close enough that Marek caught the scent of metal and oil.

"As Akron said, I'm Cael. Your trainer. Which means I'm your worst nightmare and your only lifeline for the foreseeable future."

"You always this friendly?" Marek asked.

Cael didn't smile.

"I had a brother once," he said, voice quieter now. "He died screaming in my arms."

That landed hard. Marek's expression faltered.

Cael didn't blink. "I stopped wasting time on pleasantries after that."

Silence stretched between them.

Then, more evenly, Cael added, "You've lost people. I can see it in your eyes. But you're not alone in that."

Marek looked away, jaw tight.

"Most Wardens carry that kind of pain. It's part of the cost. We're not chosen because we're perfect. We're chosen because we survive—because we almost died fighting for the innocent."

He paused, considering. "Pain is the best teacher. If you can take that pain and rage you're feeling and turn it into purpose, you may survive."

Akron nodded once. "He's in your hands."

Then, with no further ceremony, Akron turned and vanished into the Rift—leaving Marek standing alone with a stranger who seemed carved from the same stone as the fortress itself.

Cael watched him for a beat longer, then jerked his chin toward the hall. "Come on. I'll show you your room. Try not to die on the way."

They moved through a wide corridor that opened into an elevated walkway running along the spine of Arckus. The wind was cool here, dry but charged. The sky beyond stretched in all directions—no horizon, no stars, just endless space washed in shifting colors.

A slow ripple of violet and gold moved across the heavens like liquid starlight, casting the stronghold in a perpetual glow that didn't come from any sun Marek could see.

"What... is that?" he asked, slowing as he stared at the sky.

Cael didn't stop walking. "That's the Riftlight. It flares in phases—First Riftlight, Highflare, Dimfall, Voidphase. It's how we track the cycle here. Think of it like sunrise, noon, dusk, and night—minus the sun, moon, or stars."

Marek squinted upward. The pale shimmer had deepened slightly since they arrived—less pearlescent now, more gold at the edges.

"So, there's no sun at all?"

"No. No moon either. No real sky. Just the Rift breathing above us. You'll get used to it."

"Feels alive."

"It is," Cael said, glancing at him. "Time doesn't flow the same here. Arckus is anchored to Earth's hours, but between phases... you can lose track. You stay here too long, you start to feel like you're dreaming while you're awake."

"Sounds great," Marek muttered.

Cael looked at him, irritation evident in his gaze. "Training begins at First Riftlight. That's the start of the cycle—when the sky goes from silver to pearl. It causes everything to pulse a little faster.

"You'll know it because you'll feel it. It'll drag you out of a dead sleep, like an internal alarm you can't snooze... really fucking annoying. You'll get used to it... or not. Not my problem."

"Technology works here too," Cael continued, "so you could use an alarm clock, but you'll find the pull of First Riftlight much more effective."

"So, phones work?" Marek asked.

Cael nodded, pulling out his own. "Texting is Akron's preferred form of communication. For such an ancient, he's really into tech. I hate the damn things, personally."

"How long do I have?" Marek asked.

"About twelve hours. Enough time to think about how much pain you're going to be in tomorrow."

Marek noticed Cael had smiled then... Not a great sign of how this would go, if his trainer only smiled at the prospect of pain.

They reached the barracks—sleek stone structures carved into the inner walls of the stronghold. The door to Marek's chamber opened with a low, harmonic chime. Inside: a bed, a weapons rack, a basin, and a narrow window that framed a view of the open sky and the glowing rivers of Rift energy far below. There was a small dresser in the corner as well.

"You're not here to get comfortable," Cael said, leaning in the doorway. "You're here to become something useful. Every cut, bruise, trial, and lesson I give you will be to hone you into a soldier—one without fear or mercy. Both those will get you killed. The Seven Realms are not human. They hate humanity. And they hate us, the protectors of humanity, just as much. If you show mercy to Realm-born creatures, you will die."

Marek turned to face him fully. "You don't think I'll make it."

"I think most won't, because most don't. I think Akron sees something in you." Cael straightened. "It's my job to find it, mold it—then harden it."

He stepped back into the hall.

"Training starts in twelve hours. Be ready."

And then he was gone.

Marek stood alone in the dim light of Voidphase, the hum of the stronghold still alive beneath his boots, the sky pulsing with its strange, celestial breath.

Tomorrow, at First Riftlight, his training would begin.

He had a feeling he wasn't going to enjoy it.

Chapter 32

Akron

As he turned his back on Arckus, his thoughts returned to Marek's transformation.

The moment Marek took the Essence, Akron had felt it—seen it. If only just for a moment.

Not just the surge of power, not just the Oath taking root—but something deeper. Something ancient and impossibly vast. A thrum in the air surrounding Marek.

It had resonated through Akron's bones, setting his teeth on edge and his instincts aflame.

It was that brief flash of golden energy—there and gone again the next instant. It shouldn't have happened. No newly made Warden had ever had a flare like that.

Marek Tomlinson wasn't like the others. He was a puzzle piece that didn't fit into the mold it was made for.

Akron hated puzzles—things that didn't fall into place in his ordered universe.

He needed to know why Marek was different, and he knew right where to start looking. When you want to understand someone, you look to their past.

He reached out to the Rift energies, and they responded like an old friend. He had one destination in mind as he willed the Rift to take him where he wanted to go.

He materialized just outside the NYPD precinct where Marek had spent most of his short yet accomplished career in law enforcement. He wrapped himself in a veil of invisibility and proceeded to walk up the steps into the bustle of the lobby—sidestepping criminals and officers alike as he made his way to the elevators.

He hit the button for the fourth floor, where Human Resources was located.

He bypassed the elevator's card reader with a focused spark of Rift energy, molded to his will to unlock the floor he needed. The panel sparked and shorted out—it would need repairs, a part of him noted, but that wasn't his problem.

He did the same at the badge reader outside the employee file room. Another pulse of energy. A spark. The lock disengaged.

He made his way to the drawer marked with a **"T,"** as it appeared everything was sorted by last name. Sliding open the drawer, it didn't take him long to find Marek's file.

Tomlinson, Marek J.
Detective, NYPD Homicide
Age: 28
Mother: Ellen Tomlinson
Father: Unknown

Akron's breath caught.

Ellen. The name rang like a bell, triggering a memory to surface.

It seemed only a moment ago he had been soaked in rain and blood and regret—standing outside a suburban lawn, across from the house of the woman Jax had given everything to love.

He'd seen her only once—her face framed by yellow light through a bedroom window. Young. Beautiful. Radiating...

something. A pull that he felt in his bones as he looked in on her after he had taken the life of Jax.

She was the reason Jax—loyal and dedicated—had violated the sacred Oath.

Jax's last words still haunted him.

"She gave me peace."

Akron's hand tightened around the file. If Marek was twenty-eight now, and Jax died twenty-nine years ago...

A whisper of possibility stirred in his mind—one that clawed its way up from a vague feeling and formed into terrifying certainty the more he thought on it.

If Jax hadn't just broken his Oath in order to love a human—if he'd fathered a child, and that child was now a Warden...

He didn't know what that meant—for Marek, for his role as a Warden, or even if he *was* a Warden... or something else.

Akron's world spun. There was no rule for this. No law set down by Onos to handle it.

No—that wasn't true. There was a law, but Jax had broken it.

Akron closed his eyes, breathing deep—trying to find calm despite the swirling doubts and questions making their way through him.

He needed to be sure before he jumped to conclusions. Scanning further down Marek's file, Akron made a note of the address under Ellen's name in the emergency contact section.

He closed the file with shaking hands, returned it, then stepped into the Rift.

He stepped out in front of the house—déjà vu slamming into him. The small home hadn't changed much.

Same faded brick. A new paint job looked to have been done fairly recently—it was still the same home. Akron stood across the street, hood drawn low, shadows clinging to him. He didn't need to approach. He just waited.

And then he saw her.

Through the window, warm and golden with lamplight. She was older now, of course. Lines at the corners of her eyes. Silver in her hair.

That she was the same person Jax had loved, however, was undeniable. She folded laundry, slow and steady, her expression soft.

Time bent around him, memory pulling him back to that night.

How the wind carried the scent of rain and roses. How Jax's body fell at his feet. How Akron had reassured him:

"I'll spare the woman."

And now here she was. Living. Breathing. And Marek—Marek was her son—he had to be.

It hit him just then how much Marek looked like Jax.

It should have been so clear when he first saw him on the rooftop—after Akron had taken care of the second Drakyn. He had no reason to look for the impossible, though, so he missed it.

His legs nearly buckled as the pieces fell into place.

Marek's raw strength. His speed. His capacity for Essence. How he moved in combat and could hold his own against the Drakyns—as a human.

That was why he didn't feel the compulsion to take Kaycee's life. He must have had enough Essence in him from Jax that the Oath recognized Marek as something not human.

He wasn't just any Warden. He was Jax's son. That explained the Essence he felt—faint but there—prior to Marek's transformation.

As he thought back on Marek's transformation, he was hit with another impossible question: what else was

Marek? Because being Jax's son didn't explain the other power flare he had felt.

That gold-white energy that speared through Marek before disappearing just as fast... Akron would recognize that energy anywhere.

A memory as old as time rose up within him... Onos, broken and dying on the battlefield. Akron, newly made—being given oaths, knowledge, Essence.

The same gold-white energy crackling around Onos as he gave the last of himself to create the Rift, then fading from existence...

Could it be? Akron thought.

But only the silence of the night answered him as he turned from Ellen's house and vanished into the Rift.

Chapter 33

Grief settled thick over the SCU briefing room, a second skin Kaycee couldn't shrug off. Outside the glass walls, New York bled its usual noise and chaos, but in here, silence ruled. It wasn't the peaceful kind. It was the kind that came after a storm, where only wreckage remained.

She sat at the head of the table, spine straight, arms folded tightly across her chest like they might hold her together if she squeezed hard enough. Her tactical uniform was crisp, every crease precise, but her eyes betrayed her: red-rimmed and haunted. The weight of what had happened—of who had been lost—clung to her shoulders like chains.

Prior to this meeting, she had begged—pleaded with Akron to release her from her binding orders. The ones preventing her from telling humans about Wardens or the Realms. She argued that her team needed to know—that they were already exposed and deserved answers. That they couldn't continue to operate in the dark.

Akron had relented—grudgingly. He'd released her from the binding, but not without warning: only those who needed to know. No more.

Chen sat in a wheelchair, arm braced and heavily bandaged. Her jaw was tight, but her eyes were glassy, swimming with unspoken grief. Harper stood behind her, one hand on the chair, the other gripping a tablet too tightly.

Tucker—still in a coma, still barely hanging on—was absent in body but not in presence. His name hung over the team like smoke.

Marek was gone. Marcus and Malik were dead.

Kaycee took a breath that felt like glass in her lungs.

"I owe you the truth," she said quietly.

They all looked at her. Not with accusation. Not yet. But with need. They needed something to make sense.

So, she gave it to them.

In measured words, she told them about the Rift, about how it was breaking down. About the Realms. About the creatures that slipped through the cracks. She told them about the Wardens—guardians of Earth. She told them about her Oath.

And then she told them about Marek. What he had become, and where he had gone.

When she finished, no one spoke. The silence was heavy with something new: understanding.

Harper sank into a seat, arms loose at her sides. "You should've told us sooner," she said. Her voice wasn't angry. Just tired.

"I know," Kaycee replied, and for once, her voice cracked.

Chen looked up slowly. "So, what do we do now?"

Kaycee looked around the room. These weren't just agents. They were what remained of her family.

"Now we decide what to tell the rest of the world. The Bureau isn't ready. Earth isn't ready. But we are. We keep fighting. We hold the line. And when the time comes... we choose what side we stand on."

Each of them nodded, slowly. Quietly. A silent pact in the shadow of everything they'd lost.

But her day wasn't over.

———◆———

She stood in front of FBI Director Green in their conference room, the video conference showing her boss's very unhappy face in high definition on the big screen. He was tall, sharp-suited, and colder than anyone had a right to be.

"You lost half your team," he said.

"Yes," she answered.

"You lost Agent Tomlinson."

"He wasn't lost," she said. "He made a choice. And I allowed it."

"You allowed a federal asset to walk off the grid."

"He isn't just an asset. He's also a person who suffered a trauma—the loss of his partner and friend—he needs time," she said. "But I believe he'll come back on his own."

He leaned back in his chair, expression unreadable. "And what came through the Bowery breach? The report says something humanoid. Aggressive. Resistant to anything we threw at it."

"Something we weren't ready for," she replied.

"Then get ready."

"I need more." She stepped forward. "More clearance. More funding for specialized gear. A response team that doesn't get gutted every time something walks through a hole in reality."

He didn't blink. "You'll get what you need. But screw up again, and I won't be able to shield you. And believe me, Gordon, you're very close to the edge."

"Understood."

He ended the call abruptly, and her shoulders immediately sagged. She sank into a chair and sat for a long time—staring at her shaking hands.

Then, with a deep breath, she got up from the chair and left the conference room. She had to make some calls—she prepared herself to inform Marcus and Malik's families that they had died in some sort of training exercise. It was bull-shit, but it was policy for classified operations like theirs.

That night, she stood in the quiet of Tucker's hospital room at the SCU medical facilities. The only light came from the monitors—a soft, rhythmic glow that cast ghostly shadows across his face. Tubes ran from his arms. Machines chirped quietly, marking the space between heart-beats.

She sat beside him, took his hand.

"Get better soon," she whispered. "Marek needs you now more than ever... I need you... for him... for us."

No response. Just the soft beep of machines.

Behind her, Harper hovered, tablet in hand. She watched the monitor, then blinked.

A pulse. Not from the heart monitor. From the bioscan overlay. A flicker. Rhythmic. Familiar.

"That's not right," she murmured.

Kaycee turned. "What?"

Harper didn't answer right away. She tapped the screen, zoomed in, ran it again.

There it was again. A pulse. Not biological. Resonant.

Kaycee leaned over the bed. "Is that...?"

Harper nodded slowly. "It's not Essence, not from how you described it to us—not exactly. But it's similar. Maybe?"

They looked at Tucker, but he didn't stir. The machines kept beeping. And something inside him kept humming.

It wasn't over. Not by a long shot.

Chapter 34

Marek—Arckus

The pull woke him—a rising current under his skin, like someone had tied a string to his spine and tugged. Marek sat up with a curse on his lips before he even opened his eyes.

The room hummed. The bed was warm, the air sharp and clean. Through the narrow window, the sky had begun to shift. What had been a soft shimmer of silver was now bleeding into a pearl-colored white, threaded with slow pulses of lavender and blue.

First Riftlight.

"Cael was right. That's really fucking annoying," Marek muttered.

He swung his legs out of bed and stood, joints popping. He could see now why no alarm clock was needed.

He dressed quickly—black armor of the same make as what Cael and Akron wore. He had found the armor waiting for him in the dresser after Cael left last night.

Malleable, flexible, and hard as steel. As he put it on, it adjusted to his frame instantly—rippling and sliding like liquid metal. It clung to him—a second skin—and hummed faintly against his body.

The moment he stepped into the corridor, the lights shifted. The Riftlight running through the walls flared softly, then dimmed again, pulsing with the cycle.

Footsteps echoed.

Cael appeared at the far end, already armored in that matte black armor he always wore. Similar to Marek's, Cael's was perfectly molded to his body.

"You're up," Cael said, like it surprised him. "I see you found your armor. You must wear it always while you are in the field. You can wear it for training too."

"Follow me," Cael said as he turned and started walking. "We'll eat first and then see what you're made of."

The dining hall of Arckus looked like it had been designed by a war god with good taste. Long stone tables ran the length of the chamber, flanked by benches carved with Warden emblems—some fresh and detailed, others so worn you could barely make them out. The vaulted ceiling was high, with beams made of some type of hardwood.

The smell of food was earthy and sharp—roasted meat, bitter roots, spices Marek didn't recognize. It made his stomach growl.

At least two dozen Wardens were scattered across the hall, most already eating or sharpening weapons while they talked. Some looked up when Marek entered—quick glances, assessing gazes. A few didn't bother hiding their curiosity.

Cael grabbed a tray and handed one to Marek without a word. They moved down the line: dark bread, slices of something red and steaming, a thick stew that smelled like pot roast.

They sat at the far end of one of the long tables. As soon as Cael dropped onto the bench, a pair of Wardens further down looked over.

"Well, well," one of them said—a tall woman with copper hair and runes covering her armor, "Cael got another trainee. This one as bad as the last one?"

Cael didn't look up from his stew, a non-committal grunt the only response.

The other Warden, lean and pale with eyes like ice, snorted. "Didn't the last one die in training? Something about letting her anger get the best of her? Seems like you have a type, huh? You think this one'll be any different?"

The tall woman leaned over to peer at Marek. "Looks like he wants to fight the world."

"I think," Cael said, finally looking up at them, "that he's sitting right here, and if you've got shit to say, you can say it to his face."

Marek smirked around a mouthful of bread.

The copper-haired woman raised her hands in mock surrender. "Relax. We're just saying hello. Welcome to the crazy, kid."

"Thanks," Marek said, nodding. "Looking forward to getting my ass kicked."

"Don't worry. That part's guaranteed—especially with this one here. Good luck." The pale one said, gesturing at Cael.

Cael just kept eating as the two of them left the table and walked to the exit.

When they were done, Cael stood without a word, and Marek followed, tray cleared and nerves rising. The food had settled in his gut like lead—doing nothing to dull the unease curling in his chest.

This was it. No more awe. No more talk. Time to get to work.

◆

The training yard was cut into a plateau on the western edge of Arckus, open to the sky.

The surface was packed black stone—scarred, scored, and stained from centuries of training. Circles were etched into the ground for drills. Racks of weapons lined the walls. Basic swords, spears, shields... It looked like a Renaissance surplus store had vomited its contents onto the racks.

Cael walked over, pulled two wooden staves from where they hung, and turned back to Marek.

"This isn't combat training," he said. "Not yet. This is me figuring out what the hell I've got to work with. I move; you move. I observe. And if you fail, I adjust, and we repeat."

"Good," Marek muttered. "Whatever we need to do."

"Let's start with Martial Forms."

Marek blinked. "Sorry, what?"

Cael's brow twitched. "Martial Forms. They are our foundation—sword drills designed to imprint movement into muscle and memory. They're not about power. They're about discipline. You mimic the form until your body knows what comes next, because you don't have time to think about moves and counter-moves during combat—it has to become ingrained in your bones."

"Like katas?"

Cael nodded. "But ours were developed by Akron himself to combat residents of the Seven Realms. Each species is brutal, aggressive, and strong. They like to gang up on us because most cannot face us alone. These forms are designed to teach us how to combat multiple assailants."

He tossed Marek one of the wooden staves—it was made in the slightly curved style of traditional Warden swords.

"Also, please don't try to impress me—I've seen Akron fight. Just move."

Marek caught it with one hand. It was heavier than he expected—designed to be weighted like a regular sword.

"The sword is not just a tool," Cael said. "It's meant to be an extension of your will and intent. Your will needs to be strong. Your intent, sharp."

Cael stepped back, his own stave at his side, and raised it to a ready position. "Watch first. Martial Form One. No commentary, no improvisation."

And then he moved.

Slowly at first. Each strike a breath, each pivot grounded and exact. Marek watched the way his shoulders turned, the way his hips coiled before each step. There was grace there—but not softness. It was the kind of motion that could split a man from shoulder to hip without a sound.

The form flowed from strike to parry to low sweep and upward feint, then ended in a grounded stance with the blade pointed slightly downward—ready, not resting.

"Now, you follow me," Cael said.

They moved side by side. Cael led; Marek mirrored—or tried to.

At first, Marek kept pace. But halfway through, his blade dipped too fast. He turned his hip too soon. His follow-through overreached, and Cael snapped:

"Stop. Reset. You need to learn how to master your newfound speed and strength. Learn control and precision first, and your speed and strength will kick in automatically."

So he stopped, reset, and worked on the forms.

Again.

And again.

And again.

By the fifth repetition, Marek dripped sweat from his jaw. His breathing grew harsh. He could feel the strength in his arms trying to override the subtlety of the movements.

"Control," Cael barked.

"I'm trying—"

"You're trying to move the sword, and that's your problem. The sword is an extension of you. You don't try to consciously move your arms, do you? No, it just happens.

Listen to your body, let the sword move with you—guided by your thoughts and intent."

And then, as Marek moved through the form again, something shifted. A moment. A flicker.

One transition—a high guard to an angled shoulder cut—just clicked. Like his muscles remembered something they'd never been taught, the stave feeling like an extension of himself.

Cael stopped mid-step. Watched. Just for a second.

Then said, "Again."

They continued until Marek thought his arms were going to fall off, then Cael allowed him a small reprieve, tossing him a water bottle.

The sweat on Marek's back hadn't yet dried from the Martial Forms by the time Cael announced the rest break was over.

He stepped back into the training circle, and tossed Marek a small towel.

"Hand-to-hand," Cael said, rotating his shoulders once. "Let's see what you think you know."

Marek rolled his neck, wiped sweat from his brow, and dropped into a defensive stance—orthodox boxer's frame, fists up, lead leg forward, eyes sharp.

Cael's mouth twitched almost like amusement. "Predictable."

And then he moved.

No warning. No buildup. One moment Cael was standing still. The next he was inside Marek's guard, low and fast—sweeping at his knee. Marek, off-balance from the sweep, allowed Cael to follow up with a palm strike that slammed into his chest. The blow didn't hurt—but it knocked Marek off balance just enough for Cael to end the bout with a crushing sidekick.

Marek's feet lifted off the ground, and he went airborne. His back hit the stone floor with a grunt. The breath punched out of him.

Cael stepped back. "Up."

Marek climbed to his feet, fists up again. His pride stung worse than his ribs. The bastard was fast.

Marek pressed this time—*his* way. No drills, no rules. Marek swung with everything he had, short jabs and sharp elbows, leading with his strengths—what he knew from his training at Nelson's Gym as a youth. His footwork was crisp. Aggressive. He moved faster than he'd ever moved—his body responding almost too fast for his brain to follow.

He clipped Cael with a knee. Made him step back with a hook to the ribs.

Got him, He thought.

Then Cael pivoted low, caught Marek's wrist mid-swing, and twisted. The world flipped and Marek slammed into the ground hard enough to see stars.

◆

He's fast, Cael thought as he watched the boy recover, lips pressed tight as Marek rolled onto his side, coughing hard.

Faster than he should be.

That was the problem. Speed was easy. Speed without discipline was a knife without a handle—use it wrong, and you could end up hurting yourself.

Marek moved like he wanted to hurt things—people, creatures, whatever got in his way. But there was no real focus. He was power without shape. And that made him dangerous.

Not just to enemies. To everyone.

Cael circled the training ring slowly, arms loose, breath even. He hadn't broken a sweat. Not yet. But he was watching everything.

The tension in Marek's left shoulder. The stutter in his breath. The way his eyes locked onto openings too early. It was all catalogued.

And yet... There was something under it.

Some instinct—old and buried deep—that flickered when Marek fought. A flash of clarity behind the wildness. A beat of timing that Cael felt more than saw.

Like the boy's body had muscle memory he wasn't yet aware of.

Cael narrowed his eyes.

He moved again—striking low, then high, letting Marek counter out of instinct. The boy had better reflexes than most full Wardens. That should've worried him.

It didn't. Not yet.

He needed to know more. Push harder. Break him down to the bone, and see what crawled back out of the wreckage.

◆

Marek didn't know how long they'd been going. Minutes? Hours? It felt like forever.

His body was on fire. His ribs ached. His right arm and wrist throbbed from blocking too many of Cael's sharp, brutal strikes. But still—he stood.

"You're stronger than you know," Cael said, stepping back into place. "But you fight with too much anger and aggression. Your focus slips as you get frustrated, and you make mistakes."

Cael stood there, tapping his chin in thought. "There's something else too. You start hesitating when you really start moving. Like you're afraid of your speed. Your power."

"I'm not afraid of anything."

"You should be," Cael said. "Because if you don't learn control, that strength and speed... that rage and aggression... is going to get someone killed. Maybe you. Maybe someone you care about."

Marek's jaw clenched. A flicker of memory—Marcus's scream. Malik's blood on the pavement. Tucker, unmoving.

"I'm not going to lose anyone else," he ground out.

Cael nodded once. "Then let's make sure you live long enough to keep that promise."

He extended a hand. Marek hesitated—then took it.

The older Warden pulled him to his feet.

No smile. No praise. But where there had been irritation when they'd first met, now there was only assessment.

"I think I've got enough baseline to work with," Cael said. "Now, let's go to the Armory and see if we can find you a weapon to bond with."

"Bond with?" Marek asked.

Cael smiled and started walking. "You'll see. I'd hate to ruin the surprise."

Chapter 35

T hey were met at the entrance to the Armory by the Forgemaster, Teliz—a senior Warden who had been around about as long as Akron. Rumor was that he was the first Warden to be turned by Akron.

"Good luck, Trainee Marek," he said as they walked through the two large entrance doors. "I hope you find what you are looking for."

Cael and Marek both dipped their heads in acknowledgment.

As the doors snicked shut behind them, they were greeted with a silence so deep, it seemed to have its own weight.

The floor beneath Marek's feet seemed to mute the sound of his boots—like it didn't want even the sound of footsteps intruding on the stillness. The ceiling was partially shattered, open to the sky where Riftlight spilled through in soft columns, drifting like smoke. A faint wind tugged at the edges of the room, carrying no chill—just a sense of age.

The walls curved outward into a perfect circle, lined with weapon racks that gleamed under the ambient light. Dozens of blades, spears, glaives, halberds, and stranger instruments Marek had no name for. They all were mounted on the wall and racks throughout—some looked ceremonial, others deadly, all etched with the scarring of use or the perfect symmetry of preservation.

"As I said before, this is the Armory," Cael said softly behind him. His voice was quieter than usual, stripped of sarcasm.

"Each weapon is forged with Rift energy by Teliz. This makes them unique, capable of bonding with a Warden. Every Warden finds their weapon here and bonds to it. The Rift energy they're forged from, is designed to call to the Essence within you," Cael said.

He continued, "A bonded weapon becomes an extension of you, designed to work in perfect harmony with who you are—it chooses you, giving you the weapon you need, not the one you want. Take your time. You will find the one that calls to you. It will be a pull you are unable to resist."

Marek moved forward, trying to shake off the fatigue coiled deep in his joints. He reached for the first blade that drew his eye—a broad-shouldered longsword inscribed with pale-blue runes.

Nothing. The hilt was cold in his palm. No pull. No hum. No response.

He tried another. A curved saber with an obsidian edge. A spear so light it felt hollow. A glaive. Still nothing.

No hum of resonance. No irresistible pull like Cael described. Nothing he touched responded to him.

He moved down the line, frustration mounting with each failed attempt. The silence was deafening now. Not passive silence, but the kind that watched. Judged.

The twin knives didn't answer him. The collapsible staff hummed faintly but fell silent the moment he touched it. The ritual blade—the one shaped like a ripple of liquid metal—flared briefly before dimming again with a sigh of disappointment.

Behind him, Cael said nothing. Just watched. Waiting.

Marek's hands curled into fists. "I don't feel anything."

Cael gave a slow nod. "Then keep going. You will."

So, he kept going. It seemed like hours passed, and still he felt nothing.

And then—he felt it. Saw it. Recessed behind an archway, barely illuminated by the Riftlight overhead, was a large wooden cabinet with two glass windows stretching from top to bottom.

Unlike the other displays, this one didn't invite with shiny colors. It was simple, made from black wood, designed to be passed over. The shadows here felt deeper. Older. Like the light was choosing not to touch the cabinet and its contents.

Inside, two massive ninja-style swords—six feet in length—were mounted in a crossed pattern across a velvet-black panel. Lying next to the swords, there was what looked to be a crossed back scabbard, made from some type of black metal that drank the light.

The swords didn't seem to be made of steel. They weren't made of anything Marek recognized. Their edges were straight, symmetrical, and the blades had a mirror-like surface.

His feet moved without permission.

◆

At first, Cael didn't register the shift in Marek—the direction of his focus.

Trainees always wandered. They got desperate when the weapons didn't respond. It wasn't uncommon—most searched for something dramatic, something that would mark them as special. Many tried too hard to force a connection. The Armory never answered desperation.

But as Marek stepped beneath the shadowed archway, Cael's gut twisted.

Marek's posture changed—his gait shifted from frustration to focus. His movements slowed, not with hesitation, but with gravity. Like his bones knew exactly where they were supposed to go.

Cael straightened, tension bleeding into his spine. "No," he said, low. Then louder: "Marek, no!"

He stepped forward, fast now. "Marek," he called, sharper. "Don't touch that—**stop!**"

The cabinet sat like a coffin—upright, silent, black, humming with the kind of magic that whispered warnings across the skin. It wasn't just protected. It was sealed. Runes danced across its face in ancient, shifting patterns, each one woven from divine language and anchored in Rift-forged Essence.

No one had opened it. Not since the last war between Onos and his godlike children—and not for lack of trying.

Those blades were not heirlooms. They were the last blades of Onos, forged by him and for his battle-form. Imbued with the power of creation—so volatile that no one but Onos had ever held them, or wielded them.

Hell, no one had gotten past the wards on the cabinet—wards Akron himself had made—to test that theory. Any who tried simply ceased to exist. No ashes. No remains. Just... gone. Unmade.

"Marek!" he barked. "Back off. That's not for you. That's not for anyone. Those blades belonged to Onos—"

But Marek didn't stop. Didn't blink. Didn't hesitate.

Cael broke into a run.

———◆———

Marek barely registered Cael's voice. It was there—sharp, warning—but it sounded far away, like thunder from a distant storm rolling in behind the silence that had swallowed everything else.

His body moved without instruction.

With each step closer to the cabinet, the pull became stronger. It wasn't a conscious choice. It was stronger than compulsion—it was gravity, and Marek was helpless against it.

The Riftlight in the ceiling dimmed, drawn inward.

The cabinet's surface pulsed faintly as he approached. The runes didn't resist him. They didn't lash out like they should have, burning him to nothing. They diffused as he neared, seeming to burn away in recognition.

The blades started glowing faintly, the mirror-like surface beginning to flare in golden pulses that mirrored his heartbeat. The flares were accompanied by a sound—like a thousand whispers threading through the back of his mind—that grew louder the closer he got to them.

He felt it in his teeth. His ribs. The back of his eyes. The whispers grew so loud that it became hard to think. Hard to breathe.

His hand rose, and the final wards on the cabinet flared once before dissolving in threads of silver light.

The cabinet opened with a hiss that didn't come from metal, but from a soft exhale—like something taking a breath for the first time in thousands of years.

He reached inside, and the moment his fingers closed around the hilts, everything inside him locked into place.

Alignment. Ownership.

The blades sighed inside his head in relief and acceptance, the whispers quieting their crescendo as if pleased with their new owner. They immediately adjusted to him, shrinking down to a size that fit his form perfectly.

Then, like a storm waiting to be unleashed, a blinding surge of heat and light filled his skull—and then—he was somewhere else. Someone else. Some... *time else.*

The sky above him burned. Fire and Riftlight churned in the clouds like a storm. Mountains collapsed in the distance. The Realms bled together into a shattered battlefield.

And in the center of it all he stood—Onos.

Not the gentle and benevolent creator from the murals. Not the myth.

This was a warrior-Titan in his final hour.

He towered over the broken earth, wreathed in molten light, wrapped in blazing gold-white armor that flickered with radiant inscriptions. His face was carved in pain. In resolve. His twin blades in his hands—shining with a golden radiance.

Across from him, was Nyxia. His daughter. The first and the last of his rebellious children.

Her form twisted with wings of darkness, her hands drenched in the blood of Realms. She was terrible. Beautiful. Broken.

"You chose them," she hissed. Her voice cracked the stone. "Over us. Over me."

Onos said nothing.

She charged.

They clashed in a cyclone of light and shadow, screams and thunder, blades crashing with the sound of mountains dying. Nyxia fought with rage. Onos with purpose.

His blades tore through her illusions, her magic, her grief.

And then—he struck her down. Twin blades buried in her chest.

She didn't scream in pain. She just looked at him—eyes filled with hate—and whispered, "Humanity should have been ours to rule."

His voice rolled across the battlefield like a concussive blast in answer, **"NO DAUGHTER... HUMANITY WAS NEVER FOR YOU. YOU WERE FOR HUMANITY. YOU LOST SIGHT OF THAT. I AM SORRY."**

And then—faster than he thought possible, she pulled one of his blades from her chest.

He jerked back, but she had timed it well, and with the last of her strength, she drove it into his heart.

Onos crumbled. One knee hit the ground. The second blade slipped from his hand, slick with divine ichor.

Nyxia screamed, and Onos's head bowed. Then the sky shattered.

◆

Marek came back hard—like falling into his body from ten stories up.

He gasped, stumbling, blades still in hand, arms locked, heart thundering.

The chamber had gone still. No sound. No wind. No breath.

Even Cael, frozen just a few paces away, stared at him with something like awe. Or horror.

Marek's knees nearly gave, and just before he could drop the blades, the whispers stirred again inside his mind, but not as loud as before.

The swords were *alive*, Marek realized, and they were whispering to him in voices that weren't voices, but memories.

Cael couldn't move.

The moment Marek touched the swords—*truly* touched them—he'd frozen, eyes rolling up into the back of his head, vibrating and twitching as if being electrocuted.

Then there was utter stillness—as if Arckus itself had drawn a breath and stopped everything that wasn't essential.

The air changed. The resonance of Arckus shifted—in acknowledgement. Like the bones of the stronghold had recognized something returning home.

The Riftlight above didn't flicker—it simply stilled, frozen mid-wave, like time had taken a step back to watch.

And the blades—they hadn't resisted. They'd answered. Like they had been waiting all these millennia for Marek.

Cael watched them adjust their size to fit him perfectly, like they remembered him.

Cael stared, his mouth dry, his pulse thudding in his ears. He couldn't recall the last time he'd felt fear without adrenaline. Without being able to take action.

He took one slow step forward, eyes never leaving the blades.

Cael had no framework for this. No precedent. No story in Warden history that ended with someone touching those swords and still breathing—much less getting past the wards on the cabinet.

Yet Marek stood there—breathing hard—and the blades seemed to vibrate in his grip like they were just waking up.

Cael shook his head once, disbelieving, and for the first time in decades, words failed him.

"Well..." he muttered quietly. "Fuck me."

Chapter 36

T he mess hall felt louder than it should have. Not from volume—no one was shouting, no trays slammed onto stone, no chairs scraped obnoxiously across the floor.

The noise was quieter than that. It was the rustle of Warden cloaks, the low hum of whispered conversations, the occasional clang of cutlery against metal bowls. But all of it—every sound—hit Marek like static in the ears. Disjointed. Too bright.

The moment he stepped through the archway, the weight of the blades on his back felt heavier.

The twin swords were strapped to his back in the crossed scabbard that had been in the case with them—the scabbard also adjusting to fit their new size.

They moved with him now like they had always been there. They hadn't made a sound when he walked, yet he could feel the way they whispered in the back of his mind.

Eyes followed him as he passed. Shock, wonder, and fear in equal measure crossed each face.

Cael moved ahead of him without comment, his gait easy, posture relaxed, but Marek could see the tension in the way his shoulders carried his armor. He wasn't at ease. Not anymore.

Cael had pulled out his phone shortly after they left the Armory, texting someone.

Probably reporting on me to Akron... Marek thought.

They crossed the length of the hall without a word, cutting through rows of long communal tables flanked by Wardens. Some returned to their meals. A few stared a beat too long before turning away. One Warden—bald, eyes pale green—glanced once at the blades on Marek's back and went absolutely still, then hurried off in the other direction.

Marek found a seat at the far end, where the stone bench met a view of the sky beyond the arched windows. Highflare had begun outside. The Riftlight overhead had taken on a golden shimmer—like pearl washed in blood, rippling faintly in the sky that had no stars.

Cael dropped a tray in front of him—bread, roasted meat, and some kind of starch he couldn't name.

Marek didn't speak. He didn't touch it.

His stomach twisted, not with nausea, but with unease. With the weight of what he'd seen in the Armory—what he was now carrying.

Finally, Cael sat down across from him, chewing a piece of dark bread, his expression unreadable.

They ate in silence for a while. Or rather—Cael ate. Marek only stared at the food.

Then, without looking up, Cael spoke.

"You were somewhere else after you touched the swords."

It was more observation than question—but spoken in a way that demanded explanation.

Marek's eyes drifted across the table, past the edge of the bench, to the faint glint of his own reflection in the polished metal of the tray.

"I don't know what that was," he said. "A vision, maybe. A memory. Something burned into the blades."

"And?"

"I saw a war, realms splitting, chaos. Two beings killing each other—one was massive, towering, and plated in shining gold armor. The other was darkness and death, beautiful and terrifying."

That pulled Cael's gaze up. He studied Marek now—not in judgment, but in confirmation. Like he'd expected the answer and hated being right.

"Onos and Nyxia?"

Marek nodded slowly. "I don't know how I know that, but it was them. I watched them fight. I watched him kill her. I watched her... pull the blade from her own chest and drive it into his."

Cael went still, setting his fork down.

"The blades whisper to me... even now," Marek said, voice low. "They carry memories. Knowledge..."

Cael was quiet for a long moment, and then said, "They chose you."

Marek just nodded.

"I didn't just see what happened," Marek said, rubbing at his chest. "I felt it. I felt the blade in my chest when she killed him. I felt the silence after. Like the whole world was in mourning."

Cael watched him carefully now. Not skeptical. Just calculating. Evaluating.

"No one has touched those blades in thousands of years," Cael said. "Not even Akron. He won't touch them. It's why he put those wards up."

"Because of what they carry?"

"Because of what they are. What they represent," Cael answered. "They were forged to end gods and goddesses—Onos's children. And Onos poured himself into them when the Realms turned against him. What's in them now... it's more than memories. It's a piece of the Titan himself."

Marek exhaled. "I know."

Cael nodded, then pushed himself to his feet. "Come on, follow me. We've got more to do. The day is not over yet."

———◆———

The Lore Hall sat in the lowest tier of the stronghold—carved from stone so old it had worn to a shining finish. The walls were etched with murals, golden-rimmed, each one stretching high into arched vaults, their subjects painted in mineral pigment and shifting illumination. Windows lined the ceiling, illuminating the space in Riftlight.

Seven murals stretched across the chamber—one for each Realm.

Cael walked slowly now, letting the silence settle as they passed the first.

"To understand what is expected of you as a Warden, you first must understand why we were made in the first place. For that, I will tell you a tale of love and jealousy that eventually led to the Final War, millennia ago—the conclusion of which you most likely saw in your vision."

Cael continued, "Onos—Creator of the Rift, Wardens, and the Realms—first created humanity.

"At the time, the Seven Realms didn't exist. Only us—humans. We started as an experiment—a fragile, flawed, and short-lived race with freedom of thought, choice, and emotion. We were brilliant. Alive in a way nothing else was. He didn't create us to worship him, but instead made us because it pleased him. He created us to find joy in what we could become. What we could create—in turn, he received great pleasure in watching us.

"It was his grand design—an experiment to answer a question: what would a race that had complete freedom of thought and will, become over time? He watched us stumble and learn and rise again better. Stronger."

Cael glanced at the ceiling, where Riftlight flickered.

"But Earth was wild. Humanity, vulnerable in our infancy. So, he created seven stewards—his children. Immortal beings created from clay and Onos's divine power. Each was given a purpose. Each was meant to guide humanity, to help it rise without ever taking control."

Marek chuckled. "I'm guessing it didn't go as planned, huh?"

"No." Cael's voice darkened.

"They walked among us, and over time, we taught them things Onos never intended for them to learn. Not just love or sorrow—but ambition. Fear. Desire. Jealousy. They didn't turn on humanity all at once. It happened slowly, over the course of centuries. They started desiring more. More power. More control. They began to think that they should rule humanity because they were immortal, stronger, wiser."

Cael's boots echoed softly against the stone as they approached the second mural—its surface a swirl of bronze and storm blue, depicting a towering figure with a hand outstretched in protection over a kneeling human child.

"They went to Onos and demanded that he give them dominion of Earth," Cael continued. "They believed they should rule humanity, shape it, control it—because they knew better. They had walked among us, studied us, loved us, envied us. And started to find us unworthy. And in that pride, they believed themselves our rightful gods."

Marek's eyes narrowed, a memory triggered from his vision. "And Onos said no."

Cael nodded, solemn. "He said never. Earth was not a kingdom to rule. Humanity was not a people to be tamed. We were his creation, meant to be free—not theirs to possess."

"He banished them from Earth, and Onos took over the guidance of humanity himself—no longer trusting his children to shepherd what he now saw not just as creation, but as a legacy."

Cael's voice softened then, but there was iron beneath it—the kind you only heard from someone who had lost something sacred. "He gave each child a realm of their own making. A place to rule, to shape a life of their own, to reflect the ideals they believed Earth lacked. To see if they could do better. It wasn't meant to be punishment. It was mercy. A second chance."

Marek frowned, brow furrowing. "And that worked?"

"For a time," Cael said, stopping in front of the third mural. This one was riotous—chaos rendered in motion.

Seven figures, each unique, each powerful, branching away from Earth. In front of them, holes tore into existence like open wounds in the fabric of reality. Within each, a different world bloomed—a reflection of each of Onos's children.

"They became gods and goddesses to their Realms. Worshipped. But Nyxia, his firstborn, couldn't let go. Not truly." Cael continued. "She whispered amongst her siblings, using her powers to play upon their jealousy. She manipulated them to a consensus that they were the rightful rulers of humanity."

He moved on. The fourth mural was darker. Bleaker. A field of black stars and broken cities. The outline of a massive figure—Onos himself—stood at the center, twin swords lowered, head bowed. Around him were his children. Only they hadn't come as children, but as adversaries.

"Eventually, they returned," Cael said. "Not to guide. But to rule—to claim. Left on their own in their worlds, their ideals had become twisted over time. Order became tyranny. Protection became control. Desire became domination. And love turned to jealousy. They believed Earth was lost without them—and they came to correct the mistake of their exile. To prove to their father that he was wrong."

"And Onos?" Marek asked, quieter now.

Cael's jaw tightened. "He stood alone, against his children."

The fifth mural towered above them, stretching nearly to the vaulted ceiling. It showed the Final War—not as a battlefield, but as a cataclysm. Realms colliding.

Beings of impossible scale locked in combat across skies, oceans and burning cities.

He stepped back, allowing Marek a clearer view of the centerpiece of the mural—Onos, his sword planted in the chest of an achingly beautiful figure, wings of darkness stretching behind her—Nyxia. Her hand extended forward, blade plunged into Onos's chest. A perfect moment of mutual destruction, frozen in painted light.

"He ended them—and in turn was ended." Cael's said, voice dropping to a near whisper.

"That's what I saw—what I felt—in my vision," Marek murmured, rubbing at his chest again in remembered pain. The silence that followed felt heavy. Hollow.

"Most think that all Onos's children perished in that final war, but Nyxia's body was never recovered. Yet still, some believe that she dragged herself off to slumber in stasis, waiting to wake and finish what she started."

Marek stepped forward slowly, eyes tracing the detail in the artwork. The blood painted in faint streaks of Riftlight. The wound in Onos's chest. The look on Nyxia's face—a mix of hate and fury.

Marek absently rubbed at his own chest—massaging the spot where he'd felt the blade slide into his own chest in the vision.

Then Cael moved them to the final mural.

It was different. Less chaotic. Less divine.

It showed a lone warrior standing at the heart of the battlefield—Akron—bathed in golden-red light. Bent over him was Onos—wreathed in flame, his form fracturing at the seams as raw power surged from within.

The mural showed him coming apart, piece by radiant piece, until his body shattered into streams of blue-white energy that spread outward like wings, wrapping the Earth in a final, protective embrace.

"This was his final act," Cael said. "He created the Rift to act as a shield for humanity. His raw power given form and shape to act as a last barrier between the Realms."

"Before giving the last of himself to create the Rift, he created Akron, the First Warden, and within him, he placed his Essence. His power. His purpose. He left behind a vial of his own essence and a command for Akron to grow the ranks of Earth's protectors."

Marek's chest tightened as he listened to Cael's words. He couldn't look away.

"He created us to guard the Rift. He imbued Akron with power—but also without freedom. He is bound to the Oath. Onos's laws are stitched into the very fabric of who he is. It is his job—yours, mine, and every other Warden here—to protect Earth from the Realms. From what they became. From what they still want."

Marek looked at Cael now. "And the Realms?"

"They're still out there," Cael said. "Still ruled. Not by the gods—but by their firstborn. Each Realm crowned its own sovereign—a being shaped in its creator's image. They are not divine, but they are powerful, Immortal creatures infused with a portion of the power of their gods or goddesses. Each devoted to the memories of their makers."

Cael was quiet for a period of time, and then shook himself—as if coming out of a trance.

"Enough depressing shit for one day. Let's get to the fun part," he said, rubbing his hands together like it was Christmas.

He motioned for Marek to follow him as he walked back through the corridors of the Lore Hall.

Marek mumbled under his breath, something about misguided notions of fun, as he followed a reinvigorated Cael to their next adventure.

Chapter 37

As Marek followed Cael down what felt like an endless staircase of polished stone, descending toward what his mentor referred to as the Rift Chamber, he couldn't tell if the sensation of the walls closing in was just exhaustion—or if the walls were literally closing in.

Who could really tell with this place? he thought.

The deeper they went, the more the air thickened. Not with heat, not even with magic exactly—but with density. Like every breath he took came with a subtle weight.

The stone here wasn't like the rest of Arckus—these walls had no murals, no glowing runes, no torches or light. The illumination seemed to seep from the steps themselves, a faint pulse that seemed to grow in strength the further they descended.

His legs ached. His back burned. The twin blades in their crossed sheaths hadn't stopped whispering—not out loud, but within him.

He also began to feel a low and steady hum. The further they traveled, the more the hum turned into a tension, like pressure building behind his sternum, waiting to be released.

By the time the stairs finally opened into a vast, domed space carved into the base of Arckus, the hum in his chest had risen to a crescendo. He also became aware of static in the air, causing his hair to stand on end.

It become clear why he felt this way when they stepped into the Rift Chamber.

The space was circular, seamless, and alive with energy. No windows. No visible seams. The walls pulsed with branching veins of blue-white Rift energy. The floor was a series of wide, concentric rings etched into pale stone, each ring marked with script that shimmered faintly as Marek stepped closer.

At the center stood a raised platform with three steps leading to the top plateau. What looked to be mass of blue-white lightning churned in the space above it.

"This is the Rift Chamber," Cael said, stepping into the room like it didn't make his skin itch. He seemed completely unbothered. "The oldest part of Arckus still intact."

Marek moved slowly. Every breath felt heavier. Every step harder. The static electricity building.

"It feels like what Akron took me through to get here," Marek said as he motioned to the platform.

"It is, in a way," Cael said. "That was the Rift at full flow. This is a conduit—a small vein siphoned from it. Safer. Stable. Wardens train here in order to touch it without risk of drowning in it."

Marek frowned. "Why would that be a risk?"

"Because it can burn you out if you can't control it."

Cael turned, arms crossed, eyes dark.

"The Rift is Onos's last gift to the world—raw divine energy stretched between Realms. It is his pure power, given form. It will respond to the Essence in you, allow you to manipulate it with your will. However, if you allow it, your Essence will drink of the Rift energy without limits. Even full Wardens are not meant to handle that magnitude of power. I have seen several fail to gain control and then burn to ash."

Marek blinked. "Essence. As in...?"

"The divine breath of Onos that Akron gives to every Warden," Cael said. "It's what gives us our strength. Our immortality. Our speed. It is what lives inside you now."

He let the words sink in.

"So I have to learn control, before it controls me?" Marek asked.

Cael nodded. "The older you are, the more your Essence grows. That's why Akron is so powerful. He's had millennia to deepen his bond and learn control—his capacity to handle Rift energy is beyond any Warden living. But the Rift doesn't respond to strength alone. It responds to will. And that will has to be honed. Tempered."

Marek stood at the edge of the circle of rings, heart pounding.

"And you want me to step up and into... that?" he said, pointing at the churning mass of energy.

Cael gave a small shrug. "Better here, where the current is shallow, than out there in the deep end. Come on, I don't have all day."

Marek made his way slowly through the concentric rings toward the platform. The closer he got, the more... excited the energy became.

The moment Marek stepped onto the platform, the concentric rings lit up, and the Rift energy started vibrating in a different rhythm... seeming to stand up and take notice.

It pressed into him—not violently, but with curiosity. Like something sniffing at the edges of a locked door.

"Close your eyes," Cael said.

"Don't reach outward. Reach inward. Find that place inside you where your Essence lives. Draw it up and use it to reach for the energy within the Rift."

Marek did as he was told—he reached inward. Tunneled down inside himself—somewhere behind his sternum, beneath bone and blood... searching.

And when he found the Essence—everything changed.

The Rift Chamber vanished. So did his body, the floor beneath his feet, and the walls around him. All of it dissolved like dust on the wind.

He drifted—weightless and untethered—immersed in a reddish glow that pulsed gently, like a heartbeat. The Essence twined around him, coiled like warmth given shape. Welcoming. Familiar. Alive.

Then something tugged.

It came from beneath. Sharp and sudden. He resisted at first, clinging to the comforting glow. But the pull grew stronger, more insistent.

In the next breath, it yanked him down.

He plunged—deeper, farther—through himself.

Until he landed, if it could be called that, on the edge of a vast, cavernous expanse.

Before him lay a pool of absolute darkness. Its surface was still, glass-like, but beneath it... something slumbered. Something ancient. Immense. Timeless.

It didn't speak. It didn't move. It simply waited.

Waited for him to touch it, to break that surface. Waited to draw him down... down... down... into—

Marek recoiled, yanking his hand back as his breath caught in his throat. Panic—pure and primal—flared in his chest. Whatever that thing was, whatever lay beneath the surface of that pool, it wasn't just the Essence. It was something else.

It was part of him now. Or always had been.

And it terrified him.

Walls slammed up inside his mind as instinct took over. He severed the connection, climbed back from the edge of that chasm within himself, gasping—shaken and afraid of how close he'd come to falling into... whatever that was.

But with the acknowledgement that there was something within him, the Rift energy pulsed once with recognition—and then it moved.

Power surged into him in a crash of light and heat, like reaching out and grabbing hold of lightning. It was immediate. Total. A current that buckled his knees and tore a cry from his throat. His vision flared white.

The blades on his back felt like they woke up—whispers growing in volume, seeming to eagerly drink in the energy like roots—thirsty, so very thirsty.

And the Rift saw him. Saw the Essence within, and the added Essence of Jax.

And it answered.

Marek tried to pull away, but he couldn't. The power was in him now—coiled in his chest, threading through his limbs, searching for purpose.

What he could do with this power—it was exhilarating, and terrifying.

"Let go!" Cael shouted from across the platform. "You're drawing too deep—Marek, let go!"

"I'm trying!" Marek gritted out.

The power flared around him, blue-white light arcing across the platform. Symbols ignited in rings around his feet. The air bent. The room pulsed. The Rift was no longer passive. It was eager, as if sensing the potential inside him.

Marek raised his hands. Energy crackled between them—untamed, raw. A weapon without shape.

And then, without knowing how—driven by instinct and a memory not his own—he formed a shield.

A curved barrier of light and force shimmered in front of him—unstable, unfinished, but real.

He held it for a heartbeat, maybe two, before it shattered—the backlash dropping him to one knee.

Cael reached him a moment later.

"Are you alright?"

Marek nodded, barely.

"I felt... all of it. Too much."

Cael's gaze was steady now, voice low.

"That was the Rift showing you what's there—not what you can control. You pulled from the conduit, but you also reached further and tapped directly into the Rift itself. You see how vast it can be, how quickly it can get out of control."

Cael rested a hand on his shoulder. "This is why we train."

Marek's voice was rough. "I understand now."

"Good. Because if you let yourself forget, you'll burn out... and I've already invested too much time in your sorry ass to lose you now," Cael said, slapping Marek on the back.

◆

Later that night—Arkus Barracks—Marek

The door hissed shut behind him with a quiet chime.

Marek stood still in the center of the room for a long time, arms loose at his sides, breath slower now but still shallow. The twin blades rested in their crossed sheaths on his back—silent for the first time since the Armory.

His bunk sat unmade. A tray of food from earlier lay untouched. Beyond the narrow window, the sky rolled with silent colors, caught between Dimfall and Voidphase. The Riftlight painted everything in shades of cold, metallic blue.

He sat on the edge of the bed, elbows on knees, head bowed.

The ache in his body had dulled to a background hum. It was nothing compared to the noise inside his head.

What the hell was this place? What the hell was he?

A memory flickered—Kaycee's voice. The warmth of her fingers threading into his hair. Her breath against his ear in the dark. That quiet, desperate need they'd both shared the night before everything changed.

He closed his eyes. He still felt something for her—beyond the betrayal, and beyond the secrets.

Her words—when she said that what they had was real, that it had meant everything to her—he just didn't know. How could you care so deeply for someone and not tell them something that could save their life?

What they had shared that night—it had been, still was, real to him. Before he'd walked away, he'd said he needed time—to think and process everything that had happened.

The death of his teammates. Tucker's death. What happened after, between them.

Tucker. His throat tightened.

He hadn't let himself think about Tucker—not since Akron pulled him through the Rift. But now, in the silence, there was no escaping it. Tucker's last shout. How Harley had snapped his neck like he was some kind of ant, or a bug under his boot... The silence that followed.

His partner. His friend. Gone.

And now?

Now he was a weapon being forged by hands he didn't know if he could trust, in a place that didn't belong to the world he knew.

He'd always been in control.

Now he was just... falling.

◆

Earthside, New York City—Rooftop—Cael

The Rift closed behind him in a whisper of collapsing light. Cael exhaled as he stepped out onto the rooftop—an old industrial building in Brooklyn that still carried the scent of rust and rain. A familiar fallback point. Quiet. Secure.

The skyline stretched out before him—steel and glass, neon humming in the distance. Noise pulsed below.

He pulled his phone from his pocket and dialed.

One ring. Two.

Then: "About time," Kaycee's voice said, sharp but tired. "I've called twice this week."

"You know I hate tech," Cael muttered. "And I hate phones even more. There's never a moment's peace with everyone able to reach you at all times. Plus, I was ignoring you—I have a job, you know."

"You're using a phone right now, and it's your... job that I am calling about."

"Because you wouldn't stop hounding me. And since when do you take interest in my job?"

A pause. Then:

"You know since when... How is he?"

Cael leaned against the ledge, watching steam curl from a nearby vent.

"He's... exceeding expectations."

He didn't elaborate right away. Let the silence sit.

"He didn't just survive the punishment block. He kept pushing. Made it through weapons training, hand-to-hand. Then today in the Rift Chamber..."

He hesitated.

"He touched the Rift?" Kaycee asked.

Cael nodded like she could see him. "First try. No fumble. No resistance. He tapped into the main Rift too—I had to intervene. Made a shield too. It was rough but functional. No trainee has done that for me before."

Kaycee's breath hitched.

"It gets worse," he added. "The twin swords—Onos's own—chose him. You should have seen it. He burned through Akron's wards like they were nothing."

An intake of breath, and then: "You're sure?"

"I saw it happen. He moved like he didn't have a choice, and those swords... They glowed the closer he got, and once he grabbed them, they molded to him, like they'd been waiting for him."

He waited for her to speak, but she didn't. Not for several seconds.

"What is he?" he asked.

Kaycee's voice softened. "Akron called me a little while ago. He did some hunting, and it looks like everything points to Jax—yes, our Jax—being his father."

Cael inhaled sharply. "You're certain?"

"As much as anyone can be. I verified it myself after Akron told me. I found where he grew up. I stopped by his mom's house. Her name is Ellen. She's old now, bent with age, but the pictures in her house—of her when she was younger... Cael, she's the same woman Jax showed me a picture of several months before Akron killed him. Marek's a spitting image of them both. I don't know how I didn't see it sooner."

Cael frowned. "That doesn't explain the swords, Kaycee. You didn't see what I saw. They formed to fit him. The only one those swords ever did that with—and the only one who was ever able to wield them, at least from what Akron tells me—was Onos."

"What are you saying, Cael? That you think Onos has descendants out there? That he fathered someone with one of his human creations?" Kaycee asked, somewhat in disbelief.

"It's the only thing that makes any sense. Maybe it was a contingency of some sort, or maybe it was love—whatever it was, we have no idea what Marek is capable of," Cael said.

"Did you tell Akron about the swords?" Kaycee asked.

"What do you think? Of course, I fucking told him about the swords," Cael growled into the phone. "The whole of Arckus is in a frenzy because of it. The Warden Council is scared shitless about what this means... I had to tell Akron before he found out from someone who's not directly assigned to his every waking minute."

"If Marek's what you think he is, he could be the key to everything," Kaycee said.

Cael didn't answer for a long time. The wind shifted. Somewhere far below, a siren wailed.

"Or he could be the thing that breaks it all," he whispered... the line already having gone dead.

Chapter 38

Over the next two weeks, the days blurred together. Not because they were forgettable—but because they were the same.

Relentless. Repetitive. Bleeding into one another until time itself felt like just another opponent to be beaten down.

Every morning began with the annoying fucking pull of First Riftlight.

Marek woke in darkness. Always darkness. He pulled on his armor, joints stiff and aching, the inside of his armor still damp some mornings from the sweat of the day before. In the mess hall, he always found Cael waiting.

Breakfast wasn't a meal. It was maintenance. Some kind of protein, simple vegetables and starches, black tea that tasted equally plain. No one spoke to him anymore. No one lingered.

He was fine with that—he had no energy to spare for them.

Then came the conditioning. God, he hated Cael and his damn conditioning.

The stone circuits of Arckus cut paths through the cliffs like veins—and Marek ran them until he couldn't feel his legs. Pushups until his arms shook under his own weight. Plank holds until the wind sliced through him like knives and the stone ground itself into his palms.

Cael didn't shout for motivation. He barked to correct. Every movement, every posture, every ounce of effort was refined under merciless eyes. There were no encouragements. No "*good jobs.*" Only—"*Again. Again. Again.*"

Like a beat to a drum—or at least, Cael's demented version of one. He had never hated a single word so much.

Marek's body adapted faster than he thought possible—his muscles thickening, his reflexes sharpening. His lungs grew stronger, and his body and mind hardening under Cael's instruction.

Under his merciless training, he became faster. Stronger. Deadlier. But the fatigue never left. It simply sank deeper, embedding itself into his marrow until it became part of him.

Then came hand-to-hand. Forget the fancy sparring you see in kung fu movies. This was down and dirty, fight-for-your-life, learning to kill and maim with hands and feet. Like MMA—only with killing in mind.

No gloves. No mats. No holds barred.

The sparring rings were stone, scarred with blood that had long since dried into the cracks. Cael taught with brutality and precision—forcing Marek to fight without mercy, without hesitation, without pride.

Speed wouldn't save him. Strength wouldn't either. Only focus. Only control. Only the ability to read the flicker of intent in a shifting shoulder, the tightening of a jaw, the twist of hips.

Every punch Marek threw was broken down and rebuilt. Every slip of attention punished with a strike that left him gasping on the ground.

And when he let the rage get the best of him? Cael flattened him. Without fail. Every. Single. Time.

Then it was weapons.

His twin blades rode his back like heavy weights. Some days they were silent. Others, they whispered. Over the course of the next couple of weeks, he came to a realization—they were teaching him. They were embedding knowledge he'd never had before.

Moves, muscle memory, tactics—things he had yet to learn from Cael—showed up regularly throughout his training.

He trained with them too, under Cael's watchful eye.

Drills. Reactive strikes. Martial forms that burned his muscles raw. Fighting constructs made of Rift energy, used specifically for training. Smarter, faster, meaner than anything he'd faced before.

He learned to wield his blades like an extension of his own body. The martial forms combining in a seamless flow from one strike to the next. Simplistic and brutal movements designed to kill as quickly as possible.

His skill in combat grew exponentially—both from the strange whispers of his blades and Cael's relentless drills.

Lunch came next—if it could be called that.

A slab of protein. A handful of greens. Water. He ate because he had to, not because he wanted to. The hunger he carried wasn't for food anymore. It was for vengeance.

And Marek's vengeance had a target. *Harley. Dharken Mohr*, or whatever the hell he was called.

Just the thought of him—or any other creature—caused Marek's blood to boil and a haze of anger to cloud his thoughts and judgment.

His afternoons belonged to the Lore Hall.

The great chamber lay buried deep under Arckus, walls carved in an era before most Wardens had memories. There, veteran Wardens assigned to different areas of Earth's protection rotated through—teaching him more of Warden history, of the Seven Realms.

He learned that the Realms didn't just ignore Earth—they hated and despised it. Humanity was the reason Onos killed their gods and goddesses, casting their realms into chaos. Humanity was weak and unnecessary. To be ruled—or destroyed—by the more powerful.

They despised even more, the Wardens who dared to defend them.

He learned about the possible armies being bred in secret. Until the day came that the Realms could act on their need to subjugate or kill humanity.

He learned how the old alliances had rotted after the Final War—and how new ones had festered in the dark, whispering promises of rebellion, possibly even inside the Warden Order itself. Cael had his suspicions but stayed silent on the matter.

And every night—every brutal, bone-deep exhausting night—ended in the Rift Chamber, manipulating Rift energy.

Marek stood alone on the circular platform, ringed by ancient glyphs that hummed beneath the stone.

Each night he reached for it.

He became more tuned to the energy the more he reached—like a muscle adapting to use.

It soon became something he sensed automatically. Almost like a third limb. He became better at wielding it into weapons or raw power blasts, at crafting veils so humanity would ignore both his presence and the monsters he'd eventually fight.

Rift travel was slower going. Something about it made his brain rebel against using it that way.

Cael said that it was the hardest part about being a Warden. In order to travel the Rift, you had to envision what you wanted with your will—just like everything else involving Rift energy manipulation.

"It takes time," Cael had said after one particularly frustrating evening of trying—and failing.

And throughout his training, he was always aware of the presence deep within his being.

The well. Not something he had built. Something that had shown up within him—something he may have always had inside—that had been activated after becoming a Warden.

Vast. Bottomless. Alive. Terrifying.

It stirred when he reached too deep. It whispered when he pushed too hard. And though Marek barely understood it, Cael saw it—saw the thing growing inside him—and in those moments when Cael thought Marek wasn't looking, he caught it in his eyes:

Suspicion. Fear.

And maybe—just maybe—hope.

Chapter 39

The training blade cracked against Marek's hard enough to numb his fingers, but he barely flinched. He shifted his grip, twisting out of Cael's next strike and driving forward with a short, brutal shoulder-check that would've flattened a normal opponent.

Cael absorbed the hit like a stone wall, grunted once, and shoved him back with the flat of the blade.

"Better," Cael said, circling him across the rune-etched floor. "Still leading with your anger, though. It clouds your judgment."

Marek grunted in acknowledgment. Sweat dripped down his spine, cold despite the feverish heat rising off his skin. His swords felt heavier than usual, dragging at his back like anchors.

He shook it off, resetting his stance.

Cael feinted left, then lunged—and Marek was already moving, faster than thought, blades intercepting the strike with a jarring clang.

And that's when it hit him. The pulse.

A tear across his senses, like something inside the world itself had ripped open. The Rift shuddered somewhere nearby—something coming through that wasn't welcome—and Marek felt it the way a nerve feels the prick of a blade.

The breath froze in his chest.

His vision narrowed, tunneling toward the pull tugging at him, demanding him.

"Marek?" Cael called sharply.

But he was already moving. Without thinking, without speaking, Marek turned toward the pressure in his chest—toward the unseen thread binding him to whatever had torn through.

He crossed the training ring in three long strides, heat rising off his skin, sparks of Rift energy crackling faintly in the air around him.

The world folded sideways with a soundless crack. Space bent—energy wrapping around him—and Marek stepped through the Rift.

◆

SCU Team—Breach Site—Earth

The rain had picked up, a cold, relentless drizzle that turned the cracked asphalt lot into a field of dark mirrors. Somewhere in the distance, a subway rumbled past—an underground beast too far away to notice the things slipping into the world above.

Kaycee tightened her grip on the carbine slung across her chest as she approached the main warehouse. The building sagged under the weight of time and neglect, its corrugated steel walls streaked with rust. One loading dock door hung askew, creaking as the wind teased it back and forth.

This was the breach site.

Harper moved along the eastern flank, sweeping her scanner low across the ground, the soft hum of the device barely audible over the rain. Chen was in the van with Eliza, their new comms and computer genius—their replacement for Marcus.

Chen was on light duty—still healing from her last operation—and she was chafing badly under the restrictions.

And then there was Wilkinson.

Bruce "Wilko" Wilkinson moved like he had a death wish, jogging up behind Harper with an easy swagger and a crooked grin. His black tactical jacket was open at the collar, and he wore no helmet—just messy dark hair plastered to his forehead by the rain. His twin sidearms were holstered low at his hips, swinging with each bouncing step.

"Perimeter's tighter than my ex's alimony lawyer," Wilko said cheerfully over the comms. "No bogeys, no fangy bastards. Looks like a quiet night on the town."

Chen's voice crackled over the comms. "Stay sharp, Wilko. Save the stand-up routine for if we get out of this alive."

Wilko gave a mock salute and swung his rifle up to a ready grip, still grinning. "Yes ma'am."

Kaycee suppressed a sigh. She hadn't wanted a replacement for Malik or Marcus so soon—especially not someone like Wilkinson, although Eliza was turning out to be a godsend—but orders were orders. SCU needed boots on the ground.

At least Wilko could fight. She'd seen the training records: top percentile in marksmanship, breach tactics, close-quarters fighting. Highest risk tolerance on record too—which meant he was exactly the kind of liability they couldn't afford.

Or exactly the kind they were going to need. Only time would tell.

She clicked her comm once—silent signal—and motioned the team forward.

Wilko bounded ahead like an overeager retriever, rifle swinging. Harper rolled her eyes and fell in behind him.

Kaycee took point herself.

The loading dock door groaned as she shoved it open the last few inches, clearing a space just wide enough for them to slip through. Inside, the warehouse was a cavern of rusted machinery and long-dead conveyor belts. The roof had long since fell into disrepair—giant sections open to the rain outside. The air was thick with the smell of mold, oil, and something else—something metallic and wrong.

Her boots crunched glass as she moved in, scanning.

The Rift signature was faint, but it was here. She could feel it—a pressure against her skin, a low hum beneath her bones. Like standing too close to a speaker no one else could hear.

She raised a fist—halt signal—and the team froze in place.

The breach appeared near the center of the warehouse, still a fair distance from their current position. It was a shimmering distortion in the air, like heat off asphalt, barely visible to the naked eye.

As they moved closer, it pulsed once.

Then, something peeled free.

It was another Drakyn. She knew the Realm where Drakyns came from—the Realm of Shadow and Thought. What was Dharken Mohr up to? Why was he sending his shock troops in like this, jumping all over the city, trying to breach in different locations?

He always played the long game, and that is what scared her. Whatever this was, and whatever he was planning, she was sure they wouldn't be ready for it.

She brought her rifle up, lining her sights—Harper shifted to flank—Wilko muttered something sharp under his breath as they moved in toward the Drakyn.

Then, the shadows moved, and Marek stepped out of the gloom behind the breach.

One moment there was nothing. The next, he was simply there.

Kaycee froze. Her breath caught, heart racing—equal parts dread and excitement warring for space inside her.

Marek stood in the rain falling through the dilapidated roof, black Warden armor clinging to him like a second skin. Water streaming from his hair, down his face, dripping from the edges of his jaw.

The twin swords were strapped across his back—but his hands hung loose at his sides, fingers twitching with anticipation.

For a heartbeat, no one moved.

Then the Drakyn roared and charged. Marek didn't flinch. He just smiled—and stepped forward to meet it.

Later, he wouldn't remember the details—only flashes, the way time warped around him. The creature's movements seemed predictable, almost slow, like the world itself was caught in molasses—his own body moving with terrifying speed and clarity.

Two strides, and he was on it.

He slipped beneath its first swipe, pivoted, and drove his fist into its gut. The Drakyn flew backward, claws scraping gouges in the pavement as it skidded across the concrete.

Marek felt the hit all the way up his spine—bone meeting bone, sinew tearing beneath his blow—and something inside him uncoiled.

Rage—cold, bottomless, and sharpened to a razor's edge.

It wasn't enough.

The Drakyn shrieked in pain and scrambled upright but it was too slow.

Marek surged forward, caught its swinging limb in both hands, and twisted. The joint snapped and blood sprayed from the ragged socket as the arm bent the wrong way.

Still not enough.

He shattered its knee with a single, brutal kick. The creature howled—then choked as Marek drove his own knee into its face, hard enough to crush cartilage and snap fangs.

The Drakyn collapsed in a twitching, broken heap.

◆

Kaycee watched in stunned silence as Marek tore through the creature.

He was faster. Stronger. More brutal than she'd ever seen.

Gone was the man who had hesitated the first time he faced one of these things. Gone was the detective who relied on instinct and adrenaline alone.

What stood before her now was something else entirely.

There was a precision to him—a cold, efficient violence that was almost clinical. Beneath it, though, Kaycee could feel the rage—the same rage that had nearly consumed him after the team fell. It radiated from him now in every brutal strike, every unrelenting step forward.

And Onos help her, he was beautiful in that moment. Terrible and beautiful.

Her heart twisted painfully in her chest. *What have we made him into?* She thought.

◆

Marek spun as the Rift pulsed again. A second Drakyn pushed through—this one larger and faster than the first.

And Marek's had snapped out before the creature finished stepping through. He caught it by the throat, fingers digging into scales and tissue.

Lifting it bodily off the ground with a growl of rage, he threw it into a steel support beam.

It impacted with the force of a car crash. Bone splintered. Metal groaned. The creature screamed in pain, shaking its head, trying to orient itself. It had only just risen to its feet, when Marek was on it again.

His fists came in like sledgehammers—left cross, right hook, another cross—each blow thundering through the narrow space with sickening, meaty cracks, spraying black blood and jagged bits of bone across the pavement.

He didn't stop, hammering another blow, and then another. Venting his rage on the creature that had dared cross over into his world.

The beam behind it dented, bent more under the force of every hit. The creature's jaw hung slack, teeth missing, one eye crushed, its spine exposed through torn muscle—the beam grinding against its back with every punch.

Then came Marek's kick—full force—straight to its chest.

The Drakyn folded, ribs snapping audibly as it was slammed back into the beam again like a rag doll.

And Marek still wasn't done.

He drew both swords with one smooth, predatory motion, and drove them straight through the creature's ribcage. He twisted hard and pulled sideways. The blades shredded sinew, snapped bone, and burst through either side, insides spilling out in a wet cascade.

The Drakyn spasmed violently, and dropped to the ground, lifeless, but the first one was still alive—still crawling.

It dragged itself toward the Rift, broken and leaking thick trails of dark blood, limbs trembling.

Marek stalked after it. No mercy. No pause. Only the red haze of his rage.

He planted a boot between its shoulders, slamming it flat. The creature shrieked feebly as he sheathed one of his blades.

With one hand, he reached down, grabbed it, and yanked its head back hard.

His other sword met flesh, and with one clean, final slice—fast and precise—its head came free, and Marek tossed it into the dark. Red, sightless eyes locked in a silent stare.

The Rift pulsed once. Shivered. Then collapsed with a quiet sigh, like it, too, had nothing left to give.

Marek rose slowly.

Rain and blood ran down his face, traveling in rivulets down his armor, dripping from his hair. His eyes shone in the fading light.

The others just stared. No one moved. No one spoke.

Even Wilko—mid-joke before the second creature appeared—stood frozen, mouth slightly open.

Then he finally exhaled a low, shaky whistle. "Jesus," he muttered. "Guy fights like he's possessed."

There was a brittle edge to his voice. Fear, mixed with admiration.

"Brutal. Remind me not to get on his bad side," he muttered. "Guy is like a goddamn wrecking ball."

No one disagreed, because the truth of it hung heavy in the air, undeniable.

Marek Tomlinson wasn't human anymore.

Across the broken space, Kaycee stared at him. Her breath caught in her throat.

This wasn't the man she had recruited. Wasn't the man she had fought beside in the tunnels or the alleys. Definitely not the man she had made love to.

This was something else—something burning brighter, hotter—and it scared the hell out of her, because for the first time, she realized:

If Marek lost control... no one here—not her, not SCU, possibly not even the Wardens—would be able to stop him.

For a long moment, Marek and Kaycee stared at each other through the rain.

Neither spoke, as Marek's chest rose and fell in quiet, controlled breaths. His fingers flexed once around the hilts of the twin blades, still slick with black ichor.

With a flick of his wrists, he cast the blood aside—and sheathed them.

There was something in his gaze now—something colder, harder. Something that hadn't been there before.

A part of him was still grieving. A part of him was still human.

But something different had been born. Whether it was because of all he had suffered, or because of his training with Cael—all she knew was that whatever was looking back at her now was cold, calculating, and filled with rage.

Kaycee opened her mouth—an instinct, a need to say something, to tell him that Tucker was in a coma, not dead, that she... what? Loved him? Was sorry? Too many things to say in too short of a window—

And then, before she could say anything, he turned and walked into the rain, boots crunching softly over broken glass and concrete, his silhouette fading into the deepening night.

Harper's voice crackled through the comms, slicing through the heavy silence. "Gordon, we got a civvy. Kid with a phone at the fence line."

She closed her eyes briefly, dragging in a steadying breath. She holstered her weapon.

"Handle it," she said.

Harper was already moving—graceful and efficient as ever. She caught the teenager before he could bolt, plucking the phone from his hands, removing the SIM card, and crushing it underfoot.

She gave him a grand and told him to go buy himself a new phone. The kid ran off. Even if he spoke about what happened, no one would believe him.

"Phone's wiped," Harper reported. "Civilian's rattled, but no real harm."

"Good work," Kaycee said automatically, but her mind wasn't on the kid.

It was still watching the man who wasn't quite a man anymore walk away from her—again—without looking back.

The Rift was weakening. The Realms were stirring. The Warden Council was getting bolder and gaining support.

And Marek—Marek was changing faster than any of them were ready for.

If she didn't find a way to reach him soon, she knew with a painful certainty—she was going to lose him.

Not to death. But to the fire and rage that were consuming him.

Chapter 40

The rain enveloped him. It was drowning the world in sheets—a cold, endless drumbeat against the forest of concrete and metal of the surrounding buildings.

Marek barely felt it—the water running down his armor in rivulets, his hair plastered to his skull—But he kept walking, boots crunching over glass and ruin, away from the warehouse, away from the stunned faces of the SCU team.

Away from Kaycee.

He didn't look back. He couldn't.

There was too much he hadn't forgiven—too much blame. Both of himself and of her. Maybe it was harsh of him, especially as he was starting to become aware of just how binding direct orders were from Akron, especially when sworn by the power of one's Essence.

He knew if he said anything now, in his mental state, he'd open the divide further. He didn't want that.

The heat still coiled under his skin, a living thing, even as the rain tried to wash it away. His muscles ached—not from exhaustion, but from the raw force still raging inside. The same force that had driven him to brutalize those two Drakyn.

It should have been satisfying—the way he'd punished them. It should have felt like victory, but it didn't.

It didn't change anything. It didn't bring back Tucker, Malik or Marcus.

It didn't fix things with Kaycee or give him his life back—the ordered life where things made sense and facts led to convictions and jail time.

Marek stopped near the center of the street, the ruined warehouse looming behind him, streetlights buzzing and spitting overhead. His chest rose and fell in slow, ragged breaths.

He lifted his hands. They trembled slightly—a physical manifestation of the battle raging just beneath the surface.

Of the pressure—heavy, suffocating—pressing just beneath his flesh. He felt like a container that was too full.

The rage was still there. The power was still there—it was growing harder to contain.

Marek curled his fingers into fists, forcing the tremor down. Forcing the power back into the pit of himself where it belonged. His emotions—this rage—was a different animal. It fought his attempts at suppression, but he eventually pushed it down and locked it away within himself.

He gritted his teeth. He could still feel it there, ready. Waiting. Waiting for the moment he lost his grip.

And if that happened—

He didn't know what he'd unleash. Who he'd become.

A faint ripple disturbed the rain.

Not sound. Not sight. But a feeling of familiarity that followed a presence.

Marek tensed automatically, muscles coiling, fingers twitching toward his swords. He didn't turn. Not yet. He already knew who it was.

"Cael," he grunted.

"Ah, good. You are starting to feel us, the movements in the Rift—our signatures," Cael said behind him, voice low, steady.

Marek said nothing, because there was nothing to say.

Cael stepped forward, boots splashing through the shallow water, until he stood a few feet away. The older Warden regarded him with a look that was part appraisal, part wariness.

"You moved through the Rift instinctively," Cael said. "Found the breach. Without training."

Still Marek stayed silent, jaw tight, eyes locked on the glistening street ahead.

"You think that ability makes you invincible? That your power does?" Cael continued, voice like a hammer on cold steel. "It doesn't. It makes you dangerous. To others. To yourself."

Marek turned his head slightly, rain dripping from the edge of his jaw. His voice, when it came, was raw.

"I took care of things, didn't I? The Drakyn didn't stand a chance," he said, his anger and rage seeping into his voice.

"You did," Cael agreed. "But what would have happened if you were outmanned? If there were swarms of Drakyn, or something more powerful—like an Elvahr? Let me ruin the suspense—you'd have been killed. And quickly."

Cael gave him a measured stare. "You're still in training. Still learning the use of your power. You are volatile too—each emotion magnified by the need to protect Earth, the need to administer justice. The Essence of Onos heightens all emotions, creates a storm inside that you need to learn to control."

The silence between them was a living thing.

Marek swallowed hard, fists trembling. "I can feel it," he said, almost whispering. "Growing. Every time I fight. Every time I get close to the Rift. It's... changing me."

Cael's expression didn't soften. If anything, it sharpened. "And if you let it change you without understanding it—without mastering it—you'll burn yourself down. And everyone around you."

Marek's fingers flexed again. He hated how true the words felt. How much they echoed the fear gnawing at the edges of his mind.

"What do you want me to do?" he rasped.

Cael stepped closer, until his shadow merged with Marek's. "What everyone who suffers trauma must do. We Wardens are no different. It's your choice in the end, but you need to work out your shit... face it."

Marek shook his head once, water spraying from his hair. "Face what? There's nothing left. I already—"

"You're still fighting ghosts," Cael cut in, voice harsh. "You're still blaming yourself and others for things you couldn't control. You think if you had known of Dharken Mohr—Harley—the outcome could have been different? It wouldn't have—no one but Akron can fight him and win. Even then, it would be a struggle. You are filling yourself with rage, with pain, with anger. You think rage is strength. You think pain justifies your feelings of anger and therefore the acts of brutality. But all you're doing is letting it rot you from the inside out."

He reached out then, slow and deliberate, placing a hand against Marek's shoulder.

"You have to face it," Cael said again. "Before it swallows you or tears you apart. Trust me, as someone who has been where you are."

Marek stood there, frozen, the rain soaking through him, the fire coiling tighter in his chest.

And then—before he could second-guess it, before the anger and rage could get loose and harden him further—he nodded once.

A sharp, broken gesture.

Cael's hand tightened briefly on his shoulder. "Good, Marek. Good. Follow me to Arckus, to the Reflection Hall. There is something you must do," he said simply.

Without another word, Cael turned and stepped into the blue-white envelope of the Rift.

Marek followed and arrived shortly after. They were just outside the walls of Arckus, traveling again by the energy of the Rift. What once had felt disorienting and impossible now felt right.

What he once struggled to wrap his mind around and believe, he accepted just like he did gravity—or that the sun was hot.

It was as if his instinctual travel earlier had provided a key he hadn't had before. One more piece clicking into place in the new life he was building. A life he was still struggling to accept in many ways.

Marek barely registered the beauty that had once taken his breath away as Arckus loomed up ahead.

Not the massive yet beautiful spirals inscribed with curling language. Not the glowing arcs of Riftlight pulsing under his feet, nor the walkways suspended by energy—connecting the towering spires and winding towers to each other.

His mind was on other things... darker thoughts of rage, anger, and guilt. Of loss, and pain. He moved through Arckus like a ghost tethered to a stronger will—following Cael across the soaked darkness without thinking, his mind folding deeper and deeper inward.

The energy under his skin continued to simmer. Restless, coiling tighter with every step he took away from the carnage he'd left behind. A living, breathing thing that was no longer content to sleep quietly inside him. It waited, patient and hungry, knowing it would be called on again.

Marek hated the feeling. He hated even more that he was starting to crave it—the rush that came with it.

The need he felt terrified him. He'd always been stable, measured, a proponent of justice and law. The way he punished the creatures today, the way he'd taken his time to measure out pain and suffering—part of him thrilled at the feeling. At the power.

But the human part of him—the man his mom would be proud of, and the one who Kaycee believed in—was sick to his stomach.

Cael was right. Something needed to change before he lost any more of himself.

The great gates groaned open at Cael's approach, ancient metal grinding in stone, as they walked through.

But Cael didn't lead him toward the barracks, or the training fields, or the safety of the upper halls.

He led him down. Into the bones of Arckus. Into places few Wardens ever went willingly.

The air grew colder the deeper they went, the chill biting through the wet armor he still wore. The torchlight here was thin and guttering, throwing long, shifting shadows across walls that had been carved when the world was still young. Strange runes, worn down to whispers by centuries of weather and touch, twisted across the stone.

At the end of a final, narrow corridor, Cael stopped before a set of seamless black doors. They looked less like doors and more like slabs of darkness hammered into the walls.

Cael placed his hand against the surface. No gears shifted. No locks clicked. The doors simply dissolved, melting away like mist burned off by the sun.

Beyond them, waiting in the gloom, stood the Mirror.

The Reflection Hall—more of a large room than a hall—was not grand. There were no thrones. No carved banners of old victories, or images of conquest etched into the stones.

It was a simple chamber: rough stone walls, a ring of sparse torchlight guttering against the damp cold, and at the center—silent, eternal—the Mirror of Fane.

It towered above Marek, framed in tarnished silver that drank the light. The surface of the glass was so still, so perfect, it didn't just reflect the chamber—it duplicated it, every torchlight flicker and shadow cast back with impossible clarity. It was like staring into another world that mimicked this one too precisely, too completely.

Marek stepped forward without prompting.

Behind him, the doors reformed, sealing them in with a soft, final hush that seemed to echo inside his bones.

Cael stayed at the edge of the torchlight, arms crossed loosely over his chest, his expression unreadable.

Marek didn't look at him, though; his eyes were locked on the Mirror.

"This isn't a test," Cael said, his voice barely more than a murmur swallowed by the silence permeating the space. "It's a choice—your choice."

Marek stood frozen, rainwater pooling at his boots, the cold of the hall sinking deeper into him than the storm ever had. His breath came slow and shallow, visible in the thin light.

"Onos built this," Cael continued. "Before the Realms rebelled. Before Akron was created and the first Wardens took up their Oaths."

Marek swallowed hard, throat dry as bone.

"Some say he made it to better himself—to judge himself," Cael said, voice softer now. "Others say it was meant for us—that he knew we'd be needed even before his fall. So that those who would carry his Essence would first carry the truth of what they are."

The Mirror pulsed faintly—or maybe it was his heart stumbling against his ribs.

"Whatever the reason, it is here to use—look if you choose," Cael said simply, "or walk away. Either way, the Essence within you will help decide what happens next."

Marek closed his eyes.

Images rushed up to meet him in the dark.

Kaycee's scream of frustration as she tried desperately to free herself of the Drakyns to get to them. Tucker's body crumpled on the ground, neck twisted at an angle no living thing could survive. Marcus and Malik falling in rapid, brutal succession while Harley's laughter echoed through the broken alleys.

The girl in the alley. The one Marek had tried to save when he was still just a boy.

Her throat torn open. Her lifeless body tossed at his feet like garbage.

The feel of his fists clenched uselessly at his sides. The sickening weight of knowing he had been too slow. Too weak. Too human.

And through it all—the memory of Harley's voice, cruel and almost pitying:

"*You can't seem to save anyone, can you, little hero?*"

It had been a question, but it felt like a statement. An inevitability.

A sentence handed down by a reality Marek had never been strong enough to defy.

When he opened his eyes, Marek stepped forward, and the Mirror swallowed him whole.

There was no transition.

One moment, he was standing in the Reflection Hall. The next—he was back in the Bowery District.

The cracked windows gaped like broken teeth. The streets smelled of trash and blood. The rain fell harder here, thick and oily against his skin, the weight of his memories soaking through him like a second layer of guilt.

Marek knew it wasn't real, but the Mirror didn't show dreams. It showed truths, Cael had said.

In this case, truths about what happened—like reliving the past with a different perspective.

He turned—and the scene replayed itself around him in merciless detail.

Tucker standing alone, gun raised, shouting something Marek couldn't hear over the roar in his own head.

No warning. Only Harley—a blur of speed, a flash of movement too fast for human eyes.

One sharp twist. A sickening crack. Tucker, dropping without a sound, his body folding in on itself like a marionette with its strings cut—sightless eyes staring past Marek at something he would never see again.

Marek stumbled forward, reaching... but the ground seemed to twist beneath his feet, dragging him deeper into the nightmare.

Now it was Malik—firing desperately, then shedding his weapon when it had no effect. Driving in with his knife—

Then Harley, snapping his arm—his knife ripping up through Malik with the ease of shredding paper.

Then Marcus, charging forward with a roar of grief, only to have his throat torn out, dying just as easily.

Their bodies hit the ground before Marek could even blink.

Too fast. Too brutal. They didn't stand a chance.

Marek watched himself get beaten to death in the reflection. Kaycee's screams of frustration as she tried to get to him.

Harley—smiling the whole time. Mocking. Triumphant.

"You were never going to save them," the Mirror whispered, shaping Harley's voice. "You were never enough."

Marek staggered back. The world blurred again. He was younger now. Seventeen. Standing in an alley—smaller, dirtier, more forgotten.

No Rift breach here. No Drakyn. Only a girl, her throat a ragged ruin, and her eyes wide and empty.

Harley's darkness wrapping around him, holding him in place—planting thoughts of terror and failure.

He hadn't had a chance back then, not against a being like Harley, and not as a human.

"You couldn't save me either," the voice said, soft and sad, coming from nowhere and everywhere at once.

It was the girl's voice, but not. It was the Mirror, peeling back every wall he had ever built to survive.

It didn't lie. It didn't embellish. It just stripped away the illusions he had wrapped around himself to keep breathing. It had been easier to think himself a failure than to acknowledge there wasn't hope to begin with.

Another memory crashed over him.

Kaycee's voice—sharp, telling him she had been following orders, that her secrets weren't hers to share. Binding orders that she couldn't break.

The rage inside him was at her too. At her caution. At her duty to keep secrets, and to abide by protocols that had led to the deaths of his best friend.

The Mirror showed him all of it. The guilt, the rage, the betrayal, and the hollow places where his faith used to live.

How truly outmatched and helpless he had been—they all had been—against Harley. How bound by duty and orders Kaycee had been.

When the Mirror finally released him, Marek collapsed onto his hands and knees, gasping, the stone floor cold and slick beneath him.

The torches in the Reflection Hall guttered against the returning silence.

He stayed there for a long time, trembling.

He could still hear their voices. Tucker's quiet jokes and Malik's dry humor. Marcus's cool confidence under pressure, and the girl's screams in the alley.

All gone, because he hadn't been enough. Hadn't been strong enough or fast enough—would never have been as a human.

A hand touched his shoulder—not harsh, not demanding—only a steadying presence.

Marek flinched at the contact, instincts coiled, but he didn't pull away.

Cael crouched beside him, silent. Waiting.

Marek forced himself to lift his head, to look back at the Mirror, at his reflection standing there.

Cracked in spots. Splintered down the center like a sword hammered too long against an unyielding anvil.

But not shattered. Somehow—despite everything—it still stood.

When Marek finally spoke, his voice was ragged but steady. "I wasn't ready... Kaycee didn't have a choice..."

It wasn't an excuse, and it wasn't even an apology. It was just truth.

Cael nodded once, no judgment in his gaze.

"No one ever is," he said. "The human you were, stood no chance against Harley. Nothing could have prepared you for that. And orders from Akron, sworn by our Essence, are binding to us—we cannot choose to violate them."

"That is why Wardens fight for humanity. Because we *can* do something against the monsters," Cael snarled. "Because we *are* strong enough to stand when all others fall."

He rose, offering his hand.

Marek hesitated, and then he took it.

And the rage inside him—still wild, still dangerous—settled, just slightly.

As they left the Reflection Hall behind, Marek didn't look back.

He didn't need to. He would carry the Mirror's truth with him now.

Every step. Every breath. Every battle.

He would never *not* be enough again. He would do everything he could to be enough for other innocents.

He would keep his rage and emotions in check for their sake.

And Kaycee—it was no more her fault than it was his... she was as powerless in the end to warn them as he was to protect them as a human.

Chapter 41

The SCU Ops Center pulsed with low, restless energy. The heavy storm outside pressed against the glass walls, blurring New York's skyline into a smear of bleeding neon, rain carving rivers down the reinforced panels until the world beyond looked half-drowned, half-forgotten.

Kaycee sat alone at the central briefing table, her fingertips resting lightly on the spread of breach reports scattered across the polished surface.

Three Rift surges in thirty-six hours. Two partial breaches. One full manifestation—neutralized not by her team, but by Marek's intervention.

He hadn't waited for orders. Hadn't even warned them he was coming. Just stepped out of the shadows and tore the threat apart before anyone else had managed a shot.

The air pulsed behind her, the energy of the Rift pressing against her skin in equal part warning and welcome.

Kaycee didn't turn. She knew who it was.

Malen.

He stood behind her in a fitted black overcoat, tailored like a knife's sheath. Silver cufflinks. No armor. No weapons. Just the triangular insignia of the Warden Council gleaming against his lapel like a challenge.

"I thought the Council was above unannounced visits," she said flatly.

Malen smiled—thin, polite, and without warmth. "I'm not here on official business."

She gestured to the breach map. "Then you'll forgive me if I get back to my actual work."

He ignored the jab and stepped forward, palms lightly braced against the table. "I came to talk. Not to threaten. Not to lecture. Just... talk."

She didn't reply.

"You've been wasting yourself here," he continued, voice silk over steel. "This crusade—protecting humans, fighting their battles—it's beneath you. We could use someone like you on the Council. We need someone like you."

She barked a laugh. "You came all this way to offer me a seat on a council that flirts with traitorous ideals but has no real authority?"

Malen didn't flinch. "You think we're traitors because we no longer blindly worship a dead Titan's commandments? Because we've come to understand that humanity is a liability—that they are no longer worthy of our sacrifice?"

Kaycee stood, slow and deliberate. "My loyalty is to my Oath. To Akron. To the balance. To what's right.

"And humanity—flawed, messy, stubborn as they are—still deserve protection. You of all people should remember what the Realms do when left unchecked."

"I remember too well," Malen said, tone clipped. "I also remember how many Wardens we've lost in the name of shielding a species that tries, at every opportunity, to destroy itself."

Her jaw clenched.

He softened slightly. "Kaycee... you don't have to keep bleeding for a world that will never bleed for you."

She stepped around the table, slowly closing the distance between them until they stood face to face.

"If you think I'm going to abandon my post because of some empty seat at your puppet council, you've forgotten who I am."

Malen's expression cooled.

"It's not empty," he said. "We've filled two more chairs this year. There are now seven of us, with support from many Wardens. The tide is turning. Akron is losing ground. You're still young—you could be on the winning side when it happens."

"What you're saying borders on treason... does your Warden Council know you have these feelings and are communicating them to other Wardens? Something tells me they aren't as anti-humanity... anti-duty... as you are," Kaycee said, with a smirk.

Malen shifted uncomfortably on his feet, bristled, and started to speak—when Kaycee cut him off.

"Get out, before I throw you out," she said.

He flushed deeply. "You'll regret this."

She smiled a predatory smile. "If you can ever gain enough power to overthrow Akron—maybe then I'll regret this. Until then, if you ever come into my territory again uninvited, spewing these traitorous ideals, you won't have to worry about Akron—I will be the one to end you."

He was gone in the next instant—traveling the Rift as fast as he could from her sight.

◆

The medical wing was quiet. Too quiet.

Harper stood at the doorway to Tucker's room, her arms crossed, the chill of the sterile room sinking into her skin through the sleeves of her jacket.

Tucker lay motionless beneath the thin hospital blanket, his skin almost translucent under the low, flickering lights.

The monitors hummed their indifferent lullaby, green lines tracing the slow, steady rhythms of vital signs.

Normal. Ordinary. At a glance, nothing had changed.

But Harper watched the screens with the careful patience of a predator. Every few minutes—so faint it barely registered—a pulse shimmered across the auxiliary sensors. Not a heart rate. Not O₂ levels.

Something else. A golden flicker that ghosted across her monitors like a heartbeat trying to sync with a frequency the human body was never meant to carry.

Harper's hand tightened around the datapad she held, the soft plastic creaking under her grip.

She had triple-checked the readings and run them through backups.

This wasn't a mistake.

Tucker's body was resonating with an energy profile similar to what had shot through Marek during his transformation—that flare of gold-white power. The resonance was faint, but it was there—and getting stronger each day.

She didn't know what it was. Nothing she knew from talks with Gordon about Essence or Warden powers explained this.

Was it something born from proximity to Marek's transformation? Something new?

So she'd continue to monitor... continue to watch—and report to Gordon with any new updates.

Chapter 42

The morning air at the Arckus training grounds carried the scent of tempered steel, blood, and sweat. Marek moved across the training deck with a precision and calm he hadn't had a week ago—before the Mirror of Fane.

Cael circled him in loose, measured steps, a training blade held in a relaxed hand. Marek mirrored the motion, twin training blades—scaled replicas of the swords he now wore daily—held lightly at his sides. His breath was even. His stance relaxed. But his eyes were sharp, focused.

"You're different," Cael said—not a question.

Marek didn't answer.

The Mirror of Fane had left its mark—though not one that could be seen. The rage that had previously burned unchecked through him was now coiled up within. He controlled it. It hadn't vanished or dulled, but it had been honed. Like it knew its place.

Cael tested him with a feint—but Marek didn't react to the bait.

Instead, his body moved as if it had been waiting for Cael's follow-up strike. His left foot slid back, pivoted, and one blade snapped upward, deflecting Cael's real strike with the flat edge, as Marek's other came in fast—so fast Cael had to twist out of range to avoid it.

They reset.

This time, Cael grinned. "Your mind is finally clear. You are seeing past your emotions. Good!"

They clashed again, harder this time—Cael pressing him with the relentless footwork that had once overwhelmed him. But Marek didn't falter. He met Cael strike for strike, blade for blade, each movement cleaner than the last.

Every parry bled into a counter. Every dodge flowed into a riposte.

The air rang with the thwack of their staves and the distant hum of Riftlight overhead.

"You've stopped fighting your instincts," Cael said, breath catching slightly between movements.

Marek pivoted, blocked a low sweep, and twisted into a drive that forced Cael back.

"No," Marek said evenly. "I've stopped fighting myself."

The first time he'd stepped onto this deck, he'd been all raw strength, guilt, and rage—trying to prove something. To himself. To the Wardens. To Kaycee. To ghosts that never stopped haunting him. Every failure had fed the fire inside him until it threatened to burn him hollow.

But now, it was different. Now, his emotions didn't control him. He controlled them. And in that clarity, the Warden inside him had risen.

They broke apart again—breathing hard, sweat beading across skin.

Cael studied him. There was a small smile this time—approval.

And something that looked suspiciously like relief.

Without a word, Cael strode to the weapons rack and returned with his own rift-forged steel blade.

"Let's see what your instincts are worth," Cael said. "Draw your blades... trainee."

Marek drew the twin swords from their sheaths on his back in one smooth, practiced motion—the ancient metal whispering as it cleared the scabbards.

Their weight felt balanced, and a part of him. Like extensions of his limbs.

Cael raised his blade and moved into his stance. "You know what's next."

Marek exhaled once. "Yes... I won't hold back."

"Ha! Neither will I then. Come on—let's be about it," Cael said with a grin. A real, honest-to-goodness grin.

Then they launched at each other. The sound of their clash echoed across the training grounds like thunder. Sparks flared as metal kissed metal. Sweat and grunts of impacts followed close behind.

For the first time, Marek wasn't being beaten.

He was holding ground. Pressing the pace. Reading Cael's movements before they landed—guided by the whispered instincts of Onos's blades.

They had embedded their knowledge in his mind and muscles throughout his time training with Cael.

Their knowledge allowed him to fight with a skill and precision not his own. One strike got through Cael's guard. Then another.

Cael responded with tighter form, faster pacing—but Marek adapted. He pivoted around a lunge, disarmed with a hook of his pommel, and scored a shallow cut against Cael's shoulder.

The fight ended thirty seconds later—both men heaving, blades locked at the crossing point.

Cael pulled back first. He was smiling again. But this time, it was different. Proud.

"You're ready."

Marek sheathed both swords and nodded, breath still steady.

"I don't think I'll ever be ready," he said. "But I'm no longer afraid of what I am."

Cael placed a hand briefly on Marek's shoulder. "Then it's time."

"Time for what?"

Cael's gaze shifted toward the far edge of Arckus—to the Grand Circle, where the aurora flared brighter against the spires.

"Your final evaluation—taken by every Warden trainee before they are assigned a territory on Earth. The last step to becoming a full-fledged Warden."

"And what's going to happen at this evaluation?"

Cael smiled then. His crazy, sadistic smile he got whenever he invented a new and terrible physical training session for Marek.

"What happens to everyone at this point—Akron will come and kick your ass while we get to watch."

"We?" Marek asked, looking around with raised eyebrows. "I know there are Wardens here, because I've seen them in the mess hall, but no one has so much as glanced in my direction since my first day."

"That's because no one wants to get attached until you pass your assessment," he said. "Think of passing Akron's evaluation as a sort of rite of passage. All Wardens have gone through it, and no Warden will respect you until you've had your chance."

He considered Marek. "Everyone will show up to this evaluation. Some want to see if you'll survive, others will want to judge your worth on how long you last against him. But don't let that distract you. I assure you, Akron cares little for their opinion, and he will be doing his best to push you to your limit. Focus on him and only him, because in the end, his opinion is the only one that matters."

"Well, that sounds like buckets of fun," Marek replied dryly.

Cael chuckled and slapped Marek's back. "You'll be fine. Come on, let's go get some food. I'll let Akron know you're ready on the way back to the mess hall."

◆

The surge struck at midday—Highflare—as he was learning to reference it while in Arckus.

Marek was halfway through a Martial Form when the sensation hit—sharp, instinctive, like a whisper threading through his bones. He didn't hear the call with his ears. He felt it. The pull of the Rift, of something that wasn't supposed to be coming through.

Cael saw the shift in his stance instantly.

"You feel it," Cael said, not a question.

Marek nodded. "Yeah, something's trying to come through."

Cael didn't try to stop him.

Marek sheathed his blades, his breath even, movements fluid. The fire inside him didn't rage the way it once had—it pulsed. Controlled. Tethered.

He stepped into the Rift between breaths, and the world reformed in shadows and cold wind.

He emerged in a half-flooded alley off Canal Street, the scent of ozone and garbage thick in the air. Water pooled in broken concrete divots, reflecting the flicker of streetlights overhead. A crackling tear of blue-white energy pulsed in the center of the alley—the breach already destabilizing.

The tear widened further and a Drakyn stepped through.

It didn't get the chance to take a step before Marek was there in front of it.

His movements weren't wild this time. No rage. No fury. Just clean efficiency.

He slid forward in a blur, fist crushing its leg with a force that shattered bone and collapsed its stance. A pivot followed—and his fist caught the underside of the Drakyn's snout as it was falling to the ground, lifting the beast clean off its feet.

The creature landed hard. It scrambled, tried to rise—but Marek was there, pinning it in place with one hand. The other drew a blade, metal singing as it came free.

He didn't hesitate. He brought it down and pierced clean through the creature's heart. It screamed once more and then stilled, its death swift.

Then there was only silence. The Rift pulsed behind it once—then faded.

Boots splashed behind him.

"Damn it," Wilko muttered, stopping just short of the scene. "Anyone else feel kind of unnecessary right now?"

Marek looked over his shoulder, catching the trio just approaching. Kaycee, Wilko, and Harper.

He flicked his blade once, clearing the ichor, then sheathed it in a smooth, practiced motion.

"I had it," Marek said.

"You think?" Harper said, sweeping her scanner over the breach site.

Wilko stepped up beside him, glancing down at the remains, slowly turning human.

"That's the third one this week you took out solo. You're starting to ruin my whole action-hero image."

Marek gave a dry smile. "You'll survive." And turned to leave.

"Marek wait... please," Kaycee said suddenly, her voice desperate.

He stopped mid-step, glancing back. His blades were sheathed, but his posture hadn't softened.

She hesitated—just a second—then took a breath. "You should hear this from me."

Marek turned fully then, brow furrowed.

"It's about Tucker."

That was all it took. His body tensed—not the way it did in battle, but something quieter. More fragile.

"He's alive," she said. "He's in a coma... but he's alive."

For a moment, Marek didn't move. The wind still rushed down the alley. Water dripped from broken gutters. The world kept turning.

But something inside him cracked open. "Alive? But how? I saw him die—I heard his neck break..." Marek said, his voice cracking with emotion.

Kaycee took a slow step toward him. Her expression was cautious, unsure, but honest.

"I tried to tell you."

He turned to her, rain dripping from his hair, his breath suddenly heavier.

"I tried to tell you the last time," she said, "but you just walked away. You didn't let me—"

Marek raised a hand. Not to silence her, but to touch.

He reached out, fingers brushing her cheek. She went still. His hand settled along her jaw, thumb tracing a quiet line across skin still damp from the rain.

"I didn't let you," he said softly. "That's on me."

Kaycee's eyes searched his, something unspoken caught in her throat. She lifted her hand, curling her fingers around his, holding him there.

"I've been clawing my way out of a dark place," Marek said. "Didn't know if I could. But I'm getting there."

She leaned into his touch.

"Do you think..." She whispered. "Do you think we'll be okay? After everything?"

Marek huffed a quiet breath, not quite a laugh. "Well, I'm touching you. You're not punching me. And you're holding my hand. I'd say that's a decent start."

Several moments passed. Then—

"Kiss her already or leave, Romeo," Wilko called out, loud enough for the echo to slap back down the alley. "We got blood puddles and trauma reports to fill out."

Chen barked a laugh over the comms, Kaycee smothered a smile, turning her face slightly into Marek's palm.

Marek gave Wilko a slow glare. "Next time, I'll leave you with the creature."

"Rude," he muttered. "Also, fair."

Kaycee shook her head, stepping back just enough to break contact. "Are you going to see him?"

Marek nodded. "I have to."

"Good," she said. Then continued, hesitant. "They say coma patients can hear, even though they may not respond. Tell him I'm sorry. For... everything."

"I will."

He turned to go, then paused.

"Also," he said, "I'm headed back to undergo my final evaluation by Akron... Apparently, it's a right-of-passage. Cael says it will most likely end in my ass being beat in front of my peers."

She raised her eyebrows. "So soon? You must have really impressed Cael. I've never heard of him signing off on anyone so fast."

"You know Cael?" He asked, turning fully back to her with a look of surprise.

Gordon sighed, "He's the one who trained me. He's like a big brother."

”That explains a lot, actually." Marek said.

"What'd he do?" She asked warily.

"Nothing more than you'd expect of a bigger brother training the man who'd hurt his sister... let's just say he wasn't a fan when we first met. He called me newb, and didn't look too happy."

"Well, you'll just have to be nicer to me then, won't you?" Kaycee said, with a small smile.

"I'll make sure to do that." He said softly, a trace of heat in his eyes, as he turned to leave.

"Oh, one more thing," she called out. "Good luck, you'll need it—Akron is a monster in a fight."

Marek gave her a little salute, then stepped through the Rift, leaving silence in his wake.

The quiet in the SCU medical wing felt unnatural.

Too clean. Too sterile. Tucker was the exact opposite, and it felt wrong seeing him in a place like this.

Marek stood in the doorway for a long moment. Just watching.

Tucker lay motionless beneath a crisp white sheet, face pale against the pillow. Monitors lined the wall beside him, their displays glowing soft green and gold. A low rhythm pulsed across the heart monitor. Steady. Undisturbed. Comatose.

But alive.

Marek's chest tightened.

He stepped inside, boots silent on the linoleum floor. Each footfall felt heavier than it should have.

He stopped beside the bed, looking down at his friend.

Tucker looked younger like this. Softer. The constant sarcasm and sharp-eyed vigilance stripped away, leaving only stillness and vulnerability.

It unsettled Marek more than he'd expected.

He pulled a chair close and sat down, elbows on his knees, hands laced together. For a long moment, he just stared at his boots.

Then, softly, "Hey, man."

The words felt small. Inadequate.

Marek sighed, running a hand through his damp hair. Rain still clung to him from the breach site. He hadn't stopped. Hadn't even thought about changing. He'd come straight here the second Kaycee had said the words.

"He's alive. He's in a coma... but he's alive."

The world had tilted sideways in that moment.

"I should've come sooner," Marek said, voice low. "I didn't know. I—" He swallowed hard. "I didn't let her tell me. Kaycee. She tried. I just... I didn't want to hear it. Didn't want to hear anything."

He leaned back, letting his gaze drift up to the monitors, then down again to Tucker's hand resting limply on the bed.

"I've been pissed at everyone," he murmured. "At her. At Akron. At myself."

His throat tightened. "You should've seen me, man. That first night. After Harley... after the team..."

He didn't finish the thought. Couldn't.

"I lost it. I mean really lost it. I blamed her for everything," he said.

He reached out slowly, taking Tucker's limp hand.

The contact grounded him. Solid. Real.

"I wasn't strong enough. Wasn't fast enough. And I've been carrying that guilt since I was seventeen. Since that girl in the alley. I failed her. I failed the team. I thought I failed you."

He closed his eyes.

"I know who Harley is now. What he is. It's amazing I survived the encounter with him all those years ago in that alley. I carried the guilt and the blame for not saving her, but the truth is... I never stood a chance."

A flicker of heat stirred in his chest—anger, resolve, something deeper.

"I probably wouldn't stand a chance even now—but I'll get there. I'll train as hard as I need to. Do whatever it takes."

He let go of Tucker's hand and looked down again.

"And when I find Harley again..." His voice dropped to a growl. "He dies. For what he did to the girl. For Marcus. For Malik. For you."

"You always were a stubborn bastard. So, you hang on and get better... hear me? Because when you wake up, I'm going to kick your ass for making me think you were dead."

He stood and walked to the door.

His fingers hovered over the handle for a breath.

He didn't look back, but his voice carried—low and certain.

"I'm not letting this end with you in a hospital bed. You're my brother, Tucker—I need you back."

A beat of silence stretched—then a faint flicker of golden light pulsed beneath Tucker's skin. Barely there.

Marek didn't see it as he opened the door and stepped into the hall, leaving only the soft echo of boots against tile and the steady beep of the monitors behind.

Chapter 43

The fighting ring lay at the heart of the Grand Circle—an arena carved from the stone of Arckus. The space was vast and open to the sky, its perimeter ringed by towering colonnades that reached up toward the heavens.

Highflare had come and gone, and it was halfway toward Dimfall—the Riftlight still bright enough to provide plenty of light for the hundreds of spectators who had gathered.

Wardens filled the high-tiered seating, all wearing their black, form-fitting armor—many having come directly from patrolling their assigned sections of the world.

Word had spread quickly. The First Warden was testing another Warden trainee, and the sea of black-armored Wardens was a counterpoint to the aura of excitement emanating from the crowd.

Marek stood at the center of the ring, stripped to the waist, body carved from weeks of relentless training. His twin swords—the legendary blades forged by Onos—waited off to the side on a raised stand, untouched for now. This would begin as all things should: stripped down, bare, without pretense, armor, or crutch.

The testing, Cael had said, was two-part and was done to determine combat readiness. Hand-to-hand for testing physical strength and endurance, followed immediately by bladed weapons.

The fact that Akron and Marek both wielded twin blades only added to the excitement building in the arena.

Any lingering whispers of conversation were abruptly cut off when Akron entered the circle from a side door. Anticipation thick in the air, as the Wardens in attendance watched him come.

Marek studied him as he approached. Clad in a sleeveless black tunic and dark combat trousers, the First Warden looked carved from obsidian, each movement efficient, unhurried, and prowling like a lion on the hunt. His eyes met Marek's with the weight of millennia behind them—assessing him.

Cael stepped out next and walked to the center of the ring, fist over his heart in a salute to Akron. Akron returned the gesture, followed by a nod of acknowledgment.

Cael came to a stop between them, his voice booming clear and strong.

"This is a final evaluation. Full contact. No Rift energy. No killing blows. You will stop when called."

He paused for a moment, letting his words register, then said, "The first test is unarmed combat. Begin."

Akron launched first—a blur of motion, deceptively fast. Marek blocked the opening jab, parried a short elbow meant for his temple, and responded with a snap kick that forced the older Warden back a step.

No feeling each other out, and no wasted movement. It was a storm of violence from the outset. Fast. Fluid. Brutal.

Marek ducked under a spinning elbow and countered with a rising knee to the ribs. Akron absorbed it with a twist of his torso, driving a hammer-fist toward Marek's clavicle. Marek caught the arm, twisted, and brought his opponent over his shoulder. Akron tucked into the throw and landed with a roll, springing up the instant his feet touched ground.

They clashed again. Fists blurring. Feet driving forward. Elbows. Knees. Kicks. Traps. Locks.

Akron was more experienced, with millennia of combat layered into every move. But Marek had something else: a desire to prove himself, a healthy fear of getting his ass beat in front of hundreds of his soon-to-be peers, and the whispered memories from Onos's blades.

He used tight, brutal combinations, drawing from the instincts that Cael had drilled into him—and combined it with what was already embedded from the swords. Every motion had intent. Every blow followed another.

A jab to Akron's jaw.

A feint and sidestep.

An inside leg kick that staggered the older Warden for half a second.

Marek was momentarily stunned that he'd landed that blow, but a moment was all Akron needed to recover.

He swept Marek's leg from under him and came after him with an attempt to pummel him with punches from above. Marek grabbed an arm and, using Akron's momentum against him, used his feet to push and flip him in an improvised throw.

A heartbeat later, they were both back on their feet, breathing hard, bruised, and bleeding.

The crowd remained silent. A sense of awe was passing through the stands—they were witnessing something that hadn't ever happened. Someone was holding their own against the First Warden—a trainee, no less.

Cael raised his hand.

"Break."

Marek stepped back, sweat rolling down his spine. Akron nodded once, grinning with wordless approval.

Cael gestured to the weapons rack.

"Now blades."

Akron went to the rack of weapons, along with Marek. They both selected a set of twin swords that had been prepared for this duel.

Utilitarian and simple in their design, they mimicked the size and weight of their own swords—both sets of which were determined to be too dangerous to use for sparring. These blades were dulled for the occasion, but would still cut if they hit hard enough.

The hilts felt comfortable in Marek's hands. The weight familiar in a way that belied only weeks of training. He blamed Onos's blades.

They spoke to him when he used them. Whispers of knowledge. Flashes of old battles. When he sheathed them, that knowledge stayed, the muscle memory and instincts drilling deep and growing roots. They'd been doing that since he'd first bonded with them. It was thrilling and unnerving in equal measure.

He shrugged those thoughts aside as he rolled his neck and got into a ready stance—Akron doing the same.

Cael signaled the beginning of the bout from the sidelines. "When you are ready, you may begin."

They lunged at the same time. Steel struck steel as they met in a controlled fury of blows.

Marek's left sword met Akron's in a sharp parry. He spun low, bringing his second blade up in a rising slash—Akron twisted, blades whirling in tandem, and blocked both strikes.

It became a brutal yet beautiful dance as they moved around the circle.

Twin blades against twin blades.

Sweeps, feints, parries. Reversals. A showcase of perfect form and footwork.

Marek fought low and aggressive, capitalizing on angles, using speed to pressure Akron to counter before he was ready.

Akron responded with calm ferocity—every movement efficient, clean. He seemed unfazed by Marek's advance until you looked closer.

Experienced Wardens in attendance noticed that his breaths came faster and faster, and perspiration began to bead on his forehead.

The blades clashed high, then low, back up again, both fighters straining for purchase as they locked blades in the center.

Marek pivoted, sliding one sword down, gaining space to hammer his forearm on top of one of Akron's wrists. Akron was forced to disengage or lose his sword, and Marek used the freedom to slash horizontally at his chest.

Akron bent backwards, Marek's sword passing so close he felt the whistle of wind, his other sword spearing the ground for support—and he delivered a kick to Marek's ribs.

Marek absorbed it with a grunt, stepping back under the force of it. Fucker kicked like a mule.

Akron moved then in a flurry of blows, putting Marek on the defensive.

Marek parried each one of them, counter-striking in turn. Neither finding the upper hand, both of them switching the advantage as the fight reached a different tempo altogether.

In the midst of it all, Akron laughed, a grin splitting his face.

Not mocking, but in a pleased sort of surprise. That of a warrior finally finding freedom in being able to just let go and *fight!*

The guy's nuts, Marek thought. Then gave a laugh of his own as he realized he was enjoying himself just as much. *Well, I guess that makes two of us.*

The duel continued. One minute turned to three, then five. Not a soul in the stands made a sound, caught up in the display of perfect combat taking place.

They started moving faster than the eye could track, arms seeming to blur with the speed of their strikes.

Sparks flashed in the air, an accompaniment to the symphony of ringing steel.

Energy pulsed through the crowd like a live current, whispers and murmurs of surprise increasing in volume as the bout continued longer than anyone expected.

And then—abruptly—they stopped.

Marek's blade pressed against Akron's throat, and Akron's blade pressed against Marek's.

Neither moved, small drops of blood sliding down their necks where the blades rested.

The Grand Circle fell into complete silence.

Cael stepped forward slowly, raising a hand.

"Draw."

A breath.

Then the crowd roared. Exclamations of disbelief, and shouts of congratulations and praise for Marek rang out in equal measure.

Marek slowly stepped back, sheathing his blades. His chest heaved, his body trembled, but his stance remained firm. He couldn't help the huge grin on his face.

Akron stared at him for a long moment, then sheathed his own blades. He walked forward and clasped Marek's shoulder.

"You are a Warden in full now—your father would be proud," he said as he walked off.

He stopped briefly to say something low to Cael on his way out, shooting a backward glance at Marek as he did.

It took a few seconds for Akron's words to register, but when they did, it sent a shock through him.

"Wait, what? My father? What about him? Who is he? How do you know him... Akron!" he shouted. But Akron had disappeared around the corner, swallowed up in the halls as he exited the arena.

The burning questions running through him after Akron's comment overrode his thoughts, the revelation that Akron knew his father outweighing another, equally important revelation.

A revelation the rest of the Wardens in attendance were very aware of.

That, for the first time since Onos walked the Realms, someone had matched Akron.

Not a Warden with centuries of experience. Not a member of the Seven Realms. Instead, a newly anointed Warden, only twenty-eight years of age, had fought to a draw—on both tests.

As the chamber emptied out, each Warden going back to their assigned patrols on Earth, Cael walked up to Marek, a big smile on his face.

"Congratulations, Warden Marek. I've never seen anything like it in all my centuries," he said, shaking his head slowly. "You found another gear there. If you're up for it, I'd like to take you to Rufus, our very own resident tattoo artist. It's customary for new Wardens to take the mark of the Warden after we pass the evaluation—you are welcome to follow in the tradition."

Cael pulled aside his shirt and showed him a tattoo over his heart. It was of crossed swords, laid over what looked to be an image of Earth, with faint swirls coming out from the center.

"The swords represent Wardens, the Earth represents humanity, and the swirl pattern is some fancy shit added by Rufus. He swears it 'came to him' in a vision, and that it represents the Rift," Cael said.

Marek looked closer. "It just looks like fancy shit to me."

"Ha! I knew I liked you. So what do you say? You up for it?"

"Sure, why not? We'll just add it to the growing list of things I thought I'd never do," Marek said as he started to follow Cael.

"Oh, one more thing," Cael said, stopping to look at Marek. "Akron wants to meet in the Lore Hall to talk about where you'll be assigned to patrol. He thinks it's only fitting that you get the territory previously covered by your father."

Marek looked sharply at Cael. "Again, with that word. Who is my father?"

"That's the other piece he wanted to tell you. It's not my place to say more if he wants to break it to you," Cael said, shooting Marek a look that said he wouldn't talk about it further.

"Come on, let's get you some ink. Oh, and one more thing—Rufus infuses the ink with Rift energy. Something about needing to will the skin around it not to try and heal before it settles. Anyway, it hurts like hell, so try not to be a little bitch." Cael smirked as he started toward a tunnel leading out of the Grand Circle.

"I think I'll be able to keep it together," Marek said as he followed, wondering just what the hell he'd agreed to—if even Cael thought it hurt.

———————◆———————

Akron remained silent as the last echoes of steel faded into the charged air. His breath came slow and even, but his mind was anything but calm.

He kept his expression unreadable as he turned away from the circle, but behind his eyes, the battle replayed again—frame by frame, strike by strike.

He had tested Marek without holding back—though he hadn't planned on it. He had planned on starting at half-speed and working up to see how fast Marek was.

But that wasn't what had happened. From the very start, Marek had been faster, stronger, and more confident than any other Warden he'd evaluated.

Akron had quickly dropped all pretense of holding back. He had to, or he would have lost.

Through the course of the fight, he began to realize that there was something beyond just the added strength and speed attributed to the additional Essence provided by his father, Jax.

No, something else lived inside the younger Warden, he was sure of it.

There were times in the fight where Marek had moved with instincts and a level of skill that Akron knew were beyond even Cael's abilities to train.

No, this was something else. Marek hadn't just reacted. He had anticipated. Adapted. Shifted his weight before Akron had even committed to his next strike. There wasn't any training in the Realms that could explain it. That was a level of skill and muscle memory which took centuries to learn.

Akron's jaw tightened. But there were other answers.

The blades. Forged by Onos before the Final War. Shaped in a forge lit by his own power, and wrought by his bare hands. Akron had believed them to be relics—silent and dormant since Onos's death.

The swords had clearly chosen Marek. Responded to him.

Cael's text on the first day of Marek's training, after they visited the Armory, told him as much. But hearing about it, and then seeing the results of the bond the boy shared, were two different things.

He now believed that they were also teaching him.

Which meant...

Akron turned from the window, his jaw clenched. He had to be certain. He couldn't afford to be wrong. The implications were too vast.

Because if he was right—if the blades were more than relics... if they were remembering Onos's battles...

If they were responding to Marek because something in him was resonating with their ancient call...

Then Marek wasn't merely powerful. He wasn't only the son of Jax.

It was possible he was a descendant of Onos himself. The convergence of two legacies that should never have crossed—it was the only explanation that fit.

Jax's Essence ran through his blood. That alone made Marek a rarity, a prodigy born of both human and Warden lineage.

But the blades had chosen him too, and the only being they had ever answered to was their maker—Onos.

The thought left him reeling.

He'd been considering it ever since his visit to Ellen's house... ever since witnessing that golden flare of power during Marek's transformation.

Was it possible? Could Onos have left behind a descendant in humanity at some point before the Final Battle? Before his death?

Was that why he built in the Oath to not sleep with a human? Were there more descendants out there?

While Marek's use and acceptance of Onos's blades was its own kind of confirmation, it wasn't a guarantee—wasn't fact. And Akron liked his facts... needed a guarantee.

Too many questions, and not enough answers. Onos had left no instructions for this. No law or path to provide guidance.

As he made his way to the Lore Hall—to prepare for his conversation with Marek, and the inevitable questions that would arise—for the first time in millennia, Akron had nowhere to turn for answers to the questions that plagued him.

Chapter 44

The sharp scent of heated ink and sterilized steel hit Marek as soon Rufus opened the door to his "domain," as he referred to it. Marek now sat shirtless on a smooth bench, the muscles in his back tensing and jumping as Rufus prepared his tools—in anticipation of the pain Cael had promised was to follow.

Rufus was the exact opposite of what Marek had expected of a Warden. Older than Cael was—he hadn't let the centuries of life suck out his ability to enjoy life and pursue his passions.

When he wasn't pursuing creatures that broke through his section of the Rift—you could find him in here, ready to give ink to whoever wanted it.

Tattooed from neck to foot, his passion showed, and judging from the quality of the ink that was visible, there wasn't anyone else Marek would rather have apply the symbol of the Wardens.

Rufus turned to him now, grinning like a butcher with a new slab of meat. Excitement shone on his face.

"So," Rufus said, spinning a silver needle between his fingers, "you want the mark of the Warden, do you?"

Marek nodded. "That's what Cael called it."

"This is going to hurt like hell," Rufus said, grinning as he dipped the silver-etched needle into a vial of ink. "Try not to scream. Makes it awkward for people passing by. No one likes a little bitch."

"That's not very reassuring," Marek mumbled.

Rufus began his work, chuckling to himself—the first sting of the needle digging just over Marek's heart. The pain was immediate. White-hot.

The ink wasn't just physical—it burned with Rift energy that sparked from Rufus's fingertips and spiraled down the needle into Marek's skin.

He felt his body instinctively trying to fight against the process. To heal the damage that was being done.

Rufus noticed and said, "You have to accept it. Relax and take deep breaths. Tell yourself you want this over and over again like a mantra. It helps subdue our built-in instincts to heal. Makes it hurt less too."

Marek did as instructed, and it seemed to help, at least a little bit.

The tattoo took nearly two hours. Every line, every stroke etching meaning into his skin. Crossed twin blades. A faint, ghostlike imprint of Earth beneath them. Spiraling outward from the center—a stylized Rift—an abstract swirl of chaos and power.

When it was done, Marek exhaled like he'd been holding his breath. He wouldn't have been surprised if he had been. The tattoo had hurt worse than Cael implied.

Rufus sat back to look at his work. He nodded, seeming pleased with himself, then he stood and walked back to put away his supplies.

He turned to speak, as Marek began studying the tattoo, running his fingers over it.

"The Warden mark stands for three things. The Earth should be self-explanatory—it represents the Realm in which humanity resides. The swords are symbolic of protection. It's our duty and obligation to protect earth. The swirls—"

"Let me guess," Marek cut in, "they came to you in a vision?"

"Ha! I knew you'd be fun—the younger generations always are. I see you've been talking to Cael—him and his damn rumors."

His voice took on a somber tone as he added, "In all seriousness though, regardless of the debates on how I settled on the design, the swirls are meant to stand for the Rift—Onos's protection from the Seven Realms."

Marek nodded in understanding.

"But the Rift seems to be breaking down. If it was designed as Onos's last protection, why were the Wardens created? Shouldn't the Rift not let any creatures through?"

"That's a question for smarter men, but if you want to know my thoughts... I believe Onos in his wisdom, knew either that his power would one day fail, or that there were always loopholes to be found. I believe we were made as the last defense, if the Rift should fail."

Marek nodded. "That actually makes a lot of sense."

Rufus grinned again. "Just don't go telling everyone you heard it from me. I don't need the Lore Hall weirdos coming to me to discuss mystical theories and other bullshit."

Marek laughed. "Your secret's safe with me."

Marek rose and walked to the door and paused as Rufus spoke again.

"I saw your fight with Akron. I was impressed, as was every Warden who saw it. No one has stood even with Akron since the founding of the Wardens. Don't let that power go to your head. Stay humble and stay safe out there. Shit is getting crazy."

"I'll keep all that in mind. I've got too much to live for," Marek said as he opened the door to the hallway.

Rufus smirked. "Give Warden Kaycee my regards when you see her next, will you?"

Marek's head snapped to him, seeing a knowing glint in his eyes. "Who told you?"

Rufus looked surprised. "Didn't you know? Cael and she go way back."

Marek laughed. "Yeah no, he failed to mention that. Kaycee did mention he was like a brother to her though, so I guess I shouldn't be surprised."

"Oh, and Marek?" Rufus called out one last time. "Treat her well. She's well-loved among us Wardens."

Marek swallowed once, hearing the warning behind those words.

"I'll do that," he said as he exited into the hallway.

He found Cael waiting for him, leaning against the wall.

"I see you got the big brother treatment from Rufus." He said, with a smile. "That's good, means I don't have to."

"How long did you know that Kaycee and I... that we—" Marek started to say.

"Bumped uglies? Did the nasty?" Cael interrupted with a grin.

Marek just shook his head, grimacing. "Please... don't ever say that again. It sounds so wrong coming from you."

Cael snorted a laugh as he pushed off the wall. "I'll add something Rufus didn't. I know you two had a falling out, and I understand why. But a word of advice?"

Marek gave him a questioning look. "Yeah?"

"Happiness is hard to find in this line of work. If you can, work through your shit and find a way to make up. She's worth holding on to."

"I know. I think we're getting there," Marek said.

"Good." He clapped Marek on the shoulder. "Now, follow me on to the Lore Hall. You have a date with the boss you don't want to be late for."

———◆———

The Lore Hall of Arckus greeted him in its customary silence. Sound seemed muted, as though it disappeared into the vaulted ceilings. Marek walked alongside Cael as they passed shelves upon shelves of books.

They rounded a corner and found Akron, hands clasped behind his back, staring up at the picture of the *Fall of Onos*.

A vivid and powerful scene captured so well by the artist, that it had Marek recalling the memories that had assaulted him in the Armory when he bonded with his swords.

Marek had to give props to the artist for accuracy.

Akron didn't turn as they approached, only said into the silence, "Thank you, Warden Cael. You may go."

Cael shot Marek a look and said, "Good luck," before disappearing down a narrow side corridor.

Akron turned from his musing, and gave Marek a measured look, finally speaking, "You took the mark of the Wardens."

"I did."

Akron nodded. "Good. It is important to be reminded of why we exist. Especially in increasingly uncertain times."

He became quiet again, seeming lost in some internal debate or dialog.

Marek prodded gently, "You said you wanted to talk?"

Akron finally turned, his expression unreadable. "It's time you knew the truth. About your father."

Marek's shoulders tensed. "Yeah... You really messed with my head when you dropped that bomb and walked off earlier. You've got my attention."

"I'm not one hundred percent certain, but I believe your father's name was Jax," Akron said. "He was a Warden. Strong, courageous, and loyal. He was one of my best."

"What happened to him?" Marek asked. "My mother never spoke of him to me—only that I reminded her of him. That I looked just like him."

Akron sighed, a hand scrubbing over his face. "He served with honor, guarding the area you know as New York City, and the East Coast for centuries. He never faltered, was always loyal. Until he met your mother. I believe he fell in love with her shortly after they met. He gave her his heart, and eventually he slept with her."

He looked at Marek, old grief and regret shone in his eyes.

"At the very beginning, when Onos created me, with his dying breath he made me swear to uphold the laws of the Oath. That ANY violation of those Oaths would be met with death."

He looked at his hands. "Death by my hands."

"You... killed him?" Marek said, more accusation than question.

"I didn't want to." Akron said, hands and jaw clenching, "When it comes to Oath breakers, Onos ensured I would obey by placing compulsions within me. Imagine you are a passenger in your own body—your thoughts and intent being overridden by forces long-dead, but no less binding."

Marek's fists clenched at his sides. "So, you obeyed."

"I had no choice."

Marek's intake of breath was sharp—panicked—as he came to a realization. "What about me and Kaycee. We slept together. Does she die for it?"

Akron gave a hard shake of his head. "No."

"Why not?" Marek demanded—upset for a different reason now. "Why my father and not her? What makes her special?"

"It is not *her* who is special. It is *you*, Marek."

"What does that even mean?" Marek asked.

"I believe that you were born different. Jax's essence must have bonded with your cells in your mother's womb. Based on your profile and records as a teenager, some portion of that bonded Essence must have awakened on your seventeenth birthday."

Akron started pacing, "Then you came into contact with Warden Kaycee, and she exposed you to our world. I think that exposure to the Rift, and to the creatures, activated the dormant powers of your Warden heritage."

Marek stared at him in stunned silence. "How does that mean she gets to live?"

"It means that when Warden Kaycee decided to sleep with you, I believe the Oath did not recognize you as Human."

"How do you know it didn't?" Marek asked.

"Because that night I was following you, and I saw her enter your apartment. I knew what she and you had done. I believed my hand was being forced to take the life of yet another one of our kind. Yet, when I went to strike her down.... there was nothing. No compulsion, nothing driving me forward," Akron said.

"It was then that I realized there was something different about you. So, I dug into your past. I had to know more. I recognized your mother's name in your file at the precinct, so I went to the address listed. It was the same house on the same street that I was forced to take Jax's life twenty-nine years ago. She was the same woman he had fallen for."

"So that is why I am different, why I've been different my entire life," Marek said—more to himself than to the man in front of him.

"That is not all that makes you different. I cannot prove this yet, but I believe there is something else within you. Something passed down throughout generations. Lying dormant until you received the Essence and spoke your Oath."

"What is it?" Marek asked, desperate now to understand.

Akron turned away. "I have no way to confirm this by official historical accounts, but I think you may be a direct descendant of Onos."

All Marek could do was just look at him for a long moment. But slowly, he came to a realization as he reached back to brush his fingers along the hilts of the swords on his back.

"The pull I felt in the Armory. When I touched them, I saw visions of Onos fighting. Dying. I *felt* it happen. He was holding these blades. The way I feel them whisper to me—showing me memories of battles I've never fought..."

Akron nodded. "Yes. No one but Onos could ever wield those blades, much less pass through the runes I set on the case in the Armory. I believe that would be proof enough if I hadn't seen you fight."

He took a deep breath and continued, "I've fought more Warden duels than anyone living, and when we fought, you fought with a skill level and intuition that no one your age could possess."

"You think it's from the blades?" Marek asked.

Akron nodded. "Onos forged them in the fire of his own power. They'd been dormant for millennia. But now... as you've confirmed, they whisper through you. I believe they are teaching you. Filling in what time could never give."

He looked back at Marek. "You moved like someone who's lived a hundred lifetimes of war. And your father—Jax—he was skilled, but not enough to account for what I saw today."

Marek's head was filled with swirling questions. "So, what does that make me, then? If you're right that I am a descendant of Onos... what does it mean?"

"I am not sure. There's no guide for this. No record of this happening—that would have been before my time, and written histories are almost non-existent from that period. All I know is this—don't let this knowledge change who you are. You are Marek, son of Ellen Tomlinson. A good man. And a damn good fighter," Akron said with a sudden grin.

"Learn to use the gifts that are given to you. Become strong and protect Earth." He continued, as he stared up at the mural again—deep in thought.

"The Rift is weakening and more Drakyn are bleeding through every day. I have a feeling we'll need all the help we can get sooner rather than later."

He drew a deep breath, "Speaking of protecting Earth. It's time you were assigned a section of Earth to patrol. I think it's only fitting that you take over your father's section. New York City, along with the East Coast, is now yours to protect."

"Warden Kaycee is going to be your partner. Due to the heavy increase in activity in that region, we need all the help we can get, and you are both familiar with it—with each other. I imagine she'll be thrilled to find out who she'll have as a partner.

He gave Marek a wry smile. "She's been... anxious to learn where you'll be assigned."

Then, he shot Marek a parting warning. "I trust that I don't have to remind you both to not get too... distracted?"

Marek shook his head quickly. "No, you don't."

"Good," Akron said as he opened a Rift and looked back as he stepped into it, "I'd hate to have to reassign you."

Marek stood alone in the silence that followed Akron's departure,

He looked up again at the mural of Onos—the final moment of his life immortalized in sweeping color and mythic detail. The long-dead eyes of the Titan stared forward, past time, past death, past Marek.

He took a slow breath, coming to terms with the revelations of the night.

His father was a Warden. He was possibly descended of Onos, creator of the Realms and humanity.

He was assigned a massive territory, and he was going to be Kaycee's partner.

An electric sort of thrill went through him at the thought of seeing her again. Of telling her the news. He wondered how she'd react. He wondered where they went from here.

He didn't know what any of it all meant yet—but for the first time, it didn't scare him.

His hand settled over his chest, fingers brushing the new tattoo—still tender, still healing, albeit slowly thanks to Rufus's talents.

It was a mark of duty. A mark of brotherhood. He was part of something greater than himself.

He turned from the mural, the echo of Akron's words still pressing against the walls of his mind.

"Become strong and protect Earth."

He wasn't sure if he was ready for that, or what it really meant. He only knew that he would try.

Because the Rift was weakening, and NOT trying wasn't an option. Not if it meant more creatures would break through and kill humans.

Marek had a feeling that war was coming. Like a premonition that sank into his bones.

Marek stepped into the shadowed corridor beyond the Lore Hall, his blades whispering softly behind him with every step.

He had people to protect, monsters to kill, and a new partner. All things considered, things were looking up.

Chapter 45

Blue-white energy cut through the night like a knife—a tear in reality as Marek stepped out on top of the roof of SCU Headquarters.

It had only been three weeks since he was here last, but it felt like a lifetime.

So much had changed since that time. Hell, so much had changed in just the last day. He wished the world would just wait a damn minute before it dumped something else on his shoulders.

He wanted time to process... all of it.

Since the Lore Hall conversation he'd had hours ago, he hadn't stopped thinking about Akron's words.

Jax—his father. A Warden who'd broken the sacred Oath to love a mortal. Who Akron had been forced to kill.

Marek was the result of that love. And, if Akron was to be believed, he was also something new. Something that shouldn't exist but did. He didn't know where that left him.

One thing he did know, was how to follow orders, and his orders were to get stronger. Protect humanity from the Seven Realms that wanted nothing more than to destroy or subjugate them.

He could do that—and to help him, he was going to be assigned a partner.

Warden Kaycee. He was going to need to get used to that—thinking of her as a Warden.

She wasn't his superior anymore, and he'd stopped thinking of her as such since after that night they shared together.

He swiped his card at the rooftop access door, and it beeped, allowing him entry—apparently Kaycee hadn't shut off his access... yet.

As he made his way down the stairs to the main levels of SCU, the thought of seeing her again filled him with equal parts anticipation and guilt.

The guilt sat heavy in his chest—how he'd treated her after his transformation. How he'd shut her out, lashing out, never giving her the chance to explain her side. Not really.

The brutal onslaught of the transformation, his emotions raging out-of-control, and thinking Tucker had been killed... He hadn't handled it well, and she had taken the brunt of it.

He was encouraged by their last encounter, though.

Let's just hope she could find it in her to forgive him for being an ass—otherwise, it would be a long and awkward partnership.

Marek was feeling hopeful as he descended the last few steps, turning down the hallway leading to her office. It was quieter now, most of the remaining agents either off-shift or stationed elsewhere.

He found her office quickly, his feet retracing steps that seemed etched in his mind. He felt the tug of her presence before he got to her door.

And there she was.

Her door was open a crack, soft lamplight spilling into the hallway like a quiet invitation. Through the gap, he saw her at her desk—hair pulled back in a ponytail, still in partial field gear, typing up a final report. Her brow was furrowed; lips set in a patented Kaycee look of focus.

He knocked once, then pushed the door open further.

Kaycee looked up. He saw her school her expression quickly, but not in time for him to miss her reaction. Her face had lit up with something that punched straight into his chest—relief, warmth, joy maybe?

"You're back," she said, standing.

"I am," Marek said, stepping in. "And I've got news."

She arched a brow, folding her arms. "The good kind?"

"That depends on if you'd be interested in having me as your new partner," he said with a guarded smile.

Kaycee blinked. Her arms dropped to her sides. "Wait, you're serious?"

Marek nodded, as he walked further into her office, stopping a few feet from her.

"Akron assigned me to New York City—the entire East Coast actually. Effective immediately. He's worried about the steadily weakening Rift in this area."

A breath left her, like she'd been holding it for days. "Well... that's very good news."

She stepped up to him without preamble and wrapped her arms around him.

It wasn't dramatic or desperate—it was simple. Needed. Her face tucked against his chest, her body relaxing into his for the briefest moment before she pulled back.

"Sorry, I thought I'd have to deal with Cael for the next several centuries. This is a relief," she smirked.

"Ha ha, I see how it is. Just a relief, huh?" He asked.

"I mean, I have missed you too. Just a little." She held her thumb and pointer finger close together.

"I was starting to think I was alone in the missing you department," he said.

"Well, I had to give you a bit of a hard time for all you've put me through," she said, only half joking.

"About that," he said, "I was an ass. I didn't even give you a chance to explain. I was feeling too much—it was all just too much. It's not an excuse—it's only... where I was at. You had also lost your team, and all I did was lash out."

"You did hurt me. I was reeling from everything, and you didn't listen to my side." She looked up at him with unshed tears.

"You're right... about how I treated you. I didn't know how binding the orders from Akron are. I didn't see your pain. I'll do anything to make it up to you," he said, softly.

Kaycee took a deep breath. "It's not all just on you... I also should have tried to find a way to tell you more... to give some sort of clue to what we were walking into. I just didn't know how to explain everything—where to start. Then Harley showed up, and I froze. One thing led to the other, and it just became one giant clusterfuck," she finished with a whisper.

He reached for her and took her hands in his. "How about this? We both admit we were shit at communicating, and agree to not keep any secrets from each other?"

She looked into his eyes, trust beginning to bloom again—and something deeper. "That sounds good to me... partner."

"Me too," he told her, releasing her hands but not stepping back.

"Oh yeah, I forgot. Akron did warn us not to let ourselves become too... distracted. Or he'd have to reassign us," Marek said with a chuckle.

Kaycee covered her face with her hands, "Oh *Onos*.... he didn't!!"

"He did! I felt like a kid having the sex talk with his dad for the first time..." Marek shuddered.

Kaycee's body shook with laughter for just a second before dragging her hands down her face with a groan.

"I hate how hard I'm blushing right now," she muttered.

"I like it," Marek said, with a smile.

She rolled her eyes, but the smile stayed. It warmed something inside him, their renewed banter.

Before either of them could say more, the comm panel on her desk crackled to life.

"Eliza to Gordon," a crisp voice said.

Kaycee pressed the panel. "What do you have for me, Eliza?"

"Another Rift surge. Brooklyn waterfront—old construction site by Pier 34. Signature's spiking fast," she said.

Kaycee straightened instantly, her voice slipping into command mode. "Copy. We're on it."

"Eliza, huh? She pretty new to the team?" Marek asked.

"Yeah, she took over for Marcus. She's competent. No nonsense. She balances Wilko out pretty well," Kaycee said as she pulled a Katana from behind her desk and strapped it to her back.

"He's a funny one. Hopefully he keeps his sense of humor," Marek said.

"Noticed you're wearing different hardware now." Marek pointed to her sword.

"Yeah, the guns were to keep my cover when everyone thought I was human. Never really liked them, and they weren't necessary after I came clean to the team about what I am—after Harley." Her face clouded in anger and guilt.

She took a breath and gave a crooked smile. "Plus, I like my sword better. Nothing cuts like Rift-forged steel. It's my bonded blade, and I've had it for centuries," she answered as she made her way out the door.

"It looks good on you," Marek said, as he followed.

"You don't look too shabby either. I never thought I'd see anyone wear those blades... I imagine there's a story behind it." She shot him a questioning look as they got in the elevator and made their way down to the parking garage.

"I'll tell you on the way. It's a long story that almost ended in Cael having a heart attack," he said with a smile, exiting the elevator.

"Too bad it didn't take," she quipped as they got into the sleek, blacked-out SUV.

"I'll try harder next time," he said as he got in and closed the passenger door.

"Now, for that story. You've got twenty minutes before we get to the waterfront, and I'm all ears," she said as she gunned the engine and pulled onto the main road.

◆

The sky over Brooklyn hung heavy with the promise of rain, a ceiling of mottled grey that pressed low over the borough.

The air was thick with static when they pulled up and stepped out of the SUV—crisp and metallic on the tongue, like the moment before lightning strikes.

As Marek made his way up to the half-finished transit hub sprawled like a skeleton of rusted beams, he noticed how Kaycee moved beside him in a way that didn't require words or direction. Her stride matched his without effort.

He wondered if she felt his presence the way he felt hers—like a magnetic pull, a tether. He was always aware of where she was, as if something inside him tracked her.

It had been weeks since they had fought together, and he hadn't realized how much he missed it. Missed her.

He turned his attention back to the surging Rift energy emanating from deeper within the transit hub.

Kaycee's shoulders tensed, eyes flicking in the same direction. She felt it too—the energy bleeding out into their world.

Then he felt something else. A final surge of energy. He could feel it clearly now that he was a Warden, like the Rift was a door, and someone was pummeling it from the other side.

Then the Rift opened.

A vertical tear in the air, just above the ground, bordered in flickering blue-white energy. It hung like a blade through the fabric of reality, humming with power that didn't belong in this world. The Rift pulsed once—deep and low—and with it came the familiar scent of ozone and electricity.

Three Drakyn stepped through the tear, one after the other.

"Only three," Kaycee observed, "They hunt in mated pairs, so that means that one or more of them must have died trying to break through."

Marek looked at her, a brow raised in question.

She continued, "It takes a significant amount of power for a creature of the realms to pass through. Normally they die before they can. These are strong enough to make it through, so it should be fun!"

Marek chuckled. "You're nuts."

Muscles bunching, tails lashing behind them, claws gouging the concrete as they landed. Nearly seven feet tall, each of them was a nightmare sculpted in black, metallic scales. Their eyes glowed red—pits of molten hate. Their fangs flashed in jagged rows, as they lifted their heads into the air, scenting their surroundings.

They twisted in unison, low inhuman roars coming from their jaws as they became aware of the two Wardens standing nearby.

No hesitation. They charged.

Marek and Kaycee moved without a word, splitting off instantly.

There was no choreography, no planning—they simply responded to each other instinctively, moving in sync, complementing and adding to each other's strengths.

The first Drakyn charged Marek—massive, its tail whipping side to side, as it sprinted low and fast. Its fanged mouth opened, jaws stretching far too wide.

Marek dropped low into a slide beneath its first swipe of claws, boots skimming across concrete.

His blades hissed free of their scabbards as he drew them mid-movement. Twisting up from the slide, he crossed them in a brutal arc. Steel sang. Blood sprayed.

The Drakyn shrieked and reared, but Marek vaulted up, in a move that flipped him over its hulking mass. He brought his first blade down in a heavy, bone-breaking strike into the back of its neck, and his second sword finished the job—cleaving the head from its massive shoulders.

The Drakyn collapsed mid-roar, its tail spasming as the body hit the concrete in a headless heap...

One down.

The second barreled toward Kaycee.

She was already moving—fast, controlled, lethal.

She ducked the first lunge, pivoted on one foot, and rolled under slashing claws that would've cleaved a lesser fighter in half. Coming out of the spin, she drove her left blade into its side, twisting deep between its scaled plates.

The Drakyn roared and tried to crush her with its bulk.

She didn't let it.

Instead, she used her embedded sword like a handle, flung herself around its body, and drove her second blade up through the underside of its jaw—clean through the roof of its mouth.

The Drakyn staggered, gurgled once, and dropped.

"Two down!" she shouted, already pulling her blades free.

Marek didn't answer.

He was already watching the third, but it didn't charge.

It studied them—its ribbed tail swaying with serpentine rhythm, claws flexing against concrete. Breath hissed from its nostrils in quick puffs, steam curling into the thick air. It moved slowly, stalking, flanking wide.

Smarter than the other two—but that wasn't saying much.

Marek holstered one blade. The other he flung, hard and fast, like a spear.

The weapon sang through the air in a blur and struck home—driving into the creature's chest and heart. The impact threw it back, pinning it to a half-toppled rebar column.

It spasmed. Shuddered. Then went still.

The Rift behind them pulsed once more—then shrank. The blue-white light flickered erratically before the gash sealed itself with a final hiss.

Kaycee stood near her fallen target, blood streaking the side of her face, her chest rising and falling in steady rhythm. It had started to rain again—just enough to slick her armor, to trace down the curve of her cheekbones in rivulets.

Across from her, Marek calmly walked over and retrieved his blade from the body.

He was calm, collected. Eyes clear—absent of hate and rage.

She looked at him and was struck by how different he was from when he'd beaten those two Drakyn to death shortly after his transformation.

"You've changed," she said, voice low.

Marek nodded once, sheathing his thrown sword into the scabbard next to its twin. "Yeah. I had to."

She crossed the distance to him, slow and measured. No pretense now. No guard.

When she reached him, Marek stepped closer and lifted one hand. His thumb wiped a streak of ichor from her jawline, and his touch lingered there—gentle, grounding.

She leaned into it. Not much. Just enough.

"I don't know what's ahead," he said quietly, eyes still on her. "But I don't want to face it without you."

Kaycee's voice was softer than the rain, but it carried weight. "We had better face it together. Because whatever's coming... I have a feeling we're going to need all the help we can get."

The concrete beneath their boots still trembled faintly. The mist thickened. The Rift was gone, but the damage was not.

And whatever had pushed those creatures through—it was picking up the pace each day.

But for now, in that ruined stretch of Brooklyn—in the breath between one battle and the next—they stood together.

And for the first time in weeks, neither of them had to face the dark alone.

Chapter 46

O ver the course of the next two weeks, the breaches continued at the pace of one every day.

Same city. Different locations. Always the two of them to meet it head-on.

They didn't talk about the pattern. Didn't have time—they were too busy just trying to respond.

And respond they did. Together, they were unstoppable—fighting like two halves of the same blade.

The rest of the SCU had been mostly pushed to cleanup and comms support as the breaches grew more frequent.

Wilko, especially, would bitch and moan about being made irrelevant—but as the days wore on, his eyes told a different story.

Relief.

He didn't really want to be on the front line—not with the Drakyns multiplying like a plague—he just wanted to bitch about it.

When Kaycee called out a threat, Marek was already moving—fast, fluid, like he was inside her head. And when he launched into the fray, she was right behind him, cutting down anything that tried to flank him.

The fighting had changed them. Sharpened them. Pulled them closer. So close, they didn't need to speak in battle. They just knew—moving as one, reacting on a level beyond words.

And in the moments between the chaos—when the creatures were dead, and the Rift stitched itself closed—something quiet and solid settled between them.

She looked at him differently now. Not with caution. Not with that cold layer of professionalism she'd used to wear like armor.

Now, it was something else. Trust. Recognition. A softness that reminded him of the night they'd spent together before everything had come apart.

And he met her looks when he could. Gave her something back. It wasn't overt. Just steady. Present. Real.

Her touches changed too.

A hand on his shoulder after a fight. Holding his hand while they waited for intel to come through. A hug—tight and quiet—after a near miss that left them both rattled.

Small things. Tentative things. But they meant everything.

They weren't diving back into passion at full steam. This wasn't lust—though that was there, simmering under the surface.

It was also something deeper. Two people slowly rebuilding a relationship after everything had nearly shattered.

She didn't say anything about it. Neither did he. But it was there. They both felt it.

Then there was the post-battle fallout—and Kaycee handled that alone.

Every night, she reported in to Director Green.

"*Breach at 3:14 AM. Queens. Two Drakyn. Down in six minutes. Civilian injuries: zero.*"

"*New one tonight—Manhattan. Four Drakyn. Increasing coordination. Same energy signature.*"

The calls were short. Professional. Her voice always clipped and composed.

But behind her eyes, Marek could see it. The pressure. The weight. She didn't have answers—and her human bosses wanted them yesterday.

Why were the breaches increasing? Why only in New York City? Why only the dragon creatures?

Director Green never raised his voice. He didn't have to.

Kaycee felt it anyway. The disappointment. The expectation. The silent frustration bleeding through every pause when she couldn't answer their questions—either by Akron's orders, or because she didn't know.

And when the calls ended, she would just sit there, staring at the screen, jaw clenched, pulse ticking in her throat.

And then she'd stand, grab her gear, and get ready for the next breach. Because they weren't stopping.

They sent daily text updates to Akron, informing him of the patterns, the increases. He didn't have any additional insights as to why these spikes were happening. He had suspicions, but nothing actionable.

And whether they admitted it or not, both of them knew—it wasn't a coincidence.

Something was targeting New York City, And Marek and Kaycee were in the crosshairs.

◆

Marek kept his visits to Tucker quiet. He went every day.

The secure medical ward hadn't changed since the day Tucker had been admitted—sterile lights, the soft hush of pressurized air, the rhythmic blip of machines tracking vitals.

Tucker lay in the same position every time, comatose but breathing, his presence a constant in a world unraveling one breach at a time.

Marek would drop his gear, pull up a chair, and start talking. Sometimes about the field. Sometimes about Kaycee. Often about nothing in particular.

"Another two Drakyn today. Midtown. Chen thinks they're learning, maybe adapting. I'm not sure. I still think they're being driven by something—I don't think they have the intelligence for this. We took them down, but not fast enough to stop the damage. An innocent bystander got caught up in the fight and died—just by being nearby."

He'd pause, rubbing a hand over his face, letting silence stretch before continuing.

"Kaycee's taken some pretty hard hits. She doesn't flinch, though. Doesn't even stop moving. Just digs in and keeps fighting. That woman's made of iron, I swear."

Sometimes Marek would drift into stories. Half-finished memories of the times before they joined the SCU—before everything changed. Shared laughter, shared cases. Tucker making Captain Greggs laugh so hard he nearly spit his coffee across the office.

Other times, he spoke of things he didn't share with anyone else.

"I think she's letting me back in. It's slow—tentative—but real. I can feel it. Not just the way we move in the field, but something deeper. I hurt her, Tucker—bad. If you were here, you would've told me to get my head out of my ass and apologize. You were never afraid to speak your mind."

He leaned forward then, resting his palm lightly on Tucker's arm, voice rough.

"I miss you, man. I need someone who isn't afraid to call me out on my bullshit, or when I start getting in my own head. Kaycee wouldn't hesitate to do it, but she doesn't know me well enough yet. I need my brother back."

Tucker didn't stir. But Marek swore, sometimes, he could feel warmth in that unmoving grip. A pulse of something deep inside. A tether trying to reach out.

◆

By the fourteenth breach in as many days, even the most skeptical among the team had stopped pretending this was random. The surges weren't just accelerating—they were evolving.

The numbers of Drakyns coming through started to increase consistently, like the Rift was struggling to keep them out—continuing to weaken.

And the surge sites were starting to repeat in the same zones—places that had allowed the most Drakyn in.

Eliza pointed it out on the plotter.

"If you look at the pattern, it's no longer random. The attacks are getting more focused. The sites where only one Drakyn—or none—broke through last week have fallen off the grid. The ones that let in the most? They're increasing in frequency."

"She's right," Kaycee said. "We have been re-visiting the same breach locations more often. This feels like focused escalation. Like someone is trying to narrow down their attacks from the other side."

She looked at Marek, her eyes flashing with fear and something colder—like hate.

"And I think I have a suspicion of who it could be... Dharken Mohr."

Marek stilled, "Harley? How do you know?"

"Because he is the ruler of the Realm of Shadow and Thought—the place where both the Drakyn and the Elvahr reside. He's also Nyxia's General. He's been alive since the Final War between Onos and his children. He's never forgiven humanity for Nyxia's death at Onos's hands. He's committed to either killing or subjugating us. It was her last wish, apparently."

Marek pulled out his phone, "We need to tell Akron—"

Kaycee cut in. "I'm confident he already knows. But knowing *who* is behind the attacks, doesn't help us. We need to know *why* he's doing this. If I know Akron, he's searching for an answer as we speak."

"Why can't we just go in and destroy him? Attack his realm and end it?" Marek asked.

"Because Onos gave his children complete dominion over the realms he created for them. From what we know, only Onos could enter all seven. To try to break through to one of the Realms without an invitation would drain a Warden so severely, by the time they arrived, they'd be no stronger than a normal human."

She paused, then added, "And just like we can sense when something comes through our side of the Rift, Harley could sense an intruder on his. He'd be waiting, and he'd tear us apart."

Marek looked at the chart of pulsing surge points and said into the silence, "Let's hope Akron finds something—*before* whatever it is Harley's working toward comes to pass. I get the feeling we are running out of time."

Marek felt a certainty, rooted in instinct, click into place. The surges were building towards something. Something worse.

War.

And Marek knew one thing with absolute clarity: when that war arrived, it wouldn't care if humanity was ready.

But he would be. Their team would be.

Failure wasn't an option—not when the cost of losing meant watching the world burn.

Not when there were people worth protecting, and not when Kaycee was still fighting beside him.

◆

Akron stood in the heart of the Lore Hall, surrounded by silence and failure—failure to answer the questions plaguing him.

Books lay open across the long stone table in front of him—some were ancient, some were newer, none were helpful.

Scrolls had been unrolled, and half-forgotten journals cracked open again for the first time in centuries. Pages that once felt sacred now felt useless. He'd read every theory within their pages. Nothing fit.

The Rift was weakening everywhere, but the other spots were manageable.

New York City, though, was the weakest—the worst spot by far.

For months now, the breaches had been steady, manageable. One a week, maybe two. But since Marek and Kaycee had been assigned to the region, something had shifted. Now it was one breach every day, without fail. Some small, some large. All of them within that city.

He didn't blame them—not Kaycee, not Marek. He trusted them more than most.

But he couldn't shake the feeling that the increase wasn't coincidence. Something—*someone*—was pushing.

He paced the edge of the room, jaw tight, fists clenched behind his back. He looked down at his phone. At the data Kaycee and Marek had provided—the city map was displayed on his screen. And layered atop it were flashing red dots—each marking a Rift breach in the past two weeks.

There were too many.

He watched them flash in slow sequence. East Harlem. Midtown. Queens. Brooklyn. Staten Island.

Always in New York City. Always where Marek and Kaycee were.

Akron let out a long breath. He didn't want to say it out loud—didn't really need to. But the thought was already there, lodged in the back of his skull like a splinter.

Dharken Mohr.

He hadn't heard of his involvement in anything since Marek's near-death almost a month ago. Hadn't sensed him. Hadn't heard even a whisper. But this... this felt like his work.

Not brute force—something smarter. More deliberate. Like someone testing weak spots in a dam. Removing one stone at a time, until the whole thing eventually gave way.

Akron couldn't prove it, and he hated that. He didn't like acting on instincts. He liked evidence. Patterns. Logic.

But his gut had been screaming louder with every passing day.

He locked his phone, putting away the digital map, and pocketed it. He crossed to one of the long benches near the rear of the hall, where a series of hand-bound journals waited in a tidy stack. These were his. Personal logs. Old notes. The kind of things he never let anyone else see.

He sat down slowly, like the weight on his shoulders had finally caught up to him, and opened the top book. He didn't read it. Just stared at the ink, his eyes tracing the lines like they might rearrange into something useful.

They didn't.

There was no entry on how to fix this.

No instructions from Onos. No buried failsafe—no clues to what could cause this. Just silence.

Akron looked up at the mural across the wall—Onos, hand outstretched, the Rift behind him in vivid strokes of blue and white. The final gift of a Titan who had given everything to protect humanity.

He spoke to the painting, voice low... pleading.

"If you left something behind for me to find... now would be the time to show me."

But Onos stayed silent, and the Rift kept weakening.

———◆———

The halls of Arckus were silent as Malen made his way down narrow corridors toward his goal.

Malen had waited for this—waited for Akron to retreat into the Lore Hall, consumed by his latest obsession with trying to find the reason behind the weakening Rift. The First Warden's study was one of the few places in all the citadel left unsecured—not by oversight, but by arrogance.

Akron never believed anyone would betray him here—that anyone could think of betraying the Wardens.

Malen pushed the door open and stepped inside.

The study was dim, lit only by a narrow slit of daylight filtering through the high stone window. Shelves lined with worn books loomed along the far wall, and the wide wooden desk at the center was cluttered with parchment, ink pots, and hastily stacked breach reports.

No defenses. Just silence and blind trust.

He moved deliberately, gloved fingers rifling through the organized chaos on the desk. Dozens of Rift patrol summaries, casualty logs, fading ink notes written in Akron's heavy hand. Most were routine. Reports. Maps. Small annotations about minor weak points in various urban sectors.

Then he found it.

A spot on an old map of New York City. Central Park was circled with an annotation that said: *Rift weakening—paper thin—flag for special follow-up. Concern about complete failure.*

Malen's pulse quickened.

So, it was true. It was right there, written in Akron's own hand. The Rift was close to failing—not just weakening.

He hadn't expected Akron to document it so plainly—let alone flag it with concern. But here it was, evidence of the Rift nearing collapse. In the very heart of New York City.

He didn't linger.

With one last glance at the map, committing the location to memory, he slipped back into the corridor and closed the door behind him. No need to steal what was already written in his mind.

By the time the First Warden returned from his search through forgotten lore, it would be too late.

Malen would find a way to reach out to Dharken Mohr. And when that happened, he'd be one step closer to being rid of the shackles of service to humanity.

He hurried off with an eager light in his eyes—Dharken's whispered promises a silent voice playing over and over in the warped corridors of his mind.

Chapter 47

Dharken Mohr

The sky in the Realm of Shadow and Thought was always churning.

Veins of Riftlight cracked through the black canvas above, pulsing with pale blue intensity—like an exposed nerve in the body of reality.

Beneath it, Dreadfall loomed—its obsidian towers veined with ivory spirals, jutting upward like the fingers of a rotting corpse.

Dharken Mohr stood at the edge of the southern parapet, cloak dragging behind him in a serpentine trail of shadow.

From here, he could see the sea of darkness stretching out beneath the cliffs, crashing against the black rock in endless, silent fury. It wasn't water—but a mass of sentient darkness.

He turned away from the view and walked back into the War Hall, heading to his maps. To his plans.

Two Elvahr sentries knelt as he passed, shadows parting before his footsteps—His mood was blacker than the realm itself.

For weeks, he had been testing the Rift—probing, pushing, flinging his Drakyn into every weak point he could find.

New York City remained the thinnest area by far.

The last week had been very promising. Multiple Drakyn had made it through every time they tried.

But for every three Drakyns that made it through, twenty had to die in order to weaken the Rift enough to allow passage.

He was gradually narrowing his field of attack, but it wasn't enough. The current losses couldn't be sustained—or he would run out of shock troops for his army.

The Rift, even in its weakened state, was too strong.

If he kept up this pace, he would have to start over. And he was getting too close to stomach the thought of stopping—of decades more of Earth's years spent rebuilding.

He needed to find the weakest point in the Rift, but he needed more information.

He had one last possible ace in the hole. A Warden contact he had been grooming for years—slowly manipulating his mind in an attempt to place a mole in the ranks.

The traitor was convinced that he'd be allowed to rule the humans alongside Dharken when the Rift finally fell, and his plans came to fruition.

He chuckled to himself. *What a fool.* Didn't they know that he hated the Wardens most of all?

They had once been human—and worse, bound to protect them.

It was an exhausting process, manipulating a mind with his darkness—especially when outside his realm—but it may have just paid off.

He had received a message from his little traitor friend several days ago. The Warden wanted to meet. Today.

Malen said he had found information that Dharken would find valuable.

The time was close for their meeting, so he'd best be on his way.

As he ripped open the Rift and began the uncomfortable process of pushing through, he smiled.

After all, if he didn't like what the traitor had to say, he could always kill the little shit. One more dead Warden would always be worth a trip to the other side.

◆

Dharken had arrived on-time to their meeting site—Central Park—and had been waiting for five minutes when he felt the Rift before he heard it.

An electric discharge that made his skin itch. He didn't turn. Not right away.

He stood beneath the crooked branches of an old oak in the Ramble, where the paths grew narrow and the trees pressed in too close.

The kind of place where shadows didn't just fall—they lingered. Brooded.

New York City loomed beyond the tree line, humming like a tireless machine.

Here, though, the world was quieter. Colder. Older. And here, in this little knot of dark, the illusion of safety didn't quite reach.

He liked that.

He waited until Malen appeared.

The Warden stepped through the Rift with more confidence than he should have—boots landing soft in the damp grass. He kept his posture stiff, chin up like a soldier still playing at discipline.

But Dharken didn't need to see the nerves in his shoulders to know they were there—he could feel them. Smell the fear.

"You're late," Dharken said. Not loud. Just enough to cut through the silence like a knife dragged slow across glass.

Malen didn't flinch, but he didn't meet his eyes either. He stepped forward, stopping a few paces away. Not too close.

"I found it," he said, voice low and tight. "It's here, in Central Park—the Great Lawn. The Rift is almost non-existent in its protection."

Dharken didn't move, but the air around him shifted, like the night had leaned closer to listen.

"It's almost completely frayed at the edges, and no one knows why. You wouldn't need to throw your whole force at it to get through."

"You're certain?" he asked, and this time there was no cold edge to his voice—only something more dangerous. Excitement.

Malen nodded enthusiastically. "I confirmed it by stealing into Akron's personal study."

That earned the smallest twitch of Harley's mouth. Not quite a smile. Something tighter. Sharper.

Malen stood his ground. "You said I'd be part of what comes next."

Dharken smiled. Slow. Cold

Interesting, he thought, *the little traitor found a pair of balls somewhere.*

"And so you shall. When the Rift tears open—when the old world dies screaming—you'll be standing beside me."

Malen smiled and nodded to himself.

"We'll march in two days' time," Dharken said.

"Try and sow as much discord as you can between then and now." He reached out to wrap dark powers around the Warden's head, tendrils snaking inside—whispering... reinforcing his manipulations.

"I will... So, we're agreed?" Malen asked.

"You'll have your reward," Dharken snapped. "But make no mistake—if you've misled me, I will not spare you.

"Instead, you will die screaming with those humans you protect."

Dharken didn't linger. He turned and walked into the Rift, vanishing.

Dreadfall's War Hall was tense the moment he stepped through the high arch.

Voices had been raised just seconds before, sharp and overlapping in the shadow-flickering light. Now they hung in the air like heat after lightning. Twelve Elvahr lieutenants stood around the war-map, stiff in their armor, tension writ across every line of their posture. Riftlight pulsed along the room's edges, drawing jagged shadows across the ceiling.

The map itself hovered in the center, casting blood-red light onto obsidian. Earth glowed faintly beneath its shifting grid, bright and unstable—New York City pulsing at the heart of it like a cracked coal.

Dharken didn't speak at first. He moved straight to the table, cloak dragging like a whisper behind him, and raised one hand. The projection shifted, expanding.

New York City swelled, zooming in on one section. The Great Lawn of Central Park flared like an exposed nerve.

"There," he said. "That's our breach point. It is the thinnest—almost completely frayed.

"In four cycles—two human days—we attack it with everything we have. It will tear open, causing a permanent collapse in that section. No re-sealing, just a wide-open door for us to walk through."

A beat of silence, and then murmurs—quiet at first, but growing.

"How do you know?" Lieutenant Voryn asked, his voice not defiant, but deliberate.

Dharken didn't blink. "A source gave it to me."

Lieutenant Kessara's brow furrowed. "What source?"

"A Warden," he said simply.

That got them going.

The room shifted again, this time with discomfort. Voryn's jaw tightened. Kessara didn't hide her frown.

"You're trusting one of *them* to guide our assault?" Lieutenant Thalor asked, incredulous.

"He's not one of them anymore," Dharken replied. "He's been mine for years. Quiet. Watching. Waiting. And now, he's given me everything we need."

"And you believe him?" Thalor's tone was steel. "What if he's playing both sides? What if this is a ploy to lure our strength into a trap?"

"His mind is mine—there is no trap—but if there is, then I'll burn the city anyway," Dharken said.

"There is too much dissent amongst the Warden ranks. The Council bickers and chafes under Akron's old ways and has slowly turned the Wardens against him—because of this, there will not be enough Wardens to stand in our way, even if they knew."

Kessara stepped forward, her brow furrowed. "And if the Rift doesn't break?"

"It will," Dharken said, low and final. "I've *felt* it. That seam is thinning by the hour. It's not just destabilized—it's almost non-existent. That Warden gave me the last piece I was missing—the specific location. Now we force it open."

A murmur passed through the room, then silence.

He leaned in over the projection. "I want the two thousand Drakyn you have already prepared, to be at the ready—battle-conditioned, blooded. They will be the battering ram, and sow chaos."

The Elvahr Lieutenants nodded slowly, the battle plan taking root in their minds. The Drakyn were perfect for this assault. They fought. They killed. They obeyed.

"Also prepare your Elvahr elite," Darken continued. "One thousand strong as previously discussed. We'll be the surgical strike that finish off any defenses the humans or Wardens—those able to get there in time—have left after the Drakyns take their pound of flesh."

Voryn exhaled through his nose. "Four cycles. That's tight."

"We've waited long enough, and you've had enough time to gather them," Dharken said. "No more scouting. No more probing. No more bleeding resources in vain hopes that we'll find the right spot."

He looked at each of them.

"We've found it—the spot to break through. This is it. The culmination of all our plans. When the Rift finally shatters under our onslaught, we will not pass through it quietly."

He smiled, sharp and cold.

"We will *conquer*... For Nyxia!!"

"For Nyxia!!" They chorused.

Dharken's voice dropped into a near whisper, full of promise and violence.

"Four cycles—two earth days," he said.

"Then humanity learns what it means to fear. To kneel." His face split with a manic grin.

"To DIE!!"

Chapter 48

Fifteen Minutes Earlier

The Warden Council chamber was a hollow mountain of old power.

Built into the cliffs above Arckus, its stone walls shimmered with Riftlight, pulsing in time with the sky above.

A vaulted dome arched above the central table—massive, round, scarred by centuries of arguments and blood-sworn decisions. Light filtered through the skylight above, fractured into cold, prismatic rays.

They were seven now—two more chairs filled in the past couple of months.

Seven Wardens, draped in robes of their own colors, their insignias etched in silver, their expressions tight with weariness and rising tension.

"We've lost another two Wardens in the last three weeks alone," said Vara, her voice as sharp as the lines cut across her brow.

"And for what? Another city saved? Another meaningless surge repelled while the humans murder each other?"

"They are not our concern. The Rift is," replied Warden Elyos, a younger member, but one who spoke like he'd lived twice as long.

"The Rift is failing because Akron refuses to evolve," snapped Warden Malen. He leaned forward, gray-blond hair tied back, eyes burning with a quiet sort of disdain.

"We follow orders passed down like scripture, without challenge. And look where it's gotten us—death. Repetition. Nothing changes."

"Malen—" Althis started.

"No," he said, slamming a hand on the table. "I'm not saying what you don't already think. I said it before, and I'll say it again... we protect a species that doesn't know we exist, and who have become less and less worthy of our protection. They actively war and try to kill each other, for Onos's sake."

He looked at each of the Five in turn.

"Maybe it's time we aligned ourselves with one of the Realms. With a stronger force. One that could help us... reclaim order."

There were audible gasps and some outright cries at the suggestion.

Vara stood, her eyes wide with disbelief. "That's treason—we don't involve ourselves with the Seven Realms. We don't ally ourselves with them... ever."

"It's realism," Malen countered.

"Akron expressly forbade contacting other Realms... and your attitude toward humanity—Malen, if Akron heard you—" Halros began.

"He'd kill me, yes, I know."

"You speak as if there's no line you will not cross."

Malen smirked faintly. "Maybe the lines were drawn by the wrong hand."

"Maybe we should take a break. We're all upset right now, and we don't want to say anything we'll regret," Elyos suggested.

"Yes, let's reconvene after lunch," said another Warden.

The meeting adjourned moments later. They left the chamber in groups; tension folded into their silence.

Outside, in the council's corridor overlooking the sky-line lit by Riftlight, Cael stood against a pillar, arms crossed. His jaw was clenched. His gaze pinned on Malen as the Warden slipped away alone.

Cael's fingers moved quickly on his phone:

—*He's leaving. He looks shifty—like he's hiding something. I'm going to follow him.*

Akron's reply came instantly:

—*Track his signature. If he jumps, tell me where. I'll follow from the other side.*

Copy, Cael replied, already moving.

◆

Malen didn't go far—not at first. He moved with the confidence of someone used to shadows, knowing how to dodge patrols, how to bend between watchful eyes.

When he reached a blind corridor near the outer compound, he opened a Rift.

Cael waited until the last second to follow—vanishing through the same tear, a silent observer cloaked by the Rift's own hum.

Malen emerged near the edge of Central Park, just off the Loop by the Ramble—where the winding paths narrowed and the trees grew too dense for most tourists to bother with after dark.

A cold hush blanketed the park, broken only by the whisper of wind through brittle leaves and the distant hum of traffic beyond the tree line.

The New York City skyline loomed just above the canopy, flickering behind low fog like a city holding its breath.

Cael chose to arrive separately, cloaked in a veil before he even emerged. He found his spot and didn't breathe. Didn't move.

From his hiding spot behind a massive oak, Cael watched Malen approach Dharken Mohr. Every nerve in his body screamed at him to intervene, to put down the traitor before he revealed something. But that wasn't the plan. Not yet.

He focused on Malen's posture—a relaxed pose that looked forced. He was overly confident—but the Warden's shoulders also carried tension. He was trying to look calm, like he wasn't scared. That persona, however, was betrayed by the careful distance he maintained from Dharken—as though instinctively aware of the danger he courted.

If I notice it, you can bet your ass Dharken notices... Cael thought. A part of him—a very small part of him—felt sorry for Malen in that moment. He would be eaten alive by Dharken if Akron didn't get to him first.

Cael's fingers tightened around his phone, recording every damning detail of their meeting. His phone vibrated once in his hands—Akron was close. Looked like Malen's time was almost up.

Dharken was something else entirely. His presence pressed on the very surroundings, bending shadows inward, making the air seem colder—a seeping evil that emanated from his very pores.

Watching him, Cael felt a chill slide down his spine. Malen had no idea the monster he'd allied himself with.

Words exchanged between them carried to Cael—"Great Lawn... nonexistent protection... confirmed... Akron's study." Each piece lodged itself in his chest, a dagger of betrayal driven deeper with every sentence.

He couldn't say he was surprised. After all, there was always something about Malen that had rubbed Cael the wrong way. An intense disdain for the humans he was supposed to protect.

Cael felt his pulse quicken as Dharken extended his hand, tendrils of darkness snaking toward Malen—his signature power—reinforcing a manipulation that was already deeply ingrained.

He gritted his teeth. Seeing a fellow Warden compromised so completely made his stomach turn, and just plain pissed him off.

Then, Dharken vanished through the Rift, and Malen stood alone in the sudden emptiness, smiling to himself like the fool he was.

Cael waited a beat, ensuring the coast was clear, and then lunged.

His fist connected with Malen's face before the traitor could even register movement—crumpling like dead weight, hitting the ground hard and unmoving.

A Rift tore open beside him.

Akron stepped through like wrath incarnate.

"Where is he?" Akron snarled at Cael. "Where is that Elvahr filth?"

"He's gone," Cael said, eyes scanning the spot where he'd vanished moments before. "He slipped out right before you showed. But he doesn't know we were here. Doesn't know we were watching. That's what we wanted."

Akron exhaled through his nose—sharp and slow. His jaw was tight, but his voice stayed level. "Did you get it recorded?"

Cael nodded, holding up his phone.

"Got everything. Every word. Along with this little traitorous bastard as a bonus." He jerked his thumb toward the figure slumped on the ground.

Malen picked that moment to let out a low groan, starting to come to.

Akron crossed the space in two long strides, reached down, and hauled Malen up by his neck. The man's feet barely touched the ground.

Malen blinked blearily, then started choking... hands scrabbling at the immovable grip around his neck. He stilled when he saw Akron's face, inches from his own.

All the color drained from his face.

Akron's grip tightened, his voice like stone cracking under pressure. "You picked the wrong side."

Malen whimpered.

"Let's go," Akron said, without taking his eyes off him. The menace in those two words was bone deep.

Cael fell in beside him, silent but ready, as they traveled back to Arckus.

◆

They returned to the Council chamber mid-session.

The sound of the tall oak doors slamming open echoed like a thunderclap through the chamber's vaulted stone dome. Seven heads turned in unison, eyes widening as Akron stepped into the room like a storm wrapped in flesh, his black armor still crackling with Rift energy from his transit.

Malen dangled from Akron's grip, being dragged behind him. Blood matted one side of his face. His gaze was distant, unfocused—like a man watching the last light drain from a world he once believed in.

Akron didn't pause.

He reached the center of the chamber's polished obsidian floor, and flung him forward with enough force to send the Warden skidding across the inlaid rune-circle. His shoulder slammed against the marble step below the table. A crack sounded, and Malen screamed in pain.

Gasps rippled through the Council.

"What is the meaning of this?" Vara rose from her seat, her voice a sharp command, but it carried more alarm than authority.

Akron didn't look at her as he scanned the seated Council as a whole.

His voice was calm—but it was iron and rang through the room like judgment.

"Is this what you've become?" he asked, eyes sweeping the chamber. "Is this the kind of filth you welcome among your own?"

Confusion exploded into chaos.

"What—?"

"This is madness—"

"Explain yourself!"

Akron held up a single hand. The chamber dimmed as the Riftlight overhead responded to his will, casting the room in pale violet.

He tapped his thumb against Cael's phone.

The video started playing. The audio was clear—undeniable.

Dharken Mohr's voice spilled through the quiet, cold and unmistakable, followed by Malen's:

"*You're late.*"

"*I found it,*" Malen said. "*It's here, in Central Park—the Great Lawn. The Rift is almost non-existent in its protection.*"

"*You're certain?*"

"*I confirmed it by stealing into Akron's personal study.*"

"*We'll march in two days' time... Try and sow as much discord as you can between then and now.*"

"*I will... So, we're agreed?*"

"You'll have your reward..."

When the recording ended, the chamber sat in stunned quiet, punctuated only by the faint hum of Arckus.

Vara slowly turned toward Malen. Her voice cracked when she asked, "Is it true?"

Malen said nothing.

Akron took one slow step forward. The runes beneath his boots ignited faintly.

"Confess," he said with a growl.

Nothing.

"Malen," Akron said louder now, energy crackling beneath his skin. "Confess."

The traitor looked up at last.

His lips curled into something almost human—*almost*.

"I don't need to confess," Malen said hoarsely. "You heard it yourself."

Akron moved in a blink.

His hand struck Malen's chest, flat-palmed, and a bolt of Rift energy slammed into the traitor's body like a divine verdict.

Blue-white arcs raced down Malen's limbs, splitting through his veins like lightning seeking escape.

Malen screamed. It was a sound no one in the chamber would ever forget.

"I TOLD HIM!" he finally screamed, choking on every word. "The breach—the timing—Dharken Mohr's coming in TWO DAYS! And you can't stop it. You can't stop HIM."

He coughed blood then—laughing through it.

There were gasps of horror throughout the chamber as the others heard him utter Dharken's name.

"You stood still too long, Akron. You stood above us too long. You are outdated... humanity is outdated. It's time for the Realms to rise."

Then, quieter—more vicious—he added, "This is the beginning of the end."

Akron's hand moved, retrieving one of his swords from his back and, in a blur of motion, sliced through Malen's neck.

The dull thud of his head rolling to a stop several feet away, hammered like a gong through the stillness that followed.

No one moved.

The silence in the chamber was total—and carried the weight of grief, shock, and shame.

Akron stood there, motionless for a breath. Then two.

He knelt and retrieved the Essence escaping Malen's disintegrating form. He stood up—slowly—and faced the Council.

"This is what happens when we stray from the path Onos left for us," he said, voice quiet but resonating with absolute authority. "When those of you who think our ancient duty is up for modern debate."

They watched him, pale. Hollow-eyed. No one dared meet his gaze for long.

"You have two choices," he said, letting the words fall like a blade across their necks.

"Disband the Council and stand with me—gathering your Wardens in preparation to fight for humanity…"

He let the pause stretch, sword still dripping blood on the Council's floor as he pointed at Malen's still-warm body.

"Or die where you sit."

Vara rose first. Not because she was the strongest—but because she understood what was coming.

"We'll follow," she said softly.

Others fell in line and agreed. Some without speaking, some only able to raise trembling hands.

Akron didn't wait for ceremony.

He pulled out his phone and typed a single line:

—All Wardens. Meet at the Grand Circle. Dimfall—Tonight. Mandatory.

Pressing *send*, he looked up, his eyes sweeping across every face in the room.

"Send the same to yours," he said, "and be there."

They didn't speak as they scattered—shoulders tense, hands already opening phones—sending texts as commanded.

War wasn't coming—it was here.

And now, it had a time. A place. A name.

Chapter 49

The sky over Arckus had darkened into a slate of violet and charcoal by the time the Wardens began to gather.

Dimfall.

The Riftlight above casting long bands of pale-blue light across the marble tiers of the Grand Circle.

Marek stood at the edge of it all, silent, as more and more Wardens arrived—figures stepping through the Rift like flickers of thought turned solid. Their armor whispered with motion. Their faces were carved with purpose.

Not all came—some were dead, some unreachable, others perhaps unwilling—but still, any who could were in attendance. Hundreds upon hundreds. By the time the former Council members arrived with their followers in tow, the numbers had grown to nearly two thousand.

It should have been enough. It didn't feel like it.

Five hundred were still unaccounted for—many stating they had issues in their own territories to deal with.

Cowards... all.

Marek felt Kaycee arrive before he saw her. A tug in his gut and a brush of awareness against the edge of his mind—familiar, grounding. She stepped beside him, silent, her shoulders squared, her hand finding his. A single glance passed between them, and something settled inside him. They didn't need words.

Cael appeared next, offering a short nod before folding his arms across his chest.

"I recognize most of these faces—loyal to Akron and the old ways," he muttered. "Some though, are Council loyalists—whether they're here by threat or coercion, I'm glad to see them."

"Do you think any more will come?" Kaycee asked.

Cael's silence was answer enough.

Then, like a weight shifting in the air, Akron arrived. He prowled into the center of the Grand Circle without fanfare.

He didn't speak at first. He didn't need to. The Grand Circle fell into instant silence.

He stood on the ground floor, in the same spot where he had tested Marek two weeks prior. He wore his armor—black as night, etched in old scars from long-past battles—twin blades sheathed in their customary spots.

"My brothers. My sisters."

His voice cut through the stillness—quiet, resolute.

"You are here because you chose duty over fear. You answered a call that too many have ignored. We stand together now—on the edge of something that will shape not only our future, but the fate of the world we swore to protect."

He looked out across the sea of armored forms.

"Two days from now, Dharken Mohr—known to humans as Harley—will lead a full-scale assault against the weakest point of the Rift in New York City. The Great Lawn in Central Park."

A hum of dread moved through the crowd.

"He has built an army," Akron continued. "Two thousand Drakyn shock troops. One thousand Elvahr elite. All bred for one purpose—conquest. They will strike with force and precision."

"From the time his goddess Nyxia fell in battle against Onos in the Final War, his goal has been to carry out what Nyxia desired from the start. Total subjugation of humanity. He will not hesitate to slaughter any and all who stand in his way or refuse to bow to him."

He paused.

"He wants to permanently shatter the Rift, by focusing his entire force in this one section. Formerly known only to me—he now has the information because of the actions of a single traitorous Warden."

There was a loud clamor of incensed voices, shouts of rage and calls for the traitor's death.

Akron raised his hands, and the voices dropped to an angry murmur.

"The Traitor has been executed by my hand, but the damage is already done. If Dharken Mohr tries to send through even a fraction of their total number at one time, the Rift will shatter in that area. He is not expecting any resistance. He believes that when he comes through, he will slaughter humanity with no one to stand in his way—until Earth's governments kneel before him."

Akron got a nasty smile on his face then, "But we *will* be there to stand in his way."

There was a loud roar as Wardens raised their swords and cheered at the prospect.

His voice rose, echoing now with authority.

"You will cloak your signatures. You will move without being seen. And when dawn breaks in two days, you will be ready. It will be an ugly fight—the worst some of you have seen or ever will see. Our duty, as it has been since we were created, is to hold the line. If we do that, I believe we can break his army—put an end to Dharken Mohr once and for all."

The silence that followed wasn't empty. It was full of determination—etched into the face of every Warden.

Akron gave a final nod.

"Dismissed. Prepare."

And with that, he stalked out of the arena—and two thousand grim-faced Wardens followed in his wake.

◆

The next day, Marek stepped out of a Rift onto the sidewalk several houses down from his mother's house. Boots landing softly on the concrete. He had veiled his presence so no one would notice the portal behind him crackling with blue-white energy, before collapsing into nothing.

He looked around, ensured no one was close by, and dropped the veil—at least from all but the twin swords resting on his back. Cael had shown him that handy trick... he didn't want to be anywhere without them.

As he walked towards his mother's house, he enjoyed the simple and comforting sounds of his childhood neighborhood.

Birds chirped. A sprinkler ticked somewhere nearby. The world here still turned in its quiet, predictable way.

He stopped at the entrance to their lawn and took a moment to just breathe it all in.

The house hadn't changed. Same green shutters. Same crooked wind chimes on the porch. The flowerbeds had been freshly turned, the soil rich and dark around neat rows of rose bushes and flowers.

His mom had clearly been at work that morning.

She appeared around the side of the house a moment later—garden gloves on, a sunhat slanted over her brow, a trowel in one hand and a half-empty tray of seedlings in the other. She paused when she saw him, then straightened slowly, mouth curling into a soft smile.

"Well," she called across the yard, voice dry with affection, "look what the cat dragged in."

Marek smiled back. "Hey, Mom."

She crossed the lawn in a few determined steps and threw her arms around him. The hug was full and fierce—one of those bone-deep embraces that didn't rush, didn't release until something wordless had passed between them. When she finally stepped back, she looked him over like she was checking for bruises.

"You look tired," she said, squinting at him.

"I'm fine," he said. "There's just been... a lot going on."

"There always is in your line of work, isn't there?" she said, brushing dirt off her gloves. "Come on, porch swing's waiting."

They walked together toward the front of the house. The steps groaned beneath them, but Marek didn't mind. The porch swing swayed slightly in the breeze, its cushions still bright from the last time she'd replaced them. They sat, shoulder to shoulder, as the wooden frame creaked in a comforting rhythm.

She poured him a glass of iced tea from a pitcher she always seemed to have waiting—even when she had no reason to expect company.

"So," she said, nudging him with her elbow, "you gonna tell me how you've been, or do I have to ask yes-or-no questions like one of your interrogations?"

Marek chuckled. "Work's been... wild. Busier than usual."

"I gathered as much," she said, giving him a look. "Last time you disappeared for this long, you came back with a cracked rib and a stitched-up eyebrow."

"This time it's fewer stitches. More... pressure."

She nodded, silent. Understanding. Waiting for him to talk, like she always did.

They talked for a while about life—her neighborhood, the little girl down the street who was now apparently running a lemonade empire, the new couple that had moved in two doors down who hadn't yet learned about the raccoons in the trash bins. Normal things. Human things.

It grounded him.

Eventually, she looked over her glass and said, "So. Are you still seeing that agent you told me about? What was her name again... Kelsey?"

"Kaycee," Marek corrected, smiling faintly. "Yeah. W e're... yeah. We're good."

"Mm." Her eyebrows lifted. "That sounded a little dodgy. Good how?"

He hesitated, then leaned back and ran a hand through his hair. "It got complicated for a bit. We were both dealing with a lot. I almost ruined it, but we figured it out. Things are solid now."

"Is she the one who makes you disappear without a word for weeks on end?"

He gave her a sidelong glance. "One of them."

"Is she worth it?"

He paused, then said, without needing to think too hard, "Yeah. She is."

Ellen smiled into her glass. "Tell me about her."

Marek exhaled, but there was a smile tugging at his mouth as he did.

"She's brilliant. Not just book smart—though she is—but sharp. Strategic. She doesn't miss a damn thing, even when you wish she would. She's... intimidating sometimes, but it's just because she knows what she wants.

"She's got this way of carrying herself, like no matter what hell is breaking loose around her, she's already working on a plan to fix it."

Ellen rested her chin on her hand, watching him speak with a quiet kind of delight.

"And you like her?" she asked, teasing.

"I do," he said. "A lot."

"And her? Does she feel the same?"

"Yeah," he said, voice softening. "I think she does."

Ellen reached out and gently squeezed his forearm.

"That's good. You deserve someone who challenges you, Marek. Not just someone who makes you feel warm and safe, but someone who sees what you carry and says, 'let's carry it together.'

That's what real relationships are made of. The ones that last."

His throat tightened unexpectedly at her words.

"She's... kind of exactly that," he said, and the words were truer than he realized.

"Well," Ellen said, leaning back with a satisfied little nod, "then you're not allowed to screw it up."

He laughed. "I'll do my best."

"I'd like to meet her," she added, nudging him gently. "I mean it. Next time you have a window—bring her by. I promise not to tell her embarrassing stories of your youth. Maybe."

Marek's smile widened, and he laughed out loud.

"I'll bring her," he said. "Soon."

"Good," Ellen said. "Just don't make me wait another month to see you... and her this time. I might send a search party."

They sat together a little longer, not needing to fill the space between them. It was the kind of silence that came from trust, from the knowledge that no matter how infrequent he visited... no matter how dark things got in his world, or how many secrets he kept, this place would always be home. She would always love him.

Eventually, Marek rose.

"You're heading out on assignment?" she asked, though she already knew.

He nodded. "Early morning tomorrow."

Ellen stood with him and gave him one of her fierce hugs... and Marek soaked it in.

"Be safe," she said, voice quieter now.

"I will," he promised.

Marek stepped back and made his way down the cobble-stone steps to the sidewalk. He turned, and she gave him a wave with a bright smile.

He held on to that moment like a keepsake as he continued down the sidewalk. He walked for a little while, just moving to the flow of his own thoughts.

He found a secluded spot and opened the Rift. It hummed in recognition, and he stepped through—back to Arckus and everything he didn't want to face tomorrow.

◆

The glow of the bedside lamp painted Marek in shades of gold and shadow later that night, the light catching along the cut of his shoulders and the Warden tattoo inked into his skin.

He sat at the edge of his bed, shirtless, focused—his twin blades gleaming nearby, freshly oiled and resting like sleeping wolves. His hands had moved with quiet purpose for the last hour, but his mind had long since drifted ahead.

To the coming fight. To the blood. To the storm he knew was waiting for him.

He didn't hear the door open. He didn't need to—he'd felt her long before she reached his room.

Kaycee stepped inside without knocking, her silhouette framed by the hallway's dim light. Her jacket was off, eyes already locked on him. She said nothing. Just closed the door with a soft click and crossed the room with intent clear in every step.

Marek looked up, started to speak—but she was already there, her hands sliding into his hair as she kissed him.

Slow. Searching.

Her mouth brushed his like a question, and when he opened to her, she answered with a kiss that spoke volumes. They stayed that way—lips locked, breath mingling, desire building steadily—until she pulled back, eyes dark and full of heat.

He rose, his hands moving gently to her hips, but she placed a palm on his chest and whispered against his lips, "Let me."

His heart skipped a beat, and he allowed her to guide him backward until he sat again on the edge of the bed. Kaycee's eyes never left his as she slowly removed his shirt, fingertips tracing gently along his chest, mapping scars and muscle alike.

The air between them felt charged—weeks of unspoken words and longing glances finally coming to life.

His breathing quickened, eyes locked onto hers. "Kaycee..."

She kissed him in reply, then stepped back—peeling her shirt over her head, each motion deliberate. Then came the rest—layer by layer—until she stood in nothing but the soft lamplight, shadows and warmth dancing across her skin, highlighting the strength and softness that defined her.

There was no hesitation in her. Only trust.

He stood again, moving slowly to meet her, cupping her face in his hands. Their eyes met, unspoken promises hanging in the air as he kissed her softly, reverently.

His lips followed the curve of her jaw, lingered at the hollow of her throat. Her hands clutched at his shoulders as she leaned into him, bare skin against bare skin—heat and electricity crackling between them.

"Marek," she whispered, her voice filled with quiet urgency and need.

He gathered her into his arms, lifting her without effort, laying her gently onto the bed like something sacred. Their eyes never broke. Not as he settled beside her. Not as his hands found hers, fingers twining together.

The outside world faded—Only this. Only them.

His touch roamed her skin with reverence. Her breath came in shallow pulls, her body arching to meet his every movement. When he kissed her again, it was slow and consuming, a promise folded in every pass of his mouth over hers.

He pulled back just enough to whisper, "I love you."

Her hand moved to his chest, resting above his heart, where the Warden mark pulsed faintly beneath his skin. "I love you too."

Her voice dropped to a tender plea. "Just... stay alive tomorrow—I need you, Marek."

He nodded, eyes closed. "I'm not going anywhere."

"Promise me," she repeated gently.

"I promise."

And in the stillness of that room—before the chaos, before the war—two warriors came together, finding each other.

Tangled not just in limbs and desire, but in something deeper—older than the realms themselves. Something unbreakable.

Chapter 50

The next morning, Arckus was tense with the focused energy of last-minute preparations. The quiet calm before the storm.

Marek and Kaycee dressed in comfortable silence, each helping the other strap on gear and weapons. Neither said anything—because last night, they had said everything they needed to.

Showed each other everything that couldn't be said.

Their phones chimed in unison—a message from Akron:

—Rift activity spiking. All hands to Central Park. Take up defensive positions. Rift failure within the hour.

Up and down the barracks, and throughout Arckus, the air vibrated and sparked with the static hum of Wardens traveling the Rift to their predetermined assignments.

Marek looked at Kaycee. "Are you ready?" he asked, holding out his hand.

She took it, her grip firm, and nodded once. "Remember your promise—survive today."

He nodded, and they stepped through the rift.

Marek and Kaycee moved in silence as they stepped from the Rift onto the Great Lawn of Central Park, their boots pressing into damp earth. Behind them, the last of the Warden forces slipped into position—two thousand strong—dark shapes moving between trees and stone like shadows cast from another world.

Marek reached for the Rift's power and drew a veil around him. The air shimmered slightly, then stilled—his presence erased. Beside him, Kaycee mirrored the motion. Still visible to his sight, but erased from the gaze of humanity.

The veils required focus. Will. Most of them would fail the moment the first blade was drawn.

Across the lawn, the Wardens stood in perfect formation. Silent. Still.

They looked like obsidian statues—living armor wrapped in centuries of duty and pain. Dark sentinels poised on pristine grass where families once picnicked, where joggers and lovers had passed the day without fear.

It felt wrong. This peaceful ground, defiled by necessity.

Marek's gaze swept the line. Some faces he knew. Most he didn't. All of them ready to die.

His heart thudded once, deep and hollow.

"This is it," Kaycee said softly beside him. Her eyes were locked on the tree line in the east, where the wind tugged at the upper branches like warning fingers. "Whatever's coming... it happens here."

Marek nodded. He felt it too. A tension in the earth. A pressure behind the air, like a fault line beginning to groan.

He touched the hilts of the twin blades across his back. The runes hummed low, the blades a muted whisper—once an intrusion, they were now a quiet anchor in the back of his mind.

He looked at her then.

The first light of dawn stretched thin across the horizon, casting a soft amber glow through the mist. It caught the edge of her jaw, the sharp line of her cheekbone—illuminating her.

God, she was beautiful. Marek thought.

Next to him, Kaycee stood still and steady, her face calm, eyes locked ahead. Focused. Alive.

This woman—once his commanding officer, now something much more—had become the one constant in a world threatening to split apart.

"You still with me?" Marek asked, voice low, steady.

She didn't turn. Didn't need to. She simply reached out and laced her fingers through his, squeezed once—firm and sure—before letting go.

"Always."

A ripple passed through the Veil—subtle at first, like the air holding its breath. Then came the pressure.

Heavy. Insistent. Like a force battering against the fabric of reality itself.

Marek felt it before he saw it—a low-frequency thrumming that vibrated through his bones, through the earth beneath his boots. Around him, every Warden stiffened. Heads turned. Instincts sharpened.

They knew. Something was coming.

The next pulse hit like a thunderclap—deep, resonant, as if a giant had begun slamming its fists against the door of the world, trying to punch through.

Then the sky above Central Park split.

It didn't shimmer or pulse like the smaller breaches Marek had seen before. This wasn't a ripple. It was a jagged, vertical gash in the morning sky, folding back from the center like paper that had caught fire. It stretched a hundred feet wide and ten feet tall, and the world it connected to, glowed with the bruised violet-black light of a Realm that was never meant to touch this one.

And it didn't close.

For the first time since Onos forged the barrier between realms, the Rift had shattered. It stood wide. Permanent. A wound in the world that would not heal.

A sound followed, a vibration felt underfoot. Then came the monsters.

They didn't crawl or hesitate—they poured through in a rush, fanning out onto the lawn.

Drakyn—dozens at first, then hundreds, then thousands. Hulking and covered in gleaming black scales, their bone-tipped claws gouging the grass and asphalt as they surged into position. Their roars tore the air—grating—like static fed through a loudspeaker.

Behind them came the Elvahr.

Where the Drakyn were brute force, the Elvahr were surgical death. Tall and impossibly graceful, clad in living armor that pulsed with the shadows of their realm, they marched with deliberate purpose. Each bore blades like curved scythes, crescent-shaped and silent. Their eyes—cold, sharp, calculating—swept the battlefield like predators.

And then, he stepped through—Harley.

Marek saw him emerge like a general from legend—arms spread slightly. One long sword on his back, and a smaller sword at his hip.

Taller than the other Elvahr, his armor shimmered with etched silver patterns—writhing with living shadows.

He paused just inside the wound in the world, head tilting slightly. Observing. Sensing.

Then—he smiled.

"Well," he murmured, silver eyes flicking across the field. "Seems I was expected."

Harley hadn't expected the Wardens to be assembled—not all at once. He'd anticipated delays, some resistance by scattered arrivals. But Akron had been busy... and it seems his traitorous friend had failed.

He smiled anyway, surprise barely registering. He wasn't worried. Let the old wolf bring what he could.

This would be a harder fight than expected. But it would still end in his victory. He raised one arm and gestured forward, fingers curling.

"Kill them all."

The Drakyn surged like a tide, and the Wardens answered.

Their veils fell all at once—two thousand warriors stepping into full view, every rune-lined blade and armored silhouette catching the first light of dawn. Steel sang. Rift energy flared. And the Great Lawn became a war zone.

They met with a collision so violent the earth trembled.

Marek exploded forward with Kaycee at his side, their blades flashing in rhythm. His twin swords hummed with voices only he could hear—singing a soft chorus he didn't fight anymore—a knowledge he now welcomed.

Drakyn lunged toward them—he met one with a vertical strike that split it down the middle. Kaycee dropped another with a precise slide beneath its lunge, her blades finding vulnerable gaps in the scaled chest.

Around them, Wardens clashed with Elvahr elites, steel on steel. Bodies spun, blood sprayed, Rift energy blazed hot and then vanished. It was teeth and fire and energy and old rage let loose all at once.

Marek ducked under a pair of clawed arms, drove both blades into a Drakyn's gut, and turned in time to see a shape materialize from an opening in the rift just above the battlefield—falling to the earth in a glowing arc of blue-white energy.

Akron.

The First Warden slammed down like judgment it-self—straight into Harley's path.

His blades drawn before he touched the ground.

And then—they collided.

Steel met steel in a shower of sparks. Harley's strikes were feral and fast, a blur of rage and precision. Akron countered with brutal efficiency, each move honed by life-times of battle.

They fought like gods in mortal skin.

But Akron was tired. Worn. Weeks without rest piling up. Months of silence and weight and foreboding had leeched him thin. His strength was immense—still enough to level armies—but not fresh.

Harley was. He'd sacrificed Drakyn to open the Rift—not his own energy. He was sharp. Powerful. And full of his long-dead goddess's purpose.

A spin. A cut. A feint—Harley caught Akron's side with a slashing kick, then followed it with a clean thrust that Akron couldn't deflect in time—digging into his side.

Nearby, Marek turned in time to see Akron stumble.

Kaycee caught it too.

"Akron's in trouble!" Marek shouted. He blocked a de-scending blade, twisted beneath it, and drove his elbow into the Elvahr's throat—finishing with a cut that severed its head from its shoulders before spinning toward her.

"I'll draw Harley off—get to Akron. Pull him out!"

Kaycee nodded once, and they split.

Marek charged forward, slicing through Drakyn and El-vahr without slowing. His body moved before conscious thought—his blades pulling him like compass needles to-ward where he wanted to be.

Across the field, Harley drove Akron to one knee—one hand clutching a blood-slick wound. His blade hung heavy. His breaths came fast and shallow.

Harley raised his sword overhead.
"Goodbye, old wolf."

———◆———

"Harley!" Marek shouted from across the battlefield.

Harley turned, eyes widening for the briefest moment as he saw Marek cutting through the smoke toward him.

He smiled. Of course it would be him—Marek, the one who kept getting away.

"Well, well. Our little hero returns," Harley sneered, stepping away from Akron, letting the old Warden fall to the ground in a heap. "Tell me—do you enjoy punishment, or are you just too stupid to stay down?"

Marek didn't answer. He stood in silence... waiting.

Harley's grin cracked wider.

Behind them, Kaycee appeared in a shimmer of Rift-light. She knelt beside Akron, wrapped him in her arms, and vanished.

Harley's head jerked back toward Akron, just as she vanished with him.

The First Warden—stolen. Snatched away at the brink of death.

"Fuck!" He cursed, as he turned to Marek, silver eyes narrowed to slits.

"You little shit! I've been waiting millennia to get Akron on his knees," he said, voice a low growl. "You'll pay for that."

Marek didn't answer. He just motioned with his blades. "Come on, then. Let's do this, you and I."

The twin swords of Onos flickered with a pale golden sheen. The runes on the hilts flared, pulsing in time with Marek's heartbeat—seeming to react to Harley's presence.

Harley's gaze locked on them—and something in him cracked.

Recognition flashed across his face. Then fury. A fury so deep it drowned out all other rational thought.

Those weren't just weapons. They were history. They were sacrilege.

"Those... those are HIS," he breathed, almost disbelieving. "Onos's blades—the blades that killed my Nyxia!!"

His voice turned savage. "How? How do you carry those—her *murderers*?"

The scream that followed wasn't human. It tore from Harley's throat in a sound of rage and frustration that had built over millennia.

Then he came at Marek. Blades spun to life, and the space between them vanished. Their first clash rang like a bell struck by lightning.

Harley pressed in fast—his swords whipped in tight arcs, heavy but relentless, aimed to overwhelm and tear through.

Marek met him blow for blow. The force of the blows rattled Marek's bones, and caused the ground to shudder beneath his feet.

The twin swords of Onos moved like they had minds of their own—his own hands barely keeping pace, guided by whispers—memories and instincts imparted by the blades, combined with his own knowledge.

He ducked under a slash. Pivoted into a counter. Let Harley's rage drive him forward—then redirected it. Used it against him.

Harley overreached, and Marek punished him for it.

A gash across the upper arm. A shallow cut across the ribs. Marek was Controlled. Efficient.

Harley howled and came harder. The fury driving him to move faster, and hit even harder—but it also blinded him.

Marek kept his center, using the momentum, drawing his enemy in like a tide pulling on a drowning man. For the first time, it felt like he might actually win.

And then Harley changed.

The rage didn't fade—it shifted, sharpening into a focused fury.

The millennia-old General of Nyxia's armies had returned to the fight.

Marek could see it—the rage fading from his eyes, his movements sharpening. The wildness bled away, replaced by cold discipline. His strikes now had intention—calculated combinations designed to exploit Marek's weaknesses.

Marek was quickly outmatched.

The next blow came in a blur—slashing across Marek's forearm. Not deep, but enough to sting. Enough to slow him.

Then another. A thrust to the ribs that Marek barely twisted away from in time.

A third followed—clean across the chest, slicing through his armor deep into his flesh.

Pain lanced through him. He staggered, blood spilling down the front of his armor.

Harley didn't let up. "You think being a Warden makes you special?" He spat, his blade hammering down on Marek's guard.

Marek blocked high. The force drove him to one knee.

Harley leaned in, smiling a feral, predatory smile, his darkness sliding out and trying to wrap around Marek—trying to find a way in—to corrupt his thoughts.

A small piece slipped in, burrowing deep into his mind.

"You couldn't save that girl in the alley." He hissed. "You couldn't stop me in the street when I carved your team apart like meat."

Marek gritted his teeth. Fought to rise. Fought against the whispered failures that were getting louder inside his mind.

Another strike—this one to his ribs—drove the air from his lungs. His legs buckled. His vision blurred, and his resolve slipped.

More of the darkness slipped through. Images of his failures starting to cascade against the walls of his mind. A rising tide that was slowly crushing his will to fight.

"You can't stop me now. You're not a Warden," Harley said, sheathing his sword. "You're a fraud in borrowed armor—unworthy of the title."

Then he kicked him—hard—square in the chest.

Marek's body skidded across the battlefield and slammed into a massive oak with bone-shattering force. His arm snapped on impact, falling limp at his side as he crumpled to the ground.

One of his twin blades spun from his grip, landing just beyond his narrowing field of vision.

He lay there, chest heaving, the sky a spinning blur above him.

Harley stalked forward, slow and certain, like an executioner on parade.

"You're going to die, Marek," he said, voice rising with every step. "Then I'm going to finish what I started—with your woman. With your city. With your world."

The hum of rotor blades split the air.

Faint at first. Then louder. Steadier. Multiplying.

Marek turned his head and saw them.

Helicopters. Dipping beneath the clouds, their cameras rolling. They circled the Rift like vultures—drawn by the light. By the roar of battle.

Civilian drones darted across the sky. On the outer edges of the park, more were coming—reporters flooding the perimeters, crowds gathering behind hastily thrown-up barriers.

A few brave souls tried to get closer to the battle, and were ripped apart by Drakyn claws or Elvahr swords.

Phones recorded it all. Streams lit up globally. News anchors fell silent mid-report as the feeds took over. The whole world was watching in horror.

And Harley saw it too.

He smiled.

"Yes," he said softly. "Let them see. Let them remember the day their world ended."

His eyes locked back on Marek's.

"I'm going to take my time with you. You've proven unworthy of my swords, so I'll destroy you with my hands. And they'll all look on—witnesses to just another failure by our little hero."

◆

The next punch crashed into Marek's jaw—an explosion of pain that sent stars streaking through his vision. His head snapped sideways. Blood sprayed from his mouth as his cheek split open on impact.

The second came to his ribs. A dull, crunching thud. Something gave—maybe one, maybe three somethings. Marek gasped, but no air came. Just wet static and blood in his throat.

He raised an arm to block—too slow. Harley slammed a fist down across his forearm, shattering the already-broken limb. Marek screamed, the sound choked and gurgling.

"You couldn't save Malik," Harley growled, slamming his fist into Marek's sternum, and he felt something deep within him break.

A clawed hand followed—raking across Marek's chest, tearing through blood-slicked armor and flesh.

"You couldn't stop me from draining Marcus."

Another strike—this time to the gut. Marek collapsed forward, knees buckling, vomit and blood spilling from his mouth.

"You let me snap your friend's neck—some friend you turned out to be."

Harley grabbed him by the collar, lifted him off the ground like he weighed nothing, and slammed him back into the base of the oak.

The impact echoed. Bark cracked. Blood painted the trunk.

"You fail everyone around you."

Marek tried to fight—mentally pushing against the tide of blame, inadequacies, and failures that were hammering into him from Harley's power.

Why even bother... I'm nothing. He's right. I am no good to anyone. I'm a failure and the world would be better off without me.

It was at that moment that Marek lost the fight against the darkness.

Harley saw the moment pass behind Marek's eyes and smiled. He drove his claws through Marek's shoulder, pinning him to the tree.

Marek screamed in pain and anguish.

Harley leaned in, breath hot and wet with venom.

"Ah, it's good that you see it now. Your uselessness. I watched you fail in that alley all those years ago. Watched you freeze while I drank that poor girl's life. You were worthless then as a boy. You're worthless now as a man."

He pulled his claws free and let Marek drop.

Marek crumpled to the earth in a heap of torn limbs and fractured pride. Blood pooled beneath him. His good hand twitched once, then went still.

Above him, the world narrowed to shadow and light—fractured and spinning. The wind roared. His thoughts too—suffocating in their intensity.

The Rift pulsed like a second sun above the battlefield. Helicopters hovered in the distance; cameras locked on the broken man beneath the tree.

And still, Harley didn't finish it.

He stood over Marek's crumpled body, watching him bleed out in front of the world.

"Not even worth killing," he muttered, shaking his head in disgust. "You'll bleed out knowing you failed every-one—lost everything."

Marek tried to breathe.

Couldn't.

Tried to rise.

Couldn't.

He closed his eyes and crawled inside himself, trying to spiral down and hide from his pain and failures.

Chapter 51

Marek retreated into himself, spiraling away from the pain, the shame, and the inadequacies that were clogging his mind in an inky darkness—Harley's influence that he was powerless against.

The deeper he fell, the more his thoughts gained tangible weight—dense with guilt, compressed by regret, they became their own gravity.

As he descended, the darkness took shape, turning into walls. Corridors of memory. The hallways of his mind trying desperately to shield itself from the darkness raging inside.

Each thought that passed through him gained speed, like a stone dropped from a great height.

And then—he noticed the pull.

He was no longer falling with no direction. He was being drawn toward something immense. Past the place the Essence lived deep within, then deeper still.

He slammed through a barrier of his own making—landing hard, breathless, on a floor more felt than seen.

Before him, a vast lake waited.

He had been here once before, he realized. During training. In a moment of panic he hadn't understood, he'd withdrawn from it in shock and denial, building up his own walls—not ready to face what was within.

Before, the lake was a vast pool of darkness, calm on the surface. An ancient presence lying just beneath, patient and waiting.

Now, that calm lake churned and roiled. Golden energy and white lightning arced from the surface.

He stood at the edge—barefoot, bloodied, and hollowed out by loss. Golden-white arcs of luminous energy curling upward like tendrils of smoke reaching for a spark they had long yearned to reclaim.

Then they touched him.

Where they touched, Harley's darkness burned away. The whispered failures ceased, the oppressive weight of guilt and shame lifted.

They wrapped around him with warm, aching intent. Like a forgotten god reaching for its last hope. The power greeted him with familiarity and acceptance—like it knew him—had always known him.

This power—the power behind creation itself—felt as if it had watched in silence through every wound, every failure, every moment he wasn't enough.

And it had waited. Waited for him to fall far enough... fracture deeply enough to finally be willing to reach for it.

He was so tired. Tired of carrying his guilt, shame, and failure. Tired of not being able to save anyone he cared for.

He wanted to be whole—stronger. And so, with a breath of surrender, Marek stepped forward and opened himself up to it.

Tendrils of brilliance wrapped around his limbs, thread-ing into his chest, his spine, his skull. It wasn't warmth. It was an invasion. Intimate. Total.

The light didn't just touch him—it consumed him, filling every part of his being with something ancient. Vast. Divine.

Marek's world exploded in light and pain.

The pain wasn't physical, at least not in any earthly way. His body felt distant, more concept than reality, but the soul—that deepest version of himself—shuddered beneath the tidal wave of power pouring through him.

This wasn't magic. This was the power that had built worlds. The primal design that had shaped humanity, realms, and gods alike. The same power of the being who had once lit stars with his will alone—Onos.

And now that power surged through him.

His consciousness screamed beneath the pressure. It was too much. Too raw. Too alien. The very power of creation itself surged forward in relentless waves, smashing against the fragile walls of his humanity like ocean waves against crumbling stone.

He felt his thoughts fray, his sense of self begin to crumble under the crush of power. He saw galaxies whirling behind the light. Felt time fracture and bend, folding across eons.

Watched planets rise and fall like sparks from a dying flame. This power wasn't interested in lending him strength—it sought to remake him into an image it understood—that of a Titan.

Whatever was left of his mortal self, buckled beneath it. His flesh, if it still existed, stretched thin around infinite force. His memories blurred. His name dimmed. Every emotion, every failure, every flicker of human instinct—eroded beneath the tide.

And that tide was rising.

It promised peace. Power without pain. Clarity beyond grief. Absolute justice at the cost of mercy.

It lured him with the same dispassionate detachment that had once ruled Onos—the cold, incorruptible precision of a being who had risen so far beyond feelings that he'd no longer remembered what it meant to hurt, or love, or live.

In that light, Marek saw what he could become. A being without doubt. A weapon without mercy. A force above pain, above failure, above need.

But it wouldn't be him. He wouldn't be human.

If he let go... if he allowed the current to burn out his humanity, to take him into that upper realm of logic and supremacy—of pure power—there would be no one left to feel the warmth of another's hand.

No one to remember what it meant to weep, to make love, or laugh, or tremble in fear but keep standing anyway.

There would be no one left to love, and no one left for Kaycee to find.

His knees gave. His spirit cracked. A scream built inside him, not from agony, but from uncertainty—because he no longer knew if he could hold on to the pain, the grief, and the struggle that was his humanity... or if he even should.

And then—through the blinding roar of stars, fire, and the overwhelming weight of divinity—he heard her.

Her voice. Kaycee's voice—breaking through.

Not distant. Not imagined.

"Marek!" He heard her scream.

She wasn't calling for a god, or a savior. She was calling for *him.*

The sound of his name on her lips cut through everything—the fire, the logic, the seduction of control. It shattered the creeping, calcified truth that had begun to take root inside him.

She didn't need a Titan. She needed the man who still bled when he fell, who still stood even when everything had been stripped away. Who loved her—who had promised he wasn't going anywhere.

And that was enough—love was enough.

With a cry—not borne of pain, but of defiance—Marek reached into the storm.

He seized the vast golden power of creation. Not as a child begging for power, and not as an heir to a throne—but as a man, desperate not to lose the pieces of himself that mattered. He gripped the power in his hands, felt it burn through his veins, and refused to let it erase his humanity.

Summoning every shred of willpower he had left in him, every ounce of love he had for Kaycee, he shaped it. Bent it. Wrapped it around his scars, around his guilt, around his still-beating heart.

He didn't let it consume him. He gave it a new direction—and a new master to serve—and slowly, it bowed to his will.

The pressure didn't vanish. It was still a colossus living under his skin—it would never vanish. Would always threaten him with the lure of cold and dispassionate thought.

But now it moved through him with purpose, not domination. The transformation was no longer conquest—it was communion.

He rose.

Ribbons of golden light cracked from his skin like lightning breaking the surface of a storm. Symbols blazed across his arms and chest, burning sigils of a lineage not just divine, but chosen.

He stood at the center of the void left by that power—power that lived and breathed within him now.

He was still himself—still Marek—But also so much more.

He turned toward the surface of himself, toward the battlefield that still raged above.

Toward her. His lifeline. His savior.

"*Kaycee*," he whispered.

Then he surged upward in a blaze of power.

Back to the world outside—back to her.

———◆———

The battlefield trembled.

Not from footsteps or gunfire. Not from the fury of monsters tearing through Warden lines.

But from a pulse—a soundless crack that echoed through every living thing.

For one breathless moment, the air went still.

Then a column of gold-white energy erupted from Marek, splitting the air like a divine spear. It tore upward—through flesh, through cloud, through storm—before coming spiraling back down. It slammed back into him with a sound like a bell tolling at the end of time. The shockwave burst outward in a perfect impact crater, leveling everything within a hundred feet—stone, beast, and body alike.

Harley was catapulted back, slamming into bodies like a bowling ball.

Drakyns screamed and fell, clawing at their skulls as if trying to tear the resonance from their minds. Elvahr staggered back, their weapons falling silent in trembling hands. Even the Rift itself pulsed in response, the fabric of it rippling out its tendrils toward the energy surrounding Marek.

And at the center of the impact crater—hovering just above the shattered earth—was Marek.

He didn't land—he descended. Lowered by the power of what he'd become.

His boots touched the broken concrete, his figure radiant and terrible in the center of the storm. His coat had been burned away. His armor—torn and ruined—was now laced with golden fractures, light glowing through cracks like veins of molten ore beneath the surface of flesh.

The twin blades of Onos floated at his sides, spinning slowly in the air like satellites bound to his will. They pulsed in time with his breath. His heartbeat. His Essence.

His eyes opened—and they were not the same.

Gone was the pure green of the man who had once doubted, once hesitated.

Now they burned with the power of creation—swirls of radiant gold mixed with his own green, deep as nebulae, fierce as suns. There was no fury in them. No confusion.

Only clarity. Complete. Absolute.

Harley, picking himself up off the ground and untangling himself from limbs and dead bodies, turned back to the blazing light and froze.

He had seen power. Wielded it. Bent monsters and realms to his cause.

But this—this was something else. Something ancient—something he recognized from the Final War between a Titan and gods.

"Onos?" Harley whispered, the name trembling past his lips.

Marek stepped forward. "Not Onos," he said, his voice resonant and clear, both intimately human and impossibly vast. "But something like him."

Harley's eyes went wide. Then narrowed. The fear in them didn't vanish. It calcified into rage.

"You should have chosen death," he growled.

"You think that light makes you untouchable? You think I care what you've become?"

He sprinted across the space between them. Swords drawn and teeth bared.

Marek didn't flinch. He simply watched him come.

Harley brought his blades down, full of impossible force built out of his rage and fury.

And Marek caught them. Barehanded.

Steel shrieked against his glowing palms. Sparks flared, and for one suspended heartbeat, they stood locked together—General against... something else.

Harley's breath hitched. He grunted once, then twice—struggling to withdraw from Marek's hold.

Marek's grip tightened—steel twisting under the vast strength now coursing through him.

"You don't get to touch this world anymore," he said.

And then... he let go.

Not of Harley, but of restraint. A pulse of raw, golden power surged from Marek's hands like a supernova. It didn't throw Harley back—it held him in place... and unmade him.

For a split second, Harley's eyes widened in horrified understanding—too late. His body cracked outward in burning lines of light, golden power tearing through flesh and bone. He tried to scream, but the sound never came.

Then—he was gone. Vaporized. Not even ash left behind.

The flare of light rippled outward. Then faded... into silence.

Marek lowered his arms, chest heaving, the twin blades stopping their rotation, and coming to rest in his hands.

Then, he turned to the war going on around him.

The Wardens, bloodied and scattered, stared in stunned silence.

The Drakyn and Elvahr—those that hadn't fled—charged in desperation.

And Marek moved. Not like a man. Not like a Warden. But like a god of war on a path of destruction.

He became motion. A blur of light and blades, cutting through the tide of creatures with a precision that defied explanation. The swords were no longer weapons—they were extensions of his will, painting arcs of golden fire across the battlefield.

Every strike vaporized. Every movement shattered. Where he stepped, Elvahr and Drakyn ceased to exist. Where he raised his voice, Wardens found their feet again. Their hope.

He moved through the battlefield—death incarnate—unstoppable.

Around him, silence reigned. Not from fear, but awe. No one dared make a sound.

And when the dust began to settle—when there was nothing but the sound of the wind, and silence bloomed in the wreckage—only one other thing still pulsed with power.

The Rift.

Still open. Still shattered.

Marek turned toward it, the light of his power flaring and pulsing around him like a dying star.

He could feel it—like a broken piece of a stained-glass window. Out of order, cracked, but needing to be knit back together.

He was drawn to the tear with an overwhelming need to heal. The light pulsed wildly through his chest, wanting to be spent, needing to be poured back into what had been broken.

He reached the Rift's edge, willed his blades into the scabbards on his back.

He looked for Kaycee on the battlefield—found her some distance away, and spoke into her mind:

"I love you... never forget that. I need to do this—heal the rift. I'm not sure what will happen, but whatever does, I will find my way back to you."

He saw her eyes widen in understanding, as she shouted, "Marek, wait... Please!"

Before he could change his mind, he stepped into the wound in the world.

Golden energy surged from him like blood from a burst heart—threading through the rupture, knitting torn seams of reality together with raw, divine force.

The Rift became greedy, pulling at his power. Demanding more. As if it sensed, for the first time, the chance to finally be whole.

And he gave. More than he should have. More than he knew he had.

Until at last—the Rift closed with blinding flash, and Marek collapsed unconscious to the ground.

The battlefield was still. Quiet. The storm above finally easing to mist.

And through the smoke—Kaycee was running toward him.

◆

Kaycee saw him fall in his fight with Harley.

One moment, Marek was standing—fighting like hell to hold the line against him—and the next, he was broken and bleeding at the base of a tree, his body crumpling under Harley's final assault.

"No—"

The word tore from her throat. Her eyes locked on him as he was shattered by a kick to the chest, one of his blades spinning free upon impact with the tree, the other still clutched in a limp, bloodied hand.

She felt something fracture in her chest.

And then she ran.

"Marek!"

Her voice screamed across the battlefield as she threw herself into motion, blades already swinging. The Drakyn in her path didn't last a heartbeat. She didn't even see them—just movement, threat, and then meat, carved apart by the fury at the core of her.

Elvahr charged to intercept her. She didn't care. She moved through them like a storm, every step laced with desperate precision. Her blades cut clean. Her soul was on fire—love and desperation adding their strength.

"Marek!"

She screamed it again, pushing herself harder, every instinct driving her toward him. She could see him now—bleeding out, unmoving, one hand twitching, his light fading.

No. No, no, no. Not him. Not now. Not after everything.

He couldn't be dead. She wasn't ready to lose him.

And then—he moved.

Barely.

A flicker. A tremble in the air around him. A spiraling light rose from his chest. It was faint at first, then built into something deeper. Wilder. She felt it before she understood it—like a rising pressure beneath the skin of the world.

"Marek...?"

She slowed, hesitated, and then it hit.

A pulse of golden-white energy erupted from his body into the air, and then came back down, slamming into him in a shockwave that burst outward in a perfect impact crater, leveling everything within a hundred feet, lifting her off the ground with the force of it. Drakyn and Elvahr were slammed backwards or flattened.

And in the center of it—

He rose. Hovering just above the shattered earth, his body cracked with burning light. Runes—old, sacred—blazed across his chest and arms. His skin glowed in seams of gold, as if something divine had poured itself into the shape of a man and barely managed to contain the flood.

His armor—torn and ruined—was lit underneath by golden fractures like veins of molten ore beneath the surface of flesh. And his eyes—

She couldn't breathe.

His eyes were no longer only green.

They swirled with the golden power of creation—threaded through with the green she'd come to know and love.

They shone like stars.

Beautiful. Powerful. Terrifying.

"Marek," she whispered, tears spilling freely down her cheeks.

He hadn't died.

He had become something different. Something the realms hadn't seen in millennia—but she didn't care.

He'd heard her—had come back for her.

The blades of Onos floated to his sides, orbiting him like planets around a star. When his feet touched down again, the light in the air didn't vanish—it bent around him, drawn to the gravity of what he now was.

Harley charged him, screaming something unintelligible and she caught her breath as his blades arced down toward Marek's neck.

A scream of warning died in her throat when Marek brought his hands up and *caught* the blades.

Metal shrieked against glowing flesh. Sparks screamed into the air. Harley froze mid-strike, his face twisting in shock.

And when Marek spoke, it was his voice—but deeper, layered with a resonance that shook the air around them.

"You don't get to touch this world anymore."

Light surged from his palms in a blinding eruption. A pulse of power so pure, so absolute, it didn't just strike—it unmade.

Golden-white energy exploded outward, wrapping Harley in a wave of radiance that consumed everything it touched.

Kaycee flinched, one arm raised against the glare.

When the light receded—Harley was gone. Vaporized. Not even ash remained.

She watched as he took his swords in hand and decimated the remaining Drakyn and Elvahr forces, in a blur of light, motion, steel and power. Where he moved, none were left standing.

He finally came to a stop next to the Rift and turned slowly—like he was being drawn to the gash in the world that should never have existed.

He straightened and started walking. There was no hesitation in his body. No fear. He moved like a man who had already died—and come back knowing exactly what was at stake. The twin blades flared once, then sheathed themselves across his back as he approached the gaping tear in reality.

The Rift jerked and rippled... as if it recognized him—seeming to pulse out toward him like a man dying of thirst in the desert.

He turned to her then, speaking into her mind... words she'd never forget. "*I love you... never forget that. I need to do this—heal the rift. I'm not sure what will happen, but whatever does, I will find my way back to you.*"

She screamed his name, begged him to wait, but he turned and stepped into the Rift—giving himself to it.

Golden light spilled from his body like lifeblood, lacing through the edges of the wound, pouring into every fracture of the sky. She could feel it—feel the pressure of his power unraveling, not in death, but in sacrifice.

He wasn't just pouring energy into the breach. He was stitching the world back together with himself.

The Rift shrieked louder, lines of rupture convulsing as they slowly began to draw inward, filling in the gaps—healing.

And still—he gave more.

"Marek," Kaycee whispered, her voice trembling.

Energy swirling around him began to flicker, and his body swayed.

He was giving too much.

"Marek—stop. You have to stop—" she shouted.

But he didn't. He gave more. And more. Until the Rift let out one final sigh—then closed.

The tear sealed with a thunderclap that shook the city, the blue-white energy of the Rift fusing at the seams like molten glass hardening in place. A shockwave radiated outward in perfect silence.

Then it was gone. And Marek collapsed.

He fell—like something pulled his body down from the inside, all strength stripped, his limbs loose and unmoving. He hit the scorched ground beneath where the Rift had been.

"No—"

Kaycee was already moving. Her boots struck broken stone as she ran, leapt over rubble, corpses, and smoking husks of creatures, blade still in hand, breath coming in ragged sobs.

The mist was clearing now. Sunlight—thin and golden—pushed through the torn sky like it, too, had waited for this moment. The battlefield shimmered with steam, with heat, with silence.

"Marek!"

Her voice cracked as she sprinted across the last few yards and dropped to her knees beside him.

She could see the glowing tattoo still faintly visible beneath his ruined armor. Gold cracks webbed his arms and torso, the fire of the power he had carried no longer flaring—but pulsing like embers.

"Marek..." Her voice was hoarse, but she didn't care. She pressed a hand to his chest and felt the steady beat of his heart beneath her palm—still alive.

Tears slid down her cheeks as she leaned over him, pressing her forehead to his.

"You stubborn bastard," she whispered. "You can't leave me now. You promised me you'd survive this."

Her fingers traced along the edge of one glowing fracture. She'd seen men die in battle, but she wasn't ready for him to die.

"I need you," she said again, voice breaking. "I need you to fight. Come back. Don't you dare go quiet on me now."

And then—he twitched. A small movement.

His fingers moved if only slightly. He wasn't gone. Not yet.

Kaycee let out a sound halfway between a laugh and a sob, and cradled his face in her hands, gently, as if she were holding something sacred.

"You're going to be okay," she whispered. "You're going to be okay. I've got you."

Above them, the clouds finally broke.

A single shaft of sunlight poured down over the ruins of the battlefield, warming the bloodstained grass, the broken armor, the fallen beasts.

And him.

Kaycee looked up at the sky, her arms still wrapped around him. She didn't know what came next—what the world would do when it saw the truth of what had happened here.

But she knew one thing. Whatever came, he wouldn't be facing it alone. Never alone.

Epilogue

Tucker

T he machines had stopped beeping hours ago. Not because they had failed, but because they no longer understood what they were reading.

Vitals had stabilized—impossibly so. Brainwaves that had been steady for days, now thrummed with patterns too complex for the monitors to interpret. The nurses came in, checked the charts, whispered among themselves, and left—confused.

Tucker lay still, the dim hospital light casting soft lines across his face. The bruises and cuts that once colored his skin had faded to a memory.

He looked asleep. Peaceful, even.

But inside—something stirred.

It had begun as a flicker, days ago. A warmth buried deep beneath the cold stasis of his coma. It moved like sunlight filtering through murky water, slow and golden, threading into the marrow of him.

Now it pulsed, and with each beat, something fractured.

The fog that had wrapped his mind began to lift. The pain was gone. The noise, the fear, the chaos of the fight with Harley—they were distant echoes now. He didn't remember what exactly happened after Harley had broken his neck.

He just knew that Marek had done something. Something that had drawn him back from the door leading to... somewhere else.

He knew it like he knew the sound of his own voice.

An eruption of light—felt more than seen. A spark of something gold and warm, wrapping around him—pulling him back from the void of death.

His hand twitched. His monitor spiked, and a nurse beside his bed screamed and ran out into the hallway, calling for a doctor.

Then—he opened his eyes.

At first, the ceiling lights blurred. He blinked, vision adjusting slowly. He inhaled deeply, lungs filling fully for the first time in what felt like years.

Everything was... quiet. Except his heart.

It beat strong. Unnaturally strong and loud, like a bass drum in his ears.

He turned his head, slow and deliberate, and stared at the heart monitor beside his bed. The screen glitched. Just for a second. Then came back.

He didn't understand it. Didn't know why, but he felt different.

His hand lifted, fingers flexing. The movement felt effortless. Strong. The aches of old injuries that had plagued him were gone—the wounds sustained in the fight with Harley, erased.

And in the mirrored glass of the window beside him, he caught the faintest shimmer—reflected light pulsing across his irises.

They were Gold.

Not solid, and not even glowing. They were just flecks. Like embers burning bright within.

He was alive. He knew that was supposed to be impossible after what he remembered—the crack of his neck and then darkness.

People didn't come back from things like that. At least, normal people didn't.

Tucker's lips parted, his throat dry.

"...What the hell did you do to me, Marek?"

Nyxia

Far beneath the surface of the Realm of Shadow and Thought, beneath the throne carved into a mountain of living obsidian, there lay a chamber untouched by time.

It was not meant to be found.

Hidden beneath layers of sealed stone and forgotten runes of protection, the chamber pulsed faintly with residual power—Essence, fractured and dormant, wrapped in silence so absolute even sound dared not enter.

There, upon a raised altar lay the body of Nyxia.

Once the brightest and most terrible of the Seven—the one who struck the killing blow to Onos.

Her form—what remained of it—was draped in silken dark, armor cracked and scorched from the Final War. She had bled not just from the flesh, but from her very Essence, pierced by the twin blades of Onos.

Dharken Mohr, her most loyal general, had pulled her from that battlefield. Bleeding and broken—her divine light fading with every heartbeat. He had carried her—mourning, desperate—across the collapsing field of war, through the screaming remnants of the Realms' final clash.

He thought she was dead.

He placed her there, beneath her throne room. He sealed her in that resting place with every protection he knew. To allow her to be at peace, a final tribute to his fallen goddess.

But Nyxia was not dead. Not entirely.

She drifted in stasis—a half-breath from life, a flicker from oblivion—trapped in a place between death and life. And for millennia, she lay undisturbed. Silent. Preserved. Waiting.

Until now.

The chamber pulsed.

Once. Then again.

A ripple moved across the surface of her skin. A spark traced along the lines of her broken body.

And she inhaled. It was shallow and weak, but it was breath.

Her fingers twitched. The air stirred.

Eyes long shut, fluttered—once, twice—and opened.

Slitted silver irises blinked against the low light of the room. Her vision swam. Her mind remained clouded with the fragments of war, of Onos's face as she struck him down, of the silence that followed, of her loyal general's arms dragging her from the battlefield.

She tried to sit up. Couldn't.

She felt cold. Hollow.

And then—something surged against her senses—through her.

Power. It was Old. Familiar. But not the same.

She gasped, arching slightly on the stone. Her vision blurred again, this time not from pain—but from recognition.

Onos.

She had felt him. Not just his signature, but the raw pulse of his power—a blast of Essence so violent it cracked through the barriers of stasis and woke her from near death.

But it wasn't him.

Not exactly.

Her lips parted. Her voice was a whisper, dry and low, scraping across her throat like memory clawing its way free.

"...Who woke me?"

The chamber gave no answer.

But her pulse had returned. Her body, still damaged, now ever so slowly, started to heal.

Nyxia stared upward, toward the layers of stone that separated her from the world.

She did not know who carried the spark.

Only that someone did, and that meant one thing.

Onos's bloodline had not ended with him.

———◆———

Elsewhere in the Universe

In the cold spaces between galaxies—where light had never been born and time moved like slow breath—the Titan stirred.

He stood at the edge of a dying star, watching it collapse in silence, its light curling inward into singularity. Around him, reality thinned, stretched by his presence, as if the fabric of the universe remembered who he was—and what he had once helped shape.

He was one of Four.

Born not of star or matter, but of Chaos itself—the raw, wild force that predated all creation. He and his siblings had crossed into this universe eons ago, not as conquerors but as wanderers, travelers curious about the weave of potential stretched across the cosmos.

They had divided it among themselves—not through war, but through intent. Each took a domain and left their mark in quiet experimentation. But one of them—Onos—had broken from the pattern.

He had stayed.

While the others moved on, carving realms and testing the limits of form and essence, Onos had turned his gaze toward something fragile. Something strange.

He had created humans.

Not as soldiers. Not as tools. But as an experiment.

A species shaped in the image of balance—mortal, finite, and yet capable of wonder, growth, and will.

Then he had created godlike children to guide his mortal creations. The others had watched. Had judged. Had warned him of the possible cost of creating something that had free will—free to do what they wanted.

He hadn't listened—enamored with his own brilliance of creation.

And when the rebellion came, when his children were corrupted by the very ones they were created to guide and preserve, Onos had died defending them.

The others had felt it. Across stars and dimensions, they had each paused when his presence fell silent. A sibling lost to the void.

And then—for millennia—there was nothing.

Until now.

The Titan straightened. He felt it ripple through the void—faint, imperfect, but unmistakably familiar.

A pulse of power—Chaos power.

The signature of Onos, newly awakened... but changed.

He turned his eyes toward the edge of the spiral galaxy; toward the little blue planet his brother had created—bled for—sacrificed for.

Earth.

There, something had stirred.

The Titan's voice rolled across the dark, a low vibration that stirred solar winds and bent the light of stars.

"It seems you gave them your spark, brother. And now... it awakens."

He did not vanish, or rush, he simply began to walk—through nebulae, across the folds of time, toward the distant heartbeat that should not have been possible.

He was curious to see what would become of this new life.

About the author

Jay S. Scott began writing Ascension in 2017, scribbling the first 90 pages after being laid off from work—a period that sparked a quiet conviction: maybe he could actually write a novel. That early burst of inspiration stalled when the realities of how involved writing a book actually was, sank in. The manuscript was shelved, and in 2022, he returned with renewed purpose, devouring every writing lecture or video he could find—from Jerry B. Jenkins, to self-published veterans—determined to sharpen his skill and finish what he started. By 2025, he had built a foundation strong enough to carry the story to its finale.

Writing is Jay's creative outlet, and has also become a way for him to withdraw for just a moment, from the structured corridors of his career in Human Resources.

He lives in Kansas, with his adventurous three-year-old son, his supportive (and occasionally skeptical) wife, and more story ideas than he'll ever have time to write. When not daydreaming, drafting battle scenes or fleshing out ancient mythologies, he can be found running after his three-year-old son (or by himself on a running trail), balancing work and family, and building a legacy one chapter at a time.

To sign up for Newsletters, read blogs, and get updates on the progress of "*Reckoning*," the second book in the Wardens of the Rift Series, visit Jay's website https://authorjaysscott.org/